# THE
# TALLPIAN
# PRINCESS

# THE TALLPIAN PRINCESS

L.R. OBERSCHULTE

Printed in the United States of America

First Printing, 2018

ISBN 978-1983579820

*To all those who have always*
*believed in me and Gaia, Thank you.*

# Acknowledgments

To the love of my life, Jeremy. Thank you for everything. Your support, your amazing listening ears and most of all, your love. I couldn't have done this without you.

To Nic. My brother from another mother. My writing and Halo buddy. After the early days of bad writing, horrible grammar and completely unoriginal ideas, we finally get to see something in print. For always being there to listen, argue, talk me off my ledge and debate scientific principles, thank you.

To my parents. You always encouraged me to tell my stories, no matter how wild, silly or ridiculous they might have been. This book would not exist without your love and support.

To my amazing and most talented friend Katherine. You brought Gaia to life with watercolor and love. Without you, she'd still be just a vision in my head. Thank you lady.

To my editor Jeff Karon. Thank you for believing in this project. Your hours of work, critiques, edits and feedback helped bring this story to life.

And to all of my friends who have beta-read for me over the years, it is your support and feedback that have kept me going. Thank you.

# Prologue

The joys of a finely-wrought katana were unending, Nuweydon thought, distracted, as he watched his narrow blade - single-edged and lethal - slice through another neck, severing head from body. The head tumbled to the floor, and he booted the bleeding corpse out of the way, wading deeper into the fray, his weapon held aloft.

"Your Majesty, your forces have taken the lower levels. The palace is now yours." Nuweydon, his lanky frame already sprawled across the massive chair of state, took his time turning his signature blood-red eyes towards the voice, taking in the sight of his Uncle Amadeas. The Lord Commander of the Tallpian army stood at the foot of the grand dais, his immaculate grey hair disheveled and his formerly pristine military uniform stained with the brilliant red blood of their fellows. His narrow, pale face, like that of his nephew, was alight with pleasure.

"You are now king." A low bow from the waist.

"And where is my brother?"

"Awaiting your command."

"Bring him to me."

"I should have known you were behind this, Nuweydon." King Yehuda's voice was still strong, despite him having languished in a prison cell for several days. His ire carried from the base of the dais where he knelt, Amadeas's katana blade pressed against the back of his neck to dissuade any attempts at freedom or revenge.

"I'm amazed it took you so long to figure out, Brother," Nuweydon said, gloating. He had plotted for years, decades even, and now the throne was his.

"You are no brother of mine—not now, not after all you have done." The errant prince finally pulled his eyes away from surveying his new throne room, now splashed in blood, but time would wash that away. His brother, the former king of Meidonna, knelt in a quickly drying puddle at the base of the stairs. His royal silks and furs were matted and stained with more blood. His narrow, noble face was dirty, and a large wound on his neck oozed from under a dirty bandage. "Why Nuweydon?" The question was a good one, no matter how obvious the answer.

"You are a good man, Brother, but a fool. And a fool cannot be trusted to safeguard his people or their future."

"And you claim to be a good man?" demanded Yehuda. "You have murdered your own people, thrown your planet into chaos, cut us off from the rest of the galaxy. Our kind and our way of life will die because of you." He may have been beaten and bound, but Yehuda's voice still rang with strength through the empty room.

"No!" shouted Nuweydon, slamming his fists on the arms of the carved marble throne as he pushed himself to his feet. "I will bring us back from the brink. What are we now?" he sneered. "A paltry trading planet so far removed that few even know of our existence? A worn-down, wind-beaten people you have created, Brother. Have we not evolved into beings superior to those of our forefathers? Are we not superior in strength and cunning to the weak and pathetic terrans?" Nuweydon glared down at his brother with a manic smile. "I intend to lead the Tallpian race out of the dark and into the light of glory."

"By killing your brother? By killing your family?" Nuweydon paused in his descent down the stairs of the dais with another dark smile.

"That reminds me. Do tell me, Brother," insisted the new king, "where are that charming wife and daughter of yours?"

"Far away," spat Yehuda. "Away from you and your sword."

"You know I will find them."

"You already have me. What would you need with them?"

"That wailing brat of yours has already pushed me much further down the ladder of succession than I ever cared to be," he pointed out. His niece, not even two years old, had officially supplanted him as his brother's heir, not that he would have ever stood for it. "Why not ensure that my power is absolute and just kill you all?" Nuweydon asked with another evil grin.

"You will never find them," Yehuda spat. Nuweydon let out a ringing laugh. He had forgotten his brother's obstinacy in his time away from the palace. It was, after all, one of the things that had led to his downfall, Nuweydon reflected as he made his way down the remaining stairs. A thrill of pleasure rushed through him as he heard his steps echo through the room. Finally, she welcomed her true and rightful king. If Yehuda had just been willing to listen to his younger brother he might have kept his throne. No. The thought snapped through his mind like a whip crack. He would not give up the throne, the throne that long ago should have gone to him, not to some scrawny whelp of a princess. Nuweydon stepped in front of his kneeling brother, reaching for the sword still strapped to his own back. Drawing the weapon slowly, he savored the feel of the intricately carved leather hilt under his palm.

"Rest assured Brother, I will find them. And when I do, I will personally send them both to the afterlife to join you," he said, adjusting his grip with both hands. The feeling when sword bit into flesh was unique, Nuweydon reflected, far different from the jar of metal on metal during a fight, or the muted thud of metal meeting wood during training. No, it was almost a sensual feeling, as muscle and sinew and bone were parted by steel. His blade flashed out and in a single, fluid movement, sliced through his brother's neck, cutting his royal head from his royal shoulders. There was a moment of silence before the head of the king—no, former king— hit the floor with a dull thud. Flicking the vivid blood from his blade, Nuweydon turned his fierce red gaze to his uncle, who had stood aside, silent, as the former king of Meidonna was slaughtered.

"Find them."

# Chapter One

*Eighteen Years Later*

"Kill her."

The words echoed through Gaia's mind as she bolted awake, her skin prickling with fear. Glancing around, she realized, as she always did, that she was safe. Or relatively safe, all things considered. She wasn't in her small bed in her home, but instead was curled up in a ball under several sheets of decomposing cardboard, hidden in the depths of an abandoned warehouse. The air was musty, tinged with mold and old machine oil that made her nose tickle. Sitting up to stretch, Gaia could see the weak rays of late afternoon sunlight pouring through a broken window above her head. Her belly growled in hunger, and she slowly unfolded herself from her hiding place striking out in search of something to eat.

All her life, Gaia had loved the stars. Far off and cold, they still shone brightly despite the harshness of space, reminding her there were other worlds, thousands of them. As soon as she had the chance, she would leave her home and travel to them all. Not that she would ever call the planet Annui her true home, even though she had been raised there. Gritty and dirty and smelly, the factory-choked planet could not possibly be her real home. No, her real home was out there, amongst the billions of twinkling lights. Gaia had memories, jagged and vague, of her homeworld, but her mother said to forget them—they were never going back. A planet that was wild and green, harsh yet beautiful, it called to Gaia. But as much as she dreamed of that place, those memories were also tainted by fear. A voice haunted her dreams, one that ordered her death over and over again. No matter how many times she bolted awake, safe in bed in her room on Annui, she was sure the sword was about to fall.

Now, as she pulled the edge of her hood over her face, tearing her eyes from the smog-choked sky, she knew she would never look at the stars the same. She had been stargazing when they had come for her and her mother. It was her love of the stars that had saved her, but it also meant she was now alone. Almost a month ago, her mother had been arrested by the Central Core secret police and dragged from their home in the middle of the night. Nearly a month ago, Gaia had fled her home with little more than the clothes on her back, pursued by two gorths, the bounty hunters who were paid by the Central Core government to track down runaways, criminals, and undesirables throughout the galaxy. How Gaia and her mother had ended up on their list was a mystery, but one Gaia was intent on solving.

Shrugging deeper into her black leather jacket, Gaia strode down the grubby street, keeping her eyes on her boots. Eye contact was risky in general, but in this part of the city, it could be downright dangerous. Gaia struggled to blend into the crowds: standing tall and willowy with a narrow face and long, graceful limbs made her as different from the native Annuians as possible. But it was the changes that were her biggest blessing and biggest curse. Even as she marched along, she caught a glimpse of herself in a dingy shop window and saw that her previously honey-blonde hair was no more. In its place, raven-colored locks hung down around her face, echoing the color of her eyes, which had been a muted gold not three hours before. How or why the changes happened, Gaia had no idea, and she had no control over them. All her life, her mother had repeated the same warning: They would be in terrible danger if anyone discovered their secret. As Gaia grew and her hair and eye changed color daily and then sometimes hourly, she struggled to keep them hidden. But as to why the changes happened, Dyla refused to say. The fights had been frequent, but Dyla never budged.

And now Gaia was alone and on the run. Glancing over her shoulder, she tried to see if the two gorths were following her. The market was crowded, and tendrils of steam swirled among the denizens of the city's underbelly as Gaia pushed through the throng.

Starving, she decided to risk a brief stop and was just examining a vendor's display of pale, yellow-spotted pettang fruit when she felt a hard hand clamp down on her arm. Whipping around, she saw Keon, one of the two gorths, his rodent-like face alight with malicious pleasure as he held her tightly, reaching forward with a pair of handcuffs. Reacting instinctively, Gaia threw a hard upper-cut that landed square on Keon's narrow chin. Stumbling back, he released his hold on her. Taking advantage of her split-second edge, Gaia dove into the crowd, pushing people aside as she fled. She could hear Keon crow with delight as he gave chase and not far behind was sure to be Arlo, Keon's boss.

Sprinting through the dilapidated neighborhood just beyond the market street, Gaia looked around desperately for a place to hide. As the crowd thinned, Gaia saw a block of warehouses, most of them abandoned. Taking her chances, she threw herself down a narrow alley between two of the buildings, hearing the pounding of feet not far behind her. Spotting an open door, she dove through before slamming it closed and barring it. The lock was flimsy and wouldn't hold against Arlo for long, but it would give her needed seconds. Darting a look around the warehouse, she spied an air duct that ran across the ceiling. If she could just manage to reach the pipes, she might be able to avoid discovery. Racing up a nearby staircase, she was able to climb onto the railing, and with the very tips of her fingers, push into the ductwork just as the door exploded open below. Hauling herself up as quickly and quietly as she could, she shimmied into the vent before tugging the grate shut behind her. She sat hunched, arms wrapped around her knees, praying they hadn't seen her. Footsteps echoed through the warehouse, followed by a loud crashing as crates overturned and smashed.

"Where is she?" Keon's shout rang through the warehouse, followed by more noise as they tore apart the room, looking for her. "The trail goes cold, Arlo," he finally snarled. Gaia leaned to her right, glancing down through the metal slats of the grate. Arlo and Keon stood directly below her. Arlo was tall with broad shoulders and a head of black, oily hair slicked back against his pale neck. Keon was shorter with sandy-brown hair and a thin, sinuous build that reminded Gaia of a ferret. Both figures turned slowly, surveying the wrecked space.

"Fear not, Keon. Our little quarry cannot make it much further on her own." The high-pitched voice was at odds with its owner's hulking physique. His degrading taunt was one he had used many times already in their hunt, and yet she was not nearly as weak or helpless as they seemed to believe. It had almost been a full moon cycle since she had fled her home in the dark of night, staying one step ahead of her hunters.

"And then we will find her!" The sycophantic voice pulled Gaia's lip into an involuntary sneer as she rolled her eyes to herself. There was nothing worse than gorths. Universally hated, they were utilized by the corrupt Central Core government (along with plenty of other shady outer rim powers) to hunt down spies, dissenters, and anyone else deemed undesirable. It was worse on the Central Ring, where Annui was located. The closer to the Dyson Sphere that served as the home planet of the government, the worse the control. Measures meant to keep the galaxy safe and organized had broken down a millennia ago and become arbitrary and abusive. Some planets were rich and luxurious. Others, like Annui, were a mass of city-states occupied by hundreds of thousands of factories that operated around the clock, churning out goods for the Central Core. Poverty and squalor were the norms. The factories were run by the Annuians, hulking, troll-like humanoids who managed the massive equipment used for production, but most of the companies were owned by wealthy terrans who lived off-planet. Thankfully for Gaia, some of the factories had failed, and the empty shells left behind provided much-needed cover.

Sitting in the cramped vent, Gaia impatiently waited for them to finish their search and move on. Arlo and Keon proceeded to the second floor, passing not ten feet from her hiding spot but walked past, their eyes fixed on the second level, ignoring the pipes and vents that crisscrossed the ceiling. She waited until she could no longer hear their conversation before carefully unfolding herself and pushing the grate open. Gaia cautiously slid out of her hiding place, turning first one way and then the other, eyes alert for the glint of buckles on rifle straps, ears straining for the clink of chains and manacles. Carefully, she let herself down from the vent before dropping to the floor. It was a decent drop, but Gaia had quick reflexes and was able to land almost silently on her feet, her knees jarring with impact. Eyeing the hazy sky through the broken windows, it was clear the sun was not far from setting. She needed better cover and quickly. The gorths would return, and she needed to be far away before that happened.

She had gone no more than a dozen steps before a flash of white caught her eye. Glancing up, there was a square of white paint, brushed four feet square onto one of the factory walls, with a yellow slash across the center. She had seen that symbol before, she realized, stopping in shock. Suddenly, a memory surged forward in her mind: a note that had been stuck innocuously into the doorframe of her old home many years ago. The small, sturdy piece of paper bore the same symbol and two lines of hand-scrawled text: "Know you are not alone. Know there are those still willing to help you achieve your destiny." The name on the note was not her own—instead it was addressed to someone named Kallideia. Her mother had jerked it from her hand and, after reading it, proclaimed it was a mistake. The letter went into the fire, and Gaia had forgotten it. But now, the same sign was painted onto an abandoned factory wall. Staring at the sign curiously, she had barely enough time to duck when a chain came whistling through the air towards her head, intended to wrap around her neck.

"Arlo!" The shout in her ear was oily and cold, making gooseflesh break out across her skin. The answering reply came from the far side of the warehouse, just far enough to give her hope. Gaia dove to the side, throwing herself to the floor. She banged her wrist hard on a piece of metal but was able to roll away from the second chain strike. Keon, the smaller greasy creature that appeared to be part terran and part rodent, stood over her, smiling as he coiled the thick chain around his hand. He lunged and slammed her against the ground, the chain pressing into her throat. Using his weight, Keon pinned her to the grimy floor and kept leaning on the rusty chain as it started to cut into her pale flesh. Struggling to breathe, she tried to wriggle out from under his weight, but he sat back, pinning her hips to the ground.

"We've been looking for you," he said, showing a mouth full of yellow, pointed teeth as he leered at her. "Someone is real interested to meet you." Unable to breathe under the chain's pressure, she took a risk and yanked hard, pulling her left arm free of his leg, and swung. The lightning quickness of her strike caught the gorth off-guard, and she landed a solid blow against his jaw. He pitched sideways, shrieking in pain, giving her a chance to shove the length of chain away from her windpipe and gasp for air. A moment later, his backhand knocked her to the side, making stars spark across her vision. He was far stronger than his musteline-like physique would suggest. They wrestled in the dust and debris, throwing punches and snarling obscenities. A hard jab to the throat kept Keon from shouting for Arlo again, but his answering blow knocked Gaia to the side and made her head spin.

"You're coming with us, girl," he rasped, clutching his throat as he staggered to his feet, towering over her.

"I would rather die," Gaia snapped and kicked hard at his knee, feeling the joint pop and give under her boot. The rodent-faced man howled in pain and crumpled to the ground as she staggered to her feet and fled out the door.

# Chapter Two

Brexler Carrow sat with his back to the wall, facing the door. Even though he was semi-retired from the Outer Rim Brotherhood, old habits died hard, and just because he wasn't an active member anymore didn't mean he no longer had enemies. There were plenty of creatures, from the Central Core government on out to the bleak outer edges, who would love to plant a knife in his back. Watching the door was prudent, especially in a place like the one where he sat. The bar, a common inter-galaxy stopover for seedy outer-rim runners and their often seedier clientele, was dim with everything covered in a fine layer of grease. What little light managed to filter through the soot-stained windows disappeared quickly in the murky reaches of the large room, making it perfect for brokering deals that hovered just outside, or completely ignored, the law.

He was just sipping the last of his beer when a young woman—dark-haired with impossibly long legs—staggered through the door. There was a riotous game of carpo going on in the corner of the bar, and the room at large paid her no attention. Terrified young women—even breathtakingly beautiful ones—in this part of the city were unfortunate, but common. A flick of pity went through Brex, but he squashed it. Women were always trouble (he had the scars to prove it), never mind those who might need his help.

He'd been burned by that particular speeder crash several times before and didn't have any plans to repeat it in the near future. Still, he couldn't help but admire her covertly. She was tall, almost as tall as he was, with long, graceful limbs. She wasn't the classic, buxomy girl Brex tended to prefer, but there was something about the way she carried her lithe frame that immediately caught his attention. She held herself like a queen, despite the prey-like expression on her face. Her clothes were high quality (hard to find a leather jacket cut like that anymore), but it was clear that she had been living in them for some time. She had voluminous black hair, tangled and wind-whipped; her skin was fair, with an almost pearl-like luminescence, albeit smudged and dirty. Her coal-colored eyes had a calculating, wild look to them that screamed fugitive as her gaze darted around the darkened room. But as he watched her just beyond the brim of his hat, he quickly realized she may have been drop-dead beautiful, but she was also far more clever than her looks would suggest. When it became clear that no one was paying her any mind—save Brex, whom she couldn't see—she slid back into the shadows next to the door and carefully stole a dark fedora off the coat pegs on the wall. She quickly twisted her hair up, tucking it under the hat before snagging a black duster jacket that was far too large for her and shrugging into it. She pulled the collar up around her cheeks before sidling up to the bar, ordering a large mug of some dark liquid. The bartender, a bored-looking Roomajan lizard, made no comment on her unusual attire or sudden appearance. Taking her glass, the girl casually ambled to the darkest corner and sat only a table away from Brex. She guzzled down half of the drink before tipping the hat low over her eyes and sitting back, arms crossed across her chest. Brex was impressed despite himself; to an uninterested observer, she looked just like any other creature of the night, lolling drunk after too many Caldonian whiskeys. But Brex could see the flash of her dark eyes as she watched the door, waiting.

Her wait was not long. Two gorths burst through the door just a few minutes later, and Brex groaned. Of course, it had to be Arlo and Keon. The two scum-sucking bottom-feeders were employed by the Central Core's secret police (and plenty of other shady warlords and gangsters too) and, unfortunately, Brex knew them well. The bartender shook his head in resigned disgust when the door bounced off its hinges, but said nothing to the two men, undoubtedly familiar with them. Arlo strode in behind his limping lackey, pulling a black leather glove from one pale hand and then the other. Brex, like many others in the bar—including the girl at the next table—shrank back into their jackets. Few people who ran on the outer rims hadn't dealt with Arlo at some point, and many did not survive their interactions with him. Clawing his way up the ranks, Arlo had become one of the most ruthless gorths in the galaxy, so much so that Brex often forgot that he was even terran—human. Brex was one of the few who had gotten away with the herculean task of thwarting Arlo and living to tell the tale. That didn't mean they now shared a warm and intimate friendship, and Brex had made a conscious decision years ago to avoid anyone and anything associated with Arlo.

"You'll forgive us, friends, for the interruption," Arlo said in a poisonously warm voice that cut through the dense air and silenced the entire room, the gamblers in the corner subsiding meekly into their seats. "We seek someone who is very valuable, and we need to know if she has been seen here tonight." With a flourish, Keon flashed a tablet showing a wanted ad. The girl on the screen had honey blonde hair and piercing gold eyes, but it was clear to Brex that it was the same girl who sat one booth over. Obviously, she had altered her appearance in an attempt to hide from her hunters, but

Brex wasn't sure if it was going to work. When no one spoke, Keon began to prowl among the tables while Arlo stood lazily by the bar, watching as the setting sun poured through the open door and glinted off the barrel of his gun. To her credit, the girl didn't move, and Brex wondered if she would remain undiscovered. Unfortunately for them both, however, he saw one of the toads sitting at another table gesture towards their corner. Brex sighed and slugged back the dregs of his drink before subtly reaching down and cocking the hammer on one of his revolvers. Relics from a bygone age, the twin guns had been in his mother's family for generations, but they still fired bullets, and that was all that mattered to Brex. Keon slowly approached Brex's table, anticipation making his cracked lips peel away from his yellow teeth.

"Stand up, you," demanded Keon, gesturing to Brex, who sighed and stood, keeping his black hat low over his eyes.

"I am not the one you seek," Brex said in his gruffest voice, but it did him no good. Arlo's head jerked up at the sound of his distinctive drawl, and a malicious smile spread across the gorth's face.

"No," Arlo said in a delighted voice, striding forward. "You are not who I seek, but that doesn't mean we don't have unfinished business, Carrow." Brex sighed. Damn this girl, whoever she was, for leading them here. Nonchalantly, he tipped his hat back and grinned at Arlo and Keon.

"Boys," Brex drawled genially.

"Been a while, Brex," Keon sniggered, and Brex had to check the urge to slug the little weasel in the throat.

"We have unfinished dealings, Carrow," snarled Arlo.

"Yeah, about that. You see—" Arlo's grab was lightning fast, and he had his left hand wrapped around Brex's throat in a blink. Arlo's sleeve fell away from his arm, revealing an incomplete mechanized limb with shiny plating and electronics.

"That's new," Brex choked out, staring at the whirring gears that had taken the place of muscle and sinew. The new mechanics stretched from wrist to elbow, and while clearly unfinished, it already was far stronger than the human muscles it had replaced.

"Do you like it?" asked Arlo, smiling as he admired the hardware himself. "A pretty little Orchidian who ran away bought me this." Brex had no reply; he was having a hard enough time breathing while the hand gripped his windpipe. Arlo turned his gaze back to Brex. "Great for times like this." Arlo struck out, smashing his right fist into Brex's mouth while the left held still gripped his throat. The blow knocked Brex back against the table and made his whole head spin. His mouth was flooded with blood, metallic and sour, but Brex sat back up to stare at the two gorths, his grin red.

"That the best you've got?" he smirked. Both Keon and Arlo glanced at one another before they dove at him, and he disappeared under their fists.

Gaia watched the dark-haired man at the next table disappear under an avalanche of blows as Arlo and Keon attacked him. While she was sorry they were hitting him, she took advantage of the gorths' distraction to edge from behind her table and make for the door. She was halfway across the floor when there was another shout. Spinning around, she saw her neighbor had Keon in a chokehold, but that hadn't stopped the rat from shouting and pointing at her. Arlo's ugly face was alight with pleasure, having realized his prey was so close. She winced, chiding herself for stopping, and spun back for the door, breaking into the first steps of a sprint, shedding the hat and long coat she had borrowed. Arlo shoved Brex and Keon to the side and dove after her. Recognizing the predatory look on Arlo's face and knowing it didn't bode well for the girl, Brex reacted instinctively. Figuring that the enemy of his enemy was his friend, Brex kicked Keon to the floor and launched himself forward, snagging Arlo by the tail of his coat, dragging him back. But it was too late; Arlo had thrown a length of chain and managed to wind it around the girl's ankles, tangling her feet and knocking her to the floor. While she wrestled with the chain, Brex punched Arlo, trying to force the other man down long enough for him to help the girl. A knee to the groin did the trick (at least he was still human in that respect), and Brex staggered to his feet. He dashed the short distance to the girl, grabbed her hand, dragged her to her feet, and forced her out the door, Arlo's howls of pain echoing after them.

Keeping a firm grip on her wrist, Brex sprinted down the street, which had emptied of occupants once the sun had disappeared. The industrial landscape of Annui was dim and shadowed, lit faintly by the distant, orange glow of the factories that ran around the clock. They raced down one street, turned a corner, ran the length of another street and made a right before slowing to an unsuspicious walk. Wincing, he touched two fingers to his lips. Both were split open and dripping blood onto his grey t-shirt. The girl stopped walking, yanking herself free as Brex spat a mouthful of blood onto the ground.

"What are you doing?" asked Brex, staring at her in confusion as she started to back away. She stared past him to avoid his dark blue eyes and swallowed before speaking in a crisp, formal tone, her accent unfamiliar.

"Thank you for your assistance, but I must be going."

"Going?" His dark eyebrows rose of their own volition.

"Yes." The word was clipped and short. "I no longer require your help." But as she spoke, a group of dark figures detached themselves from the shadows and started down the street in their direction. Laughter, dark with anticipation, echoed off the narrow tenements as the group advanced.

"This is not somewhere we want to be after dark," Brex muttered, glancing around for an exit.

"I'll just be go—"

"You'll go nowhere," Brex growled under his breath. "I just saved your ass," he reminded her. "If you don't want both of us to be raped to death on a dirty street, I suggest you play along," he said, and quickly wrapped an arm around her hips, yanking her against him. She immediately tried to jerk away.

"Get your hands off me," she snarled, trying to pull free.

"Did you not hear me?" Brex demanded as the advancing figures drew level with them. "Play along, and we'll both see the sunrise tomorrow." Tucking her close to his side, Brex turned to face the group head on.

"Awful pretty one you got there," the lead figure said, coming to a stop just beyond the circle of light cast down by a flickering street lamp. He jerked his head at the girl, who bristled. "A little light up top, but we'll take what we can get, won't we boys?" Sinister chuckles broke out from the half dozen men who fanned out into a half-circle around their intended victims.

"Sorry," Brex said in a hard voice. "I'm not in the mood to share."

"Don't think I was asking you." As the man leaned into the circle of light, Brex could see he wasn't terran at all, but looked like an Imathine, a humanoid life form known for their penchant for drinking blood. Brex gripped the girl's narrow frame tightly, his broad hand covering almost her entire rib cage.

"Well, I'm telling you. Back up." His hand slipped down to cock one of the revolvers that hung from his hips.

"Oooh, scary," one of the dark figures to Brex's left jeered as they all drew knives from within their heavy coats. "We're shakin' in terror, ain't we?" Brex, already tired of the game, yanked the gun from its holster and fired. The clap of gunfire echoed around the street, and they all jerked around to see the speaker suddenly unable to form words around a bloody, gaping hole in his throat.

"Should we see how scary he'll look when the back of his head is blown off?" Brex asked, keeping his gun trained on the leader of the group. With a swift motion, the leader gestured to his men, who grabbed their companion who was already choking to death on his own blood and fled back down the street. As a door slammed behind them, Brex glanced down at the young woman, who was watching him intently with those liquid-dark eyes.

"What do you say we get out of here before someone else comes along and tries to kill us?"

# Chapter Three

"Where are you taking me?" Gaia demanded as Brex towed her through the dark towards a run-down airstrip, his grip like iron around her wrist and a dark glint in his eyes. Instinctively, she knew it would be unwise to challenge him at that moment. She was a bit uneasy, going along with a total stranger, but as he was no friend of Arlo's, and she thought perhaps he might be able to help her.

The airstrip he led her to appeared neglected and forlorn, as a number of rough-looking ships sat scattered around the runway in various states of disrepair. Broken windows showed the inside of buildings that had been scorched in a fire, and the watery moonlight gave everything a dark and depressed look. At first glance, the arrangement appeared random and the ships forgotten, but as they got closer, Gaia could see that it was all done purposefully. The abandoned facade worked well and made the place extremely uninviting.

"My ship is docked here," he told her, pointing towards one of the large, shapeless heaps. "If you want to get out of here alive, getting off surface is the best bet. Off the planet's surface and the hell away from Arlo and Keon, for a start." He slid her a glance as he pressed his palm against the reader screen of his ship's hull. With a dull hiss of hydraulics, a doorway opened, and a walkway descended. Brex tugged Gaia up the gangplank and hit a button, closing the door behind firmly them. "Speaking of Arlo and Keon," he said, as he released her and hit the light switches and the engine warm-up panel, "who are you and why are they so interested in you?" He leaned back against a metal storage locker as lights flooded the main bay, and the engine started to cough and sputter to life. She perched herself on a nearby stack of crates and glanced at him, letting her gaze travel over him and through the ship's bay filled with lock boxes and gun cabinets before landing back on him.

"I could ask you the same question."

"Answering a question with a question. Smart for someone who doesn't want to give anything away."

"And not answering at all, the best line of defense," Gaia retorted.

"I figure I just saved your skin, twice. Why not humor the man who rescued you and answer the question?"

"Why did you save me anyway?" she demanded instead, staring at him hard. He didn't look anything like the other men she had encountered during her life on Annui. Most of them were polished, crisp, and neat or massive, plodding, and slow. The man standing in front of her wore faded black combat pants, a blood-splattered grey t-shirt that stretched across his wide chest, and dusty, seen-better-days boots that stopped just below his knees. A pair of leather holsters seemed out of place as they hung off his narrow hips. His dark brown hair, a smidge too long, curled against his sun-tanned skin, and his dark sapphire eyes roved over her, taking in every inch. He was attractive in a rugged sort of way, and Gaia felt her cheeks flame as his eyes moved over her slowly like a caress. He scrutinized her, taking in the mass of sable curls, and the infinite depth of her black eyes before shrugging.

"I figure the enemy of my enemy is my friend. Obviously, you've got some sort of issue with Keon, Arlo, and I'm going to assume the government as well, which puts us on about even footing." She didn't respond so he shook his head. "Whatever, I'm all for getting off the planet. If you don't want to come, then fine, stay here and go to prison, if you make it that far. If you would like to come along, feel free, just pay your way."

"I'll go with you," she muttered, glancing around at the ship. "What is it exactly that you do again?" asked Gaia. Brex glanced around at the pallets, boxes, and bins with a mild smirk.

"I'm a man of many talents."

"Such as?"

"Does it matter?" he asked, grinning. She gave him a disbelieving look, waiting with her arms crossed. "Fine. I'm mostly in protection, but I'll do whatever the buyer has in mind, provided the price is right."

"So you're a mercenary." It was a statement, not a question. Brex laughed, but the sound rang of denial.

"I am not a merc." Her response was a skeptically raised eyebrow. "I'm not," he insisted. "At least not most of the time. More bodyguard than gun-for-hire, but I'll take any job I can get." His smile, as he gazed around his ship, had a roguish light to it that Gaia didn't trust for a second. Gaia followed his eyes, staring at the ship. The main bay was crowded with wooden crates, covered in all manner of text, half a dozen gun cabinets that were bursting with weapons Gaia had never seen, and metal lock boxes overflowing with ammunition. The railings and walkways were tinted red with rust, and the patchy black paint was flaking away from the walls, revealing the ancient and abused metal beneath it. "A thousand units and I'll take you wherever you want to go on the inner rings."

"Part-time mercenary, part-time taxi driver?"

"Anything for a unit, miss."

"Does this thing even fly?" Gaia asked, disbelief clear in her voice as the engine let loose a loud bang. Brex clapped his hand over his heart as though mortally wounded.

"How dare you. Of course, she'll fly. Adyta hasn't let me down yet."

"Adota?" she asked uncertainly. Brex glared at her purposeful mispronunciation of his ship's name.

"Ah-dye-ta," he spat, pronouncing each syllable. "Roughly translated it means sanctuary."

"Sanctuary, huh?" His eyes narrowed at her scorn. "Are you hiding from something?"

"Listen, missy, this ship is going to save your butt."

"I'll believe it when I see it," she snapped, jumping down from her stack of crates, but she swayed dizzily and took a step back to catch herself.

"Whoa," Brex said, lurching forward and grabbing her arm as she stumbled. She hissed and pulled from his grip but leaned back against the crates, her eyes dilated and completely black. "You alright? Listen, I—" but before he could say another word, her eyes rolled back into her head, and she collapsed.

Gaia felt a tapping on her cheek, but it was the unfamiliar voice that sounded in her ear that made her jerk awake.

"Hey, you…—um, miss?" She lurched away from the sound, instinctively glancing around for something to use as a weapon. "Whoa, easy there," said the man, stepping back and holding up his hands in surrender. "You're alright. I'm not going to do anything to you." Looking down, Gaia took in a narrow bunk, her legs covered in a light blue blanket. Staring around the cramped room that contained three more bunks and a small table, she tried to remember how she had gotten there, but the memories wouldn't come.

"Where am I?" she demanded, clenching her hands tightly, trying to ward off the waves of dizziness and nausea.

"The bunk room. You collapsed about fifteen minutes ago. I'm Brexler Carrow, and this is my ship, Adyta. I never caught your name." She eyed his extended hand for a beat before shaking. Large and calloused, his hand was warm, like his eyes as he smiled at her.

"Gaia."

"Just Gaia?" he asked, raising a dark eyebrow.

"For now, yes."

# Chapter Four

"So, Gaia, where are you headed?" Brex asked. She was perched on the edge of the control console, just within his peripheral vision as he sat in the captain's chair, guiding the ship through Annui's dense cloud layer. They passed through the smog-tinted clouds, the dusky orange light from the factories illuminating the curve of Brex's cheekbones, the slice of his nose, the puffiness of his bruised lips and Gaia had to break away from studying him to answer.

She shrugged. "I'm not entirely sure," she began but lapsed into silence, a concerned look on her face as she chewed on her lower lip. After a long pause, she spoke. "I honestly don't know where I'm going next." He raised his eyebrows at her, but she didn't elaborate.

"Well, we've got to go somewhere." He paused, trying to curb his curiosity but failed. "How come you don't know?" She hesitated, letting her gaze linger on Brex's handsome face. It unnerved her that he was helping her. Her mother had always told her that they could trust no one. She wasn't sure how much to tell him, so she decided to be vague.

"I have spent my whole life knowing certain things, and now, suddenly, those things are wrong. I fled from the only life I've ever known without any information as to why I needed to flee in the first place. Arlo and Keon were sent after me for something I don't even understand." Brex stared at her, eyes narrowed in suspicion.

"You realize that made no sense whatsoever, right?" he asked. She tossed her mane of dark hair and glared at him. Her eyes, a deep, icy cobalt blue, regarded with him with annoyance. Brex checked himself—had her eyes always been blue? Right before she had fainted, he had sworn they were as black as space itself. He shook his head to clear the weird image from his head before raising his eyebrows at her again.

"I don't understand."

"You think I understand any better?" she bit back.

"Well, you should," he said, "considering you're the one in this mess."

Gaia growled at him, an almost feline sound that came from deep within her chest, but didn't reply.

Gaia was silent for the fifteen minutes it took for Brex to navigate his ship through the final atmosphere layer of Annui. Once they hit the glittering blackness of open space, he set the autopilot and spun in his chair to face her.

"Since it's going to be very boring up here for a while, why don't you start from the beginning?" he asked.

She bit her lip, contemplating. "No," she said, climbing down from the control console and swirling out of the cockpit.

"Hey!" Brex lurched from his chair to follow her. Catching up with her on the metal catwalk above the main bay, he grabbed her arm and spun her around. "Listen, I get that you're going through some stuff right now, but don't bite the hand that feeds you, little lady. I saved your ass, for no good reason, I might add, other than the fact that I will take every chance I get to piss off Arlo. That, and I didn't really feel like dying today. Since we have an enemy in common, I figure that makes us allies." She stared at him, her eyes almost even with his own, her gaze blue, bottomless, and very tempting to get lost in. But he shook himself. "Give me something other than a name. Am I signing myself up to get killed by helping you? Who are you really?" he demanded.

"It doesn't matter who I am. Drop me on the next planet, and I'll disappear. You'll be better for having me gone," she said, tugging her arm out of his grip and marching away. He cursed his natural rescuer instinct but shook his head and followed her.

"Why?" he demanded.

"Why do you care?" she snapped, rounding on him. "You said it yourself, you didn't help me to help me. It was just to piss off Arlo—and the fact that I'm paying you, I might add." Brex stepped back, a little unsure. The fire that swirled in the depths of her midnight-blue eyes was a little frightening— not that he would ever admit it, but it spooked him. "So, do me a favor and just leave me on the next planet. I'll pay you your money, be off your ship, and you'll never see me again." She looked away, a haughty tilt to her chin. Brex set his jaw. Two could play the stubborn game.

"Fine," he spat. "My warp drive is on the fritz so it'll take a couple of hours for us to hit Prexleria. Feel free to—goddamn it!" As he spoke, the girl turned back to face him, her eyes suddenly hazy and blank. She swayed and her knees buckled as she crumpled to the floor, unconscious. "For fuck's sake, girl," Brex growled as he knelt and gathered her long frame into his arms. "What is with you?" He carried her through the ship and deposited her back into the spare bunk, leaving her there, figuring she'd be out for a while.

A half hour later, when a cluster of tiny blips appeared on his long-range scanner screen and headed right for them, Brex knew they were in trouble. So much for their head start. Sighing, he kicked up the power and switched back into autopilot so he could warn his guest. When he entered the bunk room, his heart stopped. The girl was still lying where he had left her, but instead of the dark-haired beauty that he had met in the bar, the young woman lying with her back to him was a shockingly fiery redhead. Clapping a hand to his chest to make sure his heart hadn't torn free and run for cover, he carefully approached Gaia. He poked her shoulder and jumped back when she moaned.

He slipped a hand down to cock one of his revolvers before speaking. "Gaia! Hey!" She rolled over to look at him and at the sight of gold-flecked emerald eyes, Brex felt his brain freeze. How was that even possible? He pulled his gun free and pointed it at her. "Listen here, missy, I don't know who the hell or what the hell you are, but you need to start talking, now. There is a cluster of gorth ships on our tail, and I'd like to have some fucking clue of what I've gotten myself into!"

She told him her story in bits and pieces as they returned to the control room.

"I am not a native Annuian," she began, and Brex sputtered in semi-hysterical laughter.

"No shit!" The girl, with her narrow face and slender body, was about as far from the hulking, troll-like natives of Annui as physically possible. She shot him a withering look but spoke as he gestured for her to continue.

"I'm not entirely sure where I'm from. My mother sought refuge on Annui when I was a toddler. She never told me our history, except that we were no longer welcome where we had both been born. I never knew my father or anything about the world that we left behind. The memories I have are disconnected and vague. I'm not sure if what I remember is real or just dreams." What Gaia didn't mention were the nightmares she had carried as long as she could remember: the dreams where red, violent eyes glared through the dark, and an icy voice ordered her death over and over again.

"How can you change? You had black hair an hour ago."

She shook her head. "That is another piece of the puzzle that I am not entirely sure about. Growing up, under the guise of her religion, my mother kept both her hair and mine covered. When mine started to change as I reached adolescence, she made me swear to never show another person. She revealed that hers also changed. I did not understand why and she refused to explain, saying it was not safe for me to know. When my eyes started to change, she kept me indoors, afraid someone would notice. Daily, she reminded me to never let anyone know our secret." She paused, and her face clearly showed her pain. "I resented my mother for keeping me in the dark, for refusing to tell me about my past. The only thing I knew was that if we were discovered by the wrong people, something terrible would happen."

"Because you'd probably scare the hell outta them?" Brex offered, and she threw him another look. "You glare at me a lot. You might not want to do that," he suggested, but she glared at him again through slitted eyelids. He rolled his own eyes and motioned for her to keep speaking.

"It was about a month ago when the secret police finally came for us. Someone had discovered our secret and informed the Central Core. The head of the secret police came for my mother himself. Her last act was to hide my whereabouts. They tore the house apart looking for me, and then sent Arlo and Keon after me that same night." Brex wouldn't say it, but he was impressed. For a girl—a single, solitary girl—to evade Keon and Arlo for almost a month with no help, that was a legendary feat. It was an unfortunate reality that the two gorths were very good at what they did.

"Why do they want you?" he asked.

Gaia only shrugged. "I have no idea. I have not heard from my mother since they took her." Tears pooled in her green eyes, but she shook her head and refused to let them fall. Brex had to admire her stubborn strength. The only world she knew had collapsed around her and yet here she was, still standing, still fighting, not curled up in a ball somewhere crying like most women he knew would have been.

"And what is your plan now?"

Another shrug. "I have to find out what I am, why they would imprison my mother, and somehow, by some miracle, rescue her if I can. But I have no idea where to start." She glanced at him. "I've been more concerned with running than planning," she admitted. Brex chewed this over for a long moment before speaking.

"If you make it worth my while, I'll help you."

"What?"

"Pay me, and I'll do what I can to help you track down your origins and your mother."

"How much?"

Brex contemplated for a moment. "Thirty thousand units, fifteen when we find out what you are and the last fifteen when we find your mother."

"Fifteen thousand total."

"Twenty plus any expenses or bribes. This isn't going to be easy, you know?"

"I'm well aware of that," she snapped, narrowing her eyes at him. "Where do we even start?"

"I might know someone who can help you," he temporized.

"Do you?" she asked, interest sparkling bright in her gaze.

He held up a cautionary hand. "Do we have a deal?"

"Tell me what you have in mind first."

"What, and give away my whole plan and cheat myself?"

"Are you serious?" she demanded, giving him a deadpan expression. "Does it look like I have many options to choose from? Give me an idea of what you're thinking just so I know you aren't going to get me killed."

Brex hesitated, weighing her words but shrugged a moment later. "I have a friend; he's very well-traveled and knows the far corners of the galaxy better than anyone else. A call to him could point us in the right direction."

"So call him."

"Are you going to make this worth my while or not?" Already she could tell that Brex would do almost anything for cash. He had said it himself. Gaia gave him a hard stare but then shrugged.

"Of course. Shall we say another thousand units, in addition to the original twenty, if your friend's information proves to be useful?"

"Five thousand."

"Two thousand."

"Twenty-three thousand total."

"Deal!" Gaia stuck out a delicate hand, and Brex shook. "Do you really think your friend can help us?" she asked, trying to distract herself from the warmth of Brex's touch as their grips disengaged.

"Maybe. I can't say he'll be excited to see me, though."

"Brexler Carrow. I thought you were dead." The dispassionate voice wafted through the air before the screen on the console crackled to life, and a bald man with a fat face appeared.

"Nope, Zaire, still floating around out here."

"You better hope you stay out there. If you set foot on Xael, you're a dead man. You still owe me fifty thousand units."

"I do not," Brex said, dismissing the debt with a wave of his hand. "So listen, I have something I need your help with."

"And why in the name of all the gods would I want to help you?"

"I'll make it worth your while."

"Liar. You already owe me more money that you could hope to pay."

"He'll double it," Gaia spoke from behind Brex, who whipped around in his chair with wide eyes. She stood behind him, well out of view of the screen, as he had requested before he put the call through. Her hands were planted firmly on her hips, and one red eyebrow was raised as she looked at Brex's surprised face.

"Who is that, Brexler?" Zaire's shrill voice demanded as Brex stared at Gaia in disbelief.

"That is who I need your help with, Zaire," Brex said finally, turning back to the screen, shaking his head in incredulity.

"Well, who is she?" Gaia moved to step up to the screen, but Brex put a hand on her flat stomach and pushed her back out of view.

"Picked up an interesting fare. She's searching for her origins and doesn't know where to start. Since you are a well-traveled collector of oddities, I figured you might have a guess where she could begin."

"Well, can I see her or do you expect me to guess from thin air?" Brex had to conceal a grin. He had known that Zaire's curious nature would get the better of him.

"No, you don't need to see her." Zaire glared at him through the screen, but Brex held up a hand.

"Better if you don't, my friend. Don't ask—just listen." The fat man folded his arms, waiting, one imperious eyebrow raised. Brex sighed before glancing over his shoulder at Gaia.

"Twenty-something girl. Has the ability or well, not it's an ability exactly, but the color of her hair and eyes change, randomly."

"Without dyes or infusions?"

"No way to change that rapidly or that purely. She's a red-head as if she was born that way, but when I met her a couple hours ago, she had hair the color of Mira's,—"—naming Zaire's favorite dark-haired slave girl,—"but has no idea of how or why it happens." Glancing back at her again, Brex added, "Has a tendency to fall unconscious quite a bit." Gaia wrinkled her nose at him and rolled her eyes but remained silent. "The eyes change too. Went from black to blue to the purest emerald green in a matter of hours." Zaire's piggy face went still.

"She can change the color of her irises?" The shock in the collector's voice was palpable.

Brex glanced at Gaia who shrugged before turning back to the screen and nodding. "Yep. Any ideas?"

"A moment," Zaire said as he held up a pudgy finger before he waddled away from the screen.

"Why won't you let him see me?" Gaia demanded as soon as Zaire's fat frame was gone from view.

"Just being cautious. If things go bad for us, he doesn't need to be endangered by knowing who you are or what you look like." Brex shrugged. "The less he knows, the less he can say." His statement was deliberately cryptic, Gaia realized. It implied it would keep Zaire safe, but it also meant he couldn't betray them. Brex was smarter than she initially gave him credit for.

"And how exactly do you know him?" Gaia asked, wondering if he could be trusted.

Brex smiled and ran a rueful hand through his hair. "I've had business dealings with him in the past, but over the years, Zaire has become a really entertaining friend. He makes his money by dealing in oddities and rarities from around the galaxy. Sometimes he pays me to procure certain things, sometimes he pays me to convince other collectors to pay what they owe."

"So you're a merc and a thief," she observed, her voice suddenly warm and teasing.

"Hey, I am not a mercenary! And alright, yes, I might be a thief, but at least I'm an honorable one."

Gaia ignored that. "And the fifty thousand units you owe him?" Brex laughed, but Gaia thought there was something off about the sound.

"I may have helped one of his favorite slaves escape about five years ago. She paid me to help her flee, and who am I to say no to good money? Speaking of which," he said, eyeing her carefully, "where am I going to get a hundred thousand units to pay him if this works?"

"I have the money."

"What do you mean, you have the money?" Her expression was haughty as she stared at him.

"My mother and I lived very frugally. She came to Annui with a sum of money meant to provide for us for the remainder of both our lives. If it helps me discover my past, it is money well spent," Gaia finished, unconcerned. Brex had to tear his mind away from the fact that she could just toss a sum of one hundred thousand units around like it was pocket change.

"Why not just pay someone to find your mother or to protect you from Arlo?"

"Who?" she asked. "I know no one. I trust no one."

"And me?" Brex asked.

"I do not trust you," she said, eyeing him suspiciously. "But you have helped me, so I will give you the benefit of the doubt for the time being." Brex wasn't sure how to take that. The notion of another person trusting him with their fate made him vaguely itchy, but he pushed the feeling down. Now was not the time to be thinking about Bria.

After another few moments in silence, Zaire came puffing back into the frame, a large book clutched in his arms.

His grip obscured the title, but Gaia could see swirls of gilded text crossing the leather cover.

"Well?" Brex demanded.

"Either you are very unlucky or very stupid, Brexler."

"Hey!"

"Shut up, you fool. If she has the abilities that you say she does, you may have just found one of the more rare beings in our known galaxy. Let me see her."

"No."

"Brexler!" The collector's voice was wheedling, plaintive, like a child denied a treat.

"No, Zaire. Listen, I've got a fleet of gorth patrollers about twenty clicks behind me and closing fast. Tell me what you know, and we'll go from there."

The collector grumbled audibly but made a great show of opening the book and flipping through the heavy pages before reading aloud. "She could be what is known as a Tallpian, which means chameleon in an ancient language." He glanced up to make sure Brex was paying attention. "They are a humanoid race, from the most remote part of the Western Edge. As a species, they have the ability to change their appearance at will but—" Before Zaire could finish his explanation, an explosion rocked the ship and Brex swore, barely clinging to his chair. Gaia's feet slipped from under her, and she landed hard on the metal floor. Swearing in a language Brex didn't recognize, she hauled herself to her feet, grabbing the back of his chair to keep steady. The transmission screen was snowed with static, and Zaire's voice was broken and metallic. "Wiped out…dangerous…coup… killed" were the only words that came through before the transmission broke and the screen went black.

"Shit, they must have hit one of the comm-links. We need to move fast." Brex dove under the steering console to unhook and re-attach several wires before kicking the hatch closed.

He grimaced at Gaia as he slid back into his seat. "Let's just hope this works." He glanced around. "You're going to want to hold on to something." Crossing his fingers and his toes for good measure, Brex hit the warp drive ignition. There was a loud bang, and the engine coughed hard, but Brex could hardly believe their luck as the stars started to lengthen and the ship darted into warp just as another explosion rocked Adyta.

# Chapter Five

Exiting warp not far from the planet Cunat, Brex limped his smoking ship to the planet's dusty surface.

"This is where you plan to hide?" Gaia asked, staring in disbelief as Brex maneuvered the ship to the far side of a pathetic little airstrip outside a windblown town. They landed amidst the dust and other broken-down-looking ships after a lyrical voice came over the radio and gave them permission to land.

"Until the warp drive and the rest of the damage to Adyta can be repaired? Yes." His tone left no room for argument. He left her in the ship as he inspected the damage and returned a few minutes later, slapping the dust from his gloves and looking worried, a smear of grease on his forehead. Gaia surveyed him with raised eyebrows, trying to ignore the feeling of anxiety that rose in her stomach.

"Well?" she asked.

Brex blew out a hard sigh. "Shot to hell. They landed a solid hit. It's a miracle we even made it into warp, let alone survived getting out of it." He glared and pointed his wrench at her. "If this is what I get for helping you, I'm not sure how much longer I want to be friends." She gave him an icy glare and muttered her reply in a language that Brex didn't understand. He raised his eyebrows. "Want to try that one again?"

"Trust me," she said, switching back to scornful common tongue, "the last thing I want is to be your friend. But you agreed to help me, and I'll pay you when we've found my heritage and my mother. Agreed?" Brex rolled his eyes but stuck his hand out again with a mocking smile on his face. Gaia shook his hand warily before letting go quickly. Touching him made her skin flush, and she wasn't sure why—all she knew was that she didn't like the sensation one bit.

"Agreed, lady." He looked around the ship and then out the window at the bright Cunat sun. "We can crash here for a day or two. I've got a friend who should be able to help us get things fixed." Brex grabbed a small satchel from a shelf near the door before moving to leave. Gaia followed him. "Whoa, whoa, where do you think you're going?" he asked, spinning to look at her as she marched through the doors on his heels.

"You're not leaving me here alone."

"Aw, are you scared?" he teased but immediately recoiled when she snarled at him.

"Of course not, you ass. I don't trust you out of my sight. How do I know you won't turn around and sell me to Arlo to save your own skin?"

Brex snorted in derision. "I saved your life, and you still don't trust me?"

"Not for all of the god's gifts," she retorted. Brex cocked his head to one side.

"Your gods or my gods? Who are your gods, anyway?"

"Does it even matter?" she asked, exasperated. "I'm not staying here."

"Fine. But if you're coming with me, you're not going out like that. You already stick out; let's not draw any unnecessary attention to ourselves." As if flaming red hair wouldn't make her stand out enough, her high-quality jacket, pants, and boots marked her as an outsider. Cunat was a poor planet on the far-flung South Western outer rim: its main industry was raising thin cattle on the dust-choked plains. "Come on," he said, tugging her arm, "we both need to change."

"This is completely ridiculous," Gaia said through the scarf that was wound around her head. They walked down the wide, dusty street towards the main chunk of the town that sat just beyond the airstrip.

Brex rounded on her, looking sterner than she had ever seen. "Your hair and eyes change at random. You think that won't attract some attention? Never mind the fact that you are probably one of the loveliest creatures to ever set foot here. You won't go unnoticed. If you expect me to help you, we do it by my rules. And one of my rules is to blend in as much as possible to avoid suspicion." Gaia muttered inaudible words under her breath but didn't argue. On top of the far-too-large, long-sleeve white, button-up shirt that he insisted she wear, Brex had wrapped a large, sand-colored scarf around her hair and face, leaving just her eyes visible. She had borrowed a belt, turning the overly large shirt into a dress that at least covered her legs above the knee but there wasn't much she could do about the scarf. She had re-wound it, shooting him an ugly look as she did, making it so she could breathe. Brex had changed into a pair of faded denim pants, a black button-down shirt, and a black felt cowboy hat that was perched atop his dark hair. A worn bandana was tied around his neck, for the dust, he said. The look suited him, Gaia realized, as she watched him check the cylinders of his revolvers before placing them in his holsters. He looked up from his task and met her eyes, a knowing smile creeping onto his face. Gaia looked away immediately, feeling a flush flood her cheeks, although she wasn't sure why. As they disembarked the ship, Brex slapped a long dagger in a sheath into her hand.

"What is this?" She demanded.

Brex shot her a look that brooked no argument. "If the gods, both mine and whoever yours are, are good, you won't ever need to use that. But since my luck is usually shit, I suggest you carry it for the time being. You need to be able to protect yourself." She had just held it, staring at him, so Brex yanked it from her hand. Dropping to his knees in front of her, he grabbed her leg just above the knee, ignoring her gasp of shock. Her skin was like silk under his fingers, but he couldn't even begin to contemplate what it would have been like to run his hand up the length of her inner thigh. Ignoring the lust that swirled in his gut, he slid the knife and its sheath down the length of her boot, hoping she would be able to use it if needed.

Their path through town brought them to a stop in front of a low-slung building that looked like the rest of the small city: on the verge of crumbling into the dust. Brex stopped Gaia at the door and tugged the scarf further up over her nose. He was just going to have to take the chance and hope that no one would look her directly in the eye and that she wouldn't go through any changes in the near future.

"There are people everywhere, on every planet and in every city, who are spies, informers," he explained as she tried to pull out of his grasp. He ignored her and yanked on the scarf again, covering her flyaway red tresses. "Arlo has a network that spans the galaxy. If you want to survive long enough to discover your heritage, I suggest that you listen to me." He took her hand and laced his fingers through hers, keeping hold when she recoiled. "I know what I am doing. Auggie is one of my best friends, and I've known him since, well, we've known each other a long time. We can trust him, but he's going to be really surprised to see me, so just don't say anything," he ordered as he pulled her along behind him as they stepped into the dark building.

Greeted by a jumble of engines and spare parts, Gaia looked around, letting her eyes adjust to the gloom. As Brex strode forward, towing her around the piles of junk, something caught her eye and made her stop, tugging against Brex. On the dismantled hull of a small over-land speeder, she saw the same marking she had seen in the factory, the white square with a yellow slash. When Brex looked at her in annoyance, she pointed to it. After a moment of speculation, he shrugged at her to indicate he had no idea what the sign meant—even though he did. But he wasn't about to explain to her about the Outer Rim Brotherhood right now or his place within it; their situation was complicated enough.

At the back of the shop, there was the incessant sound of metal being ground and bent against its will, and they followed it until they stopped a few feet from a workbench, where a man sat, sparks flying from his grinder.

"Auggie!" Brex shouted over the noise, and the man who sat with his back to them turned, flipping up his welding mask. After glancing at Gaia in a brief second of confusion, his eyes focused on Brex and his face split into a huge smile.

He jumped up to hug Brex and thump him on the back. "Brex! I didn't know you were still alive," he said, laughing.

Brex shook his head as he pulled back from the embrace. "What is with all of the rumors that I'm dead? Zaire said the same thing." Auggie pulled the mask from his head, revealing a head of copper-colored curls. He had fair skin despite the searing Cunat sun, a toothy smile that sat below a large nose, and blue eyes that were very close together. His lean, lanky height hinted at his youth (not much older than Gaia if she had to guess), but something about his rolling, fluid movements made Gaia suspect he wasn't entirely terran.

"I'm pretty sure it was Zaire who started the rumor. He wanted to murder you after that whole mess with Bria."

Brex laughed and shrugged. "What? She was very pretty and had a good deal of money to offer. Who am I to say no to rescuing beautiful women?" Gaia snorted in disbelief at his words, and both men turned to look at her, Auggie raising his eyebrows at Brex.

"You mean who are you to turn down good money, regardless of the job? But speaking of beautiful women," he started, but Brex silenced him with a look.

"This is Raelle," he lied, towing Gaia forward. "Picked her up on Pantonia, and she needs some help looking into her past."

"And you're her obliging tour guide? Auggie asked suspiciously, making it clear he didn't believe a word of Brex's story.

"Paid tour guide, obviously."

"So what do you need from me, Brex? You never show up unless you need a favor."

"I may have run into some old friends who decided to use my ship for target practice."

Auggie laughed and shook his head, waving a hand, dismissing them. "No way, Brex. I've already fixed Adyta too many times to count. For free, I might add."

"This is important, Auggie,"

"Then don't lie to me."

"I'm not. I'm doing you a favor," Brex said, his joking tone gone. "The less you know, the less you have to tell."

Auggie's easy smile disappeared in a blink. "I'm starting to think that you might not be doing me any favors at all. Why are you here, Brex?"

"We need help. I've got to get Adyta up and running again. As quickly as possible." The mechanic eyed them both suspiciously.

"What have you gotten into this time, Carrow?"

"You don't want to know."

"And who is going to come by looking for you in a few days?"

"More likely than not? Some of our favorite gorths."

Auggie groaned. "Really? You're mixed up with Arlo again?" Gaia opened her mouth to say something, but Brex silenced her with a gesture before turning back to his friend.

"I'll pay you, for real this time, just as soon as we find who she's looking for. But we need to get moving and moving fast." Auggie surveyed them in silence while chewing on his bottom lip, looking thoughtful. Brex couldn't entirely conceal the desperation on his face.

"Give us a minute?" Gaia asked Auggie. Without waiting for an answer, she grabbed Brex by the front of his shirt and towed him into a dark corner of the shop. He shook her off once they were far enough away that Auggie couldn't hear them. "If he can't or won't help us, is there anyone else who can?" Gaia asked in a whisper.

Brex shook his head. "No one this good." He paused and thought about it. "No one who actually likes me."

"Brex, we don't have time for this. They will catch up to us."

"If we can pay Auggie now, he'll do it, no questions asked."

"Is that all it takes?"

Brex couldn't contain a snort. "Yes, usually."

"Well, then, pay him!"

"With what? I won't have enough money until this job is over," he reminded her. "I doubt he'll cut me a break this time, considering how much I owe him."

"Will this cover it?" Gaia reached into her blouse, digging around as Brex looked on in lascivious frankness. After a moment of fishing, she extracted a golden bar, about three inches long, an inch wide and about half an inch thick, worth 100,000 units.

Brex felt his eyes go wide. "Where did you get that?"

"You mean, besides from in my shirt?"

Brex rolled his eyes. "Obviously."

"I told you, my mother—"

"Left you some money, yeah, but you said nothing about it being in gold talents," he hissed.

Gaia shrugged. "I had no idea it made any difference." To Brex, it made an enormous difference. Talents were ancient currency. Still valuable and still usable but incredibly rare. It meant the person carrying them had connections to either crime or royalty. Or both.

"Do you have any idea of how rare those are? Wait no, of course you don't. Gods, what have I gotten myself into?"

Gaia bristled. "Fine," she said, slipping the gold back into place. "If you're so concerned about trouble, don't help me." She spun on her heel and made for the shop door, but Brex lunged and hauled her back by the tail of her dress. Auggie was staring at them, so Brex pulled her deeper into the shadows of the corner and crowded her up against the hull of an ancient crop transporter, his arms on either side of her shoulders.

"Damn it, woman," he hissed, "I am helping you. I could have left you for Arlo back in that bar. I could have left you to fight off those vultures on Annui. But for some insane reason, I chose not to so whether you like it or not, we are in this together. You are paying me to help you, and that is what I am doing. But you have to trust me! I get that you've got some major issue with that, but when I take money for a job, I see it through to the end," he snapped, ignoring the guilty twist in his gut. "Whatever else, you can stake your life on that." She pursed her lips but didn't argue. Brex sighed. "We are going to have Auggie fix my ship," he said quietly, "and lay low for a day or two. Once she is back up and running, we'll aim for Xael and Zaire's."

"Didn't Zaire say—?"

"He says a lot of things," Brex said, waving the threat away. "He wouldn't actually kill me. At least, I don't think so. Anyways, he is the only person who has any clue what or who you might be. Considering how he reacted, I have a feeling asking about Tallpians will lead us straight to trouble. I'd rather start on solid, familiar ground. Xael is a good place to start, and I trust Zaire." He eyed her significantly. "And you can trust me." She hesitated just long enough to make Brex stiffen, but she spoke, overriding his sputter of indignation.

"Alright," Gaia said, extracting the gold again. She looked at Brex carefully, like she was wondering why she had agreed, before slapping it into his hand. "I'll trust you."

"Thank you." He turned away, heading back to Auggie who was doing a spectacular impression of someone who was trying their best not to eavesdrop. Brex pulled him aside and had a rapid, whispered conversation. After a moment, he pulled the gold from his pocket and offered it to Auggie, whose mouth fell open in shock. He glanced over his shoulder at Gaia before turning back to Brex and nodding.

"This will cover the repairs I've done for the last ten years. I'll get Adyta back in shape in no time, Brex. Don't worry."

"I do, Auggie, but thanks. We'll just stay out of your way, and we can get out of here as soon as she's up and running."

"You don't need to hover, Brex. Go see Willa instead. She'll be rabid if she finds out you were here and didn't stop by to see her."

"Don't you dare tell her I'm here, Auggie. I'll go see her when it's safe."

"If you think Arlo is a threat to Willa, you've lost your mind, Brex." Brex laughed in agreement with Auggie's words. "Besides, you guys will need a place to crash for the next day. I'll be making too much noise for you to relax at all," Auggie pointed out. "Go lay low."

"We'll come see you tomorrow afternoon. Take care of my girl for me," Brex said tenderly, and it took Gaia a moment to realize he was talking about his ship.

"You got it. Now get out of here, I've got work to do."

"So how do you know him?" Gaia asked, blinking hard as they stepped back into the bright sunlight outside Auggie's shop. Brex sighed as he tugged the hem of the scarf back over Gaia's face.

"He's an old friend."

"Obviously," she said dryly. "How did you meet?" Brex looked uncomfortable at her prying, but shrugged after a minute. She had agreed to give him the benefit of the doubt; he figured he could return the favor.

"We grew up together. We didn't have an easy time, so we did what we could to help the other out. We've both fought tooth and nail to get where we are, even though Auggie never really left. But he's the best mechanic in the quadrant, so he does ok."

"Grew up? You were born—"

"Here? Yes. We both were." Gaia thought that explained the distaste on Brex's face as he looked around.

"Is he…." She couldn't think of the right way to phrase it.

"Terran?" Brex finished for her. "No. Well not entirely. Like I said, we had a lot in common. Neither of us knew our fathers. His mother is terran like mine, but in terms of dear old dad, he has no clue. I know my old man was terran, but I don't know much else about him."

"I never knew my father either; my mother said he was killed when I was a baby."

"At least you know what happened," Brex said with undisguised bitterness. "My dad could still be out there, but he made it clear he wanted nothing to do with me or my mother, so good riddance."

"Brex—"

"What?" He demanded, his ordinarily warm, teasing voice suddenly icy. Gaia shook her head—she could tell from the look in his eyes he didn't want her pity. Fine, then he wasn't going to get it.

"Never mind. What's our plan now?" she asked, trying to distract him. He sighed.

"We go see Willa."

"And who is Willa?" Gaia asked as they wove through the crowds. Brex took her arm and slipped it through his, holding on as she tried to tug herself free. He raised his eyebrows at her. After a second, she acquiesced and let him pull her close. The main avenue was sprawling and dusty, the shops weather-beaten, and the people care-worn. A few glances flickered in their direction, but Gaia ducked her head down against the wind and did her best to avoid eye contact.

"She runs a…an establishment here in town," Brex said carefully. Gaia narrowed her green eyes at him over the edge of the scarf, and he shuddered. "I'll admit, it is seriously creepy that almost every time I look at you, your eyes are a different color." Another glower.

"You think I like it?" she snapped, looking away. "Every time I look in the mirror, I have no idea who is staring back at me." Her voice dropped, raw with pain. "I have no idea who I am, or even what I am. It is like being a stranger in my own body." She sounded heartbroken, and Brex felt a surge of pity. He reflected on his own past and realized how lucky he was, despite how terrible it had been, growing up on Cunat. He knew exactly who he was and where he came from. He knew his family, what was left of them anyway, and he knew where he fit into the world. It may have been working on the shady Outer Rim, but it·was a manageable life that let Brex do as he pleased. Gaia had no sense of self or knowledge of her people. Her mother had spent most of her life lying to Gaia, even if it was to protect her, and now she was utterly adrift.

"Listen, I'm sorry," he said, spinning her so she would look at him.

She glared at him. "I don't want your pity," she snapped. Brex shot her an annoyed look.

"It's not pity," he lied. "You shouldn't worry, we'll find out what your story is." He paused his walk in front of a tall, rambling house and pointed. "This is it. Brace yourself and just go along with it, ok?"

"What?" But before Brex could answer, an enormous woman in a faded paisley dress filled the doorway. Her grey hair was wound into tight curls that covered her head, and a large cigar hung from her lips.

"Brexler Carrow," she bellowed. "Haven't seen you 'round these parts in a long while!" Brex opened his mouth, but she waved away his words as she lumbered down the stairs and pulled him into a crushing hug, dropping ash on his shoulder. "I know some of the girls will be very glad to see you." She winked, but when Brex reached back and grasped Gaia by the hand, her face fell a little. "And who is this, Brexler?"

"Willa, no one calls me Brexler except you and my mother."

"Answer the question, boy."

"Willa, this is Raelle. Raelle, this is Willa." The two women sized each other up before Willa stuck out her hand.

"Never thought I'd see the day where you settled down, Brexler," she said gruffly, shaking Gaia's hand. "What am I going to tell Maggie and the rest of the girls?" she asked and Brex chuckled.

"They'll survive. Besides, the last time I was here, Maggie tried to stab me."

"You should know better than to cross her," Willa scolded him, but after a moment she nodded.

"Well come in anyways, and share your news."

"Thank you, Willa." They climbed the front stairs and entered a heavily decorated parlor. One glance at the scantily clad women who perched themselves on couches and dainty chairs and Gaia knew in an instant what kind of establishment they were standing in. She had only ever heard whispers about them, not from her mother, of course, but from mutters in the markets when she was younger about how beautiful girls could end up in houses of ill-repute if they weren't careful. But the girls seated around the room wore smiles and started to coo happily as soon as Brex stepped across the threshold. One stunning girl in particular, with a mane of dark hair and flashing, honey-colored eyes, had already climbed to her feet and started forward but froze, a scowl on her face when she saw Gaia's hand welded to Brex's. The girl shot Gaia a malicious glance before flipping her hair and flouncing from the room. Gaia tightened her grip on Brex, and he squeezed back, shooting her a look that begged her not to say anything.

"What brings you to our neck of the woods, Brexler?" Willa asked over her shoulder as she waved the girls out of the room. "Been a couple of years, I'd say, since we saw you last."

"This and that, nothing super important. Listen, Willa, would you mind letting us borrow the extra room upstairs? I'm having some work done on Adyta, and we need a place to crash until she's done."

"Anything for you, my boy. Besides, it's still too early for anyone to need it," she said, gesturing to the bright sunlight outside. Brex just shook his head and smiled. With great effort, Willa turned her attention to Gaia. "Is there anything you need, Raelle?"

"I'm fine, thank you."

"We need to get some sleep. It's been a long day," Brex said, trying to break the awkward tension. Willa nodded.

"Go on up; I'll send Poog up with some food later."

"You're a lifesaver, Willa," Brex said, smiling at her, but she just puffed on her cigar and waved him away.

Brex towed Gaia up the wide, sweeping staircase to a room at the end of a long hallway, the walls covered in portraits of gorgeous women, all half-dressed. Opening the door, he gestured her inside before closing the door behind them and locking it. Gaia immediately unwound the scarf from her head, shaking out her tumble of red curls and looking around. The room was small and rather plain, with one window that let in the bright light from outside. Faded watercolor prints of flowers hung on the walls, and a small chair and table occupied the far corner of the room. A large bed took up the rest of the space, a worn, red and white quilt covering it. Gaia ran her fingers through her hair and spoke, doing her best to avoid looking at Brex.

"Dare I ask why you seem to be a favorite visitor here?" Brex rolled his eyes at her and sat down on the bed to pull his boots off.

"I'm a notorious outer rim runner. Do you really have to ask?" Gaia shuddered and shook her head in disgust. He laughed. "I'm joking. Willa is like a mother to me. I worked here in my youth, helped take care of anyone who was rough on the girls."

"Always the hero," she muttered, and Brex shot her an annoyed glance.

"You're not exactly in a place to be complaining," he reminded her, and she narrowed her eyes at him.

"Whatever. Well, what about now?"

"I stop in for a visit every now and then. I don't make it this far south much anymore."

"No, I meant what do we do now?"

"Oh. Well, I don't know about you, but I'm exhausted. I'm going to get some sleep."

"We're being pursued by gods only know what kind of force and you're going to take a nap?"

Brex simpered sarcastically at her. "Yes, my lady, I am. I've been up for almost two straight days, and don't see much time for it in the future, so yes, I am going to get some sleep. Feel free to join me or do whatever you want, but do not leave the room."

"And why not? You don't own me."

Brex scowled, slowly climbing to his feet so he could look her in the eye, standing just inches from her face. "No, but I am being paid to protect you. If you leave, I can't do that. If you die, I don't get paid. It's that simple." He lay back down on the bed and placed his hat over his eyes to block the light. "Don't do something stupid just for the sake of being stubborn," he warned her.

Gaia felt the blood surge in her veins, and her hands twitched at her sides. Her head started to pound as frustration swamped her. She had never met another being who irked her as much as Brex did. "Fine, then move. I'm not sleeping on the floor." A grin on his face, Brex tilted the brim of his hat up to look at her.

"By all means darlin', you're welcome to join me."

She smiled a distinctly evil smile at him. "If you think I'm sharing a bed with you, you've lost your mind. Move."

"No."

"Move, or I'll make you." She flexed her hands into fists, but Brex sat up, watching her, noticing that her eyes were suddenly hazy again.

"Are you feeling…" but before he could finish speaking, she crumpled, her eyes rolled back in her head as she hit the floor. Shaking his head, Brex picked up her limp form and gently deposited her onto the far side of the bed. "You have got to stop doing that," he murmured.

A loud knock woke Gaia, and her head started to pound before she even opened her eyes. She heard Brex's voice whispering and what sounded like the clink of plates on a tray. Brex chuckled and then the door closed. She felt a hand on her shoulder, and she rolled over to find herself staring right into his dark blue eyes.

His smile immediately dropped away from his face as he stepped back in fear. "Holy shit!"

"What?" she asked, sitting up in alarm.

"Have you seen yourself?" he demanded.

She rolled her eyes at him as she scooted to the edge of the bed. "I was asleep until about thirty seconds ago, so what do you think?" He didn't say anything but only pointed to the small mirror that hung on the opposite wall. She stood wearily and stepped in front of the glass. The creature staring back at her was like nothing she had ever seen before. Her eyes were chips of amethyst, the purple color made even more striking by the silvery grey color of her hair. Gaia moaned and staggered backward to collapse onto the bed. Brex had backed away and stood in the far corner, still clutching the tray of food, his knuckles white.

"Is it really that bad?" she whispered, her magnificent silver head in her hands as she stared at the floor. Brex didn't know what to say. The girl was already one of the most beautiful beings he had ever encountered, but the silver and purple combination was utterly breathtaking—not that he was about to tell her that. Instead of answering, he just chuckled and shrugged casually as he sat at the spindly table and started uncovering the dishes on the tray.

"It's not that bad, really. I just wish I had some warning. Scares the hell out of me every time." She shot him a venomous look, and he shuddered theatrically. "Granted, at least it is only your eyes and hair. You could sprout wings or fangs or something equally horrible." She gave a weak chuckle. "Come on, at least eat something. You'll feel better." Gaia joined him, sitting on the edge of the bed closest to the table. He passed her a piece of bread spread with preserves.

"How long was I asleep?" she asked between bites.

"You went down about five hours ago. I slept until about a half hour ago. Your muttering and twitching in your sleep woke me up, so I asked Willa if she would feed us."

"Where did you sleep?" Gaia asked, ignoring his comment about her talking in her sleep. She had nightmares every time she closed her eyes, but he didn't need to know that. But then she glanced at Brex in confusion, looking around the small room.

Brex gave her a deadpan look. "Next to you, you idiot. Gods know if I touched you, I'd probably wake up with a tail or gills. I wouldn't touch you for a million gold talents."

"Liar," she said through a mouthful of food.

He grinned at her. "You're right. Maybe only half a million." She shook her head at him but giggled. She wasn't sure how to define him. He had saved her from Arlo for no good reason, and while he had demanded payment, he seemed to actually want to help her. He had made inquiries for her, and they at least had something to go on, far more than she could have ever accomplished on her own. He seemed genuinely concerned for her, willing to brave a planet he had no love for so they could rest safely. But what did he expect to gain in the end? Arlo would not stop hunting them. Was he just trying to save his own skin or was there something more to it?

After they finished eating, Gaia returned to the bed to get some more sleep while Brex slipped downstairs to return their dishes. Willa was in the kitchen with Poog the chef and two girls whom Brex recognized as Nilla and Stephie. Maggie had been standing at Willa's shoulder when he entered, but she gave him a blank stare before abruptly marching from the room. Brex looked after her in confusion but shook his head after a moment. Women.

"Thank you," he said, setting the tray down. Willa nodded without speaking and pulled a decanter and a pair of crystal glasses from under the counter before pouring him a healthy splash of whiskey. The girls disappeared with the dirty dishes and left them sitting in silence. The older woman sat savoring the last bit of her cigar before looking him over with hooded eyes. Brex chuckled into his whiskey and shook his head, knowing exactly what was going through her head.

"Just get it off your chest, Willa."

She didn't speak for a long minute, taking a drag on the barely smoldering cigar. "I'm just not entirely sure I understand what is going on with you, Brexler."

"What do you mean?"

She raised a skeptical eyebrow at him. "You, the eternal bachelor, settled down? With a girl like that?"

Brex scoffed. "Please, we aren't settled down. She's paying me to help her."

"She just doesn't seem your type, Brex," Willa said, lighting another cigar. Brex hung his head, trying not to laugh at Willa's protective demeanor. Granted she had been more of a mother to him than his own had ever been, but it still made him chuckle.

He raised his head to smile at her. "Listen, Willa, there is more here than meets the eye. I'll explain another time, but right now, Raelle is a very important person in my life."

"You mean she's the one paying your bills?" She knew him too well.

"Exactly."

"I've never seen anyone like her."

"You and me both," Brex muttered, thinking of the young woman upstairs whom he knew almost nothing about, yet it was almost more than she knew about herself.

~

They spent a restful night sleeping, eating and chatting with Willa, who finally, warily, warmed up to Gaia, though she still wore a headscarf even while indoors. They were lounging in the kitchen the next morning with Willa and several of the girls when Auggie shattered their temporary peace and quiet. He came rushing through the door, his mass of curls flying, shouting for Brex.

"August Drupmann, in the name of all the gods, what is going on?" Willa demanded as he skidded to a stop in the doorway. Brex had jumped to his feet to stand protectively in front of Gaia, who also stood, immediately watching the door behind Auggie. Panting, he leaned on the doorframe, gasping for breath.

"Damn it, Auggie, what is going on?" Brex demanded, stepping forward to shake his friend.

Willa swatted him away. "Don't shake the poor kid. Let him breathe."

"Gorths, due to arrive in minutes," Auggie gasped. Gaia felt her blood run cold. May the gods damn Arlo and his reach.

"How do you know?" Brex asked, his voice low and serious.

"Noria, who works at the airport, is a friend. Let's just say I was in her office when I shouldn't have been,—" he shot Brex a flash of a lascivious grin,—"and overheard the landing request come in from Arlo's ship. You need to get out of here now, Brex." Brex darted a look at Gaia, who rushed from the room to grab her jacket and the rest of their things.

"How is Adyta? Will she fly?" Brex demanded. Auggie stood wheezing with a hand on his chest, but he nodded.

"She may be the ugliest bitch around, but she'll fly."

"How much time do you think we have?"

"Not enough. You'll need to hide away from town in the low atmo so you don't cross onto their scanner screens."

"Where will you go?" Willa asked as more girls flooded the room, drawn by the shouting.

"Zaire's," Brex said, shrugging, keeping one eye on the staircase and the other on the street behind Auggie. Maggie sashayed through the door with several other girls and shook her dark waves haughtily, her nose in the air, ignoring Brex, but she clearly didn't want to be left out of the excitement. "Xael is big enough and busy enough that we should be able to hide out for a couple days." Gaia raced back into the room, her scarf askew. The entire room gaped at her, the silver of her hair making the purple of her eyes stand out like gems in a snowbank.

"Um, Brex, buddy, has your gal always had purple eyes?" Auggie asked, gaping at Gaia.

"No, don't worry about it. Willa, thanks for everything. Auggie, you're the man." Brex snagged Gaia's hand and drug her from the building, pausing only to pull the scarf back up over her hair.

"Are we going to make it?" Gaia demanded as they ran up the dusty main street towards the airstrip. Brex didn't answer, only tightened his grip on her hand and pulled her along. Rushing up to the ship, Brex slapped his hand to the reader panel and practically shoved Gaia through the door when it opened.

"Get upstairs and get locked in. This is going to be close." Gaia watched Brex warily, but obeyed as he raced around the ship, warming up the engine and shutting the doors. When he finally flung himself into the captain's chair, he looked like a man possessed. Without a word, he woke up the controls and sped through the take-off process. Gaia watched in amazement as his hands moved across the console, almost as if they had minds of their own. He muttered a soft thank-you to Auggie as everything booted right up and the buttons and switches glowed green.

Once they were airborne, instead of heading for space, they raced across the planet surface, leaving the airport far behind them. Gaia watched as the stark and desolate planet flashed along beneath them.

She started to speak, but Brex hushed her. "Don't," he warned. She had not seen him so serious, so she sat back in her chair and kept quiet. Long minutes passed until finally, he brought the ship to a floating idle, about a mile off the surface. Collapsing back against his chair, Brex sighed. "This should do for now. We'll hang out for another few minutes and then make a beeline for Xael. Shouldn't take too long. Once we land, Zaire can help us." His handsome face was strained and dark, so Gaia opted to stay silent.

# Chapter Six

The tense, silent trip took less than an hour in warp and finally Brex's ship landed on yet another airstrip, this time on the bright and busy planet of Xael. Soaring over the city-state of Turreni, which occupied most of Xael's larger landmass, Gaia marveled at the dazzling veins of color that seemed to flow through the sprawling city like threads in a tapestry. Great parks dotted the landscape with dark blots of greens while the surrounding neighborhoods showcased a riot of brilliantly painted buildings.

"Come," Brex said, after he had parked the ship inside a radiant yellow hanger. He agreed that Gaia could return to her normal clothes, although he insisted she leave the head-scarf in place, ignoring her stubborn glare. "Zaire is going to be very interested in you," he said as they walked down the bustling street. Gaia tried not to gape as they traversed the narrow avenues, packed with beings and creatures, most of which she had never seen before. "So just be prepared for some intense scrutiny." He tucked her hand into the crook of his arm, and they wound their way through the vibrant boulevards until they found themselves standing in front of a sprawling, mahogany-colored mansion. A beautiful slave girl with a mass of white curls and rose-tinted eyes opened the soaring doors when they knocked. A smile of recognition lit up her round, flower-shaped face, and she dimpled at Brex, giving him a lingering look of appreciation as she ushered them over the threshold. Gaia felt her eyes narrow of their own volition, and she tightened her grip on Brex's hand, making him raise an eyebrow with a knowing smile.

"Zaire is expecting you," the girl said in a lilting, breathy voice and gestured with a pale-green, almost vine-like arm for them to follow. She led them through the soaring hallways, past vast rooms of paintings, plants, statues, and jewel cases.

"My master will join you shortly," she said sweetly, before depositing them on a purple velvet couch in a room packed with cases of jewel-colored glassware. Gaia glanced at Brex with wide eyes.

"What in the name of the gods is she?" she asked in a hushed voice once the door closed. She had never seen such a being. The girl was more flower than human.

"She's an Orchidian; her name is Driana. She's been a part of Zaire's household as long as I've known him." Gaia had noticed how Brex's eyes followed the girl's narrow, swinging hips as she left the room, and Gaia was suddenly annoyed, although she couldn't quite put her finger on why. Not a minute later, Zaire came puffing into the room, his garish robe of multicolored silk rippling behind him. Both Brex and Gaia stood as the short, fat man approached them, enthusiasm radiating from his round face.

"Brexler Carrow! You finally came to see me. It has been too long," he gushed, drawing Brex into a tight hug. Brex looked uncomfortable, but there was no immediate mention of Bria or the debt. As soon as Zaire released Brex, he turned his smile to Gaia. "And you must be our mystery! Welcome, young lady. I am Zaire, collector of odd and beautiful things." He stepped up, and Gaia allowed him to kiss her hand, although his lips lingered two seconds too long, forcing Brex to clear his throat. "Please, darling girl, let me see you! Such great beauty should not be covered up!" Zaire said, gesturing to her head covering. Gaia glanced at Brex who nodded, so she pulled the scarf from her head, revealing her long silver hair and amethyst eyes. Zaire clapped a hand to his heart, shock etched into his features as he dramatically stumbled back against the other couch, gaping at her. Finally, after a long and awkward minute, he looked to Brex.

"Where in this galaxy did you find her?" Zaire asked in hushed, theatrical tones.

Brex did his best not to sigh, but sat across from his friend, tugging Gaia down with him. "We met on Annui. She seems to have drawn the attention of Arlo and whoever is paying him. The secret police took her mother about a month ago, and she has no idea why."

"Has she looked into a mirror recently?" Zaire asked, and Gaia narrowed her eyes, causing him to chuckle. "I am teasing, dear girl. But it does not take a seasoned collector to see why anyone would desire you."

"This has nothing to do with desire," she spat. Zaire looked affronted, but Gaia continued, ignoring the offended collector. "My mother was dragged from our home in the dead of night by the head of Central Core secret police. She spent her life warning me about people like them and how we must never reveal our secret." She hesitated, again, unsure of how much she should trust the two men, despite her agreement with Brex. "My mother fled our home planet with me when I was two years old. The only thing she ever said was that it was not safe for us and we could never return to the planet of our birth. She never spoke of the changes or why they happened, only that I should never show another soul."

"Plus, she doesn't always look like this, Zaire," Brex reminded him.

"Yes," the fat man said, steepling his fingers and staring hard at Gaia. "You mentioned that the hair and eyes change."

Brex nodded. "Black hair with black eyes when I met her, shifted to blue eyes, then red hair with green eyes. She woke up like this yesterday evening."

"And you have no idea how it happens?" Gaia shook her head, but Brex spoke.

"She'll pass out, sleep for a while and then wake up looking completely different."

"So not at will," the collector said, and both Gaia and Brex nodded. "Interesting. Well, as I mentioned, there is a book here in my library that speaks of the Tallpians, an ancient race that can, at will, change their appearance."

"May I see the book?" Gaia asked. Brex watched Zaire do some quick thinking, but he wasn't sure if Gaia noticed the split-second decision.

"Unfortunately there isn't much to show, young lady. The Tallpians are a very reclusive people, and there is little information that is widely available. I can tell you I know the book by heart and will answer any questions you might have to the best of my abilities." Suspicion flitted across Gaia's face, but it was gone in a blink. Zaire didn't seem to notice as he crossed his hands across his fat belly and surveyed Gaia with a cozy smile, like one settling down for a warm nap.

"Where do they hail from?"

"Originally the planet Meidonna," naming a planet that Gaia had never heard of. Brex knew of it vaguely; it was on the very north-western edge of the galaxy, but he had never had a reason to travel there. "They have been the ruling class there for the last millennia, and few other creatures inhabit the planet. They are thought to have evolved from terrans, and certainly, Tallpians are humanoids, but I'm not sure if their histories go back that far."

"Why haven't I ever seen one?" Gaia wondered if she would recognize one of her own people if she saw them on the street.

"With the way the galaxy has been going, there aren't but a handful of them left. Maybe several thousand at the most." Zaire paused, taking in Gaia's reaction, but her blank face gave nothing away. "The chatter on the black market is that their blood is almost priceless, and even a small dose would allow you to assume their appearance, at least temporarily."

"That must be why they wanted my mother," Gaia breathed, tears forming in her eyes.

Zaire nodded with a grave expression that was far too sincere for Brex to believe, and he narrowed his eyes at the collector, who pointedly ignored him. "Undoubtedly, my dear. Also, until recently the Tallpians have resisted most attempts to be brought into the Central Core alliance. Their planet is surprisingly rich in natural resources despite its remoteness; they do not need the main galaxy to supply them, so they have little interest in the rest of us."

Gaia stared at the floor in silence for several beats before raising her eyes. "Do you think it is possible that I could be a Tallpian?"

"Anything is possible, dear."

"How do I find out?"

"A blood test, done extensively enough, might reveal the DNA structure of the Tallpians."

Gaia wrinkled her nose at the mention of a blood test. "Can't you just prick my finger? Wouldn't we have a different blood color?" With thousands of species—both humanoid and not—across the galaxy, many had distinct blood colors, far different from the dull carmine of the terran race.

"The Tallpian have a bright, almost fluorescent red blood, but so do several other humanoid species, including the Weedons and Orchidians, like my Driana. A full spectrum test is the only way to tell," Zaire explained. "A bonus," he said, holding up a finger, "if your family was ever tracked genetically, your ancestors might be listed." Immediately, Gaia shrugged out of her leather jacket, revealing a black tank top that showcased her gorgeous fair skin, slender shoulders, and long arms.

She looked back and forth between Brex and Zaire as she thrust her arm out. "Take some of my blood! Test it, please, I must know."

Zaire nodded, but held up a cautionary hand. "Being hasty will do nothing for us, lovely girl. I will summon my physician, and he should be able to perform the test tomorrow morning with admirable skill. In the meantime, I suggest that the two of you get some rest before we dine. I can't imagine the last few days have been easy for you. Bathe and rest before supper, dear girl." Zaire snapped his fingers, and the same Orchidian slave girl appeared at the door. "Driana will escort you both." Driana's coral eyes immediately lit on Brex, and she gave him a slow smile that made Gaia narrow her own violet gaze. Brex didn't seem to notice, still focused on Zaire. Gaia hesitated in getting to her feet, glancing at Brex, unsure.

"You go rest," Brex told Gaia, his voice firm, eyes still on their host. "I need to talk to Zaire about a few other things."

"But—"

"Nothing to do with you," he said before smiling at her and mouthing the word "Bria.". Gaia slowly rose to her feet and slid him a look to show she did not think much of his order but allowed herself to be led away.

As soon as the doors swung shut and Gaia disappeared, Brex rounded on Zaire.

"Tell me the rest of it, Zaire," he demanded.

Zaire raised an innocent eyebrow. "The rest of what, dear boy?"

Brex fixed the collector with a knowing smile. "Don't bother lying to me; I know you well enough to know when you're trying to sugar-coat something."

Zaire eyed him in avid speculation before shrugging his shoulders and looking away. "I can't possibly imagine what you are talking about," he said in lofty tones. Brex shook his head, chuckling.

"Nice try. You're still mad about Bria, I get it. But since when have I, or even you for that matter, turned down money from the highest bidder?"

Zaire tilted his chin away pointedly, still in the game. "I may still have you killed, Carrow."

"Not while I'm helping Gaia you won't." His friend turned back with an evil smile.

"Maybe I kill you and add the girl to my collection. She is quite stunning, you know."

"I'm not blind, Zaire." Brex most definitely was not blind; Gaia had affected him far more in the last twenty-four hours than he was willing to admit. She was the opposite of any of the previous women he had been entangled with, both physically and mentally. What appealed to him most was the fact that she wasn't some swooning maiden in distress; she was fine with fighting her own battles, she'd made that stubbornly clear. She didn't need a hero; she needed a partner, a role Brex found himself more than willing to fill. He was still trying to puzzle out why.

"Then what are you going to do about it?" Zaire asked. Brex chuckled as he yanked himself present; day-dreaming about the feel of Gaia's skin under his fingertips was not productive, especially when haggling with Zaire.

He grinned wolfishly at Zaire while pulling out one of the golden talents that Gaia had given him before they disembarked Adyta. "Will this do?" He twirled the slim gold piece between his fingers, and Zaire's piggy eyes zeroed in on it instantly.

"Golden talents? Where did you come across that?"

"Doesn't matter. Does this cover it or not?"

For someone so heavy, Zaire could manage a quick snatch when the moment called for it, and the gold disappeared from Brex's grip in a blink. "My dear Brexler, thank you. All is forgiven now. Please let us forget that unpleasantness ever happened. I must ask, did dear Bria enjoy returning to her homeworld? I do miss her sweet face." Brex felt his stomach turn but ignored Zaire's question.

Instead, he fixed his friend with a stern look. "Tell me the truth about the Tallpians. I figured that asking about them outside of this room was dangerous, but why won't you tell Gaia the truth? I can tell you're hiding something." Zaire hesitated for a minute before shaking his head, rising from the couch and gesturing for Brex to follow him. They wound through the polished hallways until they stopped before a closed door. Zaire turned to him.

"I am showing you this on the condition you never speak of it. If it were to ever get out that I was associated with a Tallpian, it could harm my business interests."

"What about Gaia?" Brex asked, baffled by Zaire's secrecy. He knew Zaire was a very private person, but this was extreme, even for him. The larger man hesitated. "We are searching for her origins," Brex pressed, "not mine. She deserves to know, no matter how bad they might be."

"I'll let you be the judge of that."

Following Zaire through the door, Brex found himself in a room of telescreens and recording machines. Zaire punched several commands into a keyboard before one of the larger screens flickered to life. Brex threw himself down into a squishy black armchair and watched, feeling his eyes widen as the recording rolled. It was footage from a battle.

Instantly, he recognized the narrow faces and long limbs that Gaia shared with those on screen. The Tallpians were violent, ferocious fighters who moved with otherworldly grace. They gave no quarter and showed no mercy. They used all manner of weapons from staves to pistols, but Brex's battle-honed eye noticed many of them favored long, single-edged blades that wreaked terrible vengeance. The Tallpians also appeared very hard to kill. Worry bubbled up in Brex's stomach as he watched soldiers on the screen take several bullets to the torso and still fight on, as though nothing had happened. He wondered how it was possible. It became clear that only removing their heads would do the job. The recording rolled on and on until Brex couldn't stand it any longer. He was no innocent, hell, most of his money came drenched in blood, but the almost joyful expressions of those on the tape as they waded waist-deep in carnage was too much.

"Shut it off." Zaire obliged, pausing the screen as the lights flared back on. "I'm no stranger to war or violence— no one in the Brotherhood is—but what in the name of all the gods was that?" Brex asked. Zaire interlaced his fingers across his broad belly and looked at Brex thoughtfully. "The Tallpians are some of the most fearsome fighters known in the galaxy. They can change their physical appearance as they please, which makes them the perfect assassin. They also have rapid healing abilities, making most wounds minor inconveniences. It makes them incredibly difficult to kill, as I'm sure you saw."

"I get they're dangerous, but they don't just go around killing people, do they?" Brex asked in confusion.

Zaire raised an eyebrow at him. "It's more common than you think. They have been utilized by the Central Core since the newest prince came to power. He wrested control away from King Yehuda almost twenty years ago, murdered him, and has since turned his people into a mercenary race. Given the timeline, I would say that was around the time that your girl's mother fled with her. As to why exactly she did that, we may never know, but I can hazard a guess that it had something to do with Prince Nuweydon taking the throne. That is why I hesitated to speak of this in front of Gaia. I think you should wait to tell her until the blood test confirms it. Hers is not a warm or welcoming people."

"If Gaia and her mother were Tallpians, why would they need to flee their own kind?"

"Prince Nuweydon is ruthless and a complete madman. He murdered his brother, the king, and purged his court and family to gain power. He jails or kills anyone who disagrees with him. He is also wildly unpredictable. They say he goes from laughing to furious as quickly as you or I can blink. Rumors say it has gotten worse over the years as his power grows. Anyone who is considered even a remote threat to his throne is immediately executed. No trial, no chance to beg for mercy."

"Gods, he makes Arlo sound like a powder puff. But what about before this prince? They can't all be that bad."

"Up until he lost his throne, King Yehuda and his people had coexisted quite peacefully with the rest of the galaxy although they were fairly isolated. I have a Meidonnain opal, quite rare, that I purchased eons ago from the royal jeweler. Took me months of haggling. But no one like me has been able to trade with Meidonna since Nuweydon came to power. Most of my contacts were killed during the early purges, and the prince is highly suspicious of all outsiders. If Gaia were to turn up, unannounced, for no apparent reason, I would not expect her to survive long." Brex chewed over that information for a minute. His stomach twisted painfully as a vision of Gaia on her knees, at the mercy of those fierce blades flooded his mind.

"Do you think it's possible…?" Brex trailed off, still thinking. Zaire sat with raised eyebrows, waiting for him to finish.

"The reason her mother fled, do you think it is possible that Gaia could be…well, one of the royal family? Could she be related to the king?"

Zaire chuckled. "Come now, dear boy. How could a woman, a member of the Tallpian royal family, the queen of Meidonna, flee halfway across the galaxy with a princess and not be discovered or noticed? Besides, all reports say that the queen and princess were killed alongside the king."

"It makes sense, though. Why else would they go into hiding? Besides, the timeline fits."

"Maybe a minor noble, or a general's daughter. But a member of the royal family? A princess?"

"Find out. If anyone has more spies than Arlo in this galaxy, it's you, Zaire." The fat collector started to laugh heartily.

"Gods, Brexler, you do make me laugh sometimes."

"I'm serious, Zaire!"

Suddenly his friend's face was grave. "As am I, Carrow. Do you have any idea how dangerous the Tallpians are? If we start suddenly investigating the purged royal family, their spies and gorths will be on us faster than flies to a dead carcass, which is what we'll be when they finish with us, by the way. If she is who you think she is, I can imagine that if someone has hired Arlo to find her, they probably hail from Meidonna and they probably want her dead."

"And if her blood test shows that she is indeed a member of the race, let alone the royal family, what do we do then?"

Zaire suddenly smiled at him. "What's in this for you?"

"She's paying me to help her figure this out." Even in his own ears, the reply sounded glib.

Zaire raised a knowing eyebrow. "Are you sure you aren't developing feelings for the girl?" He smirked at Brex. "I can't say I blame you; she is one of the more stunning beings I've come across. However, that being said, I would recommend placing your affections somewhere markedly safer."

"I told you, this is just about the money. Besides, Gaia isn't dangerous."

"No, but her kin are. Consider that."

"So she is Tallpian."

"You would have to be blind not to see it." Zaire sighed, like he was finally letting go of some secret. "Yes, she is. There are no other species of humanoid that have the capabilities to change their physical appearance at will. The blood test will confirm it, but I am fairly certain she could be nothing else. Those long limbs and that fair skin, almost pearl-like? Those, too, are telltale signs, along with her changing hair and eyes."

"Hers don't change at will," Brex reminded him.

Zaire considered this for a moment. "She said her mother spent her entire life lying to her. She would have been taught how to ease through her transitions had she stayed on Meidonna. But since she knows nothing of her heritage, I can assume that she was never taught how to control it, which is why the changes seem random."

"It's usually when she is upset about something."

"Intense emotional reactions could be a trigger."

"You could say that again," Brex said, thinking of the anger that often flooded Gaia's piercing gaze, only to leave it hazy right before each collapse. He glanced up at his friend. "How do you know so much about the Tallpians anyways?"

"When King Yehuda was in power, the planet offered a large array of rare and prized artifacts. I spent a great deal of time with them in my early, early days learning their customs to better ensure their acceptance and the ease of my trades. Granted, it is a fairly miserable place, on the surface at least. Their mines are deep and vast, but at surface level, large islands make up the landmasses. The oceans are barely above freezing, and the weather is fairly abysmal. Remind me, I must show you the emeralds that also came from them, most exquisite—"

"So now what do we do?" Brex asked, cutting Zaire off, mid-rapture.

Zaire pondered the question for a moment before shooting him a knowing look. "That is for you to decide, dear boy. You and that mouth-watering girl of yours."

Driana escorted Gaia through the massive house, pointing out artifacts of interest as they passed through ornate, soaring halls. Gaia had never seen such richness in her life. Wooden paneling shined until it gleamed like gold. Intricate stonework so delicate Gaia could not imagine what kind of hands could have crafted such exquisite work. Warm afternoon sunlight poured through soaring windows, illuminating paintings, statues, and display cases.

"Here is your room," the girl said, bowing Gaia through an elaborately carved door. "My master said to tell you that you are welcome to anything in the wardrobe, and to dress appropriately for a formal supper. If you need assistance with anything, simply ring that bell"—she pointed to a silver bell on a small glass and gold table near the door—"and one of us will assist you. Is there anything else I can do for you?" Gaia shook her head, and Driana melted away like a wisp of smoke, leaving behind just the slightest hint of a beautiful, floral scent. Gaia shut the door and took in the sumptuous room, the walls dressed in pale green silk with beautiful white accents. She discovered a large white marble bathroom with a huge tub and large glass shower, stocked with fluffy white towels and robes. Unable to remember the last time she had hot water, Gaia stripped and stood under the hot stream of the shower until she was completely wrinkled. Ignoring the massive wardrobe, she chose to collapse gratefully onto the broad, inviting bed and into her first deep, dreamless sleep in ages.

~

"Miss. Miss Gaia." The voice in her ear was feminine and soft, not Brex's long drawl. Gaia opened her eyes, and the young, dark-haired maid stepped back in shock. "I am sorry to disturb you, miss, but the master said to assist you in dressing for supper. I am Mira," she said dipping a slight curtsey. Gaia sat up, glancing at the window, surprised to see the soft lavender and celadon hues of twilight already staining the sky.

"How long have I slept?"

"Several hours I should think, my lady." The girl helped Gaia into a downy robe before guiding her to the delicately carved vanity with a white framed mirror.

Sitting down, Gaia glanced up at the mirror and, with a sigh, saw that her hair and eyes had changed again. "This is getting rather old," Gaia muttered to herself as the slave carefully combed camellia oil through her hair to make it soft, before twisting it up into a loose chignon. Mira laid out several gowns on the bed, all of them more beautiful than the last. Choosing one, Gaia stood still as the maid finished the row of buttons that traveled up the back. Admiring herself in the floor length mirror that stood beside the wardrobe, Gaia wondered what Brex would think. He had only seen her desperate and dirty, but now she looked like a real being, someone who didn't spend their days being hunted and their nights terrified by nightmares. She wanted to look well for him, but pushed the reason why to the back of her mind as she followed her guide to the dining room.

~

Brex, wearing a borrowed suit, was standing in the large formal dining room with Zaire, a glass of whiskey in his hand when the soaring doors across the room were thrown open. Brex glanced up, and the room shifted sideways as Gaia stepped into the light, framed in the doorway like a statue. She was blonde now, the light platinum color of her hair contrasting with the bright, icy turquoise of her eyes. Again, he thought, immediately noticing the difference. But what caught him completely off-guard was the black evening gown she wore. Strapless and simply cut, it fell to the floor, whispering over her slight curves and showcasing her expanse of flawless, subtly-luminescent skin. His mouth dry, he met her halfway across the inlaid marble dance floor, reached for her hand and then thought better of it. Recovering, he gave her a cocky smile and toasted her with his glass, openly raked his eyes over her before speaking.

"You look…great," he said, trying to sound casual and not like he was about to choke on his own tongue. She blushed, and a delicate peach color flooded her fair cheeks, making Brex's head swim. It took every ounce of his self-control to keep a usable amount of blood in his brain. No, she didn't just look great, she looked like the single, most breathtaking creature he'd ever seen. They stood, staring at one another without speaking, her turquoise eyes locked against his dark blue ones, neither inclined to break the moment. It didn't last long; Zaire interrupted by bustling over, loudly praising Gaia's beauty, complimenting her on her recent change. She tore her eyes away from Brex to give their host a tight smile, her blush fading. But as she allowed Zaire to guide her to the table, she glanced over her shoulder and shot Brex a heated look swept from under her lashes, stealing the breath from his lungs.

After spending the next few hours at the table with Zaire and listening to him pontificate about this collection and that collection, Brex finally escorted Gaia to her room.

"I really am sorry about Zaire," Brex said, chuckling, as they reached her door. "He loves nothing better than showing off around beautiful women. He may not be attracted to women in the slightest, but he still appreciates beauty in every form. And he loves having an audience. I have a feeling he is developing a soft spot for you."

"Really, don't apologize. It was…entertaining." Her smile made Brex's gut clench. "I really don't mind. I've spent most of my life so sheltered; it is hard for me to wrap my mind around everything I have missed." Brex felt guilt surge through his body at her words, an uncomfortable feeling that he wasn't used to dealing with. He had gotten good at ignoring Bria's memories, but around Gaia, they came surging back. And now he knew more about Gaia's history than she did, but it wasn't pretty. Until they did the blood test, they couldn't say if Brex's theory might be correct. Could she be a Tallpian princess, smuggled to safety to avoid her uncle's wrath? Or was she just some girl whose life had been overshadowed by a protective and paranoid mother? She deserved to know the truth and nothing but the truth, so Brex kept his mouth shut.

"Well, he does go on and on…and on and on," Brex said, and Gaia nodded in agreement, trying to stem a laugh. "You do look lovely, though," he said, resisting the urge to run his hand down her arm. Brex could feel a slight prickle in his fingertips and was tempted to ease it by brushing them against her soft skin. Shaking himself mentally, he shoved his hands deeper into his pockets. He had to keep reminding himself that she was paying him to help her and nothing more. He had kept her safe so far, and he planned to do so until she found her people or decided otherwise. She glanced at him, and when her turquoise clashed against his dark blue, that delicate blush crept up into her cheeks again.

"Thank you. I don't think I've ever worn something this fine before."

"Well, hopefully someday that will change." Gaia didn't know what to say and just stared at him. She still could not fathom why he was so kind to her, why he had bothered helped her in the first place. But she was glad he had. Even if they didn't discover her past, she considered the thought of Brex as part of her future and found that it held immense appeal.

After a beat, the moment broke, and she smiled at him softly. "Good night, Brexler," she said, slipping through the door and closing it gently behind her.

# Chapter Seven

The next morning found Gaia and Brex seated at a delicately crafted table in the glass-walled arboretum, eating a breakfast of beautifully arranged fruits and rolls, waiting for Zaire's physician to arrive. The air wrapped around them was sultry and warm, heavy with the scent of rare flowers, and the early morning sun sparkled off the glass, throwing rainbows around the room. Brex was doing his best to not stare at Gaia like a sloppy schoolboy. When she appeared at breakfast in a burgundy silk blouse and black, high-waisted pants that were tucked into her black boots, it was all Brex could do not to completely lose his head. He had never felt like this; the feeling was unnerving, and he did his best to push it aside. Trying to shake the dizziness from his mind, Brex flicked her a lazy smile.

"Have you given any thought to what you want to do after this? I mean after the test."

"I need to find my people. Find them and see if they can't help me free my mother."

"And if you aren't Tallpian?" Even though Brex knew without a doubt what she was now, he wanted to give her a chance to think of alternatives to her long-lost planet and its race of violent shape-shifters. He shook himself mentally. Why did he care?

"We keep looking," she said simply, her turquoise eyes meeting his.

Staring at her, Brex felt his resolve crumbling. Who was he to keep her heritage from her? Regardless of what she was and what her people were, she still deserved to know, right? "Gaia, listen—" but Brex was cut off by Zaire prancing into the room, leading a short, grey-haired man with round spectacles perched on his beak of a nose. Gaia sent Brex a tight smile that looked more like a grimace, but turned her attention to their host.

A simple procedure—a small vial of brilliant red blood was taken almost painlessly—and over quickly. The doctor promised results in an hour's time. When Zaire had escorted the man away, Gaia turned back to Brex.

"What were you going to say? Before?" She stared curiously at him.

Brex shook his head. He couldn't bring himself to raise her hopes only to dash them if he was wrong. "Nothing." She cocked her head, staring at him with a smile that said she didn't quite believe him. He ignored her and the twist in his gut. "Listen, I need to head back to Adyta and work on a few things. Stay here, and I'll be back in time to hear the test results." Gaia looked surprised and opened her mouth to protest, but Brex held up a hand, cutting her off. "It isn't safe for you to be out, regardless of what you look like. A planet this big and this busy? Countless creatures would sell us out to Arlo without hesitating. You know that he has every single one of his spies looking for us. You'll be safer here."

"I don't like it," she managed, her eyebrows furrowing in concern. "They are looking for you too."

Brex shook his head, waving away her worry. "I'm a lot less distinct-looking than you are," he said, eyeing Gaia's white-blonde hair. It didn't matter what color her hair was, she was so striking she could turn heads no matter where she went, which at the current moment, was a bad thing. "I'll be quick," he said. "And besides, you're paying me to protect you, and that is what I'm doing. You are much safer here behind Zaire's walls than anywhere else right now." Still trying to argue, she opened her mouth again, but Brex shook his head at her. "You agreed to trust me," he reminded her. Slowly, she nodded.

"You're right. I did agree to trust you," she said. Brex couldn't believe his luck, but he wasn't going to give her a chance to change her mind. He jumped to his feet and rushed from the humid room before she could object.

Passing Zaire in the hallway, Brex stopped mid-stride and turned to face the collector. "I'll be gone for an hour, two tops. Keep an eye on Gaia for me."

Zaire gave him a concerned look. "What are you up to, Carrow?"

"I just need to check in with Auggie and a few other things. I won't be gone long."

Zaire heaved an exaggerated sigh. "I suppose I can be convinced to spend some time with our lovely lady." He grinned impishly at Brex, who shot him a sharp look.

"Don't do anything that'll force me to kill you, Zaire," he warned, but the fat man flapped a hand, dismissing him.

"Get out of here, boy." Brex shook his head but continued down the hall.

As Gaia watched the door swing shut behind Brex, she knew he wasn't telling her something. She may have been sheltered growing up, but she wasn't stupid. Brex's laugh at dinner the night before had been forced, despite the whiskey. Zaire was so flamboyant that she wasn't entirely sure how to read him, but her gut that said there was something more about her heritage that hadn't been brought up.

Abandoning her meal, she slipped from the steamy room. As she stepped through the door, she could hear Zaire a hallway away, giving orders to a servant. To avoid being trapped into another never-ending conversation about treasures she didn't understand, she hurried down the corridor, taking several turns before stopping to examine her surroundings. The entire house was stuffed with rare artifacts and priceless gems, most of which Gaia had no name for. Roaming the halls, she let her eyes caress everything from perfectly cut gemstones so pure they seemed to hold the light of the sun to suits of armor that were more like scales on a fish than anything else. She wasn't sure what she was looking for but knew that there had to more secrets about her possible kin buried somewhere in the sprawling house.

She wandered the mansion, opening doors at random to curiously inspect the room's contents before moving on. The first door she opened led to a room filled with brilliantly-colored insects, all pinned to crisp white backboards in perfect black frames. The range of colors was breathtaking. Opening another door revealed a room stuffed to the brim with all manner of ridiculous hats. Gaia couldn't stifle a giggle at the thought of Zaire covering his fat, bald head with any of the surrounding hats. Some boasted a rainbow of colors; others were encrusted with gems and gilt threads. She continued to explore, discovering rooms full of books, plants, statues, weapons, all seeming to go on forever. The better part of an hour passed, and her head was spinning when she pushed into a room filled with screens. One screen was paused in the midst of some film showing an epic battle. Her curiosity aroused, she closed the door behind herself and dimmed the lights before hitting the play button on a large console. The recording rolled to life, and Gaia felt her heart still in her chest. The warriors on the screen were violent, efficient killing machines, but what made Gaia's heart skip was that she knew them, instantly. Looking down at her own hands, she saw the same long fingers wrapped around sword hilts, the same fair skin that showed amongst chinks in their armor and the same narrow faces, all contorted in the rage of battle. Stifling a sob, Gaia sped through the video at high speed, watching in heartbroken awe as the action flashed by. Right before the end, one of the soldiers squared with the camera, his angry crimson eyes fixing on the lens. Chills raced across her skin; she had seen those eyes before. She resumed normal speed on the recording, and the words blared around her as the speakers crackled to life. Shouting in a language she had not heard spoken aloud since her mother had been taken, he declared that a new Tallpian regime had begun. He declared himself king and promised to wreak vengeance on those who would oppose him. The blazing eyes were exact copies of the ones that haunted Gaia's nightmares. But every gesture, every word resonated so profoundly that she no longer had any doubts as to her heritage. As she sat and stared blankly at the screen, unsure of her next move, the door burst inward, making her jump.

Brex stood in the doorway, his chest heaving and several emotions clashing on his face as he looked at her. "Gaia! Where have you been?" he demanded, frustration clear in his voice. "We've been looking all over...." His words faded when he saw the image on the screen. He glanced back and forth between Gaia and the image on the frozen screen, not wanting to break the moment, should he say something wrong.

She could barely bring herself to look at him and had to swallow several times before she was able to speak. "Did you know?" she whispered. The defiant look on Brex's face was all the answer she needed. "Why didn't you tell me?" He opened his mouth to speak, but she shook her head. "No, never mind, don't bother lying to me," she said, her beautiful face contorted in pain. She rose from her chair and pushed past him.

Zaire stood just beyond the door in the hallway, gasping for breath. "My dear, please—" but Gaia shoved him aside and broke into a run. She dodged through the corridors until she managed to find the door to her room. She grabbed her jacket, checked that her money was still in place before heading for the main foyer. She heard Brex shouting her name as she darted down the hallways, searching for the front door. Finally, she found the entry hall and had just placed her hand on the doorknob when Brex sprinted into the hall.

He slid to a stop and slammed his hand against the door, keeping it shut as she tugged on the handle. "Gaia stop. You have to listen to me."

She squared off with him as he towered over her. "I'll do nothing of the sort. How long have you known?"

Brex leaned on the door, panting as he looked at her. "Only since last night."

"And you couldn't find time to tell me?" she shrieked. "We flew halfway across the galaxy to find my heritage, and when we do, you keep it from me? I'm paying you to protect me from Arlo, not from something you think might be unpleasant, Carrow," she snarled.

He jerked—it was the first time she had used his name with such venom. "I wanted to wait until we had the blood test results before saying anything."

"You saw that film, and there is still doubt?" She couldn't stop herself from shouting. "My language, my build! Everything! Is! The! Same!"

"Gaia."

"No!" Stamping her foot now. "How dare you not tell me?"

"I wasn't sure! I knew Zaire wasn't telling us everything, but I wanted to make sure before I said anything!"

"That was not your choice to make! You should have told me."

"Listen, there is more than you under—"The tears were heavy in her eyes as she glared at him.

"I don't care," she said, cutting him off. She didn't care what he had to say now. "I knew I shouldn't have trusted you."

"Gaia, please, you need to listen."

"No. You can forget your payment; I owe you nothing, Brexler Carrow."

"Don't leave, Gaia. It's not safe," he said, reaching for her. Gaia yanked out the long knife from her boot, the same one that he had given her on Cunat. A flare of gratitude surged through him—at least she had kept it and wasn't afraid to use it. Her pale face flushed with anger as she held the long blade at chest height, but remarkably her eyes stayed clear and were not consumed by the haze that signified an impending change. She kept the knife pointed at him and jerked her head aside, indicating he should move away from the door.

Only when she pressed the point of the blade against the soft pulse in his throat did Brex move. "You may have rescued me once," she spat, keeping her weapon pointed at him as she tugged open the heavy door, "but that does not mean you will need to do so twice." With one last contemptuous look, she turned and fled down the front stairs of the mansion, and Brex stood and watched, helpless, as her blonde head slipped between the open gates and disappeared into the crowded street.

"Are you mad?" Brex glanced up at Zaire as he checked the cylinder on his revolver. The collector was pacing and wringing his hands, shouting at Brex as he readied himself to go after Gaia. "You let the heir to the Tallpian throne just walk out the door? Have you lost your mind?" Brex shot his friend a death glare as he holstered his gun. "She could be anywhere!" Zaire cried, throwing his hands up in the air and sinking onto the spindly chair next to the door. "This city doesn't go on forever. What if she makes it to the grassland and gets lost? You'll never find her! How could you have let her go?"

"I'm about to rectify that, now get out of my way," Brex snarled as he pushed through the front door. Zaire followed him down the front steps of the mansion, still twisting his hands in agitation. "If Arlo finds her before you do—"

Brex turned on the fat man dogging his heels. "That won't happen," he growled fiercely. The mental image of Arlo standing over a prone Gaia made Brex's stomach ache like he had been punched.

"How can you be sure?"

"She managed to evade him on her home planet for more than a month without help. I checked with Auggie earlier; no one knows where we are."

"That means nothing, you idiot boy. The entire underground knows that Arlo is looking for you two. Someone will turn her over before the next sundown."

A dozen streets away, Gaia pushed through the thick crowd of people who lined the sidewalks. Stalls selling spices, cloth, herbs, and trinkets were crowded along the avenues, and the mix of languages that filled the air was more exotic than anything in Gaia's experience. Her heart was still racing with the knowledge of her missing past. She couldn't believe that she finally had answers to her questions, but that new knowledge now only led to more questions. Why did Zaire and Brex seem so scared of her kin? Yes, the film showed their ability as warriors, but why should she be in any danger from her own kind? She also couldn't believe how angry she was at Brexler. How dare he keep that information from her! As she stomped through the sea of humanity, she wondered why she even cared. She had paid him to protect her and to help her find her past. It shouldn't matter that he didn't tell her right away, and it should definitely not hurt this much. Sighing, she lifted her head to look at her surroundings. She had no idea where she was but knew that if she wanted to remain unnoticed, she needed to get off the street quickly. She also knew Brex was right (not that she would ever admit it) about Arlo and his spies; they were everywhere and undoubtedly still looking for her. The buildings around her were a riot of colors, bright hues of blues, oranges, pinks, and greens. She was standing and staring, completely overwhelmed and wondering what she was going to do next when a hand descended on her shoulder. She whipped around and found herself staring into Brex's cobalt eyes.

"Get away from me," she snarled, yanking away from his grip.

He gave her a dark look. "Gods be damned, Gaia. Don't stomp off in a temper just because you're angry. It still isn't safe for you to be out alone."

"I can protect myself."

Brex snorted in derision. "One girl with one knife against Arlo and his thugs? I don't think so."

"I told you, I no longer need your help."

"Yes, you do. Do you have any idea what Arlo will do to you when—and notice I said when, not if—when he finds you?" She narrowed her eyes at him but didn't answer. Brex figured he should probably enlighten her, to hell with her feelings. "If his employer didn't specify an untouched, live delivery, he'll probably rape you, slit your throat, deliver your corpse, and walk away smiling."

She felt a cold chill snake through her, but she ignored it, squaring her shoulders as she glared at Brex. "It was not your place."

"I made a call," he said, shrugging as he looked at the crowd around them. "We need to get back. We're too exposed here."

"I'm not going with you."

"Why the fuck not?"

"Why should I? I knew trusting you was a mistake." He scoffed at her, a mocking light in his eyes.

"Get off your high horse, Gaia. I kept something from you; I didn't sell you to Arlo."

"Yet." But as soon as she spoke, she could see she had gone too far.

"Hey now," he said, his voice dropping to a growl as he yanked her close. It was all he could do not to be distracted by her perfect body, crushed against him by the crowd as he held his lips close to her ear. "I may be a lot of things, but a double-crosser is not one of them. You're paying me to do a job, and I'll see it through until the end, regardless of the outcome. You can trust that much." He looked around. "Now come on." He adjusted his grip on her upper arm and towed her through the crush. She struggled against his hold, but he ignored her, not caring if he was causing her any pain; he was too angry that she had taken such a risk. They were passing along a narrow street, full of tall, pastel-colored rooming houses when Brex heard his name being called above the din. Spinning around, Brex locked eyes with one of Arlo's goons, a towering Annuian named Uzrur. Swearing, Brex placed a hand on top of Gaia's head and shoved her to the ground, tucking her behind the stall of a startled bead vendor, hoping the tide of people would hide her. He ducked down next to her and took her chin in his hand, at the same time, passing off a five-unit note to the surprised vendor who immediately looked in the other direction, ignoring them.

"You are going to do exactly as I tell you if you want to survive this. Wait until they are following me and then run back to Zaire's. He will be able to help you."

"What about you?" she hissed. She hated the idea of him sacrificing himself for her. It didn't fit the selfish, money-hungry Brex she had gotten used to in the last three days. Not to mention she was still so mad at him, she couldn't stand the idea of him continuing to help her.

He chucked her chin with a smug grin. "It's Arlo—how bad could it be?" Before Gaia could respond, Brex straightened up and dove away from her into the crowd. She curled against the wall of the flimsy wooden stall, waiting for the goons to push through and grab her, but as she waited, all she heard was Keon's screech of "After him!"

Brex made it halfway down the street before he smashed headlong into a solid wall of Annuian muscle. The goon snagged Brex by the front of his shirt before punching him hard in the jaw. The blow knocked Brex to the ground, and he lay in the street stunned, trying to get his bearings. The light reflecting off a nearby bright red building made the whole street seem as though it had been dipped in blood, and the noise of the crowd seemed to echo between Brex's ears until another goon hauled him up by the scruff of his neck.

"Arlo would like a word with you."

# Chapter Eight

Gaia staggered to her feet, staring in the direction that Brex had disappeared. She could not fathom how they had missed her but wasn't going to question her luck. Pushing through the crowd, Gaia could still see the back of the goon's heads, Brex propped up between the two burly henchmen as they hauled him along the street. Keon was leading them, parting the crowd as though he was leading a parade. Why they hadn't stopped to look for her was confusing, but she wasn't about to question her good luck. She dove into the crush, trying to push her way forward, but as she kept her eyes on Brex's limp form, his head suddenly jerked up, and his dark eyes found her through the crowd. His midnight-colored gaze bored into her turquoise one. The look was simultaneously a command and a request—no, he wasn't requesting, he was begging her to stay where she was and not risk her safety for his. Seeing the silent plea, she slowed her walk, confused, but she stopped, refusing to break eye contact with him until he had been pulled from view and swallowed up by the crowd. Only then did she step back into the shadowy doorway of a nearby building and allow herself the luxury of a single sob.

The hit landed on his jaw like a hammer. The chair that Brex was tied to rocked back but then landed again with all four legs on the ground.

"Where is the girl?" Arlo's high, carefully modulated voice was so out of place in the dingy basement that Brex almost laughed.

Instead, he spat a mouthful of blood onto the dirt-packed floor. "No idea," he drawled back, knowing his heavy twang annoyed Arlo to no end. But Arlo only smiled before he slugged Brex again, this time in the gut. Choking back vomit, Brex shook his head up at the tall, dark-robed figure standing over him. "How did you even find us?" he demanded. Arlo offered a chuckle as he flexed his new mechanical hand, admiring the metallic sheen it threw in the low light.

Finally, he turned his watery-grey gaze to Brex. "It is amazing, the female need for revenge."

Not exactly what Brex had been expecting. "What the hell does that mean?"

Arlo gave him a smirk. "It means you should be careful who you jilt, Brexler Carrow. Pay attention to a certain lady and then ignore her for another? Doesn't inspire much loyalty. But in the end, you being an asshole did me a favor and here we are."

"Who are you talking about? We haven't even seen any other...." But as he thought back over the last two days, they had spent most of their time on Cunat. Auggie would sooner cut his own throat than give them up, but in their time at Willa's...only one person's nastiness stood out and that was Maggie's. "That bitch!"

"She was charming, actually. When I told her that I planned to kill you and the girl, she sang like a warbler. I think she fancied herself in love with you at one point."

"She stabbed me the last time I saw her."

"And you probably deserved it." Brex couldn't disagree. He probably did, thinking back on it. But he still couldn't believe that Willa had let Maggie rat them out. Another blow landed, yanking him back into the present. He winced as Arlo's mechanized fist grazed his jaw and realized it didn't matter—all he knew was that they wouldn't find Gaia if he had anything to do with it.

"Tell me where the girl is, Carrow, and I might let you live."

Brex snorted at the lie. He knew the only way he would remain breathing was if Arlo was still looking for Gaia. "Even if I knew where she was, I wouldn't tell you. But we're in the same boat now, buddy; she ran out on me hours ago, and I've been looking for her, too."

"I don't believe that."

Brex chuckled at Arlo's words, hoping it would make him more convincing. "Trust me. She owes me money. Don't you think if I knew where she was, that's where I'd be, instead of wandering the streets of Xael, looking for her?" Arlo paused, knowing Brex's love of money but then clenched his fist again.

"Regardless, I owe you for every other ounce of trouble you've ever caused me." Brex curled his lip.

"Tell you what, help me find her and I'll cut you in on the money she owes me." That was a lie but Brex was desperate. Arlo laughed, and the creepy sound echoed through the small room. He shook his head at Brex.

"Idiot boy. Do you have any idea who she really is or how much she is worth? Anything you offer me would not amount to even one one-hundredth of what I will be paid once I find her."

"Who hired you?" Brex demanded but Arlo only laughed again.

"You truly have no idea who she is, do you?" Brex rolled his eyes. He wasn't going to admit shit to Arlo.

"Let me guess, you're going to gloat about it, lord it over me and then still not tell me?" Arlo chuckled in response.

"You would be correct."

Brex shook his head, eyes on the ceiling. "Then do me a favor," he drawled, dropping his gaze to look Arlo square in the eye. "Get it over with."

*

Although Gaia wasn't sure she could find Zaire's mansion without help, after forty frantic minutes of darting through the crowded streets, she caught sight of the soaring front gates. Rushing up the steps, she pounded on the door, shouting Zaire's name. A startled footman opened the door and recognized her at once.

"I need to speak with Zaire, now!" she all but shouted as she burst through the door.

"I'm sorry miss but the master is otherwise engaged at the moment. Could I—"

"No!" Gaia cut him off. "I need to see him now! This is life or death." The man looked uncertain but still stood firm.

"I do apologize, miss, but Lord Zaire—"

"Is here." A shrill voice rang through the hall and Gaia had never been so thrilled to hear him speak. Zaire waddled in, still wearing his trademark garishly-colored robe.

"Zaire, please, Brex—"

"The boy isn't here. He went looking for you. He—"

"I know! That's what I am trying to tell you. He found me and Arlo found him!"

Zaire's fat face went pale, and his tone was bleak. "You're sure?"

Gaia vigorously nodded her blonde head. "I saw Keon and two thugs I recognize from Annui. They hit him in the street and took him away." She couldn't bring up the fact that his last act had been to push her to safety. She wasn't even sure how to process it, let alone explain it.

Zaire contemplated for a moment before raising his eyes to meet Gaia's. "I'm sorry, dear girl, but if Arlo has him, I fear there is little we can do."

Gaia barely managed to contain a shriek of rage as she frowned at the fat collector. "Brex just risked his life to save me, again. I refuse to believe that he is beyond our help."

"Even if we knew where he was, which we do not, what skills do we have that would allow us to rescue him?"

Gaia hesitated before speaking, but her voice was sure. "We don't fight our way in; we trade."

It took several moments for her meaning to become clear before Zaire shook his head at her, his fat face blanching in fear. "No. I cannot allow you to trade yourself for him." Gaia shot him an arched, regal look, and Zaire suddenly knew, without a shadow of doubt, he was in the company of royalty. "You understand that if I allowed you to do that and Brex found out, he would kill us both?"

"How dare you presume to tell me what I can and cannot do?"

"My dear girl, I—"

"No." Her voice was ice to match her eyes. She stared down Zaire, passion surging across her face. "That is enough. Brex said that you had some of the best spies in the galaxy. Make use of them now. We have to find him."

"Throw him in a cell and leave him to rot," Arlo's high pitched voice was cold, but Brex could hear it even over the ringing in his ears. "I'll get around to killing him later." The two hulking thugs who had snagged him on the streets of Xael did as instructed and hauled Brex through the damp underground halls of wherever they were. The stone walls were slimy and primitive, clearly built ages before any of them had been born. Tossed into a cell with a dirt floor, it was all Brex could do to just lie on the ground and bleed. Arlo had worked him over good. One eye was bruised and swollen, his jaw ached, and his ribs felt like fire. He was also pretty sure he was missing a tooth. He slid in and out of consciousness over the next few hours, not sure how it was possible to hurt that badly and still be alive.

"I'm going to look for him whether you help me or not."

"My girl, please—"

"Zaire, do not argue with me." Gaia straightened up to look at the fat man, after replacing her long dagger in her boot. "You can choose to help me or not, but you cannot stop me." She had returned to her bedroom to change, Zaire trailing after, trying to convince her to stay. She ordered him out of the room with a glare before changing, but he insisted on shouting through the door at her. Once decent, dressed in tan, high-waisted pants, and a white t-shirt, she yanked the door back open to see the round collector still standing in the hall, wringing his hands. Her long, blonde hair was pulled up into a high horse-tail that reached almost to her waist, and her eyes were like ice as she glared at him. Zaire collapsed onto the edge of her bed, watching as she fitted another long dagger into her boot and placed a pistol, provided by a guard, at her waist.

"Please, lady, this is not safe, especially not for you." Gaia paused, staring up with a suspicious scowl on her face.

At her look, Zaire paled. "What do you mean, especially not for me?"

Fluttering his hands, Zaire tried to backtrack. "You have little knowledge, or experience, I mean, you are a lady, I mean—…" Gaia narrowed her eyes at him and his voice trailed off. She pulled a knife free and pointed it at him.

"One more chance, and do not even think about lying to me." His face made it clear he was debating how much to tell her. There was obviously more to her history that she had still not uncovered, one more thing that Brex had kept from her. She growled in her throat, anger surging through her blood. She was going to pummel Brex when she finally got her hands on him. She glared at Zaire, who flinched. "You are going to tell me everything. From the beginning. You will leave nothing out."

# Chapter Nine

Twenty minutes later, Gaia sat on the soft, white coverlet of the bed, gripping Zaire's hands to stave off the shock. The words "royalty", "princess", "coup", and "murder" echoed in her head. The fat collector had broken down and finally told her everything that he knew about her history and that of the Tallpians, and suddenly everything made sense. The way her mother had spent her entire life keeping Gaia protected, isolated. As it turned out, Gaia was not even her real name. After trying out her old name a few times, Gaia shook her head. The word was clunky and awkward in her mouth. Gaia fit her much better.

Zaire had also received the results of her blood test after she fled, and it confirmed, without a doubt, that she was pure Tallpian.

"How do we know," she asked after several long, silent minutes. Her voice broke, and she cleared her throat and tried again. "How do you know for sure if I am who you say I am?"

Zaire hesitated for a moment and then tilted her chin so she would look at him. "Darling, darling Gaia. I think the only confirmation you truly need is how hotly you have been pursued across the galaxy by Arlo and his ilk." He shook his head. "I am sorry my dear, but the test does prove it. You belong to the royal family—in fact, you are King Yehuda's only child. I can imagine that is the sole reason they have worked so hard to find you."

"But you said, about our blood—" she protested, but he shook his head.

"That is true. Tallpian blood goes for thousands of units an ounce. But there are plenty of your people who willingly sell their own. Hunting down one wayward girl over a few ounces of blood? Seems rather extreme, don't you think?"

Gaia let that sink in. "Then someone hired them to come after us, but who?"

Zaire hung his head for a moment before answering. "You are the heir to the Tallpian throne. There is only one person in this galaxy who would be threatened by that." Gaia closed her eyes and scrubbed her face with her hands, trying to push away the memories that returned, unbidden. The red, angry eyes that haunted her dreams were now surrounded by a narrow pale face, much like her own. The voice that echoed in her mind was sharp and unforgiving. "From what I know of Prince Nuweydon, he will consider every breath you take a personal slight against him. After all," Zaire said carefully, glancing at Gaia, "he did murder his own brother—your father—to gain the throne, not to mention most of your father's supporters as well."

"Tell me everything you know about him." Her tone made it clear it was not a request.

Zaire contemplated it for a moment before speaking. "I met him once, shortly after your father was killed. I had no idea a coup had taken place and was already scheduled to visit Meidonna. I arrived days after he had confirmed himself king. Most of my contacts were killed in the purge, and I had no way of knowing what had happened." He paused to shiver theatrically. "He made it abundantly clear that my kind, any outsiders really, were not welcome now that he was king." Another shiver. "Your uncle is an unpredictable and violent man. He enjoys keeping his court on a knife's edge, waiting for a slip and blood to be spilt. He toys with people, plays games that he alone knows the rules to. He loves to hear pleas of mercy, only to condemn them in their weakness." Zaire fixed her with a strong look. "If you ever come face to face with him, which I pray you do not, know one thing: You cannot, ever, show him any weakness. He will feed on it; relish it, like an Imathine does blood. He is threatened by you—use his fear to your advantage."

"Why now?" she finally asked, looking at Zaire. "Why has he suddenly sought us out, if only to kill us? My mother and I had been living peacefully. Clearly, I knew nothing of my inheritance. Why would we suddenly become a threat?"

"You will have reached your twenty-first year by the end of the season, is that correct?" Gaia nodded wordlessly. How did he know that? Zaire offered her a gentle smile. "I know much more about you, darling girl, than you could imagine," he said, reading her mind. "You will officially come of age in a few short weeks. You are in the perfect place to seize power for yourself."

"But I had no idea until ten minutes ago that I was even part of the royal bloodline. What if I don't want to take power?"

"Your uncle does not know that, nor do I suspect he cares. Even if you are not interested in ruling, there will be those who would wish to dispose of your uncle and bring a new regime to power. You would be the perfect rallying point."

Gaia pondered that. "I wouldn't even know where to start. Even if I wanted to take the throne, I have no friends, no family, no resources."

Zaire chuckled softly. "My dear girl, you cannot say you do not have friends. You have one very good one in particular."

"Thank you, Zaire, but I couldn't ask that of you."

"I'm not talking about me, you silly goose," he said, flapping his hand at her. "I'm talking about that handsome boy who is rotting in a dungeon somewhere. Do you realize how unusual that is for him? To risk so much for someone other than himself?" Gaia shook her head, unable to speak around the iron lump in her throat. Zaire smiled at her. "I have known Brexler for many years, since he was barely a teen, scrambling to survive and keep that ancient ship of his running. I gave him one of his first commissions, and I have worked with him since. Despite being cocky, rash, impulsive, and a bit money hungry, he is, at his core, a very good man. But I still have never seen him risk so much for someone he knew so little about."

"I'm paying him." Confusion briefly flickered across her lovely features. "Was paying him."

"Maybe at first it was about the money. After you left, he could have walked away. But he didn't."

"Does he know who I am?"

"It was his thought that you might be the princess. I'll admit I scoffed at him at first. But he was right."

"He knew, and still didn't tell me?" She felt her pulse start to pound in her ears and her hands curled once more into fists at her side.

But Zaire shook his head again. "He didn't want to give you false hope. He didn't want to give you anything other than the truth."

"But it is the truth."

"We know that now. When Brex was speculating last night, that's all that it was: speculation." Gaia dropped her head into her hands.

"My gods," she moaned, "will I ever stop owing him?"

"Would you ever really want to?" Zaire chuckled and Gaia glanced at the collector, slit-eyed. "I am not blind, my dear. I have seen the way he looks at you and the way you look at him. Denial will not help your case."

"That is ridiculous," she protested, but Zaire just smiled knowingly.

"You were ready to rush off to heaven knows where to rescue him."

"I owe him a debt. He saved my life." She couldn't stand the thought of owing anyone anything, especially smug Brexler. The butterflies that flooded her stomach every time he touched her had nothing to do with it. The burning hatred Gaia felt for the sly, lascivious glances Driana gave Brex every time she saw him had nothing to do with it. He had saved her life, at least three times by her last count; it was a debt of honor. She couldn't just walk away from him now.

"Protest all you want, but this old man knows." Gaia raised her eyes to the ceiling, trying to ignore the collector's words.

"Regardless of how I feel, I owe him, and we need to rescue him."

"Turning yourself over will not get him rescued; it will get him killed."

"Then what do you suggest?" she demanded, frustrated with the old man's dithering. "If you refuse to help me, I am going alone."

Zaire sighed. "I was genuinely hoping to avoid this."

"I'm going, Zaire, you cannot stop me."

"No need for all that. I know someone who can help you."

"I thought you said your name was Raelle." Auggie's face was giant, coming through the large telescreen in Zaire's communication room as he appraised her suspiciously. "Wait, didn't you have grey hair? And purple eyes? Who the hell are you?" he demanded and Gaia sighed.

"My name is Gaia. Brex lied—"

"I knew it—"

"That isn't important now, Auggie,' Gaia chided him, and his look of superiority dropped away at her tone. "Arlo took Brex a couple of hours ago. We need to get him back."

"Wait, what?" he asked, looking confused.

"You heard me: Arlo took Brex."

"Son of a bitch!" Auggie shouted and flung the wrench he was holding. There was a massive crash in the background.

"What is the matter?" Gaia asked, stepping back in concern.

"Arlo and his goons hit Willa's yesterday afternoon."

"What do you mean?" Gaia demanded in a hard voice.

"They showed up not long after we'd left yesterday morning," he said, shaking his head, making his copper curls bounce. "I had no idea what had happened when Brex called this morning, otherwise I would have warned him. I swung by after talking to Brex and ended up helping Willa clean up. Her place is completely trashed. I've been trying to reach Brex, but all my calls kept going straight to Adyta's hard drive. I figured he was still with you."

"That must be how they found us!"

"Maggie ratted you guys out."

"How do you know that?"

"Willa told me. She kicked her out—she should have killed the backstabbing bitch, but that's up to her. I guess Arlo had them all corralled up in the front room after his boys went through and roughed everyone up." Auggie shook his head in anger. "Willa could have held them off, but when Arlo explained that he was after you and Brex, Maggie slid forward like the little snake she is and spilled her guts. Willa tried to stop her, but one of the goons stepped in. She told him to pick on someone his own size, so he punched her and gave her a black eye."

"Is Willa alright?" Gaia demanded and Auggie laughed.

"Willa is fine. Hell of a shiner, but she head-butted the goon back, and I'm pretty sure she might have killed him." Gaia couldn't even begin to digest that. Instead, she shook her head and looked up at the fair-skinned face that stared back at her.

"What do we do now?" she asked him.

"We?"

"Yes, Auggie, we."

"Why me?"

"You're his best friend!"

"That may be true, but you have to understand something, Raelle, or Gaia, or whatever your name is. This kind of thing happens to Brex all the time. If I flew halfway across the galaxy every time that Brex got into a bind, I'd never get any work done. He's a member of the Brotherhood; he's tough and can take care of himself." Gaia glanced back at Zaire, unsure. "Brotherhood?" she mouthed at him, but he shook his head at her. Now wasn't the time.

"You don't understand," Gaia said, turning back to the screen. "There is more in play here than you think. Someone hired Arlo to come after me, and I'm afraid they are going to kill Brex to get to me."

"What does that have to do with me?" Auggie asked, looking wary. It was clear he was not comfortable with the idea of Brex being in genuine danger, but he was also having trouble believing it was as severe as she said. Gaia opened her mouth to argue, but Zaire beat her to it.

"It has everything to do with you—you and the rest of the Brotherhood. Contact Kain. He'll help Brex even if you won't." Auggie's face went pale, losing what little color it contained.

"Is it really that serious? You really want to involve the entire Brotherhood in this, Zaire?" Auggie demanded, recovering enough to sit back, his arms crossed. "Brex is semi-retired anyways."

"Don't give me that, Auggie. The Brotherhood is for life. You know that, and Brex knows that. Now, this girl needs your help, Brex needs your help."

"Zaire—"

"Gods be damned, Auggie!" Gaia burst out. "We need your help. You do not understand what is at stake here!" she shouted, surprising both Auggie and Zaire.

"Then maybe you should tell me the rest of it," Auggie said. Gaia muttered a curse under her breath in her native tongue before looking back up at the screen. She didn't want to explain who they thought she was. She didn't want to believe it herself, but she couldn't think of any other way to convince Auggie that Brex was in serious trouble.

Ten minutes later, what little color that had returned to Auggie's face faded away again.

"You have got to be joking."

"Do I look like I am kidding?" Gaia demanded, crossing her arms across her chest, her turquoise eyes fixed on Auggie like knives. "I'm not asking for you to fight my battles. I'm not asking for you to help me take back my throne. All I'm asking is that we save one of your own." Auggie stared at her carefully for a long moment before shrugging.

"Well, we don't have a choice now. I'll call Kain. Shaw too. They'll spread the word."

"Tell them to meet us on my grounds. Gaia will be here with me and we can start from there," Zaire offered.

"Please do not say a word to anyone about who I am really," Gaia begged. "I have more issues than can be dealt with right now. All we need to do is save Brex."

Auggie nodded. "Brex is my best friend, I'll be there."

"Thank you!"

"We'll see you shortly."

# Chapter Ten

As Gaia paced the halls, waiting for Auggie and the rest of the Brotherhood to arrive, she finally allowed herself a moment to reflect on the last several weeks. Her mission, upon setting out, was to discover who she was and why her mother had been taken. So much had changed in the short hours since she had met Brex, and now she knew more than she could have ever thought possible. Knowing nothing about her past had gotten her where she was, and as she saw it, that was about waist-deep in disaster. Despite Dyla being a loving mother, Gaia still felt a flicker of resentment rush through her as she paced. She thought back on her childhood, and so many of the small, seemingly innocuous moments suddenly held much more weight. Keeping their hair covered, never allowing Gaia outside alone was only the start. Dyla refused to speak about Gaia's father, other than saying he was dead. Nothing about who he was or how he died. She never spoke of her homeworld or why they had left, responding to all of Gaia's questions with stony, stubborn silence. But it was the strength behind that silence that had saved Gaia's life in the end.

The night the secret police had come for them, Gaia had been on the roof stargazing. It was one of the few outdoor pastimes that her mother allowed, provided that it was done from the safety of their own roof. Following another terse argument about Gaia being able to leave the house, Gaia had retreated to the roof for some peace. A knock at the door that late at night had surprised her but, in a fit of pique, she ignored it, leaving her mother to answer. The crash that followed made Gaia jump so violently she almost fell off the roof. Raised voices echoed through the house and, peeking over the edge of the gutter, Gaia saw men in black combat fatigues flooding through the door, ransacking their home. Two firmly held her mother by the arms. Dyla's face was worried but not surprised, as if she had somehow known the visit was coming.

"She's not here." Her mother's voice was loud but calm. "I sent her away days ago." A brief pause and Dyla's voice dropped, her tone icy. "I knew it was only a matter of time." One of the dark men turned to her mother and after a moment's hesitation, delivered a ringing slap that would have knocked Dyla to the ground had she not been supported by the two other men. Gaia clamped a hand over her mouth to prevent her from crying out, but Dyla only took a deep breath to compose herself before looking back at the man in front of her. "You can tear the entire house apart. She is not here. I'm not stupid enough to not be prepared for this." Ignoring her words, the men went back to sacking the entire house. While the police were occupied, Gaia saw her mother glance at the sliding door that led to their small back garden and the narrow set of steps that led to the rooftop, where Gaia sat, shaking in fear. Peeking over the edge of the gutter, Gaia was able to catch her mother's eye. Dyla stared hard at her, as though trying to memorize her face before jerking her head ever-so-slightly to the left. Gaia could almost hear her mother's words, echoing in her head. "Go, Go!" Terrified, but with adrenaline coursing through her, Gaia slid away, making her way to the far edge of the roof. There was a small gap between their house and their neighbors, and she thought she could make the jump.

The night of her escape was cold. She crouched on the neighbor's roof as the police ransacked her house and small rear yard. Gaia couldn't bring herself to leave her mother in such distress, but she was too terrified to move. Plus, if she fled now, she left with nothing but the clothes she was wearing. She sat in the shadows and listened as their home was turned upside down. Glass broke as windows were shattered and soon her mother was pulled from their home and pushed into a waiting speeder. Two shadowy figures waited outside the door, and the tall man who seemed to be in charged stopped and spoke with them. His words carried, and Gaia didn't even have to try to overhear them.

"Find her," the voice growled. "She is the most important one. Stop at nothing, do you understand?" The voice that replied in assent would soon be burned into Gaia's mind, after listening to its taunting threats, always right behind her. The man in charge left, and the two figures leaned against the front garden wall.

"The bitch was lying; the girl will undoubtedly return, and so we will wait until she does." Arlo's voice was far too high-pitched and did not fit his broad height and build. Both figures perched themselves on the garden wall, facing the street, and sat down to wait. There was little activity in their quiet neighborhood after dark, and soon the two gorths grew restless. Finally, Arlo ordered Keon to wait and watch the house while he attended to other business. The rat-like henchman did as ordered, and settled in as the night rolled past. Soon, much sooner than she expected, she heard his light snores. Taking advantage of what she could only guess was going to a fleeting opportunity, she moved to the edge of the roof. By hanging from the gutter by the tips of her fingers, Gaia was able to drop herself almost noiselessly to the ground. She crouched low, waiting, but the small thump had not disturbed her sleeping enemy. She took a moment to lower her heart rate as her mother had taught her to do when she was angry or scared before slipping over their back wall like a shadow.

The house was an utter disaster: furniture overturned, books and papers flung free, curtains ripped down, shards of broken glass littering the floor. But Gaia could not spare a tear for her former home—not then. She tiptoed into her mother's room where she knew a significant stash of money was hidden in one of the bed-posts. She shrugged into a dark leather jacket that had belonged to Dyla before tucking all of the money she could find into the interior pockets and into her blouse. She was slowly backing from the bedroom, trying to think if anything of value was left, when she backed into a lamp that had miraculously survived the carnage, knocking it to the ground with an almighty crash. The snores issuing from the garden wall cut off and, a moment later, Keon shoved his rat face through a broken window, his narrow, menacing features twisted with excitement. He let loose a howl and tried forcing his way through the broken frame. Realizing she was probably not strong enough to fight him, Gaia instinctively spun and dashed across the wrecked room and fled into the dark, Keon not far behind.

A shout brought Gaia back to the present, and she ceased her pacing to turn and face Zaire who was puffing down the long hallway.

"They're here."

"All of them?"

"Everyone that was close enough." Zaire looked kindly at her. "They will help you and Brex."

"How do you even know about them…the Brotherhood?" Gaia asked, unsure, as they moved through the halls.

Zaire tilted his head thoughtfully, considering his answer. "The Outer Rim Brotherhood is the full name of the organization. I've never been a member myself, but Kain, their current leader, has utilized my spies on more than one occasion. I'm happy to assist them when I can. I've also worked with a number of them in different capacities over the years, but I've worked with Brexler the most. Several other Brothers have served as bodyguards or couriers in the past."

"And who are they exactly?" she asked as they turned another corner.

Zaire chuckled. "They will all give you a different answer, but for the most part, they are a loosely-associated, galaxy-wide band of beings who work together to protect the little beings that the Central Core has a tendency to stomp all over. Some call them outlaws. And it is true that many of them are petty criminals—Brexler included—but they all believe in the greater good. Many of them have no qualms about stealing from the rich or evil to provide for the weak and oppressed. It is this mission that has put them at odds with the government, which at its heart is very corrupt, as evidenced by their hiring of thugs like Arlo."

Gaia digested this. "What did Auggie mean that Brex was semi-retired?"

"Brex may have stepped away from most of his Brotherhood duties several years ago in favor of creating a different life for himself, but as any one of them will tell you, the Brotherhood is for life." They arrived at a pair of narrow doors at the end of the hallway before she had a chance to reply. "This is it," Zaire said, gesturing towards the door and Gaia nodded, squaring her shoulders, trying to organize her thoughts.

Zaire watched her carefully as she hesitated. "Are you ready for this?" She turned her cerulean eyes to him, and her gaze was already poised and serene. Zaire marveled to himself at the girl's control. She might not have known she was royalty for long, but she already wore the mantle well; maybe she had carried it all along.

"I am." Zaire pushed open one of the ornate doors that led to the terrace. Gaia stepped through and let her eyes adjust to the bright afternoon sunlight. Half a dozen men stood in the opulent garden where creepers trailed down walls, and bright clusters of flowers threw their exotic perfumes into the air. The men were as physically different from one another as possible, but their expressions of wary excitement were identical as they all stood in silence, watching her, armed to the teeth. However, it was the badge they all wore, a white patch with a yellow slash, stitched to one sleeve that made her heart stop and her head swim. Now she knew what the symbol meant, yet it was not the time to ask them about the note, the one she had found ages ago, tucked into her door. Now, it was about Brex. Auggie detached himself from the group and stepped in front of her. When he moved to bow to her, she whacked him on the shoulder.

"Don't," she warned in a low voice. "Don't you dare." Auggie looked at her, uncertain, but she shook her head. "We talked about this, Auggie. That is not important right now."

"But—"

"Drop it," Zaire advised Auggie. Gaia looked around at the rest of the group, who all wore suspicious looks on their faces. Auggie sighed in irritation, but turned to look at his companions. Waving an arm around the courtyard, he introduced them. The first to step forward was a tall, thin terran with a shock of spiky, black hair and a tablet computer under one arm. He flashed Gaia a smile, his black eyes crinkling. He stuck his hand out, giving his name as Alix. Behind Alix, leaning against the stone wall, was another terran, his shaggy, disheveled, blonde hair falling in his eyes as he surveyed Gaia up and down.

Auggie introduced him as Shaw, who gave Gaia a perfunctory nod without speaking. "He may look like a bum," Auggie said, laughing, as Shaw glared at him, "but he can shoot the dust off your boots at three hundred yards." Next to Shaw stood a massive, dark-skinned Sovarian, his broad face turned up at the sunshine. He grinned down infectiously, grasping Gaia's small hand in his large one, giving his name as Njoroge. Another Brother stood in the far shaded corner. He was short, with dark, frizzy hair that hung low and melded with his dark beard. His skin was only a few shades lighter than Njoroge's, and he had dark, piercing eyes. He grunted at Gaia, nodding in greeting as Auggie introduced him as a Dailian named Thrain. The last member of the Brotherhood uncoiled himself from a chair near the doorway when Gaia and Auggie turned to him, his movements absurdly fluid. He wore a slim, floor-length coat and what appeared to be a glass breathing apparatus, filled with an opalescent gas, that covered the lower part of his face. Gaia stared in shock, never having seen anyone move like that. He offered a wave, and she could see his gentle smile through the mask, but he didn't take her outstretched hand. Auggie said his name was Ethen and he was a Lafimen, one of the Smoke People, from the planet Landife. He declined Gaia's handshake—and almost all other physical contact, Auggie said—because her touch would be very cold to him.

"Most people just call Landife hell," Alix quipped from behind them. "The planet is almost completely consumed in flames during their day, which lasts about thirty-six more hours longer than you would ever want it to." He shook his head in disgust, and Ethen leaned around Auggie to shoot Alix a dark look.

"I'm sorry, I've never heard of them," Gaia said, glancing at Ethen, who looked away from Alix and gave her a gentle shrug.

"Hardly anyone has. They don't leave their homeworld all that much. He just happened to be in the system when the call went out," Auggie said as he waved Ethen back to his place. "His people are pretty damn rare. They can take high temperatures better than almost any other creatures in the galaxy—anything below boiling is almost too cold for them. They also have trouble with normal atmosphere," a gesture to Ethen's mask, "since Landife is mostly pure carbon dioxide. He doesn't speak," Auggie added, pointing to a faded scar that crossed Ethen's throat. "But he understands a dozen different languages just fine. He's one of our best informers. Lafimen can be very unobtrusive, and many people don't notice them; makes them great spies." Auggie looked around at the men, the expression of fraternal love clear on his face. Gaia felt her heart twist. They were here because they cared about Brex, just like she did. The men all looked at her questioningly, and she realized it was her time to speak.

She stepped into the middle of the courtyard. "Thank you all for coming to help. I'm not sure what Auggie has told you, but I need your help to rescue Brex. He saved me from Arlo and Keon on Annui three days ago. I hired him to help me investigate my origins and the kidnapping of my mother. Brex ran into Keon today while out, and they have taken him." Gaia's words were met with stony silence. "I understand that this is unusual, but I owe Brex a debt, and I refuse to let him be hurt or killed just because of his association with me. It is me they want, not him." The towering Sovarian laughed outright.

"You must not know Brex all that well, lady, if you think Arlo doesn't have his own score to settle with him."

"Njoroge—" someone warned.

"The only reason Arlo even found Brex was because of me," Gaia spoke over him.

"How did that even happen? Keon getting the drop on him, I mean," Shaw asked, suspicion creeping into his tone. "Because we all know that's hard to do."

Shame surged through Gaia, but she kept her head high. "They didn't, well, get the drop on him. Brex led them away. He was protecting me, but we were out because he had come looking for me."

"Why?" Alix asked. Gaia sighed, frustrated and a little embarrassed.

"Brex and I had an argument this morning. I stormed out of the house in a fit of temper, and he came after me."

"What was the argument about?" Thrain asked, but Gaia shook her head.

"That isn't important right now. The only thing that matters is saving Brex."

"And how are we supposed to do that?" Shaw demanded, stepping forward. His light, shaggy hair looked unkempt, but he cradled his rifle like it was an extension of his body. "We don't even know where Brex is."

"Shaw is right," Auggie said.

Gaia opened her mouth, but Zaire coughed softly, and all of them turned to look at their host. He stood in the doorway, the shadow of a servant disappearing down the hallway behind him. Holding up a small parchment envelope between two fingers, Zaire raised his eyebrows at them. "That is not entirely correct."

As the members of the Brotherhood filtered through the door, heading to arm and prepare, Auggie grabbed Gaia by the shoulder, holding her back until they were alone. Zaire hesitated in the in the doorway, but Auggie waved him away. Zaire glanced at Gaia, who nodded. Once the door had swung shut behind the fat collector, Auggie released his hold on Gaia before planting his hands on his hips, surveying her with cold blue eyes.

"Are you sure about this?" he asked her.

"Sure about what?"

"Going after Brex."

Gaia tried to keep the tartness from her words but failed. "It's a little late for that, don't you think? You're already here."

"I'm not talking about the Brotherhood." His blue gaze was skeptical. "I'm talking about you."

Affronted, Gaia took a step back. "Me? What about me?" she demanded.

Auggie let loose a hard breath through his nose. "Listen, we're going to rescue him, that's not up for debate. What I'm curious about is why you're so invested. You met him what, two, three days ago? What is he to you?" For a moment Gaia had no reply. Memories returned unbidden; the heat of his skin as he touched hers, the slight, lingering scent of fuel and aftershave that clung to him, the way his eyes raked over her like a caress as he watched her every move—how could she explain that after only three days? How could she articulate that she felt rather than saw Brexler, the way he moved, predatory and confident like a jungle cat, or how he was like a shadow, always there, just in the corner of her eye, already a part of her? Swamped by the foreign feelings, it took a moment to formulate a response that did not betray her inner turmoil.

"I told you, he saved—" but Auggie cut her off with a wave of his hand.

"You said that before but I don't buy it. You've already discovered what you were looking for. With him gone, you don't have to pay him, you could just walk away."

Insulted, Gaia drew herself up to her full height and glared at Auggie. "I can't just walk away. He saved my life, more than once. He sacrificed himself for me. How should

I feel about that?" she demanded. "I don't know what honor means to you, but to me, it is a debt that I am not walking away from until it has been paid in full."

"Why did he though?" Auggie asked. "I've known Brex a lot longer than you have, and trust me, altruism is not always a strong point for him."

Gaia raised her narrow shoulders in a shrug, and her lovely face showed her confusion. "I don't know," she answered honestly. "I've been trying to figure that out for myself."

Shoving his hands in his pockets, Auggie mirrored her shrug. "Well," he said with a rather hard sigh, "I'm not going to be the one who argues with you. I'll leave that to Brex."

"Thank you, Auggie."

"I'm not doing it for you. I'm doing it for Brex. But don't worry, I'll get the boys organized, and then we'll deliver him to your room, gift-wrapped and all."

Gaia raised an imperious eyebrow. "You're not leaving me behind."

Already taking a step towards the door, Auggie spun around to look at her. "You're not thinking of coming with us," he said in disbelief.

"I absolutely am."

"No."

"Yes!"

"No," Auggie said, his face firm. "I'm not going to be the one who has to tell Brex that we got you killed while trying to rescue him. He'd murder me with his bare hands."

"You're not leaving me here."

"Considering you're the one they're after, and you're the reason that we're even in this whole mess, I'd say yes we are."

"I don't care." Her voice was iron. "He risked his life to save mine. I mean to return the favor."

"If you are who you say you are—"

"I don't know! You heard what Zaire said—"

"Regardless," Auggie snapped, overriding her. "Princess or not, you're not coming along. You'll be more of a liability than an asset." Gaia ground her teeth and looked away for a moment before turning back to Auggie, a rather serene smile on her face. Auggie stepped back, immediately wary of her confident expression.

"I am going to rescue Brex if I have to steal your gun and go alone." She paused, staring around the empty garden. "Either you help me, or I follow you there and cause problems."

Auggie stared at her, admiration warring with frustration on his face. Finally, he spoke. "You're still a huge liability. We don't have a big enough crew to protect you and rescue Brex."

"I am more than capable of defending myself. And besides, I'm the one they want. Maybe if we can distract them long enough, we can get Brex out without them noticing."

"Use you as bait?" Auggie asked, laughing. "Yep, I'm a dead man."

"It will work, and you know it."

"No! Brex will literally kill me if we sacrifice his meal ticket," he said, eyeing Gaia up and down. "Or whatever you are to him." Unable to argue with Auggie's description, Gaia shook her head, trying to ignore the pulse in her stomach at, "whatever you are to him."

"I can be useful, I promise."

"Prove it." It was more instinct that moved her, rather than conscious thought. Gaia took two lightning-strike steps towards Auggie, yanked his pistol free from its holster, and flung her arm out, firing, all in a single, fluid movement. Both of them glanced to the right and watched as a neon-yellow bird exploded in a shower of feathers. Auggie did his best to keep his mouth from dropping open as he stared at the girl in front of him.

"How did you do that?" he asked, cautiously, suddenly aware she was not to be trifled with.

Taking a deep breath, Gaia handed the weapon back to him, grip first, trying to force as much conviction into her voice as she could. "Instinct. The first time I'd handled anything bigger than a table knife was when I threatened Brex with the blade he'd given me. Something felt so right, it was like an extension of myself." She shrugged, tossing her head back, making her long blonde hair dance. "I can't explain it," she lied. There was no doubt in her mind, after seeing the tape that morning, that weapons came as easily to Tallpians as breathing. As they stood examining one another, the door burst open, Njoroge in the lead, his own pistol drawn. Both Auggie and Gaia jumped, looking at him.

"We heard a shot," he said, drawing up short in confusion as Shaw and Ethen crowded in behind him.

"We're fine," Auggie said, slipping his gun back into its holster. "Gaia was just proving a point. Are we ready to go?"

"How does Zaire know about this place again?" Auggie whispered to Gaia twenty minutes later as their group crawled on their bellies across a tar-covered roof, just across the street from the prison where they suspected Brex was being held. The sun was hot on their backs, and they could hear the everyday hustle and bustle on the street below them.

"Besides Arlo, Brex said Zaire must have one of the best spy networks in the entire galaxy," she whispered back as they edged towards the lip of the building. "He certainly knew who I was before I did myself."

"And who exactly are you again?" hissed Shaw as he crawled along behind them. Gaia shot him a look over her shoulder, one that promised pain. Had she not made it clear in the courtyard before they left that she was just a friend of Brex, someone who owed him a debt? Despite her earlier explanation, most of the men had still eyed her with a degree of wariness. She knew the call had been put out by the head of the Brotherhood, which according to Auggie, was suspicious enough. Most calls-to-arms came from regional or quadrant leaders. But she pushed those thoughts from her mind. Who she was could wait. Brex was her only priority.

Auggie turned his wide blue eyes to his Brothers. "We agreed to help Gaia. No questions asked," he reminded them. Shaw mumbled under his breath but nodded. When they had all gathered at the edge of the building, they peeked up over it. The entrance to the prison across the street was unremarkable: the same light green as the buildings on either side. Zaire's source was an enforcer who worked in the building. A message from him told them that Brex was being held in one of the lower cells, part of an ancient tunnel network put to ground thousands of years before anyone in the group was living.

"Now what do we do?" Gaia asked Auggie as they watched the street.

He waited until they had moved away from the lip of the building before answering. "We split up," he said, pointing to out the groups as he spoke. "Thrain, Njoroge, and Alix will enter the tunnels from the sewer. Shaw will stay here on the roof and cause a diversion in front. Gaia, Ethen, and I will go through the backdoor and connect with Thrain and the others. We'll get Brex out, don't worry."

Gaia looked up from checking her ammunition and holstering her pistol with a hard smile. "Oh, I'm not worried. I'm about to give Arlo back every ounce of pain and suffering that he has inflicted on me in the last month. I am thrilled." The gleam in Gaia's eye was a little scary, but Auggie wisely chose to say nothing.

Brex was flat on his back, bound hands painfully folded behind his head. He had rarely hurt so bad in his entire life, but he was aiming for an unconcerned façade and thought he was pulling it off nicely. Lackeys rushed up and down the tunnels, and he could hear Arlo several rooms away, shouting into a telelink. By the sound of things, they still hadn't found Gaia. Brex felt a fierce surge of satisfaction (and a small amount of smugness, to be honest), knowing that she had listened to him and kept herself safe. He hoped she had made it back to Zaire's—the collector had more money and more resources than anyone Brex knew. He could get Gaia to where she needed to be.

The shouting ceased, and Brex did his best to sit up, his solar plexus screaming in protest. Arlo marched past his cell door, an angry sneer on his face, with a trail of goons and hangers-on following behind, and it was all Brex could do not to bait the angry gorth. But considering that he could barely see from his left eye, he wisely decided against antagonizing Arlo. Several quiet minutes had passed when an explosion echoed through the halls, sending a rush of hot air through the iron bars of his cell door. Muscles screaming, Brex did his best to lurch to his feet. Swearing, he grabbed the bars to keep himself upright. A tremendous amount of noise erupted far down the hall, followed by a rapid burst of gunfire that silenced most of the sound. Brex felt his heart leap into his throat. There was no way…but sure enough, a few moments later, the sound of pounding feet echoed down the corridor, and three familiar figures swam into view.

"By all the gods, I have never been so happy to see your ugly faces," Brex laughed through the bars as Alix, Njoroge, and Thrain slid to a stop in front of his cell. All three of his Brothers grinned back at him.

"Don't thank us," Alix said as Thrain dropped to one knee and set to picking the lock, "Thank your girl." Brex felt a blaze of heat flash through his stomach at the thought of Gaia rallying his Brothers to help, but he also felt a tug of worry and hoped she hadn't done anything to put herself in danger. The last thing they needed was for Arlo to get his hands on her.

"Gaia did this?"

"Her and Auggie. And the fat guy."

"Zaire?"

"Yep. Apparently, they all like you or something," Alix said with an impish smile.

"And you're risking life and limb for what reason? You barely come out from behind your computer," Brex shot back, giving Alix his own smirk. "I know they aren't paying you."

"Apparently Kain thinks you're worth saving."

"The Brotherhood is for life," Brex said, and Njoroge echoed him, nodding.

"Are you almost done?" Alix demanded of Thrain, who had the set of picks held in his enormous hands.

The darker-skinned man glared over his shoulder at the much younger one. "Would you like to do this, hacker-boy? No? Then shut up."

"We need to get moving. That stun barrier won't hold for much longer." A few more seconds and there was a clink, and the door swung open with a screech. Brex heaved a sigh of relief. Alix cut the rope holding his wrists and handed him a pistol. "Let's get out of here. Auggie, Gaia, and Ethen are upstairs waiting for us."

They rushed up the stairs to the first floor, Njoroge helping Brex with an arm around his waist. They had just broken into the lobby when they pulled up short, and Brex felt his heart stop. Arlo stood in the middle of the grey marble room, desks and chairs destroyed around him, his greasy black hair in complete disarray. He wore a triumphant smile on his face as he towered over a kneeling Gaia, a pistol held to the back of her head. Auggie lay on the ground nearby, bright, vibrant red blood pulsing wetly from a wide-open knife wound to the belly, and Ethen was sprawled across the floor a few feet away in an inky black pool that had already spread too far for him to survive. For a beat, no one spoke.

"Brex, get out of here!" Gaia's voice was panicky as it shattered the silence. Growling, Arlo reached out and snatched a handful of Gaia's blonde hair in his claw-like hand and yanked her to her feet. She shrieked in pain, but Arlo jabbed the pistol into her ribs, forcing her to bite down on her lip—so hard that Brex could see her brilliant red blood beading at the broken skin.

"Let her go, Arlo!" Brex shouted, stepping forward. His ribs objected to the sudden movement, and a hiss of pain slid from between his clenched teeth as he stopped short.

Arlo smiled at Brex, radiating smugness. "I told you I always get what I want in the end. It's a pity I didn't kill you when I had the chance." He glanced at Gaia, her pretty face contorted in pain. "I guess knowing that you will have to live with the knowledge that you couldn't save her will have to be enough."

"No!" Brex started forward again, but Thrain and Njoroge hauled him back.

Arlo pointed his weapon at Brex. "Say goodbye, Carrow." Arlo squeezed the trigger, but as he did, Gaia jerked her head back, smashing into his nose. The shot went wild, clipping Brex in the arm as he dove for cover behind an overturned desk. Snarling in pain, Arlo bashed Gaia in the head with the butt of the pistol, knocking her to the floor, out cold. Two hulking goons appeared through the front door, and one of them hoisted Gaia, unconscious, over his shoulder, her blonde hair so bright contrasted against his black shirt. Arlo turned and pulled the trigger again and again until the clip was empty before fleeing the building.

# Chapter Eleven

All Brex could hear was the ringing in his ears. Arlo had taken Gaia, Auggie was bleeding to death, and Ethen was already dead. Brex could barely focus on the foggy world around him as his remaining Brothers rushed them from the station, through the crowded streets and poured them over the threshold of Zaire's mansion. There was a great deal of yelling, blood-covered tiles, slave girls screaming, and obscenities being shouted in half a dozen languages as they all staggered through the door. Several strong footmen whisked Auggie away as Njoroge shouted for someone to find a physician. Shaw and Alix forced Brex into a chair, Shaw slapping a flask into his hand, forcing him to drink. Mira, one of Zaire's slaves, leaned down to clean and stitch the wound that was dripping blood down his arm. The heat from the whiskey sliced through him and brought reality crashing back; the noise and color were suddenly far too real. He smashed the flask to the floor and jumped to his feet, carelessly knocking Mira to the ground. Shaw helped her up with a glare at Brex, but he ignored them. Grabbing Zaire by the collar, Brex dragged him into the communication room.

"Get me Kain. Now." Zaire, never having seen Brex so intense, complied and began punching buttons on the telelink. A minute later, Alix and Shaw slid into the room behind Brex. There was some high-frequency static, and after a long moment, Kain's face swam into view. Wherever he was, it was clearly the middle of the night, evident by the large bed in the background where a dark-haired woman slept on, oblivious to the call. Kain's dark hair and beard were streaked with silver and mussed from sleep. He was younger than he looked, but he carried a heavy burden, looking after and marshaling the entire Brotherhood. His black, unreadable eyes took in Brex's destroyed face, Alix's grim continence, and Shaw's blood-soaked shirt. As the universal commander of the Outer Rim Brotherhood, Kain rarely put his boots on the ground, but he was still a part of every mission they undertook.

"What the hell happened, Carrow?" His voice was low and gravelly. "Start at be beginning."

Glancing at his Brothers, Brex explained how he had met Gaia and rescued her from Arlo without even knowing who she was. When he reached the part in his story where they discovered Gaia's history, Kain held up a hand to stop him. "You mean to tell me that after years of the Brotherhood searching for the lost Tallpian princess, you stumbled across her without even knowing it?"

Brex felt his eyebrows jump up in surprise. "You know who she is?"

Kain's dark face was unreadable. Finally, he sighed. "Yes, I do, as do the rest of the quadrant commanders. It has been a mission of the upper leadership of the Brotherhood for the last ten years to restore the bloodline of King Yehuda to the throne of Meidonna. The princess went into hiding with her mother, the queen, eighteen years ago. We were contacted by a detachment of the Tallpian army that is still loyal to Yehuda. They asked us to find her when their efforts failed."

"Why didn't we know about it?"

"We had to keep it quiet, the fact that the princess was still alive. Prince Nuweydon is insanely dangerous. If word ever got out that she was still alive, he would stop at nothing to find her."

"Well, he must know now. Even if he didn't hire Arlo, someone who works for him did."

"And now Arlo has her," Kain said darkly.

"Yes." The single word hurt Brex more than the entire beating he'd suffered at Arlo's hands.

Kain, pointing a finger at the screen, rooted them all in place with his fierce gaze. "Understand this now. We rescue her." Brex did his best not to scoff. As if he needed Kain's permission to go after them. "I won't ask if you're up for this, Brexler." Their leader eyed Brex's wounds but seemed to know that he would go charging out the door the minute their conversation was finished. "Do what you boys need to do but understand me: You will rescue her."

Arlo's words, gleeful and oily, were the first things that Gaia heard as she woke, her head spinning with pain. The voice that replied to Arlo's joy was euphoric but still cold, and Gaia could hear the malice that floated amongst the words. She lay on a cold metal floor, and she could feel the chafe of iron around her wrists, which had been yanked painfully behind her back. Peeling open one eye, it took a moment for the world to register. She was lying on the floor in the middle of the cockpit, staring at Arlo's back as he spoke excitedly into a telescreen. The face on the screen was the one that Gaia had seen many, many times now—both in dreams and on film.

"And you're sure it is her?" the voice demanded, and Arlo cackled gleefully. He gestured back to where Gaia lay, and she quickly closed her eyes. "See for yourself, Your Grace. She so does resemble your brother."

"Fine," was the curt reply. "See that you do not delay your arrival."

"Yes, Your Excellency. It shouldn't take much longer." Through slitted eyes, Gaia saw the narrow, pale face nod sharply before the transmission was cut off. Arlo turned away from the screen, smiling with smug satisfaction. She closed her eyes again, and he marched past her, completely ignoring her. As soon as she heard the cockpit door slam shut, she opened her eyes again. Stretching, she tried to adjust her wrists to relieve the knot of tension that was building between her shoulder blades. She struggled to sit up until she was able to scoot and pull her wrists under her feet, bringing them to rest in front of her. She worked her wrists around, trying to see if the bindings would give, but the iron manacles were locked firmly in place.

"There is no point in trying to get loose, you know." Gaia whipped around to see Keon sitting several feet away from her, his feet up on a crate, his rat-like face alight with pleasure. She snarled wordlessly at him, vowing silently to herself that if she were ever free again, she would make sure Keon suffered a painful and unpleasant death. He climbed to his feet and strode over to her, a delighted grin making his pointed features uglier than usual.

"You'll make us rich, you know," he said, taking her chin in his hand as he knelt in front of her. She jerked away, narrowing her eyes at him. Keon pretended not to notice. "You know your friend Brex? Arlo killed him—" Gaia froze. No, it couldn't be true. She refused to believe it. Watching Keon's face search her own, it was clear in his expression that he was hungry for her pain. She knew she couldn't let them see the cracks that Brex had created in her armor, so she tossed her head haughtily and kept her mouth shut. He would get nothing out of her. "So you're on your own now, little girl."

His smug words stung her into responding. "I managed just fine on my own for over a month. Not just some little girl now, am I?" she snapped.

Keon faltered but recovered. "That doesn't matter now. All that matters is the person at the end of the line, and he is dying to meet you."

"I know who he is."

"Then you know what he's going to do to you," Keon said with a smile.

Gaia felt fear snake down her spine but tossed her hair again, fixing Keon with a challenging glare. "That fact that he is threatened by a mere little girl," she spat with a heavy emphasis on the last three words, "what does that tell you about him?" Keon froze, and it was clear he had not thought of that. Gaia wasn't going to throw away those seeds of doubt that she had just planted. "He is terrified of me and for good reason. I am a threat, and he knows it."

"You're one girl. What could you possibly do against a king and his army?"

"An army of warriors who aren't sure where they stand. You know that my father's court was purged in the blink of an eye. How could anyone be safe with a madman like my uncle on the throne?" She paused for effect before continuing. "Besides, how many people actually know of my existence? Most of the galaxy thought I was killed along with my father. Your knowledge that I am alive makes you a liability. I don't know my uncle, but I do know one thing: That makes you a loose end."

"You won't be alive long enough for that to matter." A cold voice cut across the cockpit and Gaia turned to see Arlo standing in the doorway, his face angry. "Keon, get out of here." His rat-like henchman eyed both Gaia and Arlo suspiciously before he scuttled from the room. As soon as the door shut behind him, Arlo marched over and snagged a handful of Gaia's still-blonde hair. She ground her teeth to avoid crying out in pain but managed to throw Arlo a hateful scowl as he knelt in front of her, his claw-like hands still tangled in her tresses.

"Understand something, girl. There is only one thing that is going to happen to you when we reach Meidonna, and you know what it is." Gaia debated spitting in his face. "There is no one, not Brex, his friends, or that fat collector, who can save you."

Feeling rage build, she offered Arlo the same haughty glare she had given Keon. "By all means, make me a martyr." Arlo paused, and Gaia saw her chance. "Show the rest of the galaxy what a true despot Nuweydon is. The lunatic who was so desperate for power he had his own brother killed and murdered his niece, even though she had no desire to take the throne." Arlo glanced at her like he didn't believe her, but the doubt was clear in his eyes. Gaia could have laughed. That was one thing about gorths: They may have been strong, but they were never smart. "I'm sure someone like that will rule for ages," she said, sarcasm dripping from her words. "Even if I don't overthrow him, you can bet that his own people eventually will."

Arlo finally recovered himself. "That's enough."

"What, you don't agree with me?" she asked, arching a defiant eyebrow. "You know how dangerous he is."

"I said that is enough." Arlo snatched a rag off the console and quickly gagged her, tying it tight behind her head. She adjusted her jaw but smirked inwardly. Those seeds of doubt would sow themselves into greater things. She may not have been worldly or well-traveled, but she did know something about fear.

"Brex! You're bleeding!" Brex turned from yanking on his boots to stare at Zaire and Mira, both of them looking anxiously at him from the doorway of his room. While he had felt the trickle of blood running down from his eyebrow, he had been ignoring it.

"Has the physician looked at you yet?" Zaire demanded, but Brex rolled his eyes.

"No. Don't worry about it."

"Brex—"

"I said don't worry, Zaire."

"I understand—"

"No, you don't!" Brex shouted, rounding on his friend. "You do not understand. Thanks to my carelessness, we've handed Gaia over to the enemy—who wants to kill her, by the way! So, yes, please tell me how you understand, Zaire."

The collector narrowed his eyes at Brex. He knew that Brex's rage was covering deeper feelings, but that didn't give him an excuse to shout. "If you think you are the only person who cares about Gaia, you are wrong. But being rash will only get you both killed."

"I have to find her, Zaire."

"You will. But bleeding to death won't help her, or you." Brex growled under his breath but plopped down onto the bed. Mira darted forward, holding another needle and silk thread. The stitches on his arm still stung but he wasn't about to say anything.

She hesitated in front of him. "This is going to hurt," she warned him. "Don't knock me down again." He shot her a wane look, and she shrugged. "Don't say I didn't warn you." But Brex sat quietly, only wincing as she sewed the cut over his eyebrow closed. She dabbed at it with a wet towel before pronouncing him finished.

He kissed her cheek softly as he stood. "Thank you. Sorry about earlier." She smiled sadly at him.

"Master is right. You are not the only person who cares for the lady Gaia. If you see her, please, give her my duty." She dipped a small curtsey, and Brex felt his heart squeeze. It was physically painful knowing that he had failed Gaia and that Arlo had won, at least this round. The shame was more than he could stand. Finally, he was able to lift his eyes to at look at Zaire, who nodded solemnly.

"Bring back our girl."

In the hallway, Brex's Brothers—save Auggie—were waiting. Although their faces were grim, he felt the under-current of their energy. The Brotherhood couldn't help but be hyped for a coming fight. That is what they had signed up for: an independent force of good that could be counted on by the little people of the galaxy to do the right thing when no one else would. Kain had been very clear about their mission when he called back an hour after their first conversation. He had reached out to his contacts in the Tallpian army and explained the situation. Their main point of contact was a general who had sur-vived the purge who knew of Gaia (which they now knew was not her real name) and Dyla's flight and had contacted Kain about helping restore Gaia to her rightful throne. He could get them onto the planet and help them rescue her from Nuweydon.

Shaw sidled up to Brex and clapped him on the shoulder, giving him a sympathetic look.

Brex glowered at him. "I don't want your pity," Brex snapped, but Shaw punched him in the arm, making him wince when the blow hit his stitches.

"It's not pity, you ass, its support. Now let's go kill some gorths." A low rumble of agreement went through the group, and they trooped towards the front doors.

They were only part way down the hall when a side door was yanked open so hard it bounced off its hinges. Auggie stood in the doorway, shirtless, with a large bandage wrapped around his middle. "You guys better not be leaving without me," he barked.

Brex spun and looked at his best friend in disbelief. "They just stuffed your intestines back inside you, and you want to go charging halfway across the galaxy with a belly full of stitches?"

Auggie looked at them all as if the answer was obvious. "Well, duh." Brex couldn't help but chuckle. Of course, Auggie cared more about the mission than he did himself. It was a typical Brotherhood attitude. The idea of sitting out on a fight just because of a scratch was unheard of. But Auggie's wound was far more than just a scratch, and Brex wasn't about to let his best friend risk his life when his tethering to said life was so tenuous.

"Raise your hands over your head," Brex told Auggie.

"What?"

"You heard me; lift 'em up." His friend tried to stretch but let out a yowl of pain and grabbed his side. Brex shook his head but slung an arm around Auggie's shoulders and helped him back into his room. Jaylyn, one of Zaire's slaves, was hesitating at the end of the hall and Brex gestured for her. She rushed to their side and helped settle Auggie into his bed, plumping the pillows at his back.

Auggie winced as he settled back before he fixed Brex with a hard stare. "Kill that son of a bitch," he growled. Brex nodded and gripped Auggie's arm before rejoining his waiting Brothers.

"We should probably warn Zaire," Shaw muttered in a low voice. "Knowing Auggie, he'll make a break for it as soon as we're off-planet." Brex nodded; there was no doubt in his mind that Auggie would try and join the fight as soon as he could, ready or not.

After they were airborne, Brex set the autopilot before heading to his cabin. He dug around in a dusty box and finally unearthed a black leather jacket with the Brotherhood patch sewn onto the left arm. It had been far too long since he had worn it, but now he shrugged into it with a smile. He returned to the cockpit and rejoined Shaw who was just replacing a headset on the console.

He glanced at Brex as he settled into the captain's chair. "That was Kain," Shaw said, choosing his words carefully. Brex looked up with interest. "The general can get us onto the planet without being noticed, I guess. I've got a temporary entry code and the coordinates. Kain's also bringing in the western edge detachment for this, and said he'll meet us on Meidonna."

Brex looked at him in surprise. It was unusual for their leader to take part in any action. "Did he say why he changed his mind and is going to ride along on this one?" Brex asked, trying to keep his tone casual even though his gut was twisting, realizing just how big their mess really was.

Shaw shook his head darkly. "All he said was this was too big a fight for just one man," he said with a significant glance at Brex. Brex would have gone after Gaia by himself. He knew it, and Kain knew it, which was probably why he had rallied the nearby members of the Brotherhood to step in and help. Had he just been going after the woman he owed a debt to, it would have been one thing, but pursuing those who had kidnapped the lost Tallpian princess with the intent of putting her to death? That was a different fight altogether.

# Chapter Twelve

The landing on Meidonna was rough as high winds buffeted Arlo's ship. Gaia felt a floating sensation in her gut as the ship dropped to the ground, but it was the ice that instinctively flooded her veins that made it clear they had arrived. She had spent the rest of the silent trip debating internally. Although seeing her uncle frightened her, she hoped it would finally bring an end to her nightmares. Not that she had too many nights left, if Arlo was correct and Nuweydon planned to kill her, but it would be nice to get some decent sleep beforehand. She contemplated what it would be like to finally face him. The idea made her hands shake in fear, but she wouldn't ask him to spare her. He wouldn't even consider it; she knew that from what Zaire had told her, no matter how prettily she begged. As much as the idea of death terrified her, she knew she would die on her feet, like a princess, like a woman worthy of Brex. She did her best not to think about him—the grief of losing him was like white-hot pincers probing an open wound—but she could not keep the memories from squeezing into her mind like smoke. They had only spent three, maybe four days together and yet she suddenly realized he had a hold on her unlike anything else she had ever experienced. Just the thought of his smile and warm hands on hers made her shiver, and suddenly, she knew she could say that she might love him. She vehemently hoped that Keon was lying—the surge of anger and despair that had washed through her at his words had caught her completely off guard—and that Arlo hadn't killed Brex after she had been knocked unconscious, but she recognized that the reality was far too likely. But even if it was true, she would go to her death with her head held high; Brex would expect nothing less.

Her only other thoughts were for her mother, who was undoubtedly already on Meidonna, if she was still alive at all. Even if she only could see her for a moment, it would be enough for Gaia to tell her mother that she forgave her and that she loved her more than anyone alive.

"Time to go." A rough hand encircled her arm, and she glanced up at one of the mammoth guards who followed Arlo like a shadow. He stared at her, slack-jawed, and for a second she saw a flash of something in his eyes. Was it fear? She laughed silently to herself. How could someone triple her size be afraid? But as he hauled her from the ship, they marched past a window, and Gaia caught a glimpse of her reflection. Her blonde hair was gone, replaced by a color she could only describe as night itself. The black was pure, inky and deep. But it was her eyes that changed everything. Icy and bright, their green was beyond anything that was found in nature. The combination was startling, frightening even. Gaia felt her lips curve into a smile around the gag that was still in her mouth. This was just the look she needed to face her uncle.

They met Arlo at the door. He tugged the piece of cloth from Gaia's mouth, and she licked her lips and flexed her jaw. "You will say nothing while in the presence of King Nuweydon." Gaia snorted and rolled her eyes at the command. As if she would ever listen to him.

"You will not to give me orders I have no intention of following," She retorted. Arlo opened his mouth to protest, but she cut him off. "You are keeping us. I am sure that my uncle will not appreciate any undue delay." Arlo bristled, but Gaia simply smiled. With a glare, Arlo jerked his head, indicating that they should follow him. The door to the ship slid open, and Gaia was hit with a blast of icy wind. Heads ducked against the freezing gusts, they followed Arlo as they made their way from the ship towards a glistening white palace. Gaia could not help but gape at their surroundings. The towering white building sat perched atop a cliff that stared over an angry, iron-grey sea, and she could hear the waves as they crashed against the rocks at the bottom. The rough beauty of low, rolling green hills peppered with massive grey lumps of stone was a mirror to the planet she remembered in her dreams. She knew that this was her home—truly knew it to the depths of her soul. Looking around, Gaia could see the town spreading out into the hills, most buildings carved from the same white stone as the castle. As she let her eyes wander over the stone homes that surrounded the palace, she noticed there were few people about. They continued their march through the small town but saw no one. Curtains would twitch as they walked by, but there were no open doors, and the squares and markets were silent and deserted. Anger twisted in Gaia's gut, surprising her. The town should have been full and bustling, with children playing, vendors hawking their goods in the market square, and people visiting the shops. Instead, it was a ghost town. The anger surged again. Nuweydon had done this. Gaia threw her head back and walked tall, despite the icy wind. She knew they were being watched, and she wanted to make sure the population, what was left of them anyway, saw her and would recognize her when the time came.

They approached the castle and ascended the sweeping staircase cut from the same white stone as the rest of the town. The wind blew incessantly, and the cold sliced through

Gaia's clothes as they mounted the stairs. The guards who stood at the top of the steps nodded at Arlo in recognition, but both froze when they saw Gaia being led along behind the gorth. Gaia swept her eyes over them, keeping her expression composed, but she let her eyes narrow just the slightest degree. Both sentries jerked in apprehension. As soon as they passed, she could hear their whispers. Arlo turned and glared menacingly over his shoulder, but Gaia only smiled smugly at him, which seemed to infuriate him even more. "Serves you right," Gaia thought to herself. Two soaring doors were thrown open, and they marched across the threshold, into the royal palace of Meidonna. Never in her life had Gaia seen so many beings who looked just like her. Every one of them was tall and lithe with narrow faces, long limbs, and pale skin that matched the stone walls behind them. Understanding surged through her gut: a mixture of relief, apprehension, and frustration. Would her people recognize her? Why had she had to wait for her entire life to finally be among those like her? The crowd parted as they made their way through the palace, whispers rising at their backs. Passing through another set of double doors, they stepped into a long room where an immense dais sat opposite them. High windows let light filter into the room, but it was grey and muted. The whispers were louder here, and Gaia saw every elegant head in the room had whipped in her direction. Knowing that showing any fear would be like pouring fuel on to a fire, she settled a small, feline smile on her face and lengthened her stride, throwing her head back, and she walked through the echoing room like it belonged to her.

The figure who occupied the chair of state was like every other Tallpian in the room: long limbs and a narrow face. But that was where the comparisons stopped. The eyes that shone from the pale face were a vivid blood red. His white hair, slicked back from his forehead, hung down his back, reaching almost to his waist. His black clothes made the contrast even more distinct. Gaia felt an arrow of fear shoot through her, but then she steeled her nerve. He was afraid of her. She was the threat—not him. Arlo and his goons marched her the length of the room, stopping at the base of the dais. Slammed to the hard floor, she was forced to kneel. She ground her teeth, but ignored the pain that shot through her kneecaps. Arlo gave an obsequious greeting, and his sycophantic words made Gaia roll her eyes.

It was a long moment of silence before the voice that haunted her dreams spoke. "After all these years, Kallideia, you still look so much like your father." Of all the opening salvos, that was not what she had expected. The impulse to bite her tongue was weak, and the words tumbled from her lips before she could stop them.

"I have a feeling that even if I were your mirror image, you still would not welcome me here, uncle," she said, her voice heavy with irony as she lifted her eyes for the first time. Her uncle still sat sideways, lounging on his throne. He was young—so much younger than she expected. It took many years for the Tallpians to show their age, and it was clear that he was still in the prime of his life. His light eyebrows quirked up, somehow amused by her spirit.

"And yet, still so much like your mother."

"Where is my mother?" she demanded, and Nuweydon laughed, the cold sound echoing through the stone hall.

"Oh don't worry; you'll be joining her shortly. And then you'll die, side by side." Pain, as ragged as being sawed in half, sliced through her, and she had to glance down and bite her lip to stem the tears. Forcing herself to regain her composure, Gaia lifted her head to look at her uncle again. Knowing it was the most maddening thing she could do, she smiled and was pleased to see the ripple of concern that crossed her uncle's face. It was brief, but it was there. It was true then: He was terrified of her and the unease that she created. The thought filled her with pleasure. If she was going to die, she was going to do so on her feet, without a hint of fear. The thought made her brave and adrenaline surged through her.

She shrugged Arlo's hand off her shoulder, and climbed to her feet, using her height to her advantage as she looked up at Nuweydon with a haughty smile. "Do me a favor then," she said, borrowing a bit of Brex's drawl. "Get it over with."

"Understood. We'll see you on the ground." Brex nodded at the dark face of Kain as he disappeared from the telescreen. The Outer Rim Brotherhood was minutes away from touching down on Meidonna, and Kain had made it painfully clear there could be no mistakes.

"Do you think we can trust this guy?" Shaw asked as they descended through the layers of atmosphere towards the planet's surface, referencing the general who had contacted Kain all those years ago, in the hope of restoring Gaia—Kallideia—to her father's throne.

Brex shrugged. "I'm not sure. He's got an awful lot to lose."

"As do we."

"You mean, as do I," Brex said, shooting his friend a dark look.

"Look, man, that isn't what I meant."

"No, but you understand what I'm saying." If they failed, he'd lose Gaia forever. The thought physically hurt him.

Shaw nodded. "I get it, I get it."

"Well then get ready, because we're here."

Brex landed Adyta in a wind-whipped grass field, not far from Alix's and Kain's ships. Far off in the distance, Brex noticed a collection of long, low, stone buildings that had a military air to them. There were a dozen other crafts scattered across the field, and as they touched down, Brex could see the white patch of the Brotherhood on the hulls. They disembarked, swearing in surprise at the gusts of icy wind that flooded through the door as soon as they pushed it open. They headed towards the knot of people, clustered under the awning of a small, ramshackle building. Brex stepped up next to their burly commander. Brex was tall, but Kain was taller and wider. The leader of the Brotherhood nodded his silver-streaked head at Brex and turned back to the man in front of them. A Tallpian, he was the general who had put everything in motion. Brex, distinctly anti-establishment—like most of the Brotherhood—was immediately wary of the general's upright bearing and decorated military uniform. His silver hair was slicked back, and violet circles showed beneath blue-green eyes.

He was nodding his grey head in agreement to something Kain had said. "She arrived this afternoon. Nuweydon plans to execute her and her mother on live feed tomorrow at midday." Brex had to curl his hands into fists to keep from lashing out, but a low growl escaped his throat. Kain shot him a look that ordered him to stay calm.

"What is your plan to get them out?" Kain asked.

"It's fairly simple. Dozens of prisoners await execution. We simply draw some blood and make the switch. We'll have Princess Kallideia and Queen Dyla off-planet before morning and two other Tallpians in their place. Nuweydon will never know the difference." Brex felt an unpleasant twinge in his stomach.

"You plan to just kill off two of your own people?" Brex demanded.

The general drew himself up to his full height, his face ablaze with righteous anger. "Sacrifices must be made," he retorted. "Our futures depend on Princess Kallideia. If we must sacrifice two lives to save thousands, then so be it."

"It's still too easy," Brex said. Kain glared at him, but he ignored it and looked back at the general. "What is the hard part?"

"Getting in," he said, shaking his silver head. "The prison is almost impenetrable. Far below ground, it has one primary entrance and exit. However, there is a series of tunnels that lead down to the lower kitchens that will be utilized to sneak the princess and her mother out."

"But your plan does us no good unless we can get to them."

"I am still allowed to move freely within the palace and can smuggle you in."

"Then why are we still standing here?" Brex demanded. "How do we know he won't move everything up and just kill them?" But the general shook his head again.

"Nuweydon is a madman, but everything he does has a purpose. By airing it live, he will be reminding everyone that he has removed the last obstacle to his right to rule. There will be no one left willing to challenge his legitimacy."

"Gaia and her mother have been in hiding for eighteen years. Why now?" Brex asked. The general looked him over carefully, suspicion bright in his eyes. It was clear he was just as wary of Brex as Brex was of him.

"The princess comes of age at the end of the spring season, which is just weeks away. As soon as she is twenty-one years of age, she can, according to our laws, make a challenge for the throne."

"So he wants her out of the way before her claim becomes legal."

"Yes. And there are those who would support that claim, myself included."

"What's in this for you?" Brex asked, eyes narrowing. Kain rolled his dark gaze at Brex's disrespectful tone but let his protégé speak. The general eyed him with annoyance but spoke.

"My name is General Amadeas. My brother was King Yehuda's father. I am the uncle of Prince Nuweydon and great-uncle to the Princess Kallideia."

"You're his uncle, and you've just let him run amok for the last eighteen years?" Brex demanded, flabbergasted. How could any sane man stand by and watch as his family was torn apart by a murdering psychopath? Amadeas bristled and drew himself up to his full height, straightening his military uniform with a sharp jerk.

"How dare you! I have fought to keep myself and the rest of my family alive. Getting myself killed benefits no one."

Brex opened his mouth to reply, but Kain nudged him. "Drop it, kid."

"But—"

"I said, drop it." Brex glowered at his commander but shut his mouth. "The two of you fighting does nothing to save the girl."

"Why should you care so much about the princess?" Amadeas demanded. "You are just another hired gun." Brex tilted his chin and fixed the other man with a smug look.

"I am the only reason your great-niece is even still alive. Without me, Arlo would have delivered her days ago, and she would already be dead."

The older man surveyed him, as if debating the truth of Brex's answer, before raising his thin shoulders in the barest of shrugs. "If that is the truth, I suppose I owe you my thanks. Kallideia is the only hope we have for our civilization to survive. Nuweydon's purges, mandatory mercenary service, and unnecessary wars have pushed our kind to the brink, and we risk total destruction if he is allowed to continue."

"Then why are we standing here talking when we should be rescuing her?"

"If you storm the castle gates, not one of you will make it through alive. There are ways to enter the palace unseen, and that is how we will rescue the queen and the princess."

"Then what are we waiting for?"

"The cover of darkness—that and Nuweydon's relaxation, knowing his challengers are safely behind bars."

Gaia's haughty words were still hanging in the air when Nuweydon threw his head back and laughed again, the unnerving sound raising the hairs on the back of her neck. He pulled his lanky frame from the chair and descended the stairs towards their small party. The moment Nuweydon rose from his throne, every being in the room hit their knees, except Gaia.

She glanced around and had to stifle a frightened gurgle of laughter at the absurdity. "A bit much, don't you think?" she asked, looking at her uncle. He shrugged as he stepped down to meet her face to face.

"I like to remind people of their place," he said, eyeing her speculatively. His blood-red gaze made her shiver, but she did her best not to let it show. "You should follow their example." Gaia snorted derisively in response.

"I do my best not to encourage insanity, even when it is the most popular opinion." Anger rippled through the crimson gaze, and Gaia grinned inwardly.

"You will kneel before your king."

"You are no king of mine." To her surprise, he chuckled. She had expected anger or at least annoyance. The way he flipped between emotions was frightening, seeing it in person. Zaire had explained it to her, but now, standing eye-to-eye with the monster, Gaia knew Zaire had barely scratched the surface.

"I would shut that pretty mouth of yours," Nuweydon suggested lightly, grabbing her chin to look into her eyes, but she took a step backward and pulled herself out of his grip. Eyeing him, she spoke with irony that dripped from her lips like honey.

"Why? What are you going to do if I don't, kill me?" she asked, a slightly hysterical laugh bubbling past her lips. While Nuweydon's amused mask was firmly in place, she could see the anger building in his eyes.

"Rest assured, niece, if your death is quick and painless, you will be fortunate."

"You will be making a martyr of a twenty-year-old woman who has no desire for the throne."

At that, Nuweydon smiled. "You know, I almost believe you." He shrugged. "But it matters not. You will still die to serve your king."

"I'll repeat myself then. You are no king of mine," she spat.

"You are one of two people who disagree with me, and frankly, my dear, after tomorrow that will no longer be an issue." The thought that tomorrow would be the last sunrise she ever saw surged through her, and anguish threatened to overtake her. But she forced the feeling down. Even if Brex didn't save her, even if she was put to death, she still refused to die on her knees.

"I hope you're man enough to kill me yourself," she snapped, and she saw that it caught him off guard.

"Why would I waste my time?"

"Because you are terrified of me and you know it." There was a soft ripple of laughter around the hall at her words as one or two brave couriers tittered. Nuweydon, as quickly and easily as breathing, yanked a dagger from his hip and flung it hard across the room. There was a sickening thunk, and Gaia jerked around to see a Tallpian along the far wall sink to the ground with a gurgle, the knife buried to the hilt in his chest. Horror surged through her, and she stifled a scream. Nuweydon was more than mad: He was utterly and completely dangerous. But he was also afraid of her and any impact she might have, that much was clear. Gaia saw her chance to exploit her influence, knowing it wouldn't matter what she said; he was going to kill her regardless. She might as well do some damage while she had the chance. "I am the last threat to your throne. If you cannot manage to kill one girl, how could you be fit to run a kingdom? After all, it took you this long to even find me." She eyed him with a challenging smirk on her face. "You are mad, utterly mad, and you know what is best done with mad dogs?" she asked, keeping the smirk firmly in place. "They get put down." Her uncle turned to her, enraged, and she thought for a moment that he might strike her head from her shoulders then and there, but instead, he slapped her. It was a ringing blow delivered with the back of his hand that sent her crashing to the floor. She clutched her cheek with her hands, biting down on her tongue to keep the tears at bay. The blow hurt, but heeding Zaire's words, she ground her teeth and forced herself back to her feet. Tossing her hair out of her face, Gaia looked back into her uncle's face and found his gaze had already cooled. He offered her a smile, which completely unnerved her. He took a moment to openly appraise her, taking in her lustrous black hair and vibrant green eyes.

"Such a shame to waste such beauty," he said, his eyes caressing her in a way that made her want to scream. "Oh well." He glanced down at Arlo, who was still staring at the floor. "Get her out of here—now."

Arlo and his goons hustled Gaia out of the throne room, a tidal wave of whispers rising at their backs. They plunged into the bowels of the palace. Level after level they descended until the air was icy cold and their breath hung in white clouds. Entering the dungeon, Gaia had to stifle a cry of anguish. Row after row of cells contained all manner of beings, but it plucked at Gaia's heartstrings to see so many

Tallpians languishing there. How could her uncle imprison his own people? Many of them lifted their heads and stared at her with listless eyes, probably assuming she was just another prisoner. Moaning and weeping filled the air, and Gaia heard more than a few curses being uttered as Arlo paraded by. It was undoubtedly his fault that so many cells were occupied. They reached a cell towards the end of the farthest block, and she was pushed through the open door after the cuffs around her wrists were removed. Arlo locked the door behind her and stuck his smug face through the bars to leer at her.

"I'll enjoy watching you die," he said with relish. Gaia didn't hesitate but lashed out, catching his cheek with her fingernails, tearing four bloody scratches down the side of his face. Howling in pain, he leapt back from the door. "You bitch!" Gaia's face was hard when she glowered at him. The gorth stood frozen in place under the glare from her green eyes.

"Understand this now," she snarled, pointing one long finger at him. "If by some miracle I survive this and Nuweydon dies, you are the first person I am coming after. You and Keon," she vowed. "And there will be nowhere that you can hide from me." Shock prevented Arlo from replying, and one of his henchmen tugged him away before Gaia could speak again. As soon as they disappeared, the adrenaline that had kept Gaia on her feet during her meeting with Nuweydon melted away, and her knees gave out from under her. She dropped to the ground and burst into tears.

"Gaia?" the sound of a familiar voice coming from the far wall of her cell shocked Gaia out of her misery.

"Mother?" she asked in confusion, crawling to and pressing her cheek against the stone, trying to stop the tears and failing. She could hear her mother laughing through her own tears.

"It's me, darling. Oh, Gaia, I am so sorry!" She could hear her mother's sobs echoing off the rock walls. "I am so sorry, my girl, that everything I have done has led you here."

"Please," Gaia sputtered through her tears, "please do not blame yourself."

"I should have told you the truth," Dyla cried. "I am so sorry." Gaia could not stand to hear her mother cry.

"You were just trying to protect me. You gave me a full and wonderful life." She could hear Dyla's protests but did her best to speak over them. It was impossible for Gaia to articulate the joy that she felt reuniting with her mother, even under the present circumstances; it was all worth hearing her voice one more time.

"You have to understand, darling, if it hadn't been for your father, we would have never survived the coup. Your father forced me to flee with you, despite my protests that my place was at his side."

"He made you leave?" That was news to Gaia; it was the first information Dyla had ever revealed about Yehuda.

"To save you. He knew that if I was able to hide you away, that you might have a chance at a bright future. He made me promise to tell you, one day, when you were old enough."

"How come you never told me?" Gaia asked, thinking back to the years of silence and unanswered questions.

"Know that I wanted to. I wanted to tell you the truth, but I couldn't. Gaia, I loved your father more than any other being in this galaxy. The fact that I had left him, fled while our people were in peril, was despicable to me. I was so heart-broken that I couldn't bring myself to remember it, let alone explain everything to you. I felt like a coward."

"How could you feel that way?" Gaia asked, fresh tears tracking down her cheeks. All of the resentment she had carried for twenty years melted away in a blink. "You saved my life. You kept me safe." Gaia heard her mother laugh again through her sobs.

"Well, not exactly safe now," she said. Gaia couldn't help but give a little laugh. "How did they even find you?" her mother asked. Gaia found herself telling Dyla of her time on Annui, meeting Brex, how he had saved her and managed to bring her past to light. She described the bright colors of Xael, Zaire's kindness, and the Brotherhood's help. Her mother was silent for a beat after Gaia finished her story.

"This Brex," she finally said in a warm voice, "you have feelings for him, don't you?"

"I do – or at least I think I do. I've never loved anyone besides you," Gaia said, biting her cheek to ward of more tears. "But I can't think about him right now. This is hard enough without thinking of him."

"Do not resign yourself to a martyr's death yet, my girl," her mother said, and Gaia could hear her knowing voice through the wall. "There might be hope for us yet."

# Chapter Thirteen

Brex was pacing. There was still another hour before they could put their plan into action, and he had far too much nervous energy to sit and do nothing. Some of the Brothers cleaned and oiled their weapons, some stood in huddled groups and chatted with friends they hadn't seen since the last big gathering, and some (like Shaw) slept, returning to their ships to escape the cold, relentless wind, all of them awaiting sundown. Brex was too nervous to talk, and he would have sooner grown wings than slept. His thoughts wouldn't leave Gaia. It was odd, remembering the little things about her that he might not have otherwise noticed but now would be a crime to forget. The inquisitive tilt of her head. The way her lips curved into a knowing smile when she suspected him of being untruthful. The way she bit her bottom lip when concentrating. The lush curve of her hip in high-waisted pants. The striking contrast of her silver hair against pale skin. The flecks of gold in her bottle-green eyes. He knew that if they failed to rescue her, he would never forgive himself.

"Brex." Even from a distance, Kain's bark was unmistakable. Brex looked up at his commander who sat in the small shed, his hands held out to a small, merrily dancing fire. Kain nodded him over. Abandoning his pacing, Brex joined his leader, dropping onto an empty barrel next to the fire. He held his hands to the flame but knew no amount of heat would warm them, at least not until Gaia was safely in his arms.

The leader of the Brotherhood looked grim as Brex glanced at him. "I need you to listen to me, Brex." A little annoyed, Brex raised an insolent eyebrow.

"What, Kain?"

"Don't give me that shit, kid. This is important."

"Sorry," Brex said, shaking his head apologetically. "What is it?"

"I want you to know that you are not doing this alone."

Furrowing his eyebrows in confusion, Brex stared at his friend. "I know that. I can see—"

"That isn't what I meant." Brex was too on edge to deal with riddles.

"Spit it out, Kain," he snapped. His mentor surveyed him, his dark eyes amused and all-knowing.

"Don't forget that I've known you since you were a runty little nine-year-old, begging us older members of the Brotherhood to take you along on adventures. When we didn't take you, you stowed away and always ended up jumping into the fight, no matter how dangerous it was." Brex stifled a snicker. Kain fixed him with a dark look. "Seriously, do you have any idea what a giant pain in the ass you were as a kid?" Kain's voice was stern, but Brex could hear laughter in it too.

"You mean like the time I followed you guys to Oceris?" Kain hung his dark head, shoulders shaking as he tried to hide his laughter. He ran a hand over his face before glancing at Brex.

"You were thirteen years old! And you stole a ship."

"And you're damn lucky that I did!" Brex, desperate to belong, had "borrowed" a small, inter-planetary hopper and followed Kain and the Brotherhood leader at the time, a Necosian called Otwin, to a hostage extraction.

The planet's magistrate's daughter had been kidnapped by men employed by the Central Core in an attempt to force the planet to join the alliance. The magistrate would have nothing to do with it, and the Brotherhood was tasked with rescuing the girl. The mission had almost failed, Otwin's ship destroyed by a 420mm cannon, and they had been surrounded by the Centralized forces when Brex descended from the sky, a skinny pre-teen piloting a stolen ship. He had deftly landed the small ship, shielding Kain, Otwin, and the girl from enemy fire as they climbed aboard and escaped.

"I wanted to beat you within an inch of your life that day," Kain admitted, glancing at Brex with his black gaze. Brex nodded, chuckling.

"I figured as much. Why didn't you?"

"Otwin."

"Otwin? He barely knew me."

"No, but when we landed, and I was about to, he stopped me. Said that you reminded him of me at that age." That made Brex pause. Him? Like Kain? Kain was his hero, really the only male influence he'd ever had growing up. Even though it was fifteen years in the past, Brex felt a warm glow of pride swell in his chest. If he could be half the man Kain was, he would die happy. "You saved my life that day. That isn't something that you ever forget." Brex shook his head.

"You were as much my commander then as you are now," he said, shrugging his shoulders, hands clasped in front of him as he stared into the fire. "You were the closest thing I had to a father."

"I never wanted to be," Kain admitted, and Brex laughed.

"Of course not! Who would have wanted to? Not me, that's for sure. I was terrible."

"Haven't changed all that much."

"Nope, not much."

"But you came back," Kain said, his voice serious. Brex met his mentor's eye with effort; he recognized that dark, probing expression. The day that he'd told Kain he wanted to leave the Brotherhood, five years ago, Kain had worn the same look and asked why. Brex, with bruises and scrapes still healing from one of the worst beatings of his life, refused to answer. As much as he'd wanted to unburden himself to his leader, he couldn't—couldn't stand the shame of it. And now, he found himself nailed to the spot once again by that same dark stare. "Just like I said you would, you came back." Brex had no answer, and the only sound that could be heard was the whistling of the wind.

Kain broke the silence a few minutes later. "I just want to make sure you remember that what we're doing here today is more than just rescuing the girl. There is a whole world here at stake, and I'm ordering—no, I'm begging you—not to do anything stupid." He eyed Brex. "I know you tried to walk away from this, Brex, but I think you know as deeply as I do, that this is where you belong."

"Kain, I—" But Kain held up one massive hand.

"I don't need reasons why. I trust you, Brex, and I know that if you needed to step back, you had a good reason. Maybe you'll tell me one day; maybe you won't. But I do know you well enough to know that in your heart, you are a Brother. Maybe one of our best, provided, again, you don't do any-thing stupid." Brex tried to look affronted, but thinking back on his past, he knew there was a real chance he would do something impulsive. He shook his head.

"I can't promise anything Kain. But Gaia is my main concern, and that is where my focus will be." Kain growled at him but also shook his head.

"You're one of the best that we have, Brex. But do me a favor: Be that man. Be one of the Brotherhood. Don't be some love-stuck dumbass who goes on a tear and ends up getting himself or anyone else killed. Especially not that girl."

"Her name is Gaia."

"Is it, though?" Kain asked, his tone significant. Brex rolled his eyes.

"She hasn't gone by Kallideia since she was a kid."

"That is who she is, though. Don't forget that either." Brex was about to retort when General Amadeas stepped into the shed. Brex rose at the sight of the older Tallpian, his hand dropping down to settle on the handle of one of his revolvers. He nodded his head respectfully but eyed the military man carefully.

"I would speak with you, alone," Amadeas said politely. Kain raised his eyebrows but stood and left the shed, nodding at Brex. Raising his eyebrows at Amadeas, Brex waited. "Your commander speaks highly of you," Amadeas said, watching Kain's retreating back. "And says that you are the one who discovered Kallideia and rescued her on Annui."

"I already told you that." The general ignored him.

"Why did you save her?" he asked instead.

Brex chuckled darkly in response. "I'll tell you what I told her. At the time, the enemy of my enemy was my friend. Honestly, it was more about pissing off Arlo than rescuing a damsel in distress." Brex shrugged. "Then I got to know her, and helping her find her origins became much more important than the money she offered me. Watching her struggle with her changing appearance was harder than I ever thought it would be. Every time she looked in a mirror, she saw someone different and had no idea who she was."

Amadeas nodded in understanding. "Our children are taught as young ones how to control their appearance. I do not think that Queen Dyla ever made it a priority; rather, she concerned herself with keeping Kallideia safe." Brex understood, but it didn't mean that he agreed. However, arguing about past parenting choices wouldn't accomplish anything.

"Do you think we have a chance of rescuing them?" Brex asked.

"I do," he replied. "It will not be easy, but she is our best chance for a stable future."

"What is your plan after we get her out?"

"Kallideia will reach her twenty-first year in less than a month's time. After that, she is legally able to claim the throne. We can mount a legal coup without fear of Central-based retribution."

"We'll have to keep her well-hidden until then."

"She has made it this long. We can manage three more weeks," Amadeas said. "She'll have the best protection in the galaxy."

Brex chewed on his bottom lip for a moment before speaking. "I'm sure you're not surprised, but I don't trust you." The old general eyed Brex with a hard stare.

"That does not surprise me in the slightest. I would say the same for you. But can you put that aside for the woman we both love?"

"I do not—"

"There is no one else here who is as on edge as you are, and no one has spoken as fiercely as you. I would have to be blind not to see it." Brex chose to ignore the obvious signs. Instead, he shook his head at Amadeas.

"You haven't seen your great-niece in over eighteen years, and yet you can still claim to love her?" A smile lit up Amadeas's face for the first time since Brex had met him.

"She was the most engaging little girl," he said warmly. "So wise even as a toddler. She could have ruled the galaxy had she trained at her father's side."

"How do you know she's still that girl?"

"She will be—"

"You have no idea who she is," Brex spat, a little annoyed. Gaia had been barely two years old when her mother fled with her. How much attention would a general have paid to a child barely out of infancy? Great-niece or not, Brex didn't buy it. "She may not want the throne."

"At this point, she doesn't have a choice."

As the sun dipped toward the horizon and the temperature dropped, Amadeas gathered the Brotherhood and explained their plan of attack. All it all, it was rather simple. A quick injection and Brex and several other members of the Brotherhood would assume the identities of Tallpian prisoners. According to the general, political prisoners were very common, and it was no surprise that more and more of them were ending up in Nuweydon's cells. They would then be marched into the dungeons. The guards on duty would be relieved by other members of the Tallpian army who were loyal to General Amadeas. They would locate Gaia and Dyla, free them, and swap other prisoners into their place. If everything went according to plan, they would be off the planet's surface before the sun rose.

After Amadeas left to make final checks on their arrangements, Kain returned to the shed. Brex sat in silence, trying to work through what had just happened. There was something about Amadeas that made him inherently nervous, but it was difficult for him to put his finger on what made him edgy, so he kept his mouth shut.

They were still sitting staring into the fire when Shaw jogged up to the shed, holding a telelink screen.

"Hey, Amadeas says we need to get moving. And there is a call for Brex."

"Me?" Brex asked in surprise. Shaw nodded and handed him the small screen. Tapping a button, Auggie's face popped up. "Auggie."

He looked pissed. "Hey Brex," He sounded pissed.

"What is going on?"

"Did you tell Zaire to post an armed guard on me?" he demanded, and both Brex and Shaw burst into laughter. Shaw had called Zaire from the air and warned him that Auggie might try to do something stupid.

Trying to stem his snickers, Brex stared at his friend's face on the screen and couldn't help but dissolve into chuckles again at Auggie's martyred expression.

"That was me, dude, sorry," Shaw said, waving a hand in front of the screen.

"What the hell, man?"

"Auggie, you were almost sliced in half. They put you back together barely twenty-four hours ago."

"I'm a member of the Brotherhood. I should be there." Kain shook his head and grabbed the screen away from Brex.

"Auggie, listen to me. This is only the beginning. Much more will happen before we can close the book on this one. Stay on Xael. Get better. We'll call you in when we need you." Auggie looked like he was going to argue when Kain took a deep breath and spoke, his baritone rumbling in his chest. "That is an order, August Drupmann. If you disobey me, may all the gods help you. We don't need you charging into something you know nothing about and getting killed. Do you understand?"

Copper curls bounced as Auggie nodded. "Understood, sir."

"Good man. Rest up. Go chase a few of those girls Zaire packs his house with. That's when we'll know you're feeling better." Auggie smiled, gave a salute, and signed off. Kain looked at Brex and Shaw. "At least I don't have to worry about him." Kain's grim expression almost made Brex laugh but knew he'd get clobbered if he did. "Don't make me worry about you," he muttered, shaking his head. Another dark look between Brex and Shaw. "Alright boys, it's go time. Let's do this."

The three Brothers were joining the milling crowd of their comrades when Kain stiffened.

"Something's wrong," he said as his eyes scanned the crowd and landed on Amadeas's worried face.

Brex felt ice flood his veins. "What?"

"I don't know. Stay here," Kain ordered automatically.

"Yeah, sure," Brex snarled sarcastically. Kain observed him with a dark look but said nothing. Amadeas cut through the muttering crowd of the assembled Brotherhood members to reach Kain and Brex.

"We have a problem," the general said without preamble. "The arrival of the prisoners that you were supposed to take the place of arrived several hours ahead of schedule. They are already in their cells." Kain swore.

"You're sure?"

"I am," Amadeas said, nodding. "My men who are posted to prison duty confirmed it moments ago."

"Now what do we do?" Kain demanded. "Our whole plan hinges on getting into that palace unseen." There was a brief moment of hushed muttering before Brex spoke.

"We go as we are," he said. A stunned silence fell over the assembled men.

After a moment, Alix, who sat nearby, tablet perched precariously on his knees, chuckled. "See, this is why we keep you around, Brex. No one else is insane enough to come up with these ideas."

Brex shook his head at his Brothers' disbelief. "Don't you see? It is the perfect cover. Arlo knows me too well. He knows I'll probably do something stupid to get Gaia back. Let them think you caught us attempting to break into the palace. Drag us down to the cells as planned. Everything from there stays the same as before, we just look like ourselves."

"I'll have to present you to Nuweydon," Amadeas cautioned. "He'll be suspicious if I don't."

"All the better. That way, when I look him in the eye as I kill him, he'll know me."

"Easy there, Brex," Kain muttered, but Brex ignored him. He turned back to Amadeas.

"Do you have a plan to get your other supporters off-planet? Once we rescue Gaia, we'll be lucky if all hell doesn't break loose."

The general nodded. "My wife and those courtiers loyal to our cause will be leaving—discretely—momentarily." He checked the timepiece on his wrist. "The support we have within the royal army will leave with us, which is about two hundred soldiers. They will disable the planetary shields long enough to allow us through. Once we are safely beyond the barrier, one of my men will seal it from the inside. Hopefully, this will give us more time to get into warp without being followed."

Brex nodded, trying to find a weak spot in the plan but after a minute, found none. "Fine. Get every supporter we have off this planet because I have a feeling it could get ugly real fast."

"Are you sure this is a good idea?" Amadeas addressed Kain while watching Brex out of the corner of his eye. "Sending your men in as themselves?" Kain shook his head.

"I don't like it, but Brex is right. If we made no attempt to rescue the girl—"

"Princess," Amadeas spat, but Kain ignored him.

"If we don't mount some kind of rescue attempt, they'll be much more on their guard."

"They won't suspect subversion?" Brex laughed out loud at that, and several of the Brotherhood joined in.

"You must not have worked very closely with gorths before, General. They may have brute force on their side, but thankfully for us, they are not that smart."

Not long after, Brex stood with several other members of the Brotherhood, along with half a dozen Tallpian soldiers who were loyal to Gaia and her great-uncle, in the shadow of the palace. The soldiers were fixing manacles around the limbs of the Brotherhood that they would shed as soon as they reached the dungeon. Brex looked at the young, blonde Tallpian soldier who was locking the metal bands around his wrists.

"What's your name?" Brex asked. He realized that they were about the same age when the other man lifted his head to look Brex in the eye.

"Lathan," he said, blinking, as his eyes shifted from green to blue, mimicking Brex's own eye color. Brex shivered; he had never seen a Tallpian make use of their natural talent. Gaia's changes mostly happened as she slept and Brex, unfortunately, hadn't spent much time watching her sleep. Now he wished he had.

"Lathan, I'm going to apologize in advance," Brex said.

"For what?" he asked.

Brex stifled a laughed. "When we get in there, I am going to make your life kind of unpleasant. Figured I'd apologize now." Instead of looking concerned, Lathan smirked. "What?" Brex demanded.

"You've never actually seen a Tallpian warrior at work have you?"

"Only on film."

Another smirk. "Let's just say there is no need to apologize." Brex didn't like the sound of that, but it was too late to do anything about it.

Amadeas cleared his throat, and the small group turned to look at him. "This is it. You know the plan. We enter the palace and present you to Nuweydon. Afterward, we'll conduct you to the cells. From there, we free the princess and her mother and make our exit through the lower kitchens. Kain and the remainder of the Brotherhood will provide cover if needed. Once we are airborne, everyone is to warp to the Leconus system in the South-Eastern quadrant, specifically the planet of Miwarma. From there, I will guide everyone into the safe zone." He looked around at the faces of his men. "You understand your duty. The princess and her mother are our only priority." They all nodded. Amadeas let his eyes linger on Brex in serious contemplation. "We have to save her."

Brex nodded in reply. "I was committed to saving her from the moment I met her. We're with you to the end."

Amadeas nodded. "So be it. Time to go."

Even with the adrenaline singing through his blood, Brex couldn't help but appreciate the rough, rugged beauty of Meidonna, although he could do without the wind. The pair of guards at the front doors of the palace saluted General Amadeas as Brex and his Brothers were dragged past. Lathan and the other guards had guns pinned against the base of the prisoners' skulls to discourage them from fighting. They were hauled through the sprawling building, and even though night had fallen, the palace was alive with voices and light. A wave of whispers and chattering followed them as they headed for the throne room. Right before the doors were flung open, Amadeas looked over his shoulder and gave everyone one of them a significant glance, as if to remind them of their mission before turning back and marching into the soaring hall. There was a towering dais at the end of the room, and even from the other side of the long room, Brex could see a long, pale figure lounging in the chair, in quiet conversation with another Tallpian. Brex felt his hackles raise, knowing he was in the presence of the man who was threatening the life of the woman Brex cared about. His hands gave an involuntary yank on his chain, and Lathan gave him a tap on the rib cage with the butt of his rifle. Brex hissed in pain—his ribs were still tender—but kept his eyes forward.

"Your Majesty!" Amadeus's voice rang through the room as their group approached the foot of the stone stairs and every set of eyes was locked upon them. "I bring news that cannot fail to please you," the general said, sweeping a low bow before Nuweydon. The prince looked up in interest at their assembled party. He rose from the throne, pulling his lanky form to its full height before heading down to meet them. Every courtier in the room dropped to their knees in supplication as soon as the prince was on his feet. The Brothers were forced into kneeling positions by their guards, most of them muttering oaths and obscenities under their breath as their knees hit the cold, unyielding stone. Glancing around the room from his place on the floor, Brex felt his eyes widen in shock as he covertly watched every being in the room fix their gazes on the floor. It was terrifying to see the hold this despot held over his people. As Nuweydon descended the stairs, Brex glanced up and saw the blood-red eyes that shone from a pale face framed in snow-white hair. A shiver raced down his spine, and he vowed to himself that those eyes would not see for much longer.

"Uncle, how could you bring better news than that which I have already received today?" Brex watched as Amadeas acknowledged him with a smile and another bow from the waist as the guards and prisoner were waved back to their feet. Lathan hauled Brex up by the back of his shirt, making Brex growl low in his throat.

"'True," Amadeas said, agreeing with his nephew. "Few things are better than knowing your throne is secure, now and well into our future." Brex felt his teeth snap together at the words and suddenly understood how the old general had survived as long as he had. He sold his loyalty, and he sold it well. It was tempting to believe that Amadeas was serious, his voice was so sincere. "But I still bring tidings I think will amuse you nonetheless."

Nuweydon clapped his uncle on the shoulder. "By all means, share your news."

Amadeas turned and cast a triumphant hand, showing Brex and the five other members of the Brotherhood who stood in front of them, bound in chains. "Members of the Outer Rim Brotherhood. Some of my men interrupted their attempt to break into the dungeons. Undoubtedly they are here for her." There was no need to explain who Amadeas meant.

Brex watched curiously as several different expressions flickered across Nuweydon's face before he settled on amusement. "I must ask, Uncle, were they in any danger of succeeding?"

"Not even remotely," Amadeas said, and both Tallpians threw their heads back and laughed. Fury surged through Brex, and it had nothing to do with acting when he jerked his head back hard, smashing his skull against Lathan's face and felt the telltale crunch of a breaking nose. With his guard distracted, Brex dove at both of the still-laughing Tallpians. Two other members of the guard caught him by the arms and yanked him back, hammering their fists into his gut before he even got close. Still bruised from his recent conversation with Arlo, it was all Brex could do not to shout in pain.

Instead, he let a low growl slip past his teeth as he kept his eyes focused on Nuweydon. "Where is she?" he demanded in a bark. The two guards made to drag him away, but Nuweydon held up a hand and they froze.

"And who might you be?" he asked in a light, curious tone that Brex didn't trust for a second.

"Brexler Carrow," he spat, and there was a glimmer of recognition in the red eyes.

"Oh ho, Brexler Carrow. I have heard your name before." Nuweydon waved his hand, and a shadowy figure detached itself from the dais and stepped forward.

"Arlo," Brex snarled, and the anger was not an act.

There was glee in the gorth's eyes as he strode forward to observe his enemy cuffed and bound. "I knew you would try something stupid, Carrow."

"First time you've been right in ages, Arlo." Brex couldn't resist baiting him—it was too easy to rile him.

"I told you I'd kill you," Arlo threatened, and Brex threw his head back and laughed, letting the sound ripple through the marble room.

In his peripheral vision, Brex could see heads tilting, mouths whispering behind hands. Good, he thought, let them talk. "One for two, Arlo. I'm not dead yet."

"Yet."

Brex smiled darkly and bared his teeth. "By all means, feel free to try again." Arlo opened his mouth to reply, but Nuweydon cut across them both.

"Don't worry, Brexler Carrow. You'll have your chance to die. After the girl, though; I think I'll rather enjoy watching you watch her die." There were no words—only fury that surged through Brex, and he made another dive at Nuweydon. Amadeas stepped between them, and with an effortless blow, slugged Brex in the jaw, knocking him to the ground. Lathan was on him in an instant, the barrel of his rifle planted against Brex's temple. He froze and stayed down. The strength of the hit made Brex's head spin. The other members of the

Brotherhood surged forward in defense of their comrade, but the guards held them back, and Nuweydon chuckled to Amadeas.

"Tomorrow will be a good day. Ridding the world of two enemies instead of one, we should proclaim a national holiday." He paused. "I'm sure the Brotherhood will appreciate receiving their heads." Amadeas saluted.

"I'll see the prisoners down to the dungeons and oversee the final arrangements for tomorrow." A gesture to Lathan, who leaned down and yanked Brex to his feet none too gently before pressing his gun against Brex's spine again.

"Do," Nuweydon said with a lazy wave of his hand. "I have other pursuits." A lascivious glance flashed at one of the ladies of the court. They had resumed standing with respectfully bowed heads, but it was apparent they watched their ruler's every move. The woman's cheeks colored, and the man with dark hair standing next to her observed the look, dipped into a brief bow, spun on his heel, and left the room without a word. The young woman watched the dark-haired man depart with a slightly panicked look before turning to Nuweydon. In a blink, she composed her face into a winning smile and gracefully approached him to take his outstretched hand. Brex felt his stomach lurch and couldn't quite control the growl that slipped between his teeth. On the eve of putting his niece to death, the madman was amusing himself with one of his courtier's wives.

Amadeas shot Brex a dark look before shoving him away. "Get moving," he ordered, but the show no longer mattered. Nuweydon was no longer concerned with them.

Their small group trooped down to the lowest levels of the palace. They passed several soldiers who guarded the stout wooden door that led into the depths of the prison, all of them nodding respectfully to Amadeas. Beyond the door, in the massive, icy underground chamber, there were rows and rows of cells. Brex was surprised to see how many of them were occupied by Tallpians. Many of the prisoners recoiled as Amadeas strode through the room, shrinking back against the walls of their dark cells with muttered oaths or fearful whimpers. The reactions made Brex's hair stand on end. As they marched past row after row of cells, Brex said a silent prayer that all of those imprisoned by Nuweydon would see freedom sooner rather than later. Only when they reached the last row of cells did Amadeas slow his walk. He spun to face their group, and Lathan, showing no sign of his recently broken nose, quickly freed Brex from his manacles.

Handing him another key, he pointed to the second to last cell. "There."

Brex couldn't control the flutter that went through his gut. Glancing back at his Brothers, Shaw nodded at him. "Go get your girl." Needing no further encouragement, Brex covered the short distance in two long strides and stopped abruptly in front of the metal bars. The woman who turned her dark head to look at him was so different from the Gaia he held in his memories that he froze, unsure, but as soon as she caught sight of him, her face broke into a smile he already knew too well.

"Brex!" She jumped to her feet and rushed to the door, sliding her hands through the bars so she could grip his arms. "You're alive," she said, laughing through the tears that were suddenly pooling in her eyes.

He grinned at her. "You bet, darlin'. It's going to take more than Arlo to finish me off." A smug smile. "Besides, someone had to rescue you," he said.

She glared at him, her fluorescent green eyes bright. "Don't make me regret breaking you out of that prison," she threatened, but he just chuckled at her.

"Come on, we need to get you out of here." Pulling back, he inserted the key into the lock, and a moment later Gaia launched herself at him as the door swung open. Staggering back, he caught her and held her tight to his chest.

"Thank you," she said in his ear. He was surprised by her reaction, but the feel of her warm, supple body pressed against his drove almost every other thought from his mind. There was a cough, and they broke apart to see Amadeas standing with a dark-haired woman Brex guessed to be Dyla. Gently, he set Gaia on her feet and, remembering his manners, stepped up to her mother, taking her hand carefully and bowing over it.

"You must be Brexler," she said with a warm smile. "It is you I have to thank for returning my daughter to me." Caught off guard, Brex could only hesitate, unsure if he was being chastised for getting Gaia captured and thrown into the dungeon.

"She doesn't mean it that way," Gaia said, reading his mind and whacking his chest with the back of her hand.

"I'm sorry to break up the warm reunion, but we need to get moving." Alix's voice broke across their group, and Amadeas nodded.

"Agreed, we must hurry. Dyla, I need blood from yourself and Kallideia. Lathan, retrieve the replacements." The younger Tallpian darted off with a ring of keys as Amadeas withdrew a silver box from his coat pocket. Two needles and two vials were nested into the black silk lining. Amadeas pulled one vial free and offered it to Dyla first and then handed the second to Gaia. Both women rolled their sleeves up and pressed the sharp edge to the crook of their pale arms. Once the small bottles were full, they passed them back to Amadeas, who placed them back in the box. He turned back to Gaia.

"Kallideia, I am not sure if you remember me," he said gently. Brex could see Gaia searching the face in front of her for something familiar, but after a moment, distress wrinkled her forehead.

"I'm sorry, but I don't." She glanced at her mother, but Dyla's face was neutral and gave nothing away. Finally, Gaia shook her head. Amadeas smiled sadly.

"I am General Amadeas. Your father's father was my brother. I am your great-uncle." She nodded, silent. Amadeas appeared disappointed but shook it off after a moment. He pulled a single, different vial of blood from his coat.

"Here. This will help you change your appearance," he said to Gaia. She took it warily while glancing at her mother again.

"Give it a try first, dear," Her mother advised before turning to Amadeas. "I gave her some basic information on how to begin her simple changes. I want to see if she can manage it without help." Looking back at her daughter. "Go ahead." Gaia darted a glance at Brex but took a deep breath and closed her eyes. It took a moment, but Brex realized that her dark hair was suddenly lightening and the hue of her skin was changing, becoming a sickly grey before taking on a vivid blue tint. The hair on her head shifted and was suddenly a vivid, flawless white. When she opened her eyes, they were the same bright turquoise as her skin. Brex took a step back and couldn't stem a laugh of astonishment. Gaia spun to glare at him, and as she did, her hair shifted back to black. "You need to concentrate Gaia! It requires quite a bit of energy at first, dear, you need to focus," her mother scolded. Brex shot a guilty look at Gaia, who closed her eyes again and wrinkled her nose in concentration. A beat later and her hair was snowy white again. She opened her eyes to look at her mother and the color stayed.

"Nicely done, my girl."

"Now it is time to go," Amadeas said as Lathan and another soldier returned, leading two prisoners by their arms. They had the same lethargic air that most of the prison's occupants seemed to share and put up no protest as Lathan brought them forward. Brex ground his teeth but said nothing as Amadeas drew blood from each vial and prepared to inject the replacements. Amadeas was just inserting the first needle when a shout echoed through the long stone room. Brex whipped around and saw Arlo standing in the doorway, his face split by an evil smile.

"Shit!" Brex kicked himself mentally. He should have known that Arlo would come to gloat.

"Escaping prisoners!" Arlo shouted back into the hallway, before pulling a gun from beneath his coat and taking aim.

"Go! Now!" Brex grabbed Gaia and shoved her in front of him. In that moment, her control slipped, and her hair and skin flashed back to their previous colors. With no time to fix it, Brex simply pushed her forward to follow Amadeas, who had Dyla by the hand, dragging her towards the far end of the dungeon. Bullets started to ricochet off the stone walls as they sprinted for the exit. The Tallpians allied with Amadeas and Gaia began to return fire as more of Nuweydon's guards poured into the room. Alix and the rest of the Brotherhood followed behind Brex and Gaia, creating a protective barrier. With the sound of gunfire and Arlo's screeching commands nipping at their heels, they dodged through narrow hallways, pushing through doors before they burst into the lowest level of the royal kitchens. The entire staff stood frozen for a moment. Amadeas ignored them and shoved Dyla ahead of him.

"Go!" Brex pushed Gaia after them and paused, throwing a look over his shoulder to check that all five Brothers were still with him. When Alix slipped last through the door, he nodded and turned his attention back to Gaia. They darted through the kitchen and burst through a door on the far side. A rush of frozen night air washed over them, and a thousand yards away, their ships waited. Breaking into a sprint as gunfire opened up around them, Brex kept himself between Gaia and the palace, praying it would be enough. Nuweydon's forces spilled from the narrow door, one soldier at a time. Looking back, Brex saw that each would drop to one knee, fire, and then sprint forward as he reloaded. It was only when he heard the roar ahead of them did he take a breath. The Outer Rim Brotherhood rushed to meet them, dozens of men in dark jackets, all with the same white patch, slashed with yellow. They were halfway to the ships when Dyla stumbled, but Amadeas quickly tugged her to feet and they kept running. Charging into the crowd of Brothers, Brex noticed Kain, Njoroge, Flynn, and so many others. Their ranks closed, creating a wall between Nuweydon's army and the fleeing royal family.

Kain's Comet class ship was waiting for them, its massive hydrogen engine emitting a neon-blue glow as it idled. Brex felt a pang for Adyta, who had already been moved off-planet by one of the other Brotherhood members; with her precarious warp drive, she wasn't worth the risk to Gaia's safety. Their group rushed up the ramp and staggered on board, Brex's legs burning. Gaia collapsed to the floor, moaning and gripping her chest in pain.

"Take off, now!" Amadeas roared at the pilot, but Brex yanked his revolver free and pointed it at the Tallpian. The Brotherhood member who stood in the door to the cockpit shook his head in negation, ignoring Amadeas's order.

"We don't leave without Kain," Brex shouted. Through the still open entry hatch, Brex could see the Brotherhood's leader, his silver-streaked head distinct in the dark crowd. Their forces thinned as loyalists fled to their ships, and those that remained, returning fire, were the core of the Brotherhood. Brex gave a shout, raising his arm, and Kain's head turned in his direction. Their eyes met, and as Kain raised his arm to gesture back, a bullet tore through his chest. Rage surged through Brex, and without thinking, he dove back through the open door and sprinted across the field to where his commander stood, still firing his weapon at the oncoming horde as a dark stain spread across his shirt. Just as he reached him, Brex felt a slice of searing pain tear through his right shoulder.

Ignoring it, he grabbed one of Kain's arms with his left, just as Shaw grabbed the other. Digging deep to compensate for the extra weight, Brex put his head down, and they ran, dragging Kain with them. As soon as they staggered up the ramp, the door slid shut behind them, and the pilot punched the throttle, the ship thrusting its way into the air. They collapsed into a bloody pile on the floor of the ship's bay. Gaia shouted for bandages as Brex struggled to Kain's side.

Their leader was still alive but only just. "Brexler," he coughed, and bubbles of blood appeared on his lips.

"Don't talk," Brex advised as he stripped off his jacket and wadded it against the dark, pulsing wound in Kain's chest.

"Shut up," his commander ordered. He dark eyes strayed to the blood that was staining the shoulder of Brex's shirt. "I thought I told you not to do anything stupid."

"You need to stop talking," Brex growled, leaning on his leader's wound.

"You need to listen to me—"

"No," Brex said, putting more weight on the wound as blood continued to pulse over his fingers, despite the wadding of the jacket. "Tell me when you're stitched up."

"No." Another hard cough as more blood appeared. "Listen. You are to take my place as Commander of the Brotherhood." The sudden silence that fell over them was deafening.

"Me?" Brex demanded after beat and Kain nodded weakly. "You."

"I can't be Commander, I—"

"Shut up," Kain snapped again. "There is no one better. And if anyone can get us through this, it's you." Brex tried to shake his head, but Kain wouldn't have it and waved his bloody hand, cutting him off.

"I don't know—"

"I do. I've watched you for the last twenty years, Brex. I've known you since you were nine years old. I took you under my wing all those years ago because I saw what you could be. There is no better fit. The men respect you and will follow you. You understand what the Brotherhood means to the galaxy." He paused to draw a rattling breath. "Make me proud."

"Kain, no," Brex said, trying to shake his leader's shoulder, but Kain's eyes became fixed and dropped his head back. "No!" Brex howled, pounding his fist against the metal floor. He jumped to his feet and staggered towards the door. "I'm going to kill—"

"Brex!" Shaw grabbed his friend from behind and jerked him into an arm bar, dragging him back. Brex thrashed, howling like a wounded animal as Shaw struggled to hold onto him. One of the other Brothers, a young terran named Kyan, draped a thin sheet over Kain's body. It was only when Brex heard Gaia's heart-wrenching shriek did he stop fighting and jerk around to look at her. She stood over her mother, who lay propped up against a stack of blankets, a jagged, gaping wound in her chest pouring blood. Dyla wore a serene smile on her face as she stared up at her daughter. Gaia dropped to her knees, tears streaming down her cheeks.

"No, Mother, no!" Gaia's screams seemed to echo and redouble in the metal belly of the ship.

Her mother lifted a blood-covered hand and cupped it to Gaia's cheek. "I really hadn't planned to leave you so soon, my dear. I am sorry."

"Please, no, somebody—" Gaia darted a panicked look around the ship, and one Tallpian soldier rushed forward with a large pad of bandages, but Dyla ordered him away with a queenly glance. Gaia let out a wordless wail and yanked the bandages away from the soldier to press them against her mother's breast.

"That won't help, I'm afraid," her mother said in a calm voice. "It is too late for me. Gaia, my girl, look at me." Gaia lifted her eyes from the wound to her mother's face, tears streaming down her cheeks. "Please know that everything I've done in this lifetime, I've done for you. I love you so much." She shifted and hissed softly in pain before glancing back up at Gaia. "I so wish that I could live to see you take the throne. I know you will make a wonderful queen."

"Mother, I—"

"Please, darling, one thing…—" She pulled Gaia close and whispered something in her ear. Gaia sat back, her face flooded with confusion.

"But why—"

"Shh, it will all make sense soon, I promise. Where is Brexler?" she asked, looking blindly around the room. Brex rushed to her side and dropped to his knees next to Gaia. He landed in the puddle of blood that was rapidly spreading from Dyla's prone body. Her dark eyes searched his face. "Thank you," she rasped. "For saving my daughter." Brex ducked his head, but couldn't speak. "You will see that she frees Meidonna from him." Brex glanced at Gaia, not sure how to respond to the order. After a moment, he nodded. "Promise me you'll protect her until your dying breath."

There was no hesitation this time. "I will."

Dyla nodded in grim satisfaction before smiling back at Gaia. "I love you, darling."

"Mother, no." But like Kain, Dyla closed her eyes, a soft smile on her face as she tipped her head back and her pulse stilled. Gaia gave a howl of grief and dove against Brex's shoulder, making him yelp in pain. Gingerly he wrapped his arms around Gaia and held her as she rocked and sobbed.

"Brex, you're bleeding," Alix said, looking at his Brother in concern.

"You have no idea how many times I've heard that lately," he muttered. "It's fine," he said, pushing his friend away. He kept his arms wrapped around Gaia and carefully pulled her to her feet as Dyla's body was covered in a sheet. Gaia leaned against him, unable to cease her heartbroken sobs that shook them both. Brex ground his teeth as a shockwave of pain rushed through him.

"Brex, you need to let me look at that shoulder," Kyan said, his brow wrinkled in concern. "I think the bullet might still be in the wound."

"Damn," Brex hissed, glancing down at Gaia who still had not lifted her head. Spying a bench, he compromised by scooping Gaia into his arms, gritting his teeth at the sharp pain that shot through his shoulder. He carried her over and sat down, settling her into his lap against his uninjured left side. Kyan tore open his shirt and went to work. Shaw slid over and offered Brex a flask, which he quickly emptied, the sharp smoky whiskey sliding through his veins like quicksilver. The pain went dull, but it was his chest that hurt more than his shoulder. The physical pain of losing Kain left a raw wound where his heart once sat. His mentor from an early age, Brex would have ended up in a very different place if the leader of the Brotherhood hadn't taken a liking to him all those years ago.

One of a dozen kids, most of whom had different fathers, Brex was the youngest boy. Most of his older siblings had already taken off by the time Brex came around, and it was up to him to protect his four younger sisters. Survival of the fittest was the rule, growing up on Cunat, and familial ties only got you so far. But Brex still tried his best. His mother, lost in her own world thanks to a combination of illicit substances, poorly-made booze, and a revolving door of men, barely noticed when he was there—or not. A scrawny, perpetually hungry kid, Brex tried his hardest to make sure his sisters had enough to eat. Often, there wasn't much to go around, and he would forego eating so one of the little ones could have something in her belly.

One day, starving, as usual, he had just stolen a small savory pie from a vendor on the main avenue when a meaty hand descended on his arm and yanked him around. Brex found himself rooted to the ground by a pair of dark, deep-set eyes. But instead of punishing him, Kain had flipped a coin to the squawking vendor and hauled Brex away by the scruff of his neck without a word. A few dusty streets over, Kain asked why he had stolen it; Brex had tilted his chin proudly and lied. Kain saw through him in a second and cuffed him upside the head, telling him to try again. After a moment, the skinny, undernourished kid broke down and told Kain he hadn't eaten in three days. Kain asked why, but Brex scowled fiercely and told him it was none of his business. Kain explained who he was and what the Outer Rim Brotherhood did, how they helped people who needed it. Instantly, Brex forgot his food and asked to hear more. The idea of being strong, and being able to protect people resonated within him, even as a kid. Kain told him he was too young, but in a few years, he might have a chance, provided he kept his nose clean and stayed out of trouble. But Brex was relentless, and after several months of following Kain around like a shadow, Kain had given in and introduced him to some of the other members. They found small chores for him to do, and the coins they tossed his way kept him and his sisters fed. More nights than not, they found him curled up in a corner of Kain's shop, sound asleep under a piece of sacking. Over the years, they trained him, mentored him and finally helped him build a life. Fifteen years later, at the age of twenty-four, when Brex told his friend and mentor he was leaving the Outer Rim Brotherhood, instead of arguing, Kain had simply fixed him with that dark stare and told him he'd be back. And he had been right.

# Chapter Fourteen

After Gaia sobbed herself to sleep, Brex settled her into a bunk, the stitches in his shoulder protesting even at her slight weight. Once she was sleeping soundly, Brex returned to the ship's helm, stepping between Amadeas and Shaw.

"I'm not going to ask if you're alright," Shaw said, looking Brex over. "You look like you've been run over by an entire tank battalion."

"Thanks, man," he said, shaking his head.

"Where is Kallideia?" Amadeas demanded. Brex glanced at him, perplexed. It seemed odd that he was more concerned about where she was, versus how she was.

"Gaia is sleeping." Amadeas scowled but didn't comment on Brex's use of her name.

"We'll need to wake her before we reach Miwarma."

"We're still a distance out. Let her sleep. She just lost her mother for fate's sake."

Amadeas looked at Brex, annoyance warring with admiration on his face. "She is queen now. She needs to assume her responsibilities. She must learn to master her grief." Brex stared at him in disbelief. Considering the ragged wound that had replaced Brex's heart from losing Kain, he decided he would not pass along Amadeas's advice to Gaia.

"She's not queen yet," Brex reminded him. "Let her make the choice on her own." It irked him that Amadeas had simply assumed that Gaia would want to take the throne. Maybe she did, or maybe she didn't but that was a choice she, and she alone would have to make.

"She doesn't have a choice," the older man snapped. "If she declines to mount a coup against Nuweydon, she will spend the rest of her life as a fugitive."

"You mean unlike the last twenty some odd years?"

"This is different. Nuweydon knows for a fact that she is alive. He will never cease hunting her until she is dead at his feet."

"Let him come," Brex growled, remembering the searing red eyes of his enemy. "He'll be dead before he can get within one hundred clicks of her. The Brotherhood will protect her."

"The Brotherhood is not a private guard, Brexler. There are other problems out there that your fraternity will be faced with."

"They will do what I say."

"You cannot—" Amadeas started, but Brex rounded on him.

"No, you cannot. I am the Commander of the Brotherhood now. I know exactly what it is that we do. Do not tell me what we can and cannot do."

"Brex is right." Both men turned to look at Shaw, who shrugged nonchalantly. "Kain gave him control. What he says goes." Amadeas muttered under his breath but turned away to converse with the pilot. Shaw sidled closer to his friend.

"He's not wrong, though," he whispered.

Brex scrubbed his face with his hands, leaving a streak of blood on his cheek. "I know. But right now, this is our problem so we'll solve it, one way or another. Let's worry about the future when it gets here."

"You should contact Cayson and the other leaders; they'll need to know about Kain."

Brex took a deep breath and nodded. "Was Kain insane for thinking I can do this?" Brex asked.

Shaw chuckled, using a knife to scrape blood from the underside of his fingernails. "You are certifiably nuts," he said, shrugging, "but we knew that already. That being said, you're rarely wrong. No, I don't think Kain made a mistake."

"I'm not sure I can do this."

"I'll bet you a gold talent that Kain felt the same way in the beginning."

"No, I'm pretty sure he was born middle-aged and never doubted a thing," Brex said, and they both laughed. "Ugh, I just don't which way to turn right now. Gaia needs me. The Brotherhood needs me."

"Focus on one thing at a time. Call the Brothers. Gaia will sleep for a while."

An hour later, Brex pushed away from the telelink screen. He had reached out to all of the regional leaders of the Brotherhood to convey Kain's passing and his succession. They all expressed dismay and anger at Kain's death, but as Eliseo from the eastern quadrant had put it, Kain died doing what he believed in and what he did best. They had accepted Brex's new role and pledged to follow him as they had Kain, but it was the southern quadrant leader that had surprised him the most.

"I'm not surprised," Cayson had said, when Brex explained that Kain had chosen him as the next leader of the Brotherhood. "I'm actually more amazed that it took him this long to let you know he intended for you follow him. He's been planning it for years," he said, shrugging his enormous, lavender-hued shoulders. "He's watched you your whole life, Carrow."

"But I tried to leave the Brotherhood," Brex argued, but Cayson dismissed it.

"Everyone does at some point or another. I left for a number of years after I married my wife. It was the birth of my son that brought me back. I wanted to make the galaxy safer for him." Brex nodded in understanding. Gaia was suddenly and bewilderingly the axis on which his world spun, and he knew he was willing to do whatever it took to keep her safe.

He was still sitting in his chair, head in his hands, when he felt a feather-light touch on his injured shoulder. He whipped around to see Gaia, tall, statuesque, and heartbreakingly beautiful, standing behind him, her lovely face wrinkled in concern. Without a word, he stood, tugged her into his arms, and kissed her hard on the mouth. Without missing a beat, she molded her lean height against him, wrapping her long arms around his neck. Her lips parted under his and her kiss was sweet and cool, far better than Brex could have ever imagined. After a long, lingering moment Gaia pulled back and fixed him with her bright stare.

"What took you so long?"

"So queen, huh?" They all sat at a round table in the ship's belly, Tallpians and Brotherhood members all intermixed. Gaia sat with her slim hands flat on the table top, but when Shaw addressed his question to her, her hands curled into fists. She shot a panicked look at Brex who sat next to her, before looking back at the rest of the table.

"Honestly, I don't know."

Amadeas cleared his throat, and every head turned to stare at him. "Kallideia—"

"Gaia, please," she said, cutting across him. "I have not been Kallideia for a very long time, Great-Uncle." Her request clearly made him uncomfortable, but he gave a brief nod before continuing.

"At this point, you do not have much choice but to take the throne. Unless Nuweydon is eliminated, he will pursue you for the rest of your life."

"I have already done enough running to last a lifetime," she sighed.

"We will reach Miwarma soon. It will be a safe place to rest and train. From there, in three weeks' time, we mount our attack on Meidonna and take back the kingdom."

"How do you know we will be safe?" Brex demanded.

The general pulled his eyes away from Gaia's face and reluctantly looked at Brex. "The Leconus system is a declared neutral zone. Miwarma is sanctuary planet."

Brex did his best to not roll his eyes at the general's patronizing tone. Everyone in the galaxy knew that. "I'm aware of that, as is everyone else. But two things," holding up two fingers. "—One, how do we know that Nuweydon will respect that? How do we know he won't just come in, guns blazing, neutral zone be damned? He doesn't exactly play by anyone else's rules. And two," ticking off the other finger, "are we sure they're going to be all that happy about us training an army there, just to leave the planet and start a war?" The Miwarmans were famous for their peaceful dispositions and abhorrence of violence.

"If the shield was properly activated, they will have no way of tracking or following us," Amadeas explained, annoyance crossing his expression as he explained himself. "I have also been in contact with the heads of Miwarman leadership. They understand our need for sanctuary. The dungeons of Meidonna hold a large number of Miwarman prisoners-of-war. They are sympathetic to our cause and have agreed to shelter us. In return, we rescue and return their imprisoned citizens."

"Is there anyone in the galaxy that Nuweydon hasn't pissed off yet?" Kyan asked, leaning back in his chair. Several Brotherhood members chortled.

"No is the short answer," Lathan said. "But there are a few planets within the system that don't disagree with him, mostly just to keep up their trade agreements."

"There are thousands of prisoners from all walks of life, all objectors to Nuweydon's rule." Amadeas grimaced. "He does not take criticism well."

"Understatement of the century," Alix snorted. The rest of the table laughed, and Brex took the chance to glance at Gaia. While she slept, her hair had changed again, this time a soft, pale blonde with a darker brown layer underneath. She had swept her hair into a coil at the base of her neck that showed off the contrasting colors. Brex reached over and took one of her hands in his. Her long fingers were icy.

"Are you alright?" he asked her softly. She turned and looked at him, grey eyes brimming with tears. She smiled a blind smile, but he could see how much it cost her. Brex stood up abruptly and pulled Gaia to her feet. The rest of the table broke off their conversations to look at the pair. "Gaia needs some more rest," Brex said shortly. "And some food. We'll reconvene right before we land, understand?" Without waiting to hear the responses, he tugged her out of the room.

They were leaning against the counter in the galley, bowls of reconstituted stew in their hands. Gaia was grateful for the warmth that was seeping through the earthenware bowl. She was trying to eat but kept glancing at Brex who was tucking in like he hadn't seen food in days. She laughed softly to herself, and Brex turned to look at her.

"Are you ok?" he asked immediately, setting down his bowl.

She gave him a lopsided smile that made her bottom lip tremble. "I'm fine. I just realized that the last time I ate was at Zaire's." She smiled grimly at Brex. "I've had other things on my mind." He snorted in response and resumed inhaling his food.

"Just a few things," he said, smiling at her again before a serious expression stole across his face. Setting his food aside again, he reached out and wrapped his hands around hers as they cupped her bowl. "How are you doing? Honestly," he asked. She gave a humorless laugh and shook her head.

"I have no idea. If I start to think about everything that has happened in the last few days, I fall apart. If I think about the future, it is even worse." Again, her lower lip trembled and she bit down hard to still it. "My mother...." she trailed off, and Brex could see how hard she fought the tears. "And now, I'm supposed to be queen? I don't—" Her voice broke.

"You don't need to make a decision about taking the throne yet."

"You heard Amadeas, I don't have a choice."

Brex pulled the bowl from her hands before tipping her chin up so she would look at him. "You do. The one choice we don't have is in removing Nuweydon. But after that? You can do as you choose." He marveled at the soft pearl-grey color of her eyes as she looked at him.

"No, I can't. Someone must take the throne and I—"

"Sure, you're part of the royal family, but I'm sure you have cousins or other relatives you don't know about. They are part of the bloodline too. If you don't want the throne, one of them is next in line."

"I'm the only direct descendant."

Brex shook his head. "Maybe that's the case. But right now, all that matters is that you are alive and safe. Until Nuweydon's ugly head is on the ground at your feet, you don't need to decide." As he spoke, he wondered to himself why he was so suddenly invested. Sure, Gaia was gorgeous—you'd have to be dead not to notice—but beautiful girls could be bought for a handful of units. As he stared down at her and saw the strength in her eyes, it clicked. She had no interest in pity; his, her own, or anyone else's. She was stubborn and proud, and it was that fire that drew Brex to her most. Did he love her? He wasn't sure, but he did know he wasn't going anywhere until she stood over the dead body of the man who planned to kill them both.

Brex walked Gaia back to her cabin at her request.

"I hope I can sleep. Maybe it will help," she said, palms up in a helpless gesture. She paused in the doorway and glanced over her shoulder at him, conflict making itself clear in her expression. He scrutinized her face, trying to make sense of the emotions that warred there. Grief and heartbreak were there in her weak smile, like her control was slipping away but the warmth and what Brex thought might have been desire that flared in her steel-tinted irises surprised him. He quirked an eyebrow at her in confusion. She ignored him, disappearing over the threshold into the cabin that had been set aside for her. Brex stared around guiltily before following her into the small room. She turned and wrapped her arms around his neck again and pressed her lips to his. He couldn't help but moan as he felt all of the blood rush away from his brain. Yanking himself present, he gave a gentle grin to the girl in his arms.

"I think I know what you're doing," he offered softly. She raised a set of dark eyebrows in question. "Distracting yourself?" he said, twisting a hand in her long hair so he could tip her head back and kiss her jaw, but after a moment, he stepped back. Her eyes darkened as he pulled from her grip. "Trust me, Gaia, I've been thinking about that with you since the moment I saw you stumble through the door of that bar on Annui. But not right now. You need your rest and so do I. Besides, with your mother and Kain…." He trailed off as he caressed her soft cheek, her face crumpling as tears threatened again. He sighed internally—she was as mercurial as her uncle. "As soon as this war is over," he promised, tilting her chin up to kiss her gently. She leaned into the kiss, curling her fingers into his shirt to pull him closer. After a moment, he pulled away, gently detaching her hands from his shirt.

"I never thought I'd have to work this hard to seduce you," she muttered darkly, and he chuckled at her.

"Darlin', you don't have to seduce me, trust me, I'm all too willing. But not right now—dear gods, I can't believe I'm actually saying this, but not right now." Gaia sighed, but let him pick her up and carry her the few short feet to the bunk. He deposited her gently and sat next to her, nudging her over to make room. Gaia lay down and closed her eyes as Brex ran his fingers through her hair, freeing it from its twist. She could have wept at how good it felt; it also made her think of how her mother used to brush her hair as a child. She felt the tears building when there was a soft touch of lips to her ear.

"It will all be ok. I'm here, and I'm not going anywhere."

# Chapter Fifteen

"Bunch of wussy, whiny do-gooders," Shaw muttered in Brex's ear.

Their company stood assembled in front of their ships, blinking in the bright tropical sun, greeting the leaders of Miwarma. The race of diminutive, dark-skinned pacifists received them gladly but began their welcome with a recitation of their creed, all of it espousing their philosophy of peace and nonviolence. Gaia and Brex stood at the head of the party, flanked by Shaw, Alix, Amadeas, Lathan, and the others. The rest of the Outer Rim Brotherhood and Tallpian army were spread out behind them on the massive floating green that served as the air and water port for the capital city.

The entire planet of Miwarma was covered in a vast ocean, and over time, the local residents had built floating cities that checkered the planet's surface. All of the structures, including the immense airfield where they stood, were anchored into the seabed with posts. Attached with rings, the expansive green could rise and fall with the tides. Brex could feel the ground moving slightly under their feet, undulating with the gentle waves, and it made him dizzy. Looking around, he could see beautiful homes with lush gardens that spilled over walls and dangled into the water, a network of rope bridges and paths suspended above the sea crisscrossed between all of the buildings. Most of the structures had small boats or speeders tied up out front as well. But it was the water that fascinated him the most. The color of the water was the exact shade of Gaia's eyes from their first night at Zaire's—cerulean and bottomless. As they stood listening to their hosts, Brex admired her covertly. His gorgeous girl carried herself like a queen, no matter how much she claimed to not desire the throne. She had gracefully received the Miwarmans obeisance, despite her pants and blouse being caked in her mother's blood.

Brex snorted at Shaw's words and quickly had to turn it into a hacking cough as Gaia sent him a side-eyed glance.

Shaw pounded him on the back, making Brex gasp in pain. "Sorry, forgot about that bullet hole," Shaw snickered.

Brex rolled his eyes at his friend, not believing it for a second.

While the Miwarmans welcomed them with open arms, it was clear that they did not condone the violence that had brought them there. Gaia gave Brex a look as he coughed during the speech, and he smirked back at her. Finally, the speeches wound down, and they were directed to their temporary homes. Brex wrinkled his forehead when Gaia was led away in the direction of a small, beautiful bungalow that balanced over the water with its own gardens and dock. Brex and the rest of the Brotherhood were directed to a large barracks that floated near a soft, grassy field that was to serve as their training ground. Gaia gave him a soft shake of her head as her great-aunt, the Lady Bronwyn—Amadeas's wife—took her hand and gently escorted her away. Brex watched her go with regret before turning and following his men.

Brex, in deference to his status, was given a room of his own at the end of the barracks while the rest of the men squabbled over bunks.

After he changed into some clothes that weren't soaked in blood, Brex went in search of his Brothers. Gathering Kyan, Alix, Njoroge, Shaw, and a dozen others, he sat them down at the large, round table in the center of the long hall.

"Alright boys, now is your chance. Questions, concerns, whatever. Now is the time to talk about everything that happened and will happen." Their grim faces all stared back at him. "If you don't want to be here, this is your opportunity to leave, no hard feelings."

"I don't think any of us can walk away now, not after they murdered Kain," Njoroge rumbled in his low voice. All of the heads around the table nodded in agreement.

"I don't think any of us want to leave," Shaw pointed out.

"Do the others know?" Alix asked, lifting his eyes from the ever-present computer screen to stare at Brex. "The Miwarmans have a closed comm network, but I can break in in no time if needed." Brex shook his head.

"I already notified all of the quadrant leaders who were not on Meidonna with us. Cayson and Tyrell will both join us in the next couple of days. They are going to rally their sections to help—are you alright, dude?" Brex asked, breaking off mid-sentence to stare at Kyan, who was bright red and sweating profusely. The young medic stared back at his commander and shook his head.

"No, I'm fine, it's just a little…warm here," he said, trying not to pant. The rest of the table broke into laughter, and Kyan glared. He was from Kalki, a planet covered entirely in ice on the far north edge of the galaxy. The warm, humid climate of Miwarma in the south-east was far from anything he was used to. "What is our plan?" Kyan demanded, cutting off his Brothers' laughter.

Brex blinked hard and scrubbed his face with his hands before speaking, trying to marshal his thoughts. "Gaia will be twenty-one at the end of spring season, which is exactly twenty-one days from now. Once her birthday passes, she can legally, without fear of intergalactic retribution, mount a claim for the throne."

"What are we going to do for the next three weeks?"

"We get ready. We train. We plan. We are going to take the entire planet by storm."

"Can it be done?"

"General Amadeas seems to think that we have enough of the Tallpian army on our side, and with the rest of the Brotherhood reinforcements, we should be able to invade with no problem."

"And then what?"

"We'll figure that out when we get there."

"Please, Your Grace, I must insist."

"Lady Bronwyn, I appreciate your support, but I also must insist. I am not wearing that." Gaia pointed one long finger at the dress her great-aunt held: a giant, lacy, peach-colored concoction that looked more like a dessert than a gown. Gaia had no idea where it had come from, but there was no way she would be caught dead in something that ridiculous.

"It is proper," Bronwyn insisted again. "If you are going to be queen, you must dress the part."

"I will take your word for it; however proprieties are not high on my list right now." Gaia glanced at the young Miwarman girl standing just inside the door. When they arrived, tiny Sia had been assigned to assist Gaia with anything she might need. "Would it be possible to find something more similar to this?" She gestured down to the tan pants and white blouse she still wore.

The girl nodded. "I'm sure I can find something," she said, darting from the room.

Gaia returned her gaze to her great-aunt. "In the meantime, I am in desperate need of a shower." And some alone time to think, but she didn't say that aloud. Bronwyn huffed and marched away, the giant dress rustling in the breeze. Gaia rolled her eyes as she turned away from the door. Of all the battles she had to face, that was the last thing she had expected. She watched as her great-aunt stomped across the narrow walkway that linked Gaia's cottage to the main compound, a little worried she had just offended one of her last remaining family members. Turning away from the door, Gaia wasn't sure if she liked the gentle slapping noise of the waves that steadily lapped at the supports of her temporary home, but she had to admit the bungalow was one of the most beautiful things she had ever seen. The large, square room housed a sprawling white bed with a gauzy mesh canopy, along with a simply-carved wooden vanity table. A substantial glass shower occupied one corner of the room, and Gaia could not wait to give it a try. The small door at the back of the room led to a high-walled garden that was stuffed with exotic plants and heady-smelling flowers, all of which would have not been out of place at Zaire's mansion. Gaia turned her attention back to the small front porch, her wide-open door giving her an exquisite view of Miwarma's gorgeous ocean surface. Deciding that the sound of the waves was soothing after all, she left the screened door open, turning her attention to the waiting shower, still worrying about having affronted Bronwyn. What would her mother have done? She had been queen once; how would she have handled difficult relatives? Gaia felt her heart stutter as she tried not to think about her mother and failed as tears pooled and started sliding down over her lashes.

"I'm not very good at all of this," she muttered aloud, sniffing as she stripped off her blood-encrusted clothes, dropping them in a handy wicker basket.

"I think you're plenty good at it."

"Brex!" Gaia whirled around, snatching a towel off a nearby hook and wrapping herself in it. Her rescuer, still ridiculously handsome despite the bruises that marked his face and jaw, leaned against the doorframe, smiling at her. "What are you doing here?" she hissed, looking out the door for her great-aunt, who had made it plainly clear how she felt about Brex. "He is a common mercenary," Bronwyn had sniffed as they had watched him from a distance as he marshaled his men, waiting for the Miwarmans. "Not a fitting consort for a queen." Gaia had just smiled. "Hardly common," she had replied distractedly, watching Brex laugh with two of his Brothers. As she watched, he glanced up, and their eyes met, instantly generating enough heat between the two of them to ignite a star. Her aunt had hissed censoriously and hurried Gaia away. Now they stood completely alone in Gaia's quarters.

"Checking on you. You didn't seem happy when you left."

"I'd rather be staying with you," she admitted honestly. They both froze for a moment, thinking about the possibilities. Finally, Brex spoke, ignoring her admission.

"Be careful just leaving your door open like that; any madman could just stroll on in." He shot her a cheeky smile. Gaia rolled her eyes and tried to ignore the pulse of annoyance, irritated that Brex wouldn't acknowledge her feelings, but she shook it off.

"That was bad, even for you," she said, giving him a look.

Brex chuckled, looking around at her new room before turning his dark blue gaze back to her. "You said something about a shower?" Brex offered, mischief bright in his eyes. Gaia ignored the rushing, twisting sensation in her stomach and returned his impish grin before sashaying towards the glassed-in shower. She dropped the towel as she crossed the threshold and Brex froze. Lithe and svelte, her narrow limbs and slim hips made Brex's mouth go dry.

Gaia looked over her shoulder to see Brex standing frozen, staring at her. She raised an eyebrow in invitation. "Are you coming or not?" she asked, stepping into the shower, brushing her hand across the control panel, bringing the water to life. She kept her eyes locked on his face, and after a moment of him standing there dumb and staring, she started to laugh. "Brex!" He jerked, a dazed look on his face. "Are you going to join me or just stand there and stare?" Brex grinned, and it was infectious. He quickly shed his clothes, wincing as he yanked his shirt over his head and pulled on his stitches. Shirtless, he showed off a rock-hard core that tapered to a narrow waist and long, muscular legs. He discarded his black cargo pants before stepping into the water with her. Brex was handsome in any light, but in the low glow with steam wrapping around them both, Gaia wasn't sure if he had ever looked better. She wrapped her arms around his neck and tugged him against her, their skin meeting fully for the first time.

She gave him a lingering kiss before drawing back. "I can barely form a coherent thought with you standing there," she said, running her hands over his chest. "But you stink so badly." She wrinkled her nose, trying to stem her giggles, and it was all Brex could do not to pin her to the wall and take her.

"Fine," he grumped, but couldn't resist her smile. Snagging a bar of soap, she motioned for him to turn around. The wide expanse of his well-muscled shoulders sent Gaia's head spinning. She trailed her fingers over the sharply defined muscles, pausing to gently caress the row of stitches that marched across the back of his right shoulder. Brex flinched under her touch but didn't say anything and Gaia had to shake herself.

Would she ever stop owing him for everything he had done for her? Rescuing her on Annui had been one thing, but taking a bullet—two, actually, she realized as she admired Mira's neat handiwork on his left tricep and Kyan's even stitching on his right shoulder—in her defense was something entirely different. Pushing down the lump in her throat, she washed the broad plain of his back before reaching over and handing him the bar of soap. He circled to face her as she pulled her mane of wet hair over one shoulder and turned her back to him. His brain momentarily stopped working, staring at the expanse of her perfect, pale skin. After a beat, he was able to start running his hands, coated in soap, over her willowy length, washing away the dirt and grime and fear. Gaia relaxed under his caress and felt her troubles sliding away. Suddenly, she could stand it no longer and twisted around to face him again. His hands found her waist as the soap clattered to the floor and he took a step forward and pressed her against the cold stone wall, making her shiver. Brex dipped his head and slanted his lips over hers, his fingertips digging into her skin. As his tongue caressed hers, the only thing Gaia wanted was for him to hold her tighter. She was delighted as he read her mind and complied, crushing her body to his.

"So much for waiting until the war is over." They were lying in tangled sheets, the windows thrown open to let the cool tropical breeze could wash over their bare skin as the last bits of light left the sky. The gentle tones of a glass wind chime filled the air with a delicate tinkling sound, and the ebb and flow of the waves added a soft, steady roar in the background. Lying on her back and at peace for the first time in ages, Gaia turned her head to grin at Brex, impish delight bright in her eyes as she appraised his naked form on the bed next to her.

"What? You think I have that much self-control, especially when you start taking your clothes off?" Brex demanded with a laugh.

Gaia smiled. "I'm very glad you don't," she informed him, planting a lazy kiss on his lips. He kissed her back, and she felt the flickers of lust start to build again.

"You sure I can't stay?" Brex drawled as he broke away, tracing the line of her hip with a finger, making Gaia shiver.

"I want you to, but it might kill my aunt if she catches you here."

"Good," Brex growled darkly. He could already tell that the older Tallpian woman did not approve of him. Not that he cared, but they had enough trouble on their hands without adding a protective, angry Tallpian matron into the mix.

Gaia rolled her eyes. "She may drive me crazy, but she's some of the only family I have left."

"Darlin', you're a grown woman, about to become queen, might I add—"

"Don't say that!" Gaia rolled over to whack him on the shoulder. Brex winced as she slapped his injured left arm and her face froze. "Oh Brex, I'm so sorry—" but Brex just growled and pinned her naked shoulders to the bed. She shrieked and giggled as he held her in place.

"My little queen-to-be," he purred, kissing her throat as she struggled, but after a moment, she tilted her face to the side with a sigh. Brex sat back, watching her in concern. "I'm sorry, I know you're not super comfortable with the whole queen thing yet." She turned her grey eyes back to him.

"What if I don't want it? Even after all of this?" she asked.

Brex smiled easily in reply. "Then you don't take it."

"But what about everyone who has died already? What about my mother? What about Kain?" Brex's handsome face darkened but she ignored it. "How could I live with myself if I let their sacrifices be in vain?"

"Kain knew what he was doing. Every single member of the Brotherhood knows the risks. It isn't up to us or anyone else, I might add, whether you take the throne."

"I still have trouble with people dying for me," she snapped. "What would my mother say?"

"If she truly cared about you, she'd want you happy, regardless of the form that takes. But if that's how you feel, you might be in the wrong game, sweetheart."

"What does that mean?"

"War means people die. Either a handful of willing soldiers sacrifice their lives for you and your cause, or you die. Nuweydon needs to go. Leaving him alive would be more of an insult to those who have died fighting him. Like Kain. Like your mother."

"I'm just worried about disappointing people."

"You will disappoint no one. This is about you and your choice; no one else can make it for you."

"I'm not sure what my choice is."

"Not yet. But you'll make the right one, I know it. And even if you don't want to be queen, you still have your entire future ahead of you."

"Are those my only choices?" she demanded, her voice catching in her throat. "Queen or nothing?"

Brex made a face. "Did I say that? Even if you don't want to be queen, there are still plenty of options."

"Like what?" she demanded. Brex shrugged. He already knew what option he wanted her to choose but wasn't about to say it. He had a vision of the two of them, side-by-side for the rest of their lives, leaders of the Brotherhood. He had a sneaking suspicion that with enough training, Gaia would be as lethal as the rest of her kin. She would be an immense asset to their intergalactic company, never mind the fact that Brex already couldn't envision his future without her in it.

"You could do anything. Join the Brotherhood, strike out on your own, or just stay here in bed with me." He made his tone light and teasing, expecting her to light up, but strangely her face stayed dark. "What?"

"That's your plan, Brex."

"What is your point?"

"What if I have other plans in mind?"

"Like what?"

"I don't know."

"Well then let's not worry about it until after."

"And what if I take the throne? How does that fit into your future?"

"You don't want the throne," he temporized, sitting back and looking at her in confusion.

"I don't know what I want!" she snapped, rolling out from under him. She stood and started to pace alongside the bed, gesturing wildly. "Maybe I take it. What are you going to do then, if I'm queen and tied to my planet?"

"You've already said you don't want—"

"What about my people?" she cut across him. Brex scoffed.

"Your people? You mean the same people who turned their backs on you when your uncle went on a murderous rampage?"

"How dare you?" she demanded. Despite his agitation, Brex couldn't help but stare at Gaia's naked body.

But his shook free the thoughts that were trying to take root and spoke. "Your great-uncle let Nuweydon spend almost two decades on the throne, imprisoning people and killing them too. Why did no one else stand up to him? Or step up to help you when your father was killed?"

"Brex—"

"How can you, someone who has such trust issues, trust someone like that?" Brex demanded. "Gaia, you need to think about this."

"Maybe I don't want to."

"You need to. You can't avoid the past."

"I'm not trying to."

"Yes, you are. Your great-uncle has already essentially crowned you queen. Have you even spoken to him about how you feel? Or are you going to go along with him for the rest of your life, just like you did with your mother?" As soon as the words were out of his mouth, he knew he had gone too far. Gaia's eyes dilated to black, and she hauled back and slapped him—hard.

"Out!" she shouted, pointing at the door.

"Gaia, I didn't mean—"

"Get out, Brexler!" She snagged his clothes off her floor and threw them at him. He yanked his pants on before standing in front of her. She was still naked, hands on her hips. Just looking at her made his mouth water but the glint in her eyes was terrifying, and she was barely holding herself together. "Get out before I throw you out," she threatened, her voice and lower lip quivering with emotion.

"Gaia, please—" she pulled back for another slap but Brex saw it coming and grabbed her wrist before she could land the blow. He tugged her into his arms and planted a hard kiss on her lips before she pushed herself free.

"Damn it, Brex, get out!"

"Don't be mad at me, you know I'm right." The tears that had been building finally began to fall and she pointed at the door.

"Get out."

# Chapter Sixteen

Her heartbroken words rang in his head as Brex marched across the torch-lit walkways, shrugging into his shirt and wincing when it pulled on his stitches. Shaw saw his commander's dark face from across the water and changed his path to intercept him.

"Where have you been?" his friend asked, falling into step next to Brex on the narrow wooden bridge that lead to the Brotherhood barracks. Brex grunted at him, not wanting to explain. He had just experienced the most exquisite evening of his life, and it had suddenly turned to shit. Shaw fixed him with a knowing look but moved on.

"We need to talk about Amadeas." That stopped Brex in his tracks. The bridge wobbled slightly and he steadied himself on the railing. He looked at his interim second-in-command.

"What about him?" Brex prompted.

There was a pause as Shaw leaned his forearms against the railing, staring out over the ocean which glittered in the moonlight. "I don't know. It's nothing specific but something doesn't feel right," Shaw said with a nonchalant shrug that Brex knew was forced. Brex had been completely honest with the general on Meidonna—he didn't trust him. In Brex's mind, someone who allowed a madman to run amok for twenty years was more concerned about saving his own skin that doing the right thing. The fact that Shaw seemed to feel the same way only solidified Brex's feelings.

"What do you mean?" Brex asked.

"He spent most of the evening meeting with the Miwarmans. You weren't invited—no one in the Brotherhood was. He made sure you were busy before meeting with them."

"It could have to do with their political prisoners," Brex pointed out, trying for unbiased reason.

Shaw gave him a suspicious look. "Maybe but if it has anything with the coup, we should be a part of it."

"You're right, something already feels off. We haven't even been here for a full day, and he's already being secretive." Brex said in agreement. "Thanks for keeping an ear open. If anything changes, let me know." They resumed walking towards the barracks, but as they dropped down onto the large grassy quadrangle, a tall figure detached itself from the shadows of one of the smaller buildings.

"Speak of the devil, and he shall appear," Shaw muttered.

Amadeas stepped into the circle of light created by an overhead lantern. "A word, Carrow." Brex stopped in front of the Tallpian, trying to keep an amiable look on his face. Shaw looked at him, a questioning look on his face but Brex shook his head. Shaw shrugged and kept walking, glancing darkly at the Tallpian. Obersving the general, Brex could tell something wasn't right. The old man no longer wore a mask of polite acceptance. There was something in his face that might have been revulsion.

"By all means," he said, gesturing for the old man to begin.

"It is about Kallideia."

"Gaia," Brex corrected him automatically.

Annoyance flushed Amadeas's face. "Exactly my point. She will not be that girl for much longer."

"Are you sure about that?"

"She will step up and fulfill her destiny. She does not have a choice."

"Not that you're giving her, anyway," Brex muttered, and Amadeas growled under his breath.

"Are you determined to keep her from her destiny?"

"I'm determined to keep her happy and safe. That is all that matters to me."

"You should have care of how you manage that."

"What is that supposed to mean?"

"Your familiarity with her will create problems."

"For who? You?" Amadeas bristled but managed to control his voice.

"For her. If you care about her, you will not jeopardize her chance at taking back her throne."

"I'm pretty sure I'm going to be involved in that one way or another, whether your people like it or not."

"Are you? The new head of an intergalactic rabble of misfits and criminals?"

"You mean the intergalactic organization dedicated to doing the right thing, that was able to rescue your niece and is now committed to finishing this, regardless of how it ends?"

"If it hadn't been for me, you would have never made it into that palace." His tone was petulant.

"If it wasn't for me, Gaia would already be dead," Brex spat back. The Tallpian general drew himself up, puffing out his chest but Brex cut him off. "What is your point, Amadeas?" he demanded, getting frustrated.

"Your relationship with Kallideia endangers her claim. Our people will not accept her if they think she will be bringing in an outsider as her consort. We will have done all of this work for nothing."

"I don't want to be king, if that is what you're getting at."

The general's laugh was dismissive. "Hardly. Meidonna has been ruled by Tallpians since the beginning of time. Nothing will change that."

"Then what is the problem?"

"If you continue your involvement with Kallideia, you risk her place within our world, never mind her safety."

"I can keep her safe."

"Here, maybe. By all means, post guards or do whatever you feel is needed. And even in battle, your forces will be useful. But after? You are a mercenary, not a guard dog." Brex bristled, but Amadeas sneered at him. "If you wish to dedicate your life to her safety then go ahead. But you will never be more to her than a shield, a tool. She has the blood of the kings and queens of old in her veins. What are you, a mongrel from the gutter? She has no future with you."

Brex flexed his hands into fists to avoid swinging at the old man. "We will protect her until the day she tells me herself that she has no further need of me," he snarled. "The day that she, and no one else, says it."

Amadeas opened his arms wide with a smile. "There is no doubt that time will come. But if you care about my niece as you claim, then you will leave her be once she does, otherwise, she has no place in this galaxy."

"Her place is with me." Why he couldn't have said the same words to Gaia but was able to speak them aloud now confused the hell out him.

"Is it? Has she agreed to that?" Brex said nothing. "If that is the case, then why are you standing here speaking with me, instead of with her?" Brex remained silent, and Amadeas laughed. "Do not imagine yourself more important than you truly are, Carrow. When the time comes, she will order you out of her life. And you will go, because you will realize that, in the end, she will never be able to love someone like you."

Amadeas gave him a curt nod and walked away before Brex could reply. He watched the general march away, his spine ramrod straight. Brex stood in the shadows, trying to form coherent thoughts about what had just happened, his hands balled into fists, when Shaw emerged out of the dark and came to his side.

"What the hell was that about?" Shaw asked as they resumed walking.

"I have an idea, and I'm not thrilled."

"Do you want to talk about it?"

"No."

"Ok, then now what?"

Brex rubbed his eyes and checked his timepiece. It was late already. "I have to deal with some stuff," Brex said, scratching the back of his neck. "I've got three messages from Auggie that I've been ignoring. Zaire too."

"Clue them in."

"I'm going to; I just don't want to talk about Gaia right now."

"So that's where you were. I figured." Brex tried to look nonchalant but failed. Shaw crowed. "I knew it! How was she?"

Brex rounded on his friend. "None of your damn business, Shaw."

His friend stepped back and raised his hands in surrender but looked at Brex in annoyance. "Whoa, whoa, alright. Shit, sorry."

"Yeah, you should be."

"Wasn't that good, obviously," Shaw muttered under his breath. Brex snarled and swung, but Shaw ducked, and the blow whiffed through his shaggy blonde hair.

"Leave it alone."

"Whatever man, you'll talk when you're ready." Brex turned his eyes towards the dark sky, not wanting to think about Gaia and failing. "I had a thought, though." Seeing

Brex's look, Shaw shook his head. "Not about that. Well, it has to do with Gaia, but not like that."

"Spit it out, Shaw, before I slug you."

"Have you thought about posting guards on her?"

"Yeah, actually I have; she's not exactly security conscious. Amadeas also mentioned it." They passed into the nearly empty hall. Most of the Brotherhood had lives outside of their membership, and some had already headed for their home planets with a promise to be back in time to take part in the battle. Brex saw Alix and Kyan and waved them over as Shaw spoke.

"You were the one that made the point about Nuweydon being a raging lunatic who plays by no one else's rules," Shaw pointed out. "It wouldn't surprise me if he ignored the neutrality of this system and just came storming in here. He would aim straight for Gaia, the rest of us be damned."

"She'll go nuclear on me but whatever. You're right. And I don't trust the rest of the Tallpians." He looked around at the Brothers who remained. "You and Kyan take first watch," Brex said to Shaw. "Alix and Njoroge will relieve you guys around,—" looking at his timepiece,—"zero two hundred hours."

"You're not taking a watch?" Kyan asked innocently.

Brex glowered at the young recruit who jumped back in alarm. "No. Both of you get over there, and if anyone bitches, send them to me first."

Gaia was roused from her sleep by the low mutter of voices outside her door. Unable to distinguish the speakers, she quickly and stealthily slipped from her bed and grabbed a heavy candlestick from a small side table. Yanking open the front door to her quarters, she raised her weapon over her head but pulled up short when she realized she was looking at Shaw and Kyan, both of them posted on the small porch in front of her door, rifles cradled in their arms. She dropped her arms to her sides, and the candlestick fell to the floor with a thunk.

"What are you doing?" she demanded. They both looked at her then down at her bare legs peeking out from the long shirt she was wearing as a nightdress before looking back up at her. "Two seconds." She slammed the door in their faces and struggled into her pants before opening the door again.

"Let's try this again: What are you doing here?"

"Brex sent us."

"Why?"

"To stand guard." As if it was obvious.

Gaia felt herself go slit-eyed. "And why exactly does Brexler Carrow think that I need guards to stand at my door?"

Kyan shrugged, shifting his gun to the other shoulder. "Not my place to ask or question him," he pointed out. "But it's not exactly safe to leave you alone until Nuweydon is dead."

"Where is he?" she demanded.

Kyan took a step back, looking alarmed. "Crashed out, I think, but—hey!" Gaia shoved past them and marched along the wooden path that led to the barracks where the Brotherhood was berthed. Both guards trotted after her and when Shaw reached to put a hand on her shoulder, she whirled around on him.

"Touch me," she warned, "and I'll tear it off." She spun away and resumed her march. She burst through the barracks door, blood boiling. There were a handful of men still awake despite the fact that it was the middle of the night, some playing cards or oiling weapons, the rest asleep, their backs to the room at large. One look at her thunderous face and they all pointed towards a door at the end of the hall. Gaia all but sprinted the length of the room before yanking the door open. She expected Brex to be asleep, but he sat at a small desk, a portable telelink on the surface in front of him.

He looked up when she entered, his face exhausted. He glanced down at the screen. "Auggie, I'll call you back." He hit a button without waiting for a reply and disconnected the call. He brought his eyes up to meet Gaia's, staring at her with a raised eyebrow.

For a moment her rage was so incandescent that she couldn't speak. Finally, she was able to point at Kyan and Shaw who had followed her into the small room. "What in the name of all the gods are they doing standing on my doorstep?" she demanded.

Brex fixed her with a deadpan look before sighing. "We have no idea if Nuweydon knows where we are. If he does, we don't know if he'll violate the neutral zone. You just leave your doors open like we're not at war. At this point, I am not taking any chances. You will have an around-the-clock guard made up of Brotherhood members until this mess is resolved." Gaia opened her mouth to argue, but Brex beat her to it. "Don't bother arguing. Your great-uncle agrees with me."

"What?" she demanded, caught off-guard.

Brex shrugged. "You are the single most important person in this half of the galaxy right now. I will not leave you unprotected."

"I can take care of myself." Brex snorted, and the edge of Gaia's vision went red.

"Against an armed, trained assassin in your sleep? Sure."

"Damn it Brex, I—" but he held up a hand, cutting her off.

"You can argue all you want, Gaia, but you won't change my mind." He looked past her to Shaw and Kyan. "Escort her back to her quarters, please."

She shot a warning glance at Shaw before looking back at Brex. "If you want me to go somewhere, take me yourself." When Brex glanced at her, she was surprised at the hurt that flickered there.

He shook his head. "I have things to do. The Brotherhood has responsibilities outside of this." He glanced around her again to nod at Shaw. "Take her back, please. I'll meet with you both in the morning." He took in Gaia's stricken face and lowered his voice. "Gaia, you need your rest. We can talk tomorrow." He nodded to them all and returned to the telelink. Shaw wrapped a gentle hand around Gaia's arm, but she slapped him off and stormed from the room.

Gaia marched back to her quarters, her two guards trailing after her. She slammed and locked the door before throwing herself onto the bed, sobs wracking her body. She couldn't believe Brex. Their afternoon had been so perfect, and then he had opened his mouth. The words about her mother stung, but it was the words about her great-uncle that worried her. She hadn't told anyone, even Brex, about the words her mother had whispered in her ear as Dyla lay dying. "Don't trust Amadeas," Dyla had whispered, and before Gaia had been able to ask her why, she was gone. What did that mean? Amadeas had orchestrated their rescue from the dungeons, but Gaia was suddenly wondering why. Amadeas and Bronwyn had both already started treating her as if she was queen, and neither had stopped to ask her if she was interested in taking her father's throne. Mulling over the idea, she wasn't sure if she even wanted to be queen. Granted, if ruling meant she had the chance to save the Tallpian race, and improve the lives of her people, then maybe it would be worth it. But she didn't know, and unfortunately, the biggest wrench in the cogs was Brex. His presence in her life opened a broad horizon, even if they both refused to speak of it. He wasn't just a thief anymore: He was the leader of The Outer Rim Brotherhood. Would that new post give him an anchoring in life that he hadn't found before? Would he want her as a part of that future? She didn't know, and for the sake of her already stinging pride, she wasn't going to ask.

And she was scared. Not that she would ever admit it aloud, but she still saw Nuweydon's face every time she closed her eyes. The fact that she had dodged death only made it worse. Would she ever feel safe? Was she even capable of being queen? She had no idea—and no one to ask.

# Chapter Seventeen

The light was bright by the time Gaia opened her eyes again. She was face down and fully clothed on top of the coverlet. Lifting her head and looking around, she spotted a small stack of clothes that had been deposited just inside her door. Stretching her shoulders, she scooped up the pile before retreating to the bathroom for a much lonelier shower that her previous one.

She emerged clean and dressed, a half smile on her lips. Her Miwarman assistant had gone above and beyond delivering what Gaia had requested: a black wrap-around blouse in a light, gauzy material with a black undershirt that showcased her slender frame and leather pants, also black, fitted and soft as cream against her skin. As she moved to replace her towel, she dislodged a small, black bag that rattled as it hit the floor. Opening it, she found various makeup applicators. None of them were familiar, but she made a quick call using the speaking system built into the wall, and her assistant knocked on the door a few minutes later.

"My name is Sia, Princess Kallideia—" Gaia held up a hand to stop the girl's curtsey.

"My name is Gaia. Not Kallideia, not 'princess', alright?" She offered a smile to the girl who was maybe sixteen. Sia returned the smile brilliantly.

"How can I help you, Gaia?"

"This," she said, holding up the bag. Sia smiled again and gestured for Gaia to sit in front of the vanity mirror. Using a feather-light touch, she tilted Gaia's face first this way then that, applying a light ring of kohl around her eyes and touching a red tint to her lips.

"You look like SaBeth," the girl said stepping back a few minutes later, a little awed, naming the Miwarman's goddess of passion. In their world, hate and love were considered two sides of the same coin—the coin of passionate emotion. Like many of the outer-lying planets, the Miwarman's had their own gods and goddesses, unlike the majority of the Central Core allied planets that all worshiped under the ancient religion of Christianity, which traced its origins back to the original Earth.

Glancing at herself in the mirror, she saw at once that the soft blonde of her hair didn't match her dramatic face. Closing her eyes, she focused on her goal, as her mother had taught her in the dungeon of Meidonna. The moment was longer than it should have been: most Tallpians could make their changes in the blink of an eye, but as Gaia was still learning, it took her several beats. She heard Sia gasp and knew she had been successful. She opened her eyes. The creature staring back at her in the mirror had burgundy hair the color of the deepest wine and eyes of molten gold. Just what she needed to face Brex and her great-uncle. Smiling in pleasure, Gaia rose and swept from the room, thanking Sia for her help. Marching through her door, she nearly tripped over the two members of the Brotherhood who were standing guard. As they fell into step behind her, she ground her teeth but said nothing. Guessing that Brex would still be sleeping, she went in search of her people and found her great-aunt and uncle breaking their fast in a long dining hall set aside for the visitors. Both of them rose to their feet when she entered, Lady Bronwyn eying Gaia's clothing suspiciously.

"Princess Gaia," Amadeas greeted her, bowing low from the waist. "We hope you slept well."

Gaia nodded. "I did, thank you, Great-Uncle." Amadeas pulled out the chair from the head of the table, gesturing for her to sit. She settled gracefully into her seat as two attendants set several small plates of brilliantly-colored fruit and warm pastries in front of her. Taking small, careful bites, she glanced at her relatives, who resumed their seats. Her great-uncle's face was warm as he looked at her, a small smile on his face. Her great-aunt appeared to be on the verge of fainting, and Gaia had a sneaking suspicion it had to do with the amount of skin she was showing in her new shirt.

"Princess," Amadeas said, "I understand that all of this change is a bit of a shock. Please know that we will absolutely stand by your side and help guide you through the next few weeks. As our future queen, you have much to learn."

"Please, Great-Uncle, just Gaia."

"Princess—" Bronwyn started, but Gaia cut her off.

"As your future queen, I expect you to honor my requests," she said firmly, looking her scandalized aunt in the eye. "And as this is such a simple one, I am having trouble understanding your reluctance."

Bronwyn colored but nodded slowly. "I apologize, Gaia. You are not familiar with our ways. You will come to understand them in time." Bronwyn paused to inhale, but Amadeas settled a quelling hand on his wife's wrist before she could continue speaking.

"Let it be," he advised in a low voice.

He looked back to Gaia. "Gaia," he acknowledged. "Please know that we have only the best intentions in helping you gain back your throne. We will do our best to help you learn and become accustomed to our ways."

"At this point, what I am addressed as should not be considered a priority," she replied. "We are on the brink of war, and I feel that deserves our full and undivided attention." Her regal tone clearly caught both of them off guard. Amadeas dipped his head in acknowledgment.

"Of course. Your knowledge of war is limited, but trust me when I say we will do everything in our power to help you take back the throne of Meidonna." Amadeas began rambling about offensive strategies and weapon caches, speaking loudly for more than fifteen minutes.

Having had enough, Gaia spoke up, cutting across him. "Great-Uncle, I understand that you think me a young, weak-minded and weak-willed woman who knows nothing of the great galaxy. But if we are going to discuss battle tactics, I require all of my commanders."

"The rudeness…—" her great-aunt murmured, but Gaia just smiled.

"A lone soldier may plan a war," Gaia replied, "but the battle can only be won by many."

"I am Lord Commander of—"

"Of the Tallpian army," she finished for him. "Yes, you are. However, there are other players in this who should be consulted. This includes Brexler Carrow and the regional leaders of the Brotherhood. Since they will make up a significant portion of our forces, they will be included in any discussions we have regarding war." Amadeas's pale face flushed, but Gaia overrode him again. "As you are my Lord Commander, I request that you call a meeting so that all parties involved can be consulted. Please summon the Brotherhood leaders for a discussion tomorrow afternoon."

"Of course," he said, his voice rich and warm and indulgent. "And what am I to tell them?"

Gaia rose to her feet and smiled confidently, tossing back her rich, carmine mane. "Tell them the future queen of Meidonna requires their presence for our first strategy meeting. Now if you will excuse me," Gaia said, pushing away from the table, "I have other things I must attend to." She marched from the room before either of her relatives could reply.

With the heady rush of adrenaline singing through her veins, Gaia figured it was time to face Brex. Passing into the area that had been set aside for the Brotherhood, she saw that most of the men were outside in the floating quadrangle, some sparring with partners, others drilling with their weapons in the warm sunlight. A quiet word in an ear pointed her towards the barracks. Shedding her guards at the door with a careless gesture, she walked the length of the room before pausing in front of Brex's door. She took a deep breath, ready for the coming fight, pushed open the door and stopped dead in her tracks. Brex was sprawled across his bed, shirtless and sound asleep. He was on his back, his left arm folded behind his head. Thanks to the previous afternoon, Gaia knew Brex's body intimately, and despite her anger at him, she suddenly wanted to relive the experience over and over again. She couldn't keep herself from staring at his chiseled chest and rock-hard core that tapered down to his narrow waist. His low-slung pants sat on his hips, exposing just the slightest bit of dark hair. Gaia heard herself sigh with desire and the sound was enough to make Brex slowly peel open one eye and then the other. He watched her steadily for a moment, waiting for a reaction, but she couldn't move. His words had burned her, but she craved his kiss with a desperate need she had never experienced before. Without a word, he reached over and snagged her hand, tugging her on top of him.

"I'm still mad at you," she murmured as he kissed her. He wrapped one of his legs through hers and twisted so that she landed against the bed, hips pinned by his weight. He smiled his smug smile at her.

"Of course you are."

"I wasn't kidding." The words came sometime later, as Gaia lay on the bed facing Brex. He smiled like he didn't believe her. "I am still so mad."

"I can tell," he said, teasing. He reached over and skimmed a hand over the naked curve of her hip, and it was all she could do not to jump on him again. She wrinkled her nose and sighed. He shook his head, chuckling. "I should have found a better way to say it." She buried her head in her arms, waves of burgundy hair falling around her face, but peeked up at him a minute later.

"Is that the best apology I'm going to get?"

"For me being right? You bet."

"But you're wrong," she said, eyeing him. "My great-uncle is whole-heartedly behind me."

"For now," Brex muttered.

Gaia glared at him. "Brex, he is my family. The only family I have left, and he sacrificed a great deal to rescue me." Brex opened his mouth to reply, but she cut him off. "I don't understand why you don't like him, but I'm done discussing it," she said.

Brex grumbled under his breath but didn't reply. Instead, he sighed. "Fine." He paused, giving her a soft smile. "You know, I've got to admit," he said, running his fingers through her hair, "the new look is terrifying."

Gaia laughed out loud at that. "Good," she said, rolling over onto her back. The red tint from her lips had rubbed off and spread across his jaw where she had kissed him. "That's what I was hoping for."

"Well, my fearsome lady, since you're still mad at me, what do you propose we do now?"

Gaia sat up and stretched her arms over her head, Brex's eyes following the movement hungrily. "Actually, I want to learn to fight."

"Fight?" Brex said with a raised eyebrow. "Are you sure?" Miffed, Gaia frowned at him.

"Yes, I'm sure."

"I'm not arguing," he said, helping her off the bed. "I have a sneaking suspicion you're going to be deadly." He sent her a sideways smile. "I like it."

"I don't think I have ever had this many bruises in my entire life," Gaia groused later that afternoon as Alix and Brotherhood member Murad followed her back to her quarters. It was late evening, and Gaia had spent most of the day learning to spar with Njoroge. Brex had offered to teach her how to use a gun, but since many Tallpians preferred hand-to-hand combat or swords, she had chosen to start there. Njoroge, the smiling, laughing, almost seven-foot-tall Sovarian with skin as black as night, was the ideal choice for a trainer. He had taught her some basic moves before letting her pair off against a younger Brotherhood member. When she had bested him, she turned her smile to Njoroge, who had just returned her grin and beckoned her with one hand. It had taken a mere minute for her to learn how woefully incomplete her knowledge was. Pinned in less than two minutes, she hadn't even landed a hit. But it was Brex's worried look, as he watched from the shade where he was oiling his pistols, that drove her back to her feet.

"Again."

They boxed most of the afternoon, and by the end of the evening, she had managed to land a few solid hits (drawing just a flash of his violet-tinted blood) and once, knock Njoroge to the ground. But he had paid her back in kind, and now her pale skin was covered in rapidly-disappearing dark-purple blotches.

"You're a quick learner, lady." Murad rubbed a hand on the back of his neck. "When Njoroge taught me to spar, it took me months to drop him to the ground. I still have trouble with it." Gaia chuckled but instantly regretted it and moaned in pain as her ribs protested. Alix laughed before opening her door for her. She passed into her room before falling face down on the bed and dropping almost instantly into a deep sleep.

# Chapter Eighteen

Over the next five days, Gaia threw herself into training and did her best to absorb everything that could be learned: sparring practice with Njoroge, time on the shooting range with Brex and even a few, very interesting lessons with Brotherhood member Alix and a long, single-edged blade that he referred to as a katana.

"It isn't a true katana," Alix explained as he adjusted Gaia's double-handed grip on the hilt of the sword their third afternoon on Miwarma. "There was a time, several millennia ago on the original Earth, that the style of sword was used by a specific class of people in an ancient feudal society. Thankfully, we've improved on the blade since then. We use stronger alloys and superior forging techniques that keep the blades from being as brittle or fragile." He twisted his weapon around in a complicated pattern before striking out at the dummy they had been practicing with. The metal pole holding the dummy in place was sheared neatly in half, and the set-up collapsed to the ground.

"It's also one of the best weapons to kill a Tallpian." Gaia twisted around to see Lathan had joined them, holding a blade of his own.

Gaia raised her eyebrows, a little surprised. "Why is that?"

"I'm not sure if you've noticed, but we heal very quickly." Gaia nodded. She had noticed: the bruises left on her fair skin by Njoroge faded almost instantly and small hurts like dislocated fingers healed within minutes. "It can make us very hard to kill." Lathan raised his eyebrows at Alix in invitation. They bowed to one another before dropping into combat stances. Gaia watched as the two men sparred, very evenly matched, and after a series of feints and thrusts, Lathan moved to allow the tip of Alix's blade to clip his shoulder. Blood gushed from the wound, but even as Gaia watched in wide-eyed horror, Lathan slapped his hand tight against the injury. After several long beats, he pulled it away to reveal a tear in the shoulder of his tunic and a pink scar that seemed to fade even as they watched.

Gaia's eyebrows wrinkled in confusion as she eyed the other Tallpian. "Then why," Gaia asked, but her voice broke. She swallowed and tried again, shoving the pain and grief back down. "Then why did my mother not survive her wounds?"

There was sympathy in Lathan's eyes. "There are two sure-fire ways to kill a Tallpian. One is to sever the spine. The best way to ensure that you've done it properly is to just remove the head completely. The other is a perfect heart shot." His eyes were sad as he looked at her. "From what I saw the night of your escape, I believe this is what happened to your mother. I am sorry, Gaia. For some reason, the heart is the one organ that does not heal itself if damaged."

Brushing aside his sympathy, she spoke before her grief could consume her and drag her down into the darkness. "Why?"

Lathan shook his head. "We don't know. I know there are theories among our people that involve the idea that the gods created the weakness in us so that we might not rival them for their power." He shrugged. "I'm not sure if I believe that, but it is what it is. The best way to kill a Tallpian is to either slice off their head or destroy their heart." Gaia digested this. When she spoke, she did so carefully, trying to choose her words delicately.

"If we are going to be facing our own kind in battle, I feel this is something the rest of our forces should know." She glanced around, but Brex was nowhere to be seen. "We should tell Brex and the rest of the commanders so it can be passed on to those who will be on foot during the battle."

"I agree," Alix said, but Lathan's green eyes were troubled.

"What is it?" Gaia asked, watching him curiously. He glanced at her and Alix before shaking his head.

"I'm sorry, it just goes against everything I know, sharing that information. As much as I despise Nuweydon and everything he has done, it is still hard explaining how to kill my own kind."

Gaia sighed. "I understand. But only by fighting this battle will we be able to end Nuweydon's hold on our people." Lathan nodded, but he looked far older than his thirty-five years when he replied.

"'A man does not fight because he hates what is in front of him, rather that he loves what stands behind him.'"

Gaia gave him a twisted smile. "Now I'm not so sure about that."

Lathan acknowledged her with a rueful laugh. "You may be right. I do hate Nuweydon and everything he has done."

"And you love the people who stand both in front of and behind you."

He dipped his head in acknowledgment. "I do."

"Thank you, Lathan," Gaia said sincerely. "I promise that I will not stop until he has paid for his crimes."

"And that is why I've told you. I don't like the idea of killing my own people, but if we don't do this, our kind won't survive at all."

Bronwyn objected to Gaia's training regimens, but Gaia ignored her. Queen or not, she needed to know how to protect herself. Amadeas agreed with her, and there were no more arguments from Gaia's great-aunt.

One sunny morning, six days after they had arrived on Miwarma, Gaia was sitting in the sun with Brex as he massaged a knot out of her shoulder when Amadeas entered the bright courtyard. He dipped Gaia a half-bow, openly eyeing Brex as he ran his hands along Gaia's back.

"A word, Princess Kallideia."

"Gaia," she instantly reminded him. His face immediately broke into a smile of contrition.

"My apologies, Princess," Amadeas said, dipping his head in apology. Gaia ground her teeth. Had she requested that they not address her by 'Princess'?

Annoyed, she stared up at him. "What can I do for you Great-Uncle?"

"I would speak with you privately." Gaia hesitaed, but Brex nudged her.

"Go, you need a break anyways." He helped her to her feet before pressing a possessive kiss to her cheek. Amadeas kept his face bland, ignoring Brex. Gaia followed Amadeas until they rounded the corner of a building and he stopped.

"I must speak with you."

"You are welcome to, Great-Uncle. What is on your mind?"

"Brexler Carrow." Gaia was surprised at the annoyance in his tone.

"What about Brex?"

Amadeas appeared to marshal his thoughts before speaking, clearly uncomfortable. "You need to understand something, Gaia. Tallpians do not mix with other races. I'm concerned that your dalliance with him could affect your ability to rule."

"You think Brex will hinder my ability to be queen?" She asked, her eyebrows rising of their own volition.

"I do not speak for myself—I wish you every happiness, of course—but for the rest of our people. I am concerned that they may not accept you if they think you may be bringing in an outsider as your consort. It could damage our campaign against Nuweydon." His voice was kindly, pity warm in his eyes. "I know you care for him, Gaia, but I cannot recommend that you continue to see him."

"That is enough," she said sweetly, trying not to glare at him. "Brex saved my life and has stood by my side this entire journey so far. He has made his intentions to see this to the end very clear."

"I would suggest, for the good of your future, that you ensure he knows that your arrangement is temporary." Gaia narrowed her eyes at Amadeas.

"I will decide if and when the relationship changes its status. That is not for you, or anyone else to decide, Amadeas."

"As queen—"

"As queen, I can make my own choices, including those that involve my personal life. It is no concern of yours what my relationship with Brexler is."

"As a blood relative and your advisor—"

"Your advice is noted," she snapped. "But do not presume to order me. You are not my father."

"As the closest thing you might have to a father—"

"Do not dare to assume his place, Amadeas," Gaia snarled icily. "Where have you been for the last twenty years, if you plan to consider yourself my surrogate father?" Her great-uncle's face turned puce as he sputtered in anger.

"You will heed—"

"Your advice is noted," she snapped again. "I will not continue this conversation with you." She surveyed him carefully. "I have training to attend to." Without waiting for his answer, she spun on her heel and walked away.

"I don't know if I can take another meeting like that," Brex said to Gaia later that evening. They were winding their way back to Gaia's cottage after a particularly long, exhausting strategy meeting.

Gaia tilted her head in confusion. "What do you mean?"

Brex rubbed the back of his neck. "I don't know where they got the idea that you were going to be some malleable little weakling. How can you stand listening to them talk down to you?" he asked.

Gaia laughed. "You heard Lathan, most female Tallpians choose to concern themselves with gossip and children, not battle planning and war." Brex scowled at that.

"Not his wife," he pointed out. Lathan's wife Leona was a young woman of the Tallpian court. She had been assigned by Lady Bronwyn to tutor Gaia in the Tallpian traditions and history as well assist her in mastering the transitions that were as easy as breathing for most Tallpians. Gaia quickly conquered the natural skill of changing her hair and eye color; however, she still struggled with the full transformations. According to Leona, it required a great deal of energy and concentration to assume the physical identity of another being; she confirmed that even some mature, well-practiced Tallpians had trouble with the skill. Formal and cold at first, Leona had eased her polite stiffness after Gaia's insistence that she relax. Letting go of the formalities, Leona revealed a whip-sharp sense of humor and biting wit. Gaia liked her instantly and admired the smoldering soul under Leona's mass of curls that were usually a brilliant red.

"I believe Leona is an exception," Gaia admitted.

"You are a warrior race, known throughout the galaxy for your fighting prowess," Brex continued.

"The males, at least," Gaia said with a complacent shrug. "They will adjust to having me as queen."

"You so sure about that?" he asked.

Gaia fixed him with a gentle look. "Brex, listen, I know you don't agree with them much, but these are my people. They are what's left of my family. We have to work with them."

"Did you notice that not one of the Tallpians will look me in the eye?"

"I wouldn't take it personally," Gaia advised. "They aren't used to working with outsiders." She wasn't about to relay the conversation she'd had with Amadeas earlier in the afternoon. Brex didn't need to know about how the rest of her people felt. She didn't even know how she honestly felt and they had avoided discussing their feelings since their arrival on Miwarma.

"Regardless, I'm the Commander of the Brotherhood. Your lover or not, I deserve respect."

"I'll say something to Amadeas."

"Don't bother," Brex said, his voice tinged with resignation.

"Why not?"

"I don't think it'll do any good. Besides, I can fight my own battles."

"Brex—"

"I'm telling you, something doesn't feel right. Have you noticed how they keep saying, 'when you rule'?"

"Brex, we've talked about this."

He glowered at her. "You keep telling me you don't want to be queen but you seem to go along with everything they say. What are you going to do once we've won? Tell them you've changed your mind about ruling?"

"I haven't made up my mind," Gaia snapped, as they passed through the door to her cottage. She gave him a hard, sweet smile that made it clear that the subject was closed. "I'll decide when the time comes." Brex shut the door firmly behind them but crossed his arms as he stared at her.

"But—"

"Brex, please, don't worry about it. Trust me." She arched her eyebrows at him with a smile. "How about we do something that requires no knowledge of war and no clothes?" She snagged the edge of his pants and tugged him closer. His reluctant grin was the only response he needed.

⁓

"What do you mean you lost him?!" Brex left Gaia sleeping early the next morning and had returned to his small room to do some work when a transmission came through from Zaire. The fat collector shrugged in half-hearted apology.

"I put my best guard on him, but when Jaclyn went to check on him this morning, he was gone."

"When I get my hands on Auggie, I'm going to murder him."

"Might have your chance sooner than you think," a third voice spoke, and Brex looked up to see Alix standing in the doorway.

"What?"

"Well, Auggie sort of just landed."

"Here?" Brex demanded, slapping his hand to the telescreen, cutting off the image of Zaire's fat laughing face.

"Yep."

"He's my best friend, but I'm still going to kill him," Brex said as he stood and headed through the door, shaking his head. He and Alix were halfway across the grassy landing strip when they saw a familiar, copper-headed figure slouching towards them.

"Auggie, you dumbass, what are you doing here?" Brex shouted as they drew level with their friend.

Auggie just grinned at him. "Good to see you too, Brex."

"What the hell? You were in bed with a belly wound a week ago. How are you up and running halfway across the galaxy?"

But Auggie just rocked back on his heels, ginning and nonchalant, hands in his pockets. "I'm fine, don't worry about me. You've got enough on your plate." Brex growled wordlessly at him but watched as his friend stretched with a yawn, and he saw no trace of pain on Auggie's face. Whatever made up the other half of his genes had some serious healing abilities. An image of Auggie lying in a puddle of bright red blood flashed before Brex's eyes, and he shuddered. Losing Gaia would kill him, but Auggie was his best friend—the fact that he had come that close to death because of Brex made him eternally grateful for whatever made up the other half of Auggie's DNA structure.

"Fine. I suppose you're here to help?"

"Well, duh."

"Fine, but we don't launch for another two weeks," Brex said, still peeved.

"Whatever, man, but there are some things that you should know."

"Like what?"

Twenty minutes later, Brex sat at his desk, wondering if banging his head against it hard enough would solve all of his problems. Auggie sat in the chair across from him, a slight smile still on his lips. Perpetually amused, despite the looming brink of war, Auggie took everything in stride. Unlike Brex.

"You're sure of everything?"

"Yes, for the thousandth time, yes," Auggie spat. "A week is a lot of down time for me, so I spent a ton of hours surfing off-world comm-feeds. Nuweydon has contacted the Central Core and informed them that you guys are planning a coup. They say that if you succeed, legal or not, they'll refuse to recognize Gaia as queen and may mount a counter-rebellion."

"Hell."

"Is that the best response you've got?" Auggie demanded. It had been Brex's go-to answer for almost their entire conversation.

Brex ignored him. "What do we do now?"

"Well," Auggie said, scratching his head, "It's actually not as bad as you think. Central is more than likely bluffing. I doubt they're willing to spend that kind of time and expense for one tiny planet way the hell out on the outer edges. And most of the outer-edge planets aren't buying into the threats because no one this far out trusts Central anyways, and those that do were in league with Nuweydon to begin with. At this point, no one has fully outright promised support. I think they are all a little wary of pissing off the next ruler of Meidonna, whoever they may be."

"So they think we can do it?"

"Frankly, yes. Personal relationships have nothing to do with it. They trade with Meidonna for the money. Whether or not Nuweydon falls, they still want those trade connections to remain open, so the support is sort of nebulous at this point. The only planet we really need to worry about is Caninus. The feeds say that they are considering scrambling their army."

"As long as it is only one other planet, we can work with that. Alix thinks he might have a way to disable their fleet, and as long as we can meet them on the ground, we should be alright." Alix was one of the only members of the Outer Rim Brotherhood who actually hailed from the Central Core. A technology genius, he had defected from Central several years previously after his scientist parents were murdered by the government for what the secret police called "subversion." Alix had barely made it out alive and had sworn to spend the rest of his life to bringing down Central Core and their allies.

"There is one other thing," Auggie said carefully.

"What?" Brex growled. "No more bad news, Auggie."

"It actually isn't bad news."

"Just spit it out."

"The only thing going for us is that they have no idea where we are."

"Well, the Miwarmans did promise us safety."

"I'm just amazed you all made it into warp without being followed."

"Amadeas said that he has someone on the inside who was able to activate the planet's shields, which keeps ships from landing or leaving."

"Are we going to be able to deactivate those shields before we invade?"

"I've asked Amadeas to show Alix how to get into their system, although I'm not sure if he's done it yet. If anyone can break in and take it down, it's Alix." Auggie nodded in agreement. Their hacker was as good with computers as Auggie was with a welding torch.

"We need to update everyone including Gaia and Amadeas. Cayson and Tyrell are here, and Jehu is supposed to be back tomorrow."

"And how is our lovely queen-to-be?" Auggie asked.

"She's fine." Brex made a face as he all but spat the words.

Auggie raised his eyebrows. "That bad, huh?"

"She's not sure what to do at this point. Her mother was killed the same night that Kain died, which rocked her foundation. She's doing her best to avoid thinking about it, if she does, she completely falls apart, which isn't super productive. She's conflicted about taking the throne, and her relatives are causing more problems than they solve."

"And how does she feel about you?"

"It's complicated," Brex said, scratching the back of his neck. "We're fine, provided I don't bring up her mother, the throne, her family, or the future."

Auggie sat back in his chair, laughing. "Well, that's something. Poor girl, she's probably terrified out of her wits."

"I couldn't tell even if she was, and every time I bring anything up, she makes it clear we aren't talking about it. She may have finally found her family, but I don't trust them as far as I can throw them."

"What makes you say that?"

Brex shook his head. "I can't quite put my finger on it. The rest of her people will barely acknowledge me, except Amadeas, and he's made it very clear he doesn't think I'm good enough for Gaia."

"What does she think about that?"

"I haven't said anything to her," Brex admitted. "I'm not sure if she just genuinely believes that's the way they are or if she's just shutting her eyes to the truth because she's so relieved to be among her own kind again."

"Then what's your plan?"

"Do our job," Brex said with a shrug. "We have a job to do here, regardless of my feelings for Gaia."

"Feelings?" Auggie asked with a curved smile.

"I don't want to talk about this, Auggie."

"Fine, but just saying, you should think about it."

"Yeah, yeah I am. But we have bigger problems than how I feel about Gaia."

"And to think you could still be on Cunat, being chased around by Maggie with a knife." Brex laughed, but it turned into a groan.

"We need to focus. Central knows we're planning a coup. We still have another twelve days until we can legally mount said coup. Meanwhile, I have to keep Gaia alive, keep her from killing me, and you have to keep me from killing her relatives. How in the name of all the gods is this going to work?"

# Chapter Nineteen

"**N**uweydon has notified the Central Core and let them know what we plan to do. They say they'll mount a counter fight against us, even though what we're doing will be legal." An outburst of obscenities in multiple languages met Brex's words. They all sat at a long, narrow table in the hall set aside for war meetings. Brex had called a strategy meeting with the Tallpians and Brotherhood alike so they could hear the news brought by Auggie. "Cainus is the only planet openly declared in alliance with Meidonna, but their forces are minimal. The rest of the outer rim is waiting in the wings to see how it goes."

"You're absolutely sure?" Amadeas demanded after the noise died down.

Auggie stared down the older Tallpian, a stoic look on his face. "Yes. I am positive of my sources."

"We'll be outmanned and outgunned a hundred to one," Lathan said, shaking his head.

"If the Brotherhood is unable to deliver the forces they have promised," Amadeas said, eyeing Brex with an odd expression on his face. "We could very well fail."

"Hey, we said we'd be there. And we will be," Brex said.

"Even if you triple your force, we'll still be outnumbered," Ravi, a young but brilliant Tallpian captain, retorted.

Brex opened his mouth to reply but Gaia stood and cut him off. "That's enough." Every head swiveled in her direction. She was staring around the room with smoldering, violet-colored eyes. "After the last eighteen years of running and fear and nightmares, I refuse to back down, out-numbered or not." She balled her hands into fists. "I will not have my commanders bicker like children while we are planning to overthrow the despot who currently occupies my throne. Have I made myself clear?"

"I did not say give up. I just said that the odds are hopeless," Lathan said with a petulant shrug.

"Nothing," she snarled, "is hopeless until the last one among us gives up their final breath."

"We are simply being realistic," Amadeas replied, looking put-out at her disagreement. "If we cannot rely on the Brotherhood—"

"I think you mean fatalistic," she interrupted. She pointed a finger at the collection of men who surrounded her. "Every single one of us is a survivor, a fighter. We have all clawed tooth and nail to get where we are, and I say we are far too close to give up now." She paused to take a breath. "My challenge and claim are legal. I am the true heir to the throne. Central cannot challenge our laws without risking unbalancing themselves elsewhere. If they are allowed to contest a legal claim, what goes to say that other planet's rules and laws will remain intact? The rest of the galaxy will not stand for it."

"Now that is a queen worth following," Cayson whispered in Brex's ear. Brex smiled. He knew it. He hated the idea of losing her to her throne, but as the days passed and he watched her grow into a thoughtful and driven (although incredibly stubborn) leader, he was having a harder time convincing himself that she still belonged with him and the Brotherhood, despite his selfish wishes.

But Gaia wasn't finished. She glared at her great-uncle. "We already have a plan in place to reach the planet surface. They are unaware that we can even do that."

"I told you before: I am not sure that my spies still remain alive. Nuweydon is probably purging everyone who has ever been connected to me."

"You've said you'd give Alix the connection lines for the planetary shield," Brex said, looking at the lanky, dark-haired Brotherhood hacker. "As long as you give him those, it should be enough to at least get us safely to the planet surface."

"I haven't gotten them yet," Alix said, his black eyes fixed on Amadeas, who looked away.

"I will provide them as soon as I know for a fact they are still usable."

"I can get through anything as long as I have the basic information," Alix replied, his tone flat. "If you won't—"

"I will provide them in due course. If you are as good as you say you are, you should have no problem with them."

"If you won't work with us," Brex started, glaring at the Tallpian general. "You should just say so."

"Stop," Gaia snapped, ignoring Amadeas as he tried to answer Brex. "The only thing we need to worry about is our strategy on the ground. Alix has made it clear that he'll get us that far." She acknowledged the hacker, who nodded, his narrowed eyes still locked on Amadeas.

"Where we will be completely outnumbered," Ravi reminded them.

"I said that is enough!" Gaia yelled. "I have spent almost twenty years of my life living in fear and isolation. I finally have a chance to end all of that and I will do so, even if it means going alone."

"You are not alone." Brex stood, and squeezed her hand, smiling. "You know you'll have to beat the Brotherhood off with a stick if you don't want our help. We're with you to the end." Gaia's eyes were glittering like brands when her great-uncle stood.

"I suppose I may have been hasty in my observations."

"You think?" Brex asked sarcastically, and the Brotherhood broke into muffled laughter. Amadeas's pale face flushed red. For a moment, he glanced around the room at the collection of Brotherhood members and Tallpians. With a huff and a contemptuous glance at Brex, he turned his back on them and stalked from the room, most of the Tallpian company rising immediately and following him out. Brex rolled his eyes as the door slammed, but turned back to the remaining council. Only Lathan remained, shrugging at the older Tallpian's petulance.

"We will need to make sure that our formations are strong. Even if we are outnumbered, that does not mean we are weaker," Gaia said, resuming her seat.

"I still do not think that meeting them on an open battlefield is wise," Cayson advised, shrugging his massive set of shoulders. "Out-numbered or not." Jehu, who sat next to the Necosian, nodded.

"I know that we've discussed trying to avoid it already, but in all likelihood, hand-to-hand combat is exactly what will happen. I think it is important to continue drilling our forces with the idea that nothing short of full decapitation will stop a Tallpian soldier." He wore an unapologetic expression. "Clean heart shots in the heat of battle are going to be very difficult."

"Agreed."

"We don't necessarily need to kill everyone," Alix said from behind his screen. "Just hold them off until we can kill Nuweydon."

"Nuweydon is a madman," Lathan said, "but I doubt he's stupid enough to rush headlong into a battle himself. He will send forth his armies and wait inside the palace until the battle is on the verge of completion. He will then join his troops for their 'victory.'"

"So we split up." Every head swiveled to look at Brex, disbelief showing openly on their faces. "The main army meets Nuweydon's army on the battlefield, another group goes in to root the vermin out of his hole." After a beat, Auggie and Shaw started to howl in laughter, making everyone jump.

"See?" Shaw said as their chuckles finally subsided, wiping tears of laughter from his eyes. "I told you. This is why Kain put you in charge. No one else is crazy enough to think of something that insane," he said, still laughing, but both Cayson and Tyrell contemplated Brex with avid eyes.

The Roomajan's gaze was particularly speculative. "He's not wrong," Tyrell mused, his reptilian features looking thoughtful, the colored patterns on his skin shifting and shimmering as he tilted his head to stare at his new commander. "The plan does have a simple elegance to it."

"Thanks," Brex said, throwing an annoyed look at his two Brothers who were still snickering.

"It also sounds like a suicide mission," Alix chimed in. "Splitting up a force that isn't all that large to begin with?"

"Not necessarily." Everyone turned to look at Lathan, who shrugged. "Nuweydon is not someone to stay unguarded. He will have the best of the best with him, but it would still be possible with a small handful of talented fighters to break into the palace and engage him," he said.

"So we send our best," Brex replied, his gaze touching on Njoroge, Shaw, and a handful of others. Gaia watched him with narrowed eyes.

"If you even think about leaving me out of this…—" she warned, and he sighed in exasperation.

"How many times have I told you it's more important that you stay safe than be involved?"

"Remind me again whose throne we are fighting for?"

"Yours," Brex said carefully after a moment. She threw him a triumphant look.

"So what I say goes."

"Now Gaia," Njoroge put in, but she whipped her head around to stare at her trainer.

"Not you too!"

"Brex is right," the giant Sovarian advised her gently. "At this point, it is more important that you stay safe long enough to take back the throne. We can't risk losing you in battle."

"He is right, Gaia," Lathan said. "As queen, you should not risk yourself."

In response, Gaia stood again and slammed her fists into the table, splintering the wooden surface. "Damn all of you. This is my fight for my throne. I will be there. There is no debate."

"Gaia," but she swept Lathan a queenly glare, cutting him off.

"Do you plan to disobey the wishes of your future queen?" she demanded, drawing herself up to her full height. With her rose-tinted hair twisted into a chignon at the back of her neck and her brilliant lavender eyes flashing, she looked like one of the queens of old, beautiful enough to set atop an altar and sacrifice goats to. Brex clapped a hand over his eyes and shook his head. They had already had this argument several times over the last few days. She flat-out refused to stay on Miwarma until the coup was over, and as much as he wanted to prevent her, he knew she would figure out how to get herself there, whether he liked it or not.

Finally, he broke across their argument. "Stop. Gaia, you will be there. We cannot stop you from fighting for your throne. And you will be the one to kill Nuweydon," he promised, cutting her off at the look on her face. "We just can't lose you before then."

"You won't." Her voice was diamond hard as she glanced around the table. "You are all dismissed," she snapped before stomping from the room without waiting for them to rise from their seats.

Auggie glanced at Brex and winced as Gaia slammed the door. "I get what you mean now," he said with a grimace. Brex nodded. The rest of the council rose from their seats, chattering under their breath as they collected their things and moved away.

"Yep, welcome to my world," Brex said, slumping back into his chair.

"Would it help if you told her how you feel?" Auggie asked. "Might help her understand." Brex shrugged. "How do you feel? You never did answer me."

Brex looked around the emptying room before shrugging. "I have no idea."

Auggie gave him a deadpan look. "You two are like two halves of the same whole. You'll be finishing each other's sentences before long, you know, when she's not seething mad."

Brex shrugged again. "Sure. Gods know I've never felt anything like this before but…."

"But the idea of being in love with someone like her scares the hell out of you."

"Being in love with anyone," Brex muttered, scratching the back of his neck as was his wont when he was uncomfortable. "I don't know, dude. I've known her for what, ten, twelve days? It isn't supposed to be like this."

Auggie scoffed. "What, falling in love at first sight with a gorgeous, strong, hot-headed young woman who just happens to be a princess? I'm pretty sure that's the basis of every faerie story ever."

"This isn't a faerie story, though. This is real life." It was Auggie's turn to shrug.

"Maybe. But are you really going to risk losing someone like her because you're afraid of your own feelings?"

"Since when are you Dr. Love?" Brex demanded in irritation.

"I'm just smarter than you," his friend replied, laughing good-naturedly. "Are you going after her?"

Brex scowled. "Do I have to?" he asked, giving a mock shiver. "She's terrifying when she's angry."

Auggie laughed at him. "Go after her, you coward."

$\backsim$

"Gaia?" Brex knocked on the door to her quarters, but it wasn't Gaia who answered.

"She's not here." Sia, Gaia's Miwarman assistant, stood in front of him, her arms full of laundry. "She changed her clothes and left a few minutes ago." Sia looked apologetic. "She said something about kicking someone's ass?" Brex shook his head. She was good and mad this time.

"Thanks, Sia. I think I know where she is."

$\backsim$

The clang of metal meeting metal rang through the training courtyard as Brex wound his way through the cluster of buildings. Coming around a corner, he saw Gaia, dressed head to toe in a black, form-fitting bodysuit, wielding her favorite sword against Murad. Murad was in full body armor, and from the look on Gaia's face, Brex guessed that he needed it. Watching her swing the slim blade was like watching a bird in flight. He had observed her training with the detached eye of an expert, but she surprised even him by progressing so quickly. She had grown into her strength and quickly became a formidable opponent, regardless of the weapon. She was able to pin Njoroge in minutes now, and was almost a better shot than Brex. But it was the katana-like weapon where her passion lay. The sword was like an extension of her body, and she moved with a breathtaking fluidity. She wore a look of fierce concentration on her face, and it was all Murad could do to keep her at bay, bringing his own blade up over and over again to meet with hers, the steel ringing under the force of her blows.

Murad called for a break, and Gaia stalked away, fury written in every movement. She swung the sword experimentally, watching as the blade cut through the air and caught the sunlight.

"You're lethal with that thing," Brex said.

She whirled around but he was well out of her reach, and she glowered at him. "What are you doing here?" she demanded. Gods have mercy on him, she was a live grenade.

"Gaia, getting angry and storming out of war meetings isn't helping us right now," he chided her, trying to keep his voice gentle.

"Why should I listen to your misogynistic views?" she demanded, her lilac eyes fixed on his face with such intensity it made him want to take a step back.

But Brex held his ground. "Hey now, that's not it at all," he protested, his dark eyebrows coming together.

"Then what do you call it?" she demanded, still swishing her blade through the air.

"Genuine concern for you. If we told you that you couldn't rule because you're a woman, that's misogyny."

"I'm the one who is going to be queen."

"And we're going to do everything we can to make sure that happens without any problems. Problems like you dying," he said, giving her a firm look. "Despite what the rest of your people say, you know that we are going to stand behind you and make sure that we win this war."

"Even if you refuse to let me fight."

"Gaia! We are trying to protect you, but we are not going to stop you, how many times do I have to tell you that? It is your people that are trying to make sure you don't."

"But Njoroge—"

"Is concerned just like the rest of us. But he won't stand in your way. And if you're so mad, why aren't you telling this to Amadeas and Lathan? They are the ones trying to control what you do." Gaia paused, her mouth open but no answer on her lips. Finally, she recovered and glared at Brex again.

"I still don't like it. It is my throne, I'm going to be queen; why shouldn't I be there to fight for it?"

Brex gave a humorless laugh. "So you're going to take the throne for sure?" The thought of losing her hurt more than Brex was willing to admit, but he pushed the feeling down, trying to avoid adding any more conflict or confusion to her decision.

At once the anger drained from her face and was replaced with panic. "Yes. No. I don't know," she said, slamming her sword into its scabbard. "Some of the time I want it more than anything, and others I want to get as far away from all of this as I can." She gave Brex a desperate look. "You don't understand how badly it hurts me, knowing how my people have suffered under Nuweydon. I have the chance to fix that, Brex, can't you understand that?" Brex held out a hand to her, but she ignored it to start pacing in front of him. "But I can't stand the thought of other people dying for me, dying because of my fight! And if I choose not to take the throne, all of those sacrifices will have been in vain." She looked at him, anguished. "You of all people should understand that."

"Gaia," Brex said, once again extending his hand. "We've talked about this already. Every single person here is committed to helping you, regardless of the outcome. I know that. Lathan, Auggie, Shaw, and Njoroge, they all know that." He caught her hand as she marched past him and tugged her against his chest. She struggled, but he tightened his grip on her. "If we do nothing, your life is over regardless. But we will win this. And once we do—as I've said all along—you can then choose if you want to take the throne or not. Even if you choose not to take it, the Brotherhood is still committed to removing a psychopath from power." She stopped fighting his hold and tilted her head back so she could look at him. "But give Cayson and the others a chance. They are all seasoned soldiers; they know what they are talking about." She started to bristle, but he shook his head at her. "No, don't get mad. Take it all in stride, just like any good queen would. Accept their reservations about having you in battle and move on. You'll be there," he said, tilting her chin so she would look him in the eye. She sighed and after a moment leaned her forehead against his shoulder. Brex sighed in relief. His girl was like a thunderstorm: She broke harsh against the landscape but soon wore herself out and faded away.

"You promise you won't leave me here?" she asked, her words muffled against his shirt.

Brex laughed. "And risk having you come after me with that thing?" he said, nodding at the sword she still held in her hand. "Forget that. I want to live to see old age." Gaia laughed and then stepped back from his embrace. He ran a hand over her rib-cage and down over the swell of her hip. "I like the new outfit, by the way," he said, peeling back the collar and trying to glance down her shirt. She slapped him away with a shriek and dissolved into giggles.

"What am I going to do with you, Brexler Carrow?" she demanded, smiling at him.

He raised a suggestive eyebrow. "I have an idea."

# Chapter Twenty

Auggie was strolling back from the mess hall with Kyan late in the afternoon the next day. They had resumed their abandoned strategy meeting from the previous day, planning from early in the morning until they broke for the midday meal. They were focusing on the ground fight, pouring over troop numbers and potential battle sights. They only had eleven days until Gaia's twenty-first birthday—only eleven more days to plan and win a war.

In what Auggie considered a smart move, Brex had elected to keep their idea to split up the forces from Amadeas. Before the meeting had begun that morning, he asked all of the attending Brotherhood members not to say anything about their plan around the Tallpian general. Lathan had looked uncomfortable, but Gaia had fixed him with a stare that could have frozen steel, and he acquiesced, agreeing to keep quiet.

"I can't quite put my finger on it," Brex had said, "but I don't trust Amadeas. I want an ace up my sleeve if it comes to that," Brex had said.

Auggie and Kyan were cruising along one of the narrow rope bridges that edged along the building that served as the Tallpian part of the compound, when the two Brothers heard raised voices issuing from a cracked window about three-quarters of the way along the building. Recognizing Amadeas's harsh tones, both Kyan and Auggie slid flat against the building and sidled up to the open window. The shade was drawn, obscuring the figures inside, but the voices were clear as they issued from the room. Kyan raised a finger to his lips, motioning for Auggie to be silent as they crouched down by the window to listen in.

"I understand your perspective, but I'm not sure that your means will justify the ends."

"Justify! We are talking about the future of our world. If we do not make sure that we control our destiny, we may very well be driven from existence."

"I hardly believe that Gaia becoming queen will drive us into extinction."

"You may be willing to take that chance, but I am not."

"The repercussions would be far worse than the rewards, how do you not understand that?"

"Coward! Don't you understand what I do is for the good of our people?" It took Auggie only a moment to realize that he was listening to Amadeas arguing with another Tallpian. "And that boy is nothing but trouble," Amadeas continued. "If we do not remove his influence, we may lose all control of the queen."

"Control? She is hardly a loose cannon. She has a worthy mind and an able conscience. I think she will make a gifted ruler in time."

"Can you say that she will follow our precepts?" There was a pause.

"She may have her own way of seeing things, but surely a new vantage would not be a bad thing?"

"Our traditions are what have kept us alive. Would you allow her and those who surround her to destroy that?"

"Again, I doubt that the Brotherhood cares one way or another about how our planet is run once Gaia is queen. She has made it clear, she alone will rule."

"If you choose to believe that, then so be it."

"Carrow has openly said he has no desire to be king."

"He is lying, how could he not be? And all obstacles must be removed, one way or another."

"One way or another? She will not dismiss him. She is far too in love."

"There are other ways of severing such a bond."

"Such as what?" the voice was dismissive.

"By force, if necessary." There was another pause, longer this time.

"You are planning to kill him?" the other voice demanded incredulously. Auggie felt the hairs on the back of his neck stand on end. If it was what it sounded like it was, Amadeas wanted to kill Brex in order to get to Gaia. The thought made his stomach pulse with fury. Glancing at Kyan, he could see the same shock he was feeling etched into the young medic's face. When no answer came from Amadeas, the other Tallpian continued to speak, his voice breaking with rigid anger. "I will have no part in this! He may be terran, but he is a good leader and has a mind for war."

"Irrelevant."

"Our force cannot defeat Nuweydon. We have need of the Outer Rim Brotherhood."

"No, we do not."

"Then find another to help you because I will have no part in your plots."

"You will if you wish to remain within my army."

"Blackmail?"

"A direct order."

"Risking her anger is not worth it, even if you have no qualms about cold-blooded murder."

"You are a coward. It is worth everything we hold dear."

"Your desire for power and control corrupts your vision, General. Gaia will make a worthy queen."

"That girl has no idea of her place in the world. She will be made to understand how things work."

"I doubt it. She is much stronger-willed than you anticipated."

"Nothing is insurmountable. She will be made to understand."

"Not even you would dare."

"When will you learn, boy, I will do as I please?"

"Those days are changing. I think you should consider that."

"One way or another, that girl will take the throne."

"So you can achieve your own selfish aims?"

"Selfish!" Amadeas spat, offended. "What I do, I do for our people. And Kallideia will be their next queen whether she desires it or not."

"What if she does not?" the question hung in the air. "What if she refuses?"

"There are others in the bloodline that have a strong claim."

"Oh no," the other voice said, a cold laugh ringing out. "Don't look at me like that. We have had this conversation. I may be her cousin, but no part of me desires the throne."

"I could force you."

"You would have an easier job forcing a corpse to rise again. I feel as though I can't make myself clearer, Amadeas. I do not want the throne." A chair scraped against the floor. "Even though you listen to no council other than your own, I will still offer this. Attempt to remove Brexler Carrow from Gaia's life and you will regret it. Anyone can see that, and I hope you would be wise enough to understand." Footsteps receded from the room as Auggie glanced at Kyan, disbelief and worry flooding his face.

"Brex! Brex! Gods be damned, Brex open the door!" Auggie yelled, hammering on Gaia's door. A moment later it was ripped open, and Brex stood before them shirtless with his pants unsnapped and very annoyed, red lip tint smeared across his jaw.

"This had better be good, Auggie," Brex snarled, glaring at both Kyan and Auggie.

"You have no idea."

"What is going on?" Gaia demanded, appearing at Brex's shoulder wrapped in a sheet, her long, seafoam-tinted curls pooled over one shoulder. Auggie and Kyan froze, both trying valiantly not to stare at Gaia.

Brex reached over and slapped Kyan on the side of the head. "Stop staring and get to the point."

"Amadeas is going to try and have you killed," Auggie said baldly. A moment of complete silence followed.

"What?" Brex finally asked in disbelief.

Auggie sighed. "We were coming back from chow and heard Amadeas arguing with someone. We caught the tail end of their conversation, but Amadeas thinks you are the reason that he can't control Gaia and thinks that by getting rid of you, he'll be able to manipulate Gaia and control her once she becomes queen." He paused to take a breath before glancing at Gaia. "Whoever he was talking to is also in the bloodline, and apparently has a decent claim to the throne as well."

"What?" she asked incredulously. "Who?" Auggie shook his head.

"Never saw his face. It's one of the officers, though. I've heard the voice before."

"And you're saying that Amadeas is planning to kill me?" Brex scoffed. "I'd love to see him try."

"I wouldn't tempt him. The look on his face yesterday when everyone laughed at him in the meeting, he looked like he wanted to cut out your heart right there."

"How is that possible?" Gaia asked. "He has always been perfectly pleasant to you."

Brex snorted. "In front of you, yes, he tolerates me. But he made it very clear how he feels about me the night we arrived here."

"When was that?" Gaia asked, her forehead wrinkling in confusion.

"After I left you," Brex said gently, trying not to focus on their fight. Gaia was an emotional creature, Brex was realizing, and while he had never treaded softly in his life with anyone, he found himself being a little more careful around his lover. She was prone to intense reactions, especially whenever she thought she was being slighted or insulted. A brief conversation with Leona had confirmed that was a normal Tallpian trait.

"Oh."

"I ran into him, and for as much waffling and pontificating as he does during strategy meetings, he was transparent about the fact he thinks I'm no good, especially for you."

Gaia scowled. "I don't believe it," she said slowly, trying to ignore the pulse in her gut as she recalled her own conversation with Amadeas about Brex.

"You really doubt me?" Auggie asked, one eyebrow raised.

Gaia shook her head. "Of course not, Auggie. But I still find it hard to believe."

"We know he doesn't want me anywhere near that throne."

"But we all know you don't want it to begin with."

"I know that, and you know that. But does Amadeas?"

"But enough to kill you?"

"Think about how badly he wants you on the throne." Brex fixed her with a firm look. "He has been talking about you becoming queen before we even had you free of the dungeon and has been pushing you onto that chair since then and it's not even empty yet."

"He thinks he can manipulate her," Auggie added. Gaia snorted in derision, but Auggie shrugged. "Whoever he was talking to tried to tell him that it won't work, but obviously Amadeas doesn't listen to anyone."

"Manipulate me?" Gaia asked in disbelief. "He just wants to remove Nuweydon, like the rest of us."

"Gaia," Brex said, grabbing her arms, "I'm sorry, but you just don't see it. I know they are what remains of your family, but I'm not entirely sure they have altruistic motives."

"I don't believe that," she said, but Brex could hear the doubt creeping into her tone.

He shook his head and instead looked at Auggie. "I really want to know who he was talking to."

"Whoever it was, they are a friend of the Brotherhood. He refused to have any part in Amadeas's plans, and made it clear that the Tallpians need us if they expect to win Meidonna back," Auggie said. Brex disappeared briefly before stepping back to the door, pulling a shirt over his head.

"I'm going to talk to Amadeas."

"Don't," Auggie stalled him, holding up a hand.

"Why?"

"He'll deny it, especially to you," Auggie pointed out. "I'll take care of it."

"You sure?" Brex asked, looking suspicious.

"I'll handle it, dude. You have bigger problems to worry about." Auggie glanced at Gaia and she narrowed her eyes—today, the same shade as her mint-green hair—at him, making him laugh.

"Easy there, tiger." He looked at Brex. "I'll deal with Amadeas, you deal with everything else." Gaia scowled, but Brex just nodded before wrapping an arm around her waist and tugging her back into the room, slamming the door behind them.

"What are you going to do?" Kyan asked as he and Auggie returned to the barracks.

Auggie glanced at the younger member. "Nothing right now. Don't worry about it. I'll take care of everything." The kid eyed him suspiciously but shrugged. Not his place to argue or question with a senior member of command. Auggie waited until Kyan left, mumbling something about getting some sleep, before grabbing his pistol and a knife (not that he planned on needing them, but it never hurt to be prepared) and slipping from the room.

The sun had already begun to set when Auggie eased through the door to the main hall used by the Tallpians. It was deserted; most people were at the evening meal, but, as he had hoped, there was a light showing from under Amadeas's door. Without bothering to knock, he pushed into the office. Amadeas sat hunched over his desk, scribbling fiercely and did not immediately look up.

"You can write all you want, but this won't end the way you want it to." Amadeas's head jerked up in surprise. He surveyed Auggie for a moment before returning to his writing.

"I have nothing to say to you. Get out."

"You don't have to say anything. Just listen." Auggie sat down in one of the chairs that faced the desk, and Amadeas paused to glare at him.

"What—"

"I said you don't need to talk. But I do have something to say, and you will listen." Auggie took a deep breath and fixed an easy smile on the Tallpian commander. "I understand what you're doing here. Trying to win a war, trying to restore your brother's legacy to the throne; all very noble, we agree." Auggie paused before he glared at Amadeas. "However, should I hear you threaten Brex's life again, I will end you." As he watched, several emotions flickered across Amadeas's face. "Don't bother trying to deny it. Everyone can tell that you hate him, and I overheard your conversation earlier this afternoon."

"You heard nothing," Amadeas dismissed, but Auggie chuckled, not surprised by the denial.

"I know exactly what I heard. As did another member of the Brotherhood, along with whoever you were speaking with, who, by the way, clearly understands the need your people have of us."

"How dare—"

"I'm not the one plotting to kill the leader of an intergalactic organization for good, so yes, I dare." He fixed Amadeas with another dark glare. "If you so much as think about killing Brex again, I'll have your head off your shoulders before you can blink."

"If you think you can threaten me…—" Amadeas growled, drawing himself up. Auggie shook his head, trying not to laugh again.

"Oh, I'm threatening you, make no mistake. With your great-niece's permission, I might add. Gaia has been part of our family longer than she has yours. You may share blood with her, but do not think that gives you the right to try and influence her into getting what you want."

"And what is it I want?" Amadeas sneered, sitting back in his chair and crossing his arms. Like a rat in a trap, Auggie thought with another smile.

"You want to rule. Oh not directly yourself," he added, seeing the look on the general's face. "You know that the people of Meidonna already don't like you very much. After all, you've let Nuweydon do as he's pleased for the last two decades. It wouldn't surprise me if you helped him in the first place. I can't imagine that's made you very popular."

"My only interest—"

"—Is using Gaia for a puppet. But she won't be used, will she? I don't know if you expected her to throw herself at your feet in gratitude for rescuing her or something, but you should have figured out the day you met her that wasn't going to happen."

"I—"

"And you think Brex is the reason for that."

"He is not fit to be king!"

"And he doesn't want to be. But if you spent more time paying attention instead of scheming, you'd understand that already."

"I will do whatever is necessary to save my people."

"By trying to control your great-niece once she is queen?"

"I plan to guide and mold and lead—"

"And there is your problem. But you don't see it, do you?"

"Get out of my office," Amadeas snarled, and Auggie took his time getting to his feet.

"Sure. But remember, if there is so much as a hair out of place on Brex's head, I'll blame you. And the entire Brotherhood will back me up."

"Your gang of misfits does not scare me," he sneered, and Auggie smiled again.

"We should. The entire membership already wants Nuweydon's blood for killing Kain. You wait until they hear that you want Brex out of the way so you can abuse Gaia's power. There will be no corner of the galaxy you can hide in, because we are everywhere." Giving him a casual wave, Auggie strolled from the office. As the door swung shut behind him, he heard the distinct sound of a desk being cleared as papers were flung against the wall. Auggie smiled to himself as he sauntered across the compound, whistling, towards the Brotherhood's barracks.

# Chapter Twenty-One

"Are you sure it's a good idea to let Auggie confront Amadeas?" The door had just shut behind Kyan and Auggie when Gaia turned to Brex. He paused in stripping off his black cargo pants to shrug.

"I don't see why not."

"Do you really think he is planning to kill you?" It all seemed a little far-fetched to her. Brex snorted as he reached for her.

"I don't have a doubt in my mind."

"I don't know, Brex. Seems a little extreme, don't you think?" she asked.

Brex scoffed. "Not in the slightest." Gaia raised her eyebrows in disbelief.

"What are we going to do about it?" she demanded, placing her hands on Brex's chest to keep him from leaning in. He sighed, and cupped her face in his hands.

"We are going to let Auggie deal with it. I trust him, as you should."

"I'm more concerned about your safety."

"I can handle myself," he reminded her before leaning down for a soft kiss. "Don't you worry about it. You've got enough on your mind already. Let's just focus on the challenge at hand." She offered him a sly grin.

"And what exactly is that challenge?" He dipped his head and brushed his lips against her ear.

"I want to see just how loud I can make you moan."

The massive Miwarman sun had just begun to set as Brex reluctantly left Gaia's cottage later that evening. More Brotherhood members were arriving each day, and they all required a direct briefing from him. Gaia shooed him from the room with several lingering kisses before closing the door and stepping in front of her full-length mirror. Deciding she no longer liked her mint-green hair and eyes, she closed her eyes briefly before reopening them. Auburn curls and jade green eyes were much better. Dropping the sheet that had been wrapped around her, Gaia examined her body and realized how much had changed over the last eleven days. Her muscles were taut and strong, but her entire body looked rounder, more developed. A little surprised, she twisted around, trying to see herself from another angle. As she spun, she caught sight of the slight swell at her middle and froze—that was new. Her brain started to spin into overdrive. It took her a moment to coherently form the thought. Was it even possible? Her knowledge of physical relationships was very limited, but she had a sudden flash of horror. She and Brex had not gone a day without ending up in bed together. Could that mean what she thought it might? Trying not to panic, she hit the call button and requested the only person on the planet she felt she could trust.

"Gaia, are you alright?" Leona paused as she pushed through the door to Gaia's bungalow as Sia slipped past her, after retrieving her mistress's dinner tray. Catching sight of the stricken look on Gaia's face, Leona hesitated before shutting the door quietly. "What is the matter?" Leona looked at her queen-to-be, concern spreading across her face. "Gaia? Please say something, you're scaring me!"

Gaia lifted her auburn head and stared, horror-struck at her red-haired friend. "I think I'm pregnant." There was a long, drawn-out pause while Leona tilted her head in alarmed contemplation, her red curls vibrating with worry.

"Well," she said at last, "it is technically possible. Brex?" Leona asked, and Gaia nodded, not even taking offense at the implied possibility there could be anyone else. "You are both humanoid lifeforms. I mean, our early histories suggest that we could be descended from the original terrans, so it is, in theory, absolutely possible."

"How soon—" her voice broke. She cleared her throat and tried again. "How much longer do I have, until…—?"

"Until Brexler's child is born? Since you are Tallpian, you should, again, in theory, carry the child for four months, much shorter than most females. Our advanced makeup allows for rapid gestation." Leona tugged Gaia to her feet and looked her up and down. While it was barely noticeable at first glance, there was a definite, discernible bump forming between Gaia's hip bones under the clinging silk of her robe.

"Are you sure it's possible?" Gaia's voice was near breaking.

"Ask me again," Leona dared her, her patience already thin with worry. "It doesn't happen all that often, but that doesn't mean it can't. We start to show much sooner than a terran, and we carry for a shorter amount of time." Leona ticked the months off on her fingers. "If you're just now pregnant within the last two weeks, you should give birth no later than the beginning of the autumn season."

"What am I going to do?" Gaia had her hands splayed across her stomach, cradling the space where her child would soon swell. Leona watched as emotions clashed in Gaia's green eyes.

"What worries you the most?" Leona asked gently, guiding Gaia back to sit on the bed.

Gaia looked up, her face white with worry. "I don't even know where to start."

"Take a deep breath. One thing at a time."

"Brex. Giving birth while we're at war. Being a mother, being queen…which comes first?"

"Gaia, first things first: you have to tell Brex."

Gaia blanched, looking at her friend in horror. "I can't! Do you have any idea how much he'll worry? He already doesn't want me to fight! This will only make it worse. Never mind the fact that he didn't even know his father, what if he doesn't want his own child? He is going to freak out."

"He's going to be a parent; I think that's generally to be expected."

"What if he tries to make me stay behind, Leona? We are at war, for my crown. I can't be left out of that fight."

"Gaia, you need to tell him. He has every right to know."

"Not if it jeopardizes me going after Nuweydon."

"Gaia, this is the heir to the throne we're talking about. Your throne."

The look that Gaia suddenly fixed on Leona was icy. The panic was suddenly gone from her face, and Leona could see her future queen staring back at her.

"No, I refuse to be left out of this. This is my fight." She paused before glaring at Leona again. "You will say nothing to Brex, not a word to anyone. This is mine to share, and I will share it as I choose." Leona paused for a moment, narrowing her eyes as she tried to collect her thoughts.

"Gaia, as your friend and advisor, I don't agree. Brex is going to be a father. You are bearing first and foremost, his child. The fact that he or she will be the heir to your throne is second. Tell him."

"No."

"Either you tell him or I will. Friends or not, my queen or not, I swear I will tell him. He has every right to know, and you have no right to keep this from him." Gaia hissed between her teeth, surprised as the other woman's threat.

"This war is bigger than any one being, Leona," Gaia said, trying for reason.

"That won't matter to Brex. Tell him. And then start working on your argument about staying in the fight." Gaia opened her mouth to retort when the speaker in the wall crackled to life, urgently calling Leona. Leona moved to the wall and replied into the speaker that she would be right there.

"Promise me you'll say nothing until I'm ready," Gaia demanded. "I'll tell Brex, I swear, I just need to think for a bit." Leona surveyed her friend before nodding and heading for the door.

"Alright, Gaia, alright. I won't say anything."

"Pregnant? You're sure?" The young Miwarman girl nodded her dark head. Amadeas slammed a fist onto his desk. "Gods be damned." He glanced at the girl. He couldn't remember her name, but he couldn't deny her usefulness. He was grateful that his wife had persuaded the child to spy on her new mistress. But as he thought about it, maybe this turn of events could be used to his benefit. Maybe this was the card he needed to finally force Kallideia to do what was necessary, what was required of her. "This is what you must do," he said, outlining his plan in a few cool words before dismissing the little spy who bobbed a brief curtsy before fleeing from the room. "This changes everything," he muttered to himself, reaching for his telelink.

Brex sat at his desk, just having closed his connection with Zaire. The collector was doing them a favor and keeping his ear to the ground, listening for any murmurs in the trading world about what Nuweydon might be doing in preparation for the coming war. He had just pushed back from the screen when there was a soft knock at his door. He called for them to enter, and Brex was surprised to see Sia, Gaia's Miwarman assistant, poke her dark head around the edge of his door.

"Gaia would like a word with you," she said, dipping in a brief curtsey, her eyes on the floor. Brex cocked his head, confused. He had left Gaia planning to go to bed. Why wouldn't she just come to him herself? Reading his reluctance, the girl spoke again. "She said it was important." Confused and a little concerned, Brex rose to his feet.

"I'll go see her now," he said, moving past her. She stepped back out of his way, and in a very soft voice that he thought he might have imagined, she whispered, "I'm so sorry." Brex glanced at her, but her dark face was bland.

Brex was passing through a dark part of the village when he thought heard the wooden bridge creek behind him. Before he could turn to investigate, something hard struck the back of his head, and the world went black.

Amadeas made sure there was no one around to notice them before he gestured two strong Tallpian soldiers to step from the shadows and lift Brex from the ground where he lay unconscious.

"Quick, into the dungeon."

The small, subterranean room was one of the few cells on the entire planet. The Miwarmans had little use for them, since their peaceful nature allowed them to reason their way through almost any conflict. It was only outsiders who made any use of the cells, often at odds with their hosts' peaceful nature.

Amadeas's men deposited Brex in the musty stone room, chaining his wrists to a ring set deep in the wall. Amadeas was tempted to stay and gloat, but he had work to do. Observing the prone form of the Brotherhood leader for another moment, Amadeas blinked and suddenly another Brex stood in the doorway. He glared at his men.

"Whatever you do, do not let him escape."

Amadeas made his way through the torch-lit compound, forcing himself to acknowledge each Brotherhood member he came across. If his ruse was successful, he wouldn't have to worry about the rabble or their leader for much longer. He paused before Kallideia's door and squared his shoulders. Careful to act as Brexler would, he pushed through the door without knocking. Kallideia was sitting at her vanity, amber hair pooled over one shoulder, evergreen eyes regarding Brex warily.

"Sia said you had something you wanted to talk about?" he asked. Amadeas had been careful to ensure that it was Sia who carried the message to Brexler and not Leona. The other Tallpian woman was infuriatingly close to Kallideia. Bronwyn had instructed her to keep her distance, but instead, their warnings had fallen on deaf ears, and now the two young women were close friends. Kallideia nodded slowly in response to his question.

"Yes, there is." She looked up at him with fear in her eyes. "Brex, there is no easy way to say this. I'm pregnant." Amadeas made sure the shock showed on his face.

"What?"

"I am carrying your child." It made her jump when Amadeas slammed his fist into the wooden door frame.

Amadeas managed to smother the glee he felt at the heartbroken look spreading across the narrow, pale face in front of him.

"You're sure it's mine?" he demanded, glancing at her.

Gaia shot him a withering look. "You know it is." He raised an eyebrow in suspicion, and she bristled at him. "How dare you even suggest that?" she snapped, glaring.

"How should I know, Gaia? I've known you for two weeks! I don't know what your past looks like."

"I can say for sure that it is far cleaner than yours is, Brexler."

"How do you even know? We've only been together a few times." Amadeas was guessing, but if she was pregnant, it would have only taken once.

"Tallpians can conceive and start to show within eight days of conception," she replied tonelessly.

"How could you let something like this happen?" he said, starting to pace. "Do you have any idea how terrible this is? How could you let this happen?" The anger that flooded Kallideia's face almost made Amadeas smile. It was too easy.

"This isn't just something I did, Brexler," she snarled. "As they say, it takes two."

"How could you be so stupid? We're at war!"

"How dare you!" she spat again, jumping to her feet. "You think I did this on purpose?"

"Of course you did! Why didn't you think to be careful?"

"I'm not a whore, Brex. That's not something I thought about! I didn't even know it was possible!" Tears started to pool in her green eyes.

"Well, obviously it is! You've ruined everything." Horror flooded Kallideia's face as she glared at him.

"You really think that?" Her voice broke as she collapsed back onto the bench in front of the vanity. Amadeas almost felt bad as he glared at her. Almost.

"Of course! You think I want to be a parent? Did you think I'd want to stay with you after this?"

"But—"

"We never planned a future, and I sure as hell don't want one!"

"Brex! How can you—"

"Forget this, Gaia. You screwed up, and now you can fix it. Alone." Gaia's mouth dropped open as he slammed his way out of the room, trying to hide the look of unadulterated joy that threatened to consume his face.

Even on an ocean planet that spent almost every waking hour blasted by tropical sun, the dungeon was still dark and dank. Salt formed white crystals that covered the stone walls like frost, and Brex wondered if he was below the ocean surface. His head still hurt from the blow that had knocked him unconscious—when? He had no idea how many hours he had been in the stone room before coming to. It was all Amadeas's fault, Brex just knew it. Amadeas was up to something and Brex going to kill him just as soon as he got loose. Whatever his plan was, Brex knew it couldn't be good news for him or Gaia.

The hours passed slowly, Brex pacing as far as the chains would allow. Rage and worry rushed through him. Where was Gaia? What was Amadeas doing?

Finally, it seemed like days even though it was only hours later, the stout wooden door swung open with a grating noise. Dim light filtered down the staircase just beyond the door. Clearly, it was already morning. Brex didn't recognize the Tallpian soldier who stood in the doorway. But in a swift movement, they stepped aside for Amadeas as he entered the small stone chamber.

Brex felt his eyes narrow. "What is going on?" demanded Brex, yanking on the chain. There was no reply as Amadeas entered the cell and closed the door firmly behind himself. He paused, staring at Brex with a frightening amount of dislike in his eyes. "Tell me what is going on! Why am I down here?"

"You cannot imagine the things I have done for the sake of my family and my kind," Amadeas said finally.

"That sounds like a threat."

"Could be," the general said, giving him a grimace. "But it is up to you if it becomes a significant one."

"I've told you before, old man, speak plainly."

"If you care about my niece as you say you do, you'll take the offer I'm about to give you and never look back."

"No," Brex said, yanking on the chain again. "Not after this—"

"A half million talents." That brought Brex up short. He stopped yanking on the manacles to gape at the general.

"You have got to be fucking kidding me."

Amadeas leered at him. "What, that isn't enough?"

"You are desperate enough to try and pay me off to leave Gaia?" Brex demanded, trying to ignore the twist in his stomach at the thought of half of a million talents. That was serious money. He could quit smuggling, set up a small ranch, maybe on Xael.—"No." His voice broke through his own thoughts. "No, I am not leaving Gaia." And then something dawned on Brex, and he started to laugh, which made the lines around Amadeas's mouth deepen. "I get it now," he said, chuckling, and looking at the general. "Auggie told me. I know you want me dead. But you realized that if you had me killed, Gaia would have your head off your shoulders the second she found out. And that's not where you want to be, so you figured you could pay me off instead. Probably a lot less messy." Brex shrugged. "If you were smart, you would have led with that. This is going to be much harder for you to explain."

"Fine. Make it a million."

"A million gold talents?" Brex asked in disbelief, trying not to choke. Not even Zaire had that much money.

Amadeas nodded, his face cold. "On your ship and gone within the hour, and you swear on your life to never look back."

"Fuck you," Brex said, his lips curling back in disgust. "What makes you think that money would be enough to make me leave Gaia?"

Amadeas shrugged. "You're smarter than I originally gave you credit for, Carrow." Another look of intense dislike. "At first I thought you were just amusing yourself with my niece, hoping for an easy tumble and a decent payday." The older man shrugged. "But I see where it is headed now. She's falling in love with you, and if I don't get rid of you now, I'll never be free of you. I won't permit a mongrel like you near the throne of my forefathers." He examined Brex with a critical eye. "Kallideia will make a fitting queen, one day, with my guidance."

"She wouldn't listen to you even with me gone. You burned that bridge twenty years ago when you let your nephew murder her father."

"Oh, I think she'll come around eventually."

"She's much smarter than that. She doesn't trust easily, and I know she doesn't trust you." That may not have been entirely true, but the doubt had begun to show in Gaia's eyes after Auggie informed them of Amadeas's planning.

"Does she trust you?"

"I've saved her life two or three times now; I think I've earned it."

"Will she trust you when she finds out about Bria?" Brex felt his blood freeze, but he scoffed at Amadeas.

"She knows I helped Bria escape from Zaire's. What about it?"

"Does she know that Bria is dead because of you?"

"How do you know about that?" Brex snarled, jerking on the chains, making the rock around the ring crumble ever so slightly. The old Tallpian smirked at the show of force. "How the hell do you know about Bria?" he asked again.

Amadeas chuckled. "I have sources you couldn't even dream of. I know much more about you, Brexler Carrow, than you could ever imagine." Brex had no response. Amadeas smiled maliciously. "I wonder how Kallideia will feel when she learns that the girl paid you, only for you to abandon her, no wait; you didn't just abandon her, did you? All Kallideia will hear is that you sold out the girl to save your own skin when the going got tough."

"I...—" Brex tried to argue but the day in question surged back, far clearer than Brex ever wanted it to be. He had known Bria for a few years, from his visits to Zaire's. A pretty little Xoian, she had been stolen from her homeworld as an infant, her jewel-like appearance making her very valuable to someone like Zaire. Brex remembered that her diamond-like skin had a particular way of sparkling when she laughed, which was not often. While Zaire was a kind master, Bria craved her homeworld more than people on Landife craved water. Over the years, she had amassed a small fortune, stealing coins here and selling trinkets there. When she finally had enough money, she approached Brex, knowing he would help her for a price. They were less than a day away from her homeworld of Xoi when Adyta was hit by drifters; brutal, bloodthirsty marauders who scavenged on the farthest edges of the galaxy. Captured and brought aboard the drifter's ship, Brex was sure they were both going to die. But the drifters were far more affected by Bria's beauty, and a fight quickly broke out over which of them had the rights to her first. In the midst of their arguement, Brex disarmed the captor holding his chains. Having a choice between facing down an entire drifter crew and surely dying, or fleeing, Brex made the split-second decision and fled back to Adyta when the drifters set themselves on Bria. He had made the mistake of glancing over his shoulder to see if he was being pursued and instead all he saw were Bria's topaz-tinted eyes staring over the shoulder of one of her captors as he raped her, her eyes begging him to save her. Instead, he had ducked his head and ran. It was a mistake that would haunt him for the rest of his life, and he could still hear her screams in his nightmares. He had told no one the story, hoping to put it behind him. It was the guilt that followed that drove him to leave the Brotherhood. Not only had he betrayed Bria, but he had betrayed everything that the organization stood for. Even when Kain had asked, Brex hadn't been able to bring himself to tell his mentor. The shame burned red-hot once again. He had hoped no one would ever find out.

"How will Kallideia feel, I wonder," Amadeas asked, jerking Brex back to the present, "to know that Bria trusted you to help her return home safely and, in the end, you gave her up to save your own skin? The girl died, screaming in agony, ravaged by drifters as you ducked and ran away like a coward. Do you think she'll trust you after that?" *"How do I know you won't turn around and sell me to Arlo to save your own skin?"* Gaia's voice rang in Brex's head. She had asked him that question when they landed on Cunat. Fear surged through his middle.

"I'll tell her," Brex said, trying not to let the panic creep into his voice. "I'll tell her what happened." But Amadeas only smiled.

"Oh, I'm sorry. Did I not mention it? I already told her." Brex felt his mind fragment and shatter. No. Gaia. She would be heartbroken; she would never trust him again. It was like being stabbed in the gut, more painful than Brex ever imagined possible. "She was very upset, as you can imagine. I comforted her as best I could, but she was crying as though her heart would break." Amadeas didn't even trouble himself to hide the glee in his voice.

"May the gods damn you, Amadeas. I'm going—"

"You're going to, what? Kill an unarmed man? Not even your misfit, pitiful excuse of a Brotherhood would approve of that. Good luck explaining yourself out of this one." Amadeas gave Brex one last contemptuous look before sweeping from the room. A few minutes after he was gone, a Tallpian soldier Brex was not familiar with, entered the cell and unlocked the manacles around Brex's wrists. He was hauled to his feet and strong-armed from the cell. As soon as they reached daylight, Brex yanked his arm from the guard's grip. Surprisingly, the man let him go. After throwing a dark look over his shoulder at the passive-faced soldier, Brex hurried away into the sunlight towards Gaia's cottage.

"Gaia," he called as pushed through the door without knocking. "Gaia, we—"

"How dare you?" she shouted, snatching up a small vase from the vanity near her bed and throwing it at him. Brex, caught completely unaware, caught the glass vessel in the side of the head.

Growling in pain, he glared at her. "What the hell, Gaia?" he demanded, rubbing his temple, his hand coming away smeared with blood.

"How dare you come back here after what you did?" she shrieked, her dark eyes heavy with tears. She leaned back against the vanity, one hand on her chest as she gasped.

Brex watched her, shame and fury searing their way through his bones. "Gaia, I—" but she held up a regal hand, cutting him off as she fought back tears.

"I don't care to listen to anything you might have to say, Brexler Carrow." She swept him a queenly glare. "Get out."

"Gaia, wait, you have to listen—"

"I told you, I don't care what you have to say."

"Gaia!" he shouted, catching her off guard. "You have to listen to me!" he said. She couldn't bring herself to answer, but could only glare contemptuously. "I'm sorry but—"

"You think that you can come back and just say sorry, after something like that?"

"I wasn't—"

"I don't care what your excuses are." She fixed him with a glare that could have frozen steel. "I have nothing to say to you Brexler. Get out."

"Gaia….—" She fixed her onyx-colored eyes on him, and he saw the queen she was destined to be.

"You are dismissed, Carrow. We no longer have need of your services." A beat passed before Brex could bring himself to speak.

"You're sending me away?" Brex asked in disbelief. How had this happened? What had Amadeas done?

"You heard me. Get out. I never want to see you again."

"Gaia, why—" but she turned her back on him, cutting off his words.

"I have nothing more to say to you," she repeated.

"Damn it, woman, listen to me! Amadeas—"

"That is enough!" she shouted, rounding back on him. "There is nothing in this galaxy that will absolve what you've done. Go." His heart breaking and pride (and temple) stinging, Brex gave her one long last stare, but she refused to meet his eyes. He sighed once before turning his back on her and marching out the door, slamming it as hard as he could behind him.

Brex was halfway across the compound in a blind march before he rebounded off a tall figure with a shock of red hair.

"Hey!" Leona grabbed his arms, trying to stay upright, but he pushed past her. "What the hell, Brex?" she demanded, but he kept walking without answering.

Slamming his way into the barracks, Brex saw his men all jump to attention, but he ignored them. White-hot rage seared through his veins, and it was all he could do to keep walking. He pushed his way into his small room. He didn't have much: just a few changes of clothes and his weapons. He was stuffing his pants into a rucksack when Auggie pushed through the door.

"What is going on, Brex?" he demanded, standing in the doorway. "Leona said something…." Brex turned on his friend as he spoke, unable to keep the grief from his expression. Auggie trailed off, unsure.

"She threw me out, so I'm gone." Whatever Auggie had been expecting, clearly that was not it.

"What? Is that why you're bleeding?"

"Amadeas told Gaia about Bria, and she threw me out after throwing a vase at me. So I'm leaving."

"Wait, what? How can you leave? We're about to invade—"

"The Brotherhood is about to invade. I don't have to do shit. If she doesn't want me here, then fine, I won't be here."

"I don't get it. She threw you out just because you helped Bria escape?" Brex felt a knife twist in his gut. Auggie still didn't know the truth. No one did, or so he had thought, until Amadeas had proven him wrong.

"There's more to the story than you think. Let's just say I fucked up big time."

"Still," his friend said, "it's not like you killed her or anything." Anger made Brex spin around to face Auggie.

"See, that's where you're wrong, Auggie. I did, I did kill her. I may not have pulled the trigger, but I left her for dead, which is just as bad. Amadeas told Gaia, and now she won't have anything to do with me. Good riddance at this point." Auggie knew the rage was real, but so was Brex's heartbreak.

"Just talk to her—"

"I tried!" yelled Brex, rounding on Auggie again. "I tried, but she won't listen to a word I have to say. She ordered me out, so I'm out."

"So you're just leaving?" Distaste made Auggie's voice flat.

"You guys don't need me for this. You guys don't need me at all."

"Brex—"

"I said no, Auggie. You guys stay. Help her win back that cursed throne if you want, but I'll be damned if I stay where I'm clearly not wanted." With his rucksack packed, Brex buckled his holster around his hips before staring at Auggie. Auggie could see the pain in his best friend's face.

"Maybe just try—"

"No. I may be nothing but a hired gun, but I'm not stupid."

"Like hell you aren't."

"What?"

"Don't you see? Amadeas is getting exactly what he wants! He wanted to drive a wedge between you and Gaia, and he's done it! And because of your stupid pride, you refuse to try and work things out with the woman you love."

"I don't care anymore, Auggie. I tried, but I'm not going to get burned twice. Besides," his voice was ironic and bitter. "It was a royal command."

"Brexler. Can't remember the last time I heard from you." The lilting female voice was dry.

"Hello, Mia. It's been a while."

"What have you been doing?"

"The usual stuff."

"Where have you been?"

"You know, here and there."

"What do you want, Brex? You never call me unless you need a favor."

"I need a place to crash for a while."

"What have you done now?"

"Doesn't matter. I just need to lay low for a few days until I can get some shit figured out."

"Well, you know where the key is."

Brex's landing on Dail was quiet. Mia's house was on the outskirts of a small mining community, and most of the planet's activity was below ground. The sun was just setting and had tinted the waving grassland around the small ranch house a brilliant red. Retrieving the key from its hook under the eave, he let himself into the foyer. No sign of Mia's husband Marcus, which was a good thing, but Brex could hear humming and the sounds of cooking issuing from the kitchen towards the back of the house. He stepped into the narrow doorway and smiled at the dark-haired young woman who stood with an apron tied around her slim waist as she removed a dish from the oven.

"Hello, gorgeous," he said, keeping his voice low. Mia whirled around, uttering a soft scream.

"Brex! What are you trying to do, scare me half to death?" She set the dish on the counter before rushing across the room to wrap her arms around his neck. He gripped her svelte form in a tight hug.

"You look great, Mia." She slid him an amused smile as she pulled away, and her dark blue eyes flashed.

"It's good to see you. It's not often my big brother makes an appearance."

Mia was the only sister Brex was still in contact with. After their difficult childhood, most of their siblings had gone their separate ways, but he saw Mia every few years. She let him crash in her tiny spare bedroom whenever he needed to escape from the real world. But it had been years - almost five to the day—since they'd last seen each other.

Mia let her gaze rove over him. "You look like shit, by the way," she said, gesturing for him to sit at the tiny, round table tucked against the windows. Her kitchen was small, cozy. Domesticity fit Mia, but no matter how hard Brex tried, he could not fit the image of Gaia into something similar. She would never be barefoot and pregnant in any kitchen, let alone his.

"You have no idea how many times I've heard that in the last few days," he said wearily, dropping into a seat.

"Well, what is it this time, debts or women?"

"Both. Neither. I don't know." He ran his fingers through his hair, looking up at his sister, and she could see the lines of pain etched into his face.

"Oh no, what'd you do? It's bad this time isn't it?" She moved to the cupboard without waiting for his answer and pulled out a dark bottle.

"I'm pretty much scum," he said with a bitter laugh before he slammed back the shot of whiskey she handed him.

"It can't be that bad." She settled at the table next to him and waited expectantly.

"The woman I'm in love with threw me out. Because of what happened with Bria. And I let her." Mia's mouth tightened. "But all I need right now is to sleep and hope all of this is a nightmare that I'll wake up from tomorrow."

The sound of the waves lapping against the supports of Gaia's cottage was the only sound she could stand to listen to. Over the waves, she could hear soft whispers outside her door.

"Has she said anything?"

"Nothing."

"She needs to eat."

"She won't see anyone."

"It's been almost a week."

"What are we going to do?" Gaia grabbed a nearby stone statuette and slung it at the door, causing it to shatter against the wood. The voices quieted, and Gaia grumbled, rolling over to try and get some sleep.

"Gaia?" The voice jerked her awake right as she had been slipping back into a doze. She looked around for something else to throw but had already exhausted her reachable supply of breakable ammunition. "Gaia, its Leona. We need to talk." There was a pause. "It's important." Gaia was getting ready to order her away when the other woman pushed through the door and shut it firmly behind her, a tray of food balanced in one hand. Immediately, she fixed a firm stare on Gaia. Her queen's face was pinched, dark shadows under her eyes showing mauve against her pale skin.

"Gaia, when was the last time you ate?" Leona demanded. Gaia ignored the question and rolled over in bed, her back to the room. Leona sighed hard through her nose before marching across the room and grabbing Gaia's arm, rolling her over so they were eye-to-eye.

"You may be upset, you may be heartbroken, but for gods' sake, you need to eat! This isn't just about you anymore!" Gaia's answering smile was bitter, but she wouldn't look Leona in the face.

"Maybe it should be," she said, her voice disconnected and far away. "It's ruining everything."

"It will be your child and your heir Gaia. You cannot do this to yourself."

"I didn't do this." Gaia's voice was breathy and childish. "This isn't my fault."

"If you both fade away, it will be."

"He left," Gaia said, looking Leona in the eye for the first time. "How could he leave?"

"I don't know, Gaia, and I'm sorry. But you have to take care of yourself." Leona was smart enough not to point out that Brex had left on Gaia's orders.

"All I want to do is sleep."

"As long as you eat first, that's fine." Gaia grumbled under her breath but finally sat upright and allowed Leona to slide the tray into her lap. Leona planted herself on Gaia's feet and crossed her arms across her chest, making it clear she was going nowhere. Over the next several minutes, the only sound to be heard was cutlery against china as Gaia ate. As soon as she pushed the tray away, Leona removed it to the floor before joining Gaia on the bed again.

"Gaia, I know you are struggling, but there is something else." The dead look in her queen-to-be's eyes scared Leona.

"I do not care."

"This is important. Amadeas is planning something."

Gaia sighed and waved a hand to dismiss the other woman. "He's always plotting. He is always planning. I no longer care."

"This is different. Lathan said that they are going to try to declare you incompetent." Gaia stared blankly. Leona tried to hide a sigh of exasperation. She didn't know how to explain just how much danger Gaia was in. "If Amadeas succeeds in doing so, not only could he have you jailed, but he might make an attempt to take the throne himself." Gaia felt a dull flicker of rage in her chest, but it did little to penetrate the ice around her heart.

"Tell him he is welcome to have it. I want nothing to do with him or that throne ever again."

Gaia moved to lay down, but Leona grabbed her arm and tugged her upright. "Don't you understand?" she demanded, her fingers digging into Gaia's skin. "Amadeas is the reason we are even here! He was the one who first plotted to kill your father all those years ago and set this whole war into motion. He knew Nuweydon only needed to be prodded to commit murder without hesitation. He planned to rule through Nuweydon, but he underestimated just how dangerous and mad Nuweydon is. Once it was clear he had no power over his nephew, he set his sights on the next closest heir, who just happens to be you. Now that you're proving unsuitable,—" Leona sneered her way through the word,—"—Amadeas is trying to find a way to remove the last obstacle between him and the throne. I think he's finally given up the pretenses."

"How do you even know that?" Gaia asked dimly. She couldn't even begin to contemplate the implications of her friend's words. Her father's death seemed so far away, so far removed from where she was now. Had he truly died because of his uncle's influence?

"Lathan," she said shrugging. "He was close to Amadeas for years after his own father was killed in the purge, but in the last few days, he has begun to see a whole new side of him come to light. Lathan has made it clear that he does not approve of Amadeas's methods, but Amadeas won't listen. Our loyalty lies with you, Gaia. Not Amadeas."

"Why are you just telling me this now?" Why hadn't they told her this when they first met Amadeas? Dyla had given Gaia her warning the day they'd been rescued, but why, if this was such common knowledge, hadn't she been told? Leona seemed to read Gaia's mind.

"We thought that Amadeas might have changed when he declared his interest in rescuing you. We all thought that seeing what Nuweydon was capable of might have set him straight. But it is clear he hasn't changed. He has always resented being the second son, passed over for the crown on multiple occasions, same as Nuweydon. He's been trying to keep his saint's hat by making it look like he is helping you retake your birthright. Now that it is clear he won't be able to rule through you, he is resorting to martyrdom." Leona placed a hand at her breast and adopted the low, lugubrious tones Amadeas was known to use. "'Only for the good of the people would I take the throne'," she mimicked with a nasty expression on her face. "'I would never consider it otherwise.' The only problem is as much as our people hate Nuweydon, it is nothing compared to the loathing they had for Amadeas. They blame him for the death of Yehuda, all those years ago. It would start an entirely new civil war that would drive our race to extinction." Gaia struggled to wrap her mind around the new developments.

"I still don't understand why I wasn't told," she snapped, giving Leona an icy glare. The other woman offered her a gentle shrug but didn't answer the question.

"Lathan also thinks Brex leaving might have something to do with Amadeas, but he can't prove it." Gaia felt her heart stutter at the mention of the Brotherhood's leader. "He said that Amadeas was plotting something but never gave any specifics."

"We know why he left, Leona." Gaia's voice was a snarl. "He clearly wants nothing to do with me or his child."

"What if that wasn't true?"

"Why are you telling me this?" Gaia demanded instead.

"If Amadeas ends up on the throne, he will be even worse than Nuweydon. Amadeas thought he was going to be able to manipulate you into being his puppet queen. He would rule through you. But now he is working to have you declared unfit. Afterward, he will probably have you killed and just take the throne himself. You have to do something. We must stop him."

"Every single horrible thing that has happened to me in this lifetime has been brought about by him," Gaia said, and Leona nodded in agreement. She grabbed Gaia's hands in hers and stared beseechingly into her face.

"You have got to come back. You cannot let him win."

"I can't allow him to live, not after what he has done." Gaia reached for the knife she kept at her bedside.

"No!" Leona said, grabbing the knife away and holding it behind her back out of Gaia's reach. "No. If you levy this against him, he will call you mad, addled, sick of the mind. It will only give him the ammunition he needs to move forward with this charade. Please. You need to come back and come back stronger than ever. If you take back your power, we have a chance to stop him. We cannot let him win this, not when he has won at everything else."

"It's been almost a week, Brex. This is getting out of hand." Brex lay face down on the narrow bed in the spare room, window shades closed against the bright sun outside. He opened one eye. Mia stood in the doorway, hands on slim hips, staring around at the mess. Whiskey bottles littered the floor, and whole plates of food sat on the dresser, uneaten.

"Forget out of hand; it is fucking disgusting." The voice of Mia's husband cut through the stale air.

"Marcus! You are not helping."

"He may be your brother, Mia, but enough is enough." Brex heard the heavy tread stomp away. Mia's dancer-like steps entered his room, and there was a soft creak as she sat at the foot of the bed.

"Why did you marry that dick?" Brex asked, his voice muffled by the mattress.

"He takes very good care of me."

"Do you love him?"

"I don't think you're allowed to lecture me about love, Brex."

"He's still a dick."

"He's also right."

"Hey!" he protested, finally sitting up. Mia raised her dark eyebrows at the giant stain marking the front of his t-shirt. Brex looked down and grimaced before pulling the shirt over his head and tossing it into a corner. Mia wrinkled her nose at him in disgust.

"Gods, Brex, you're only making his point for him. Do you have any idea how bad you smell right now? This has got to stop. You cannot wallow here in misery and filth for the rest of your life. You need to man up and make a choice."

"I already made one. And look where it got me."

"Make another one then." Mia's voice was steely. Brex flinched. "I don't care what it is, but living in my spare room reeking of booze and sweat is not one of the options."

"Since when do you snarl like that?" Mia had always been so soft and gentle. It was one of the reasons why Brex had worked so hard to protect her when they were kids. She gave a sad shake of her head.

"I had to get my backbone from somewhere."

"And you got it from who, Mom?" Brex asked in confusion.

"No, you idiot, I got it from you." She sighed. "Brex, this isn't like you. I understand your pride is wounded, but there is more to it than that." She surveyed him with a keen eye. "You love her. I can see it as plain as day. But if you love her, you should fight for her, no matter what she might have said. Instead, you've spent the last five days wallowing in whiskey and your own dross, hiding from the rest of the galaxy at your sister's house." She paused. "You're heartbroken."

"Hey, I am not, I'm just trying to plan my next move."

"Brex, you haven't done a damn thing since you've gotten here but get drunk and sleep. You finally found the one woman who makes you happy, and you walked away because you got your feelings hurt."

"So what if I did?" he asked with a sarcastic, lopsided smile, spreading his arms wide. "But I've fucked it up good now. I could never go back. Gaia will never forgive me."

"Do you love her?"

"More than anything," he admitted. Mia fixed him with another steely glare and pointed a finger at him.

"Then get up off your ass and prove it!" His face held for a moment and then crumpled.

"I wish I could, Mia. But I can't. I've let her down. I can't go back now, not since she threw me out. And not just her, but my Brothers too. Kain was wrong. I wasn't built for this." Brex flung himself back down on the bed and turned his face to the wall.

"Gaia!" Amadeas, so surprised to see her appear silhouetted against the morning sun, was shocked into using her preferred name. "You look well." She smirked at the surprise in his tone and gave him a saccharine smile, shaking her pearl-colored hair away from her face as she marched into the room. Her storm-colored eyes surveyed the surprised expressions around the room with bitter amusement. Six days had passed since Brexler left, and Leona finally convinced her that she needed to return and take command—her very life depended on it. There were five days until the invasion, and she couldn't allow Amadeas to call the shots any longer, not if she wanted to survive to take back her father's throne.

She strode across the hall, dressed head-to-toe in her usual black, Leona only two steps behind her. Amadeas's eyes lit on Leona's suspiciously passive face before returning to Gaia.

"Thank you, Great-Uncle. You sound rather surprised." She stood at the head of the table, next to the chair that

Amadeas currently occupied. He hesitated, giving her a dark glance before removing himself and taking a chair on the side of the table.

"Absolutely not. We were simply concerned for your health. But it appears that you are once again well, thank the gods." Gaia took her place at the head of the breakfast table as an attendant pulled out the chair for her. She sat gracefully before staring down the table at Amadeas, locking her grey eyes to his.

"I have been most neglectful of my affairs this last week. However, it will not continue." She could tell from the look on his face that he was waiting for an apology for her disappearing act, but she wasn't about to give him one.

"That is reassuring to hear. We would have carried on in your absence –"

"I am sure you would have. Hence my return." She shot him a dark look before smiling back at the rest of the Tallpians around the table who sat, enjoying their breakfasts and watching the exchange. "There is nothing to fear. I have not given up my desire to return my father's bloodline to the throne. The line of Yehuda does not run from a fight." The look she fixed on Amadeas was one of frozen steel.

"Brex, you have a call."

"Unless it's Dwar himself, tell them I'm not here."

"I don't think even the god of the underworld wants anything to do with you right now, Brex."

"Thanks, Mia," Brex shot back sarcastically.

"Take the call."

"No."

"It's Auggie."

"Fuck," Brex said, finally sitting up to look at his sister. "Did you tell him I was here?"

She gave him an exasperated look. "Of course not. He called me. He's not stupid you know. He knows you well enough to guess you'd be hiding out here."

"I don't want to talk to him," Brex mumbled, turning away.

"You're talking to him if I have to tie you to a chair first. Man up, Brex."

"Jeeze, when did you turn into such a hard-ass?"

"I'm only like this when the people I love are being stupid." She smiled coldly at him before thrusting a telescreen into his hand and marching from the room.

Auggie's pale face stared up at him, and Brex watched as his typically jovial best friend regard him coldly, his pale blue eyes hooded. "Brex."

"Auggie."

"What the fuck, man?" Auggie exploded his normal, easy-going demeanor nowhere to be seen. "I can't believe you actually left! Kain puts you in charge and you just bail?".

Brex winced "Hey, listen, you know there is more—"

"Don't care, dude."

"That isn't fair—"

"Neither is what you did to Gaia."

"Listen to me—"

"No. After what you did, I don't think I need to."

"Auggie—"

"Shut the fuck up and listen to me, Brex." Brex obeyed and shut his mouth. "You're my best friend, but I've got to admit this is low even for you. Running out on Gaia is one thing, and we'll get to that, but first and foremost you left your Brothers. You. Our new leader. Tucked his tail and ran without so much as a word of explanation. Why should we follow a man like that?" Auggie demanded. Brex was wholly taken aback. Never had he seen Auggie so mad. He hadn't given the Brotherhood much thought as he'd fled, his thoughts only on Gaia. But he had betrayed his Brothers, the men who trusted him to lead them and take care of them. The shame that welled up in his chest almost made him physically ill.

"You don't under—"

"Secondly," Auggie said, overriding him. "You took off and left the woman that you swore to protect at the mercy of her family. Not to mention you broke her heart." Auggie narrowed his eyes and scrutinized Brex's stubbled face.

"If you recall, she threw me out."

"And you just went? The Brexler I know would have stayed and fought it out."

"Fought it out? She threw a vase at me."

"Coward."

"I won't stay where I'm unwanted."

"She loves you, and you love her. I'm not sure how that makes you unwanted."

"Amadeas—"

"If you believe anything Amadeas tells you, you're an even bigger idiot than I thought."

"Auggie, she wouldn't listen to me."

"Then you make her listen."

"How?"

"You'll figure it out."

"No way, I'm not coming back."

"You have to. Amadeas is planning something."

"How do you know that?"

"I'm not nearly as stupid as you are. Amadeas realized that if he had you killed, Gaia would murder him the minute she found out. Making you leave of your own volition puts you out of her heart and out of her bed. Now she has no one to listen to but him." He sighed. Brex could suddenly see the heavy burden he had left on his best friend's shoulders and felt the guilt rush through him. "We're trying to support her, but he keeps trying to shut us out of meetings.

Lathan and I are doing our best, but Amadeas is a crafty old bastard."

"Lathan? He wants nothing to do with us. He's just Amadeas's shadow."

"Not anymore. Things are changing Brex, you need to get back here and help Gaia."

"She doesn't want my help. Amadeas is her family, remember?"

"That's a bullshit excuse, and you know it."

"Who cares? Let her be Amadeas's puppet."

"If she doesn't pull out of this funk, he'll take control with or without her."

"Is she ok?"

"I'm not telling you shit."

"Why not?" he demanded, suddenly angry with his best friend.

"Because," Auggie said, fixing Brex with a steely glare, not unlike Mia's. "You left. You chose to walk out on the one girl in the entire galaxy who is the perfect match for you. You don't deserve to know."

"Just tell me she's ok."

"What the hell do you think? Do you think she's doing ok? You're obviously not," Auggie said with another dark look.

"What did Mia tell you?"

"Nothing. I know you, Brex, much better than you think I do."

"Why did you call, Auggie?"

"I've been looking all over for you, and it finally dawned on me that there is only one place you go when you really feel like scum, and that is your sister's."

"Scum doesn't even begin to cover it."

"Good," Auggie snapped. "Because frankly after this shit, I don't think you deserve Gaia."

"Then why are you calling?" Auggie shook his head, looking like a man stuck between a rock and a hard place.

"I think you deserve to rot, but you need to come back here."

"I can't. Not after this."

"You don't have a choice. If you truly care about Gaia, you'll get your ass on that ship and be here by sunset."

"Why?"

"Amadeas is planning to kill Gaia."

*The Previous Day*

"What do you mean, kill her?"

"That's all I heard. It was in a link to Jio, who is still on Meidonna." Ravi's pale face was flushed as he looked at Auggie's skeptical expression. "Listen, I don't know if he was serious, but it sounds like he is trying to make sure she dies in battle, even if by friendly fire. If he is serious, Gaia is in danger." He hesitated. "Why would Amadeas go through all of this trouble to save her, just to decide to kill her?" The Tallpian looked uncomfortable at the thought of Amadeas plotting to kill his great-niece.

"Something's happened that's forcing his hand," Auggie mused. He glanced at Shaw. "Whatever it is, it can't be good." Shaw looked up, speculative.

"We all know that he wants to control her once she is queen. What could possibly motivate him to suddenly want her dead?"

"All I know is that we can't let that happen," Auggie said, reaching for a nearby telelink. "Thanks, Ravi," he added. The Tallpian nodded.

"Amadeas may be my general, but Gaia will be my queen one day. I know where my loyalty lies."

✍

"You don't have a choice, Brex," Auggie snapped. "I don't care what she said to you—if you don't get back here tonight, you'll hate yourself for the rest of your life."

✍

"Well I hope it doesn't take another monumental fuck-up for you to come visit," Mia said, wrapping her arms around Brex. He pursed his mouth at her, but she smiled. "You know I love you, Brex. I'm proud of you."

"Thanks, Mia," he said, returning the hug. "And thanks for putting up with me for the last few days."

"I'll probably never get the smell of bourbon out of the drapes, but that's ok." Her dark eyes flashed at him as she shrugged. "I'm just glad you're doing the right thing."

"You were right," he said, mirroring her shrug. "I don't think Gaia will ever forgive me, but I have to try."

✍

It may have been her discovery of Amadeas's plot to remove her from power that brought Gaia surging back to her former energy, but Leona was careful to avoid mentioning the dark-haired leader of the Outer Rim Brotherhood. When he was brought up, Gaia alternated between heart-broken, soul-wrenching tears, and pure, unadulterated fury. Unfortunately, neither was very productive.

"What am I going to do?" Gaia whispered later in the evening of the day she returned to court. She sat, hands resting on her stomach, as Leona helped her get ready for bed.

"You need to get some rest. Try not to worry so much right now, and we'll figure everything out as it happens."

"Leona," Gaia said, looking up at her friend, "thank you."

"Of course, Gaia. It is my pleasure."

"I mean it. You had no reason to be so kind to me. Thank you."

Leona smiled at her future queen. "Anyone can see that you will do great things in your life, Gaia. I am proud to call you my friend."

Ten minutes later, Gaia was sound asleep, and Leona slipped from the room, nodding at the two Brotherhood members who still stood watch outside the door. Despite the departure of their leader, Auggie had kept the rotation active, making sure Gaia was guarded around the clock.

Leona was marching across one of the rope bridges when she spotted the curly mop of copper hair she was looking for. Auggie's face darkened when he saw her worried expression but changed his course to meet her.

"I need to talk to you." They both spoke at the same time and laughed.

"You first," Leona said.

"I've had word that Amadeas is trying to have Gaia killed."

"What?" Leona demanded. She had not been fond of Amadeas on Meidonna—he had always appeared far too enthusiastic for Nuweydon's rule—but now she felt hatred flood her mouth like poison in the mouth of a viper. From having her declared unfit to outright murder in just a day?

"We aren't sure what's caused it, but I guess there is a plan to make sure she dies on Meidonna during the fight." Suddenly, Leona had a sneaking suspicion as to what might have pushed Amadeas over the edge. How had he found out? Only she and Gaia and Brex knew….

"I have an idea, and you're not going to be happy about it."

"Well, that isn't everything."

"What else?" Leona demanded, wondering if it could get any worse.

"Brex is coming back." Yes, apparently it could.

# Chapter Twenty-Two

Brex passed through the last layers of Miwarma's atmosphere and landed his ship on the floating airfield as the sun made its way past the horizon, the ocean surface throwing off diamond glints of light. The broad green spread out in front of him like a rug, the color reminding him of Gaia's eyes. He could see a trio of figures waiting at the edge of the grass, lit by the orange glow of the setting sun. Lathan, tall and blonde, stood sandwiched between his bewitchingly pretty red-headed wife and Auggie, all of them wearing identical, cold expressions on their faces. He steeled his nerve. He knew there was no welcome home celebration waiting.

"You can do this," Brex whispered to himself as he buckled his holsters around his waist and disembarked. They waited for him, making him march across the entire field to reach them. Reaching them, he opened his mouth to speak when Lathan stepped forward with languid grace and slugged him in the jaw. The blow was like a hammer strike, and it knocked Brex to the ground, making his whole head spin. Cuffing blood from his split lip, he glared up at them from the ground. When they didn't move, he struggled to his feet alone.

Looking at the three stony faces in front of him, he sighed. "I guess I deserved that."

"I was in favor of feeding you to the sharks," Leona snapped. "But I was overruled." She shot a facetious smile at her husband, who ignored her.

"You understand that if you run out on her again, I reserve the right to hunt you down and murder you with my bare hands," Lathan threatened him. "And you know what I'm capable of."

"If I don't get to him first," Auggie growled. Brex gave his oldest friend a disbelieving look.

"Hey—"

"We'll work out our issues later, Brex, but you need to be brought up to speed right away. Some things have changed since you left."

"I figured. How is Gaia?"

"She doesn't know you're here yet," Leona said. "We think you should go see her first."

"By myself?" His voice almost broke.

Auggie laughed coldly. "You should be scared, dude. Real scared."

"Getting back in her good graces is only the first step, but it is the most important."

"Hell. Might as well get it over with then."

"One last thing," Leona said, and with a strike like a snake, she reached out and yanked on the belt for his holsters, ripping the guns from his hips.

"Hey! I might need those!"

"Oh don't worry," she said, stepping out of his reach, "I'll keep them plenty safe and give them back, provided you survive." The glint in her eye was far too satisfied at the thought of Gaia killing him. Brex shook his head but moved away, crossing the rope bridges in the fading light towards the little bungalow. He nodded at the two sentries on duty in front of Gaia's cottage. He ground his teeth in frustration—not at Auggie, he would be eternally grateful that his friend had stepped up to care for Gaia in his absence—but at himself for being so proud that he had run out on the woman he loved and the men he led instead of fighting it out. Like Kain would have done. Both sentries looked at him in shock, but he shook his head, motioning for them to remain silent. They stepped aside and let him pass. He hesitated at the door: Should he knock or just walk in? Finally, he tapped softly on the door-frame as he pushed through. Gaia sat at her vanity table, framed in the setting sun's light, her back to him as she brushed her pearl-tinted hair, staring into the mirror. She slowly set down the brush and glanced over her shoulder, her beautiful grey eyes listless. The look of pure shock that etched itself onto her face when she recognized him would have been comical in any other situation, but Brex had never felt less like laughing in his life. Her mouth tightened as they stared at one another before she suddenly erupted to her feet, screaming at him.

"What the hell are you doing here?" she shouted, glancing around for a weapon. Brex crossed the room in two long strides and wrapped his arms around her. She shrieked and yanked herself out of his grasp, shoving him away. "How dare you come back here after what you did?"

"Gaia, you are going to listen to me. I am going to explain everything that happened—"

"No!"

"Yes!" Brex shouted back. She took a surprised step backward. "Gods be damned, Gaia, I love you!" Saying it aloud wasn't as hard as he would have imagined. In fact, he felt lighter at the admission. But it wasn't what Gaia wanted to hear.

"If you loved me, you wouldn't have left."

"You threw me out."

"You still should have stayed."

"You aren't making any sense, woman!"

"I don't care what your excuses are."

"You shouldn't," he said, shrugging, and he could see she was caught off guard. "But you are going to listen to me explain anyway."

"I don't—"

"Damn your stubborn pride, Gaia! Listen to me. Hear me out, and if you still don't want anything to do with me when I'm finished, I will walk back out that door and never bother you again." He hoped, with all of his heart, that wouldn't end up being the result. "But until you have heard everything I have to say, I'm not leaving." She sat, folding her arms across her chest, glaring at him. He figured that was as close to getting her permission to speak as he was going to get. He marshaled his thoughts quickly and began to speak; giving voice to the story he had played over and over in his head for the last five years. "I want to tell you the story of someone named Bria. It was five years ago. I told you I met her at Zaire's—what are you looking at me like that for?" Gaia was gaping at him already, mouth open in offended silence.

"You think this has to do with another woman?" she demanded. Brex felt confusion swamp him. Of course, it all had to do with Bria.

"Well, yeah. I mean I thought I told you about her—"

"Brex, what are you talking about?"

"What are you talking about?" he asked, thoroughly confused. "You said you could never forgive me for what I did."

"You blamed me! You said it was my fault and that you wanted nothing to do with it."

"What are you saying, Gaia? How could it be your fault? I didn't even know you five years ago."

"Brex, you aren't making any sense!"

"Neither are you!" Feeling the frustration grating at his nerves, Brex tried to take a deep breath. "Explain what you're talking about, Gaia." She fixed him with a stare, her grey eyes liquid and threatening to spill over. "What did I blame you for?"

"When I told you. About the baby—"

"The what?" The small bungalow was suddenly airless.

"Brex, I'm pregnant."

As Gaia watched, the blood drained from Brex's face. No, she couldn't go through this again. She rose to throw him out but froze when he spoke.

"Are you sure?" His voice was off, wrong. He was staring at her in such wonder; she couldn't believe this was the same man who had stormed from her room six days ago, swearing he would have nothing to do with her or the child.

"I'm positive. I told you that six days ago. Right before you stormed out of here, swearing you never wanted to see me again."

"Gaia, I would never—"

"You did!"

"I wouldn't!" he shouted back. "Gaia, six days ago Amadeas attacked me and locked me in one of the cells. He left me there overnight and only came to see me the next morning. He offered to pay me to leave you, and then he blackmailed me when I wouldn't take the money."

"Blackmailed you? With what?"

Brex sighed. "Bria. The girl I told you about—Zaire's slave that I helped to escape. I didn't get her home like I promised. We were attacked. I managed to fight my way free but at the price of Bria's life." He paused, his shoulders heavy, and Gaia could see the tears in his eyes. "I was so terrified that if you knew, you wouldn't trust me. I had a hard enough time convincing you to the first time around. I thought if you knew about her, you would expect me to do the same to you." Gaia paused. Hadn't she expected it, at first?

"I did expect it," she admitted.

"I would never. I told you that the first time."

"That had more to do with your honor as a thief—"

"Hey, I am not a—"

"Regardless," she said cutting across him, "You left."

"You threw me out!"

"I told you I was pregnant and you swore—"

"Gaia, how many times do I have to say it? That was not me!"

"If it wasn't you, then who was it?" The expression on Brex's face was clear he thought her stupid.

"Gaia, you belong to a shape-shifting race! Who do you think it was? Who would benefit most from us fighting?" It hadn't even occurred to her that it might not have been Brex who had thrown the pregnancy back in her face. If it had been Amadeas or one of his soldiers….

"Do you think…?"

The look on Brex's face was stormy. "I know it was." Before Gaia could answer, there was a knock at the door. Brex answered it, barely cracking it before pulling it wide open. Auggie and Leona stood waiting, framed in the soft mauve of twilight.

"We have a problem," Auggie said without preamble as he stepped into the room, Leona on his heels.

"What else could be going wrong?" Gaia snarled.

"Amadeas is coming," Auggie said, looking between Brex and Gaia's angry faces. "He heard Brex is back, and he is coming to tell you everything about Bria, Gaia."

"If we are going to keep you alive, we have to present a united front," Leona said. "I understand you two still have quite a bit to work out. You can be as mad at each other as you like in private, but for right now, your family needs to think that you two are still in love. We have to keep you safe, Gaia. This is the only way." Gaia glared at Brex with hard eyes, trying to find a fault in the plan.

"And you cannot say anything to Amadeas about his posing as me," Brex said, ignoring Auggie and Leona's confused faces. "For now, let's keep that to ourselves until we can definitively prove it."

"Fine," Gaia snapped. She glanced at Leona. "Go with Auggie, I'll be alright." Leona glared daggers at Brex before stomping through the door and disappearing into the oncoming night with Auggie. The door slammed hard.

"I am not happy about this," Gaia growled as Brex immediately began to unbutton his shirt. "What are you doing?" Gaia recoiled as Brex reached for her.

"I get that you're pissed at me—"

"Oh pissed does not begin to cover it, but please, continue," she offered sarcastically.

"Gods, I'd forgotten how stubborn you can be."

"That is your own fault," Gaia snapped back at him.

Brex sighed. "Gaia, please, I know you're angry with me, but you have to understand that wasn't me. I won't ask you to trust me, because I know you don't right now. I'm going to ask you to follow my lead instead. Let me get us through this." He glanced at her, his look pleading. "I'm trying to save your life."

"Fine," she snapped again. "What do you suggest?"

"Kallideia, I insist on speaking—what in the name of all the gods is going on here?" Amadeas stormed through Gaia's door without knocking before stopping short. Brex and Gaia were standing locked together in the center of the room, the straps of her sleeping gown slipping down her shoulders, Brex's shirt discarded on the floor. She had initially planned to just press her lips against Brex's—she was still livid from his rejection, real or not—that she didn't want to touch him. But when he had slanted his lips over hers and tunneled his fingers in her hair, she felt heat explode in the pit of her stomach, heat she hadn't felt in days. His tongue touched hers and the warmth raced through her, setting her nerves on fire, bringing her body back to life. She couldn't resist, and her fingers curled onto the edge of his pants, tugging him closer. It was with extreme reluctance that she pulled her lips away from his to deal with Amadeas. Without untangling Brex's finger's from her hair, Gaia turned a steel-colored glare over her shoulder at her great-uncle.

"Can I help you, Amadeas?" she demanded.

The old general's face shifted rapidly from red to purple to prune. "What is he doing here?" Amadeas thundered, pointing a finger at Brex. Brex offered a smug look over Gaia's head.

"Saying hello to the woman I love, what are you doing here?" he asked, deepening his drawl, knowing it annoyed the Tallpian.

"I warned you," he snarled at Brex as he took a step forward. Gaia cut him off.

"Brex has told me everything." Amadeas stopped in his tracks, his rage frozen on his face.

"I beg your pardon?"

"He told me the entire story about Bria. He apologized for leaving me in my time of need." She glared archly at Amadeas, so tempted to throw his failure in his face, but she managed to keep the words from spilling out. "I have forgiven him." Amadeas stood sputtering for a moment before regaining his composure.

"I do not feel that was a wise choice, Niece, but it is your choice to make." With an abrupt bow, Amadeas left the room, the door slamming behind him. The second the door closed,

Gaia wrenched herself from Brex's grip, but he was too busy staring after Amadeas to notice.

"He took that far too well," Brex mused, still watching the closed door.

"What is your point?" Gaia demanded, wiping her mouth on her arm.

Brex rolled his eyes at her. "No need to be so dramatic." He had felt her respond to his kiss, but he knew rubbing it in her face was not a wise idea.

"I am not happy about this."

"Clearly," he retorted. "But in case you've forgotten, I am trying to save your life, something I've been doing since the day I met you."

"You left me."

"You threw me out!"

"How can I trust that you won't leave again?"

"You think I'll ever leave you again after this?" His laugh was humorless. "Trust me when I say you're never getting rid of me now. I'm not about to let the woman I love go charging off to war carrying my child."

"Oh, so you are making my choices for me now too?"

"It's my child too!"

"And this is my war!"

"So you think it's perfectly ok to keep a secret like this, something we both have a stake in?"

"You mean like how you kept my heritage from me?" she demanded. Brex checked at that.

"It's not the same thing!"

"It absolutely is!"

"No, it is not. There is a life at stake here."

"There are thousands of lives at stake. Does one more make a difference?"

"Of course! It isn't safe for you or for the child."

"This is my choice."

"No, it's not."

"Be careful, Brexler," she warned him, her voice chilling. "You're dangerously close to turning into Amadeas and trying to make my choices for me." The insult hit home, and Brex's face flushed dark red.

"I am not trying to manipulate you," he growled. "I am trying to protect you! For the gods' sake, I love you!"

"If you truly love me, you won't stop me from fighting for my birthright."

"And what if something happens to you? I lose both the woman I love and my child?" His tone sent a thrum of reassurance through her, but she refused to let it show.

"Nothing is going to happen to me."

"You can't know that."

"I swear, Brex, you have to trust me." As she spoke, he burst into bitter laughter.

"You realize how ironic this is, right?" he demanded as he stopped pacing again to stare her down. "Telling me I need to trust you when you refuse to trust me?"

"You can't blame me for not wanting to!"

"I can and I will. I've told you, it wasn't me."

"I don't know if I can believe you!"

"Believe this!" Brex lunged forward and grabbed her, pressing his lips against hers. It was the same electric shock she had felt before, and it took every fiber of her being not to moan and collapse against him. She tried to push him away, but he kept his arms wrapped tightly around her, molding her lithe form to his rock-hard body. His kiss was aggressive but tender, demanding yet submissive. He was begging her to trust him again, to love him again. What she couldn't tell him—not yet, anyhow—was that she had never stopped loving him.

"Gaia," Brex spoke after pulling away slowly, "I told you before, that was not me. I would never react like that. And I'm back now, so you can continue to dwell on the fact that I left or accept that I am indeed human and made a mistake. I could have taken off into the wilds and never resurfaced, but instead, I'm back here, doing everything I can to help you." He hesitated, his eyes brushing over her midsection. "You and the kid." Gaia had no response and Brex sighed. "Get some rest," he said, pressing a soft kiss to her forehead before she could push him away. "We've got a lot to handle in the next few days." He shrugged back into his shirt and gave her one lingering look before slipping out the door and into the night.

"Well, that went well." Kyan chuckled. He had been relieved of guard duty as Brex left Gaia's bungalow and offered to accompany his commander back to the barracks.

Brex shot the kid a dark look. "That went well?" he asked incredulously. Kyan shrugged.

"She didn't even throw anything at you. I got hit by a bookend a couple days ago. You got off easy."

"She got me before I left," Brex said, touching the bruise on his temple.

"No offense, sir, but you deserve it." The kid shrugged again when Brex glanced at him.

"You don't seem mad about me leaving," Brex said, watching Kyan's expression.

"The whole Brotherhood is a little ticked," the young medic's voice didn't conceal his sarcasm, "but I figure you must have had a good reason." The kid looked him square in the eye. "I respect you, sir. I know you wouldn't do something like that unless it was really bad."

"Amadeas was blackmailing me," Brex admitted. He liked the young recruit and trusted him too.

"We figured as much. Auggie knew it was something big but didn't tell us much other than it had to do with someone named Bria."

"You know about that?"

"Everyone knows about that," Kyan said as they pushed through the doors to the barracks. Brex hung his head as they moved through the room.

"Gods did I fuck up."

"Sure," Kyan acknowledged, "but what are you going to do about it now?"

"Everything I can to fix it."

The next morning Gaia rose before the sun and scaled the wall in her back garden. She had discovered the small platform on her roof several days before and found it was a perfect place to sit and watch the sunrise. There was a war meeting after the morning meal, and all of her commanders would be attending. The Brotherhood and those loyal to them were meeting just after sunrise to formulate a plan of attack on Amadeas. Gaia had retreated to her roof for a brief respite before the work began. She couldn't remember the last time she had felt wholly at peace—actually, she could, she realized. It had been their first day on Miwarma, and the hours she and Brex had spent making love for the first time before he had opened his big mouth. Her hand dropped down to caress the swell of her stomach with a sigh. Brex had left before they had a chance to further discuss her pregnancy. She wondered if she even wanted to. She couldn't risk losing him again. Watching him leave again, the physical heart-break might kill her, she thought. But as she mused, she somehow knew Brex was being honest with her. And if the Brex who walked out on her truly had been her great-uncle or one of his minions…she couldn't think straight for a moment as the rage swamped her. Her great-uncle was not the person she had originally thought him to be. He played his part so well, that of the concerned relative, doing the honorable thing by returning his nephew's legacy to the throne. But now, if it was true that he was plotting against her, there was no way she would stand for it.

She was still musing when she saw Leona stalking the waterways on her way to help Gaia dress. Gaia smiled. She had developed a soft spot for the other woman, who was passionate and brave and outspoken. Gaia quickly scaled the roof and dropped back into the garden, fearing the scolding she knew would come if Leona caught her on the roof in her condition, even as early along as she was. Beating Leona to the door, Gaia opened it and smiled warmly at her friend.

"What happened last night?" Leona demanded as she stepped into the room and automatically moved to the wardrobe, removing options for Gaia to wear.

"I was kissing Brex when Amadeas just barged in. He wasn't thrilled, to say the least."

"And you?" Leona asked, one eyebrow up as she debated between two blouses.

Gaia rolled her eyes. "I was almost less thrilled than he was."

"No surprises there," Leona snorted. But she paused as she handed Gaia one of the blouses in her hand. "But you don't have much of a choice, unfortunately."

"What?"

"We have to present a united front to Amadeas. If he is in fact behind all of this and is plotting against you, we can't have any division on our side."

"But—"

"Gaia," Leona snapped, catching her friend off-guard. "Gaia, you need to listen to him. Something isn't right with all of this. Please, if even just for today, give him the benefit of the doubt."

Gaia was silent as she shrugged into the shirt. "I can't let my personal quarrels with Brex interfere with the bigger picture, I guess," she finally said.

"Spoken like a true queen," Leona agreed. "No, not that one—it makes you look fat," Leona said, pointing at the blouse Gaia had just put on. "What? We don't need to broadcast that you're with child. Tell everyone when you're ready, but don't let them guess."

"You said yesterday you think Amadeas knows," Gaia said, pulling off the offending blouse and taking another one that was white, flowy and very low cut.

"What else could have pushed him this far? Even if it wasn't him who masqueraded as Brex, whoever did will have told him all about it by now, even if it wasn't on his orders. If he's trying to make it look like you've been killed in battle, it means he doesn't want you on the throne at all. He'll get us to kill Nuweydon, have you killed, and take over himself. Since you're suddenly carrying an heir—and Brexler's child to boot—I can't imagine Amadeas sees his prospects of remaining in control as being all that great." Gaia glanced at Leona, horror stealing over her face.

"We'll have to tell them," she said, trying to control the panic in her voice. "How else can we explain his shift?" Leona shook her head.

"Amadeas is insane, we've all realized that. We don't have to tell them anything until you are ready."

They were spread around the large, round table in the middle of the Brotherhood's barracks, Lathan, Ravi, and a handful of other converted, trusted Tallpians sitting amongst the Brothers. Most of the men had welcomed Brex back into the fold, with promises from him to explain everything that had happened.

"This is going to suck," he muttered to Auggie, who sat to Brex's left. His friend shrugged at him.

"Self-inflicted, dude." As soon as Auggie had heard Brex's full explanation, he had reverted to his easy-going, laid-back demeanor.

"I knew it had to have been bad," Auggie had said after hearing about Amadeas and Bria. "I didn't think there was really anything that could pull you away from Gaia. But I get it now—that isn't something I'd want hanging over me, either." Brex had never been so grateful to his friend and yanked him into a hard hug.

"Thank you, Auggie."

"Don't thank me. We're Brothers; it's what we do."

They were all waiting when Leona marched in. Brex admired the young woman, even though she wasn't fond of him. She fixed her mint-colored gaze on him as she stomped across the room.

"She's coming," Leona said, stepping up to the table. "I've persuaded her to listen to you. This is your only chance, so I suggest that you don't screw it up." There was an outbreak of chuckles from the rest of the table.

"Hell hath no fury," one of the men muttered under his breath. Leona's green eyes flashed, but she was saved from answering by Gaia's entrance. Brex swiveled around in his seat and felt his mouth go dry. Gaia was dressed head-to-toe in black, a pair of high-waisted leather pants hugging her curves like a second skin. The black, short-sleeved blouse was sleek, and showcased her creamy skin. Her hair was a stunning honey blonde, and her eyes were like chips of sapphires. She strode across the room, her steps echoing around the hall. Every man at the table jumped to his feet, with Lathan and the other Tallpians bowing low from the waist. She flicked her hand in a regal, casual gesture, releasing them. They all waited until she had taken her seat before sitting down. She turned her face towards Brex but didn't meet his eyes. He guessed it was his chance.

"Before we talk about the war for Meidonna, I would like to explain what happened, what drove me to…leave," Brex said. "First, I want to tell you the story of someone named Bria…,"

As Gaia sat and listened to Brex explain how he had met, helped, and then abandoned Bria, she found herself swamped with a swell of emotions, horror being the primary one, at the thought of the poor girl's fate. Vindication surged through her as Gaia thought to herself that she had known trusting him had been a mistake but as she listened, she couldn't help but understand a young man's mistake and fear for his own life. His anguish was apparent—the mistake had haunted him for years. He described meeting with Amadeas and being forced to leave, after seeing Gaia, thinking she knew the whole story.

"Amadeas told me you knew the entire story. When you reacted the way you did and threw me out, I assumed that was what caused it," Brex said, nodding at Gaia. She paused, trying to collect her thoughts. She hadn't wanted to admit publicly that she was pregnant, but it seemed like she didn't have a choice. She squared her shoulders and looked around the table.

"Eight days ago, I discovered that I'm pregnant." There was an outbreak of surprised noises from the people sitting around the table. Gaia ignored it and lifted her head higher. "I had no idea it was even possible, but it has been confirmed. We discussed," Gaia said, letting her eyes touch on Leona, who dipped her head in acknowledgment, "that the first thing I needed to do was tell Brex. Leona was called away, so I sent Sia."

"I got your message but never made it to you," Brex said, looking angrier every second.

"But someone did. And that someone looked exactly like you."

"I swear it, it was not me." Looking around at the table, Brex grimaced. "It was Amadeas. He had me attacked and thrown in a cell overnight. When I went to speak with Gaia the next morning, she was already angry with me, and I thought I knew why."

"Are we sure it was Amadeas?" one of the Brothers asked. Several heads nodded vigorously, including Lathan.

"Absolutely."

"How can you be sure?" Njoroge asked.

"Like this," Lathan said, and as they watched, he blinked and another Brex suddenly appeared at the table, sitting next to Leona, who curled her lip and leaned away in distaste. Several Brotherhood members lurched back, Kyan falling out of his chair. Cries of shock echoed around the room.

"What in the name of the—"

"It's a typical Tallpian ability," Lathan said, blinking again, and in an instant, his trademark blonde hair and green eyes were back in place. Leona smiled fondly at him.

"Then why do you look like that? Why not go around looking like other people all the time?" Murad asked in surprise.

"Just because we are capable of doing it doesn't mean we always want to. It requires quite a bit of energy to assume another person's being, especially someone who is not full Tallpian." He nodded to Leona who blinked, making her red hair disappear. A mass of mahogany curls appeared, and when she opened her eyes, they were a deep storm-grey. "Transitions like that are far easier and don't require nearly as much effort. But it can be done, without a doubt."

"So the possibility of Amadeas posing as Brex—"

"Is completely realistic. In fact, I am positive that is what happened," Leona said. "I was called away from Gaia just minutes after we discovered the pregnancy."

"Sia came back to deliver my clean laundry," Gaia added, "and I asked her to deliver a message to Brex."

"And we know what happened from there."

"How did Amadeas figure it out?"

"Does it matter?" Auggie asked. "He knows, and now he's planning to have Gaia killed."

"Amadeas was the one who planned King Yehuda's murder twenty years ago," Lathan said in his low, even voice. "He desired the throne even then and has never been able to cope with the idea of being the second son. He pushed Nuweydon into killing his brother, knowing Nuweydon suffered from the same resentment. After Gaia was born," he nodded to her, "both of their places were in even greater danger of being usurped by a child." Gaia wrinkled her nose at him but said nothing. "When Dyla fled with Gaia, Amadeas was content to let them live out their lives somewhere in the galaxy, provided that Dyla never encouraged her to take back her birthright."

"We know how the rest goes," Brex said. "Nuweydon is insane. Amadeas realized he had backed the wrong man."

"He played his game very well," Lathan said. "He was the one who reminded Nuweydon that Gaia would soon be twenty-one, knowing that Nuweydon would do whatever it took to have her found. On the other hand, he also had a plan in place to rescue her and crown her queen since his plans to control Nuweydon had failed. Amadeas realized that Nuweydon was no longer under his influence and decided it was time for him to be removed."

"And yet, Amadeas is now planning to kill me," Gaia spat.

"He never realized how much like your mother you are," Lathan said with a grin. "Granted, none of us did. You are far more willful and stubborn than any other Tallpian woman he has ever met—well, except maybe one," Lathan covered hastily, glancing at his glowering wife. "The point is, he thought that by driving Brex from your life that he would be able to control you more easily. He thought Brex was the problem."

"Only one of them," Brex said wryly, glancing at Gaia. She couldn't control the flutter that went through her stomach, but she kept her face impassive. Gods damn that boy, she thought, for still being able to give her that rush.

"So now that he knows he has no chance of controlling me whatsoever, he is planning to what? Have me die in battle and take the throne himself?"

"Something like that," Ravi offered.

"He thinks he can play with our futures as he pleases," Gaia snapped. "I no longer fit into his plans, so his answer is to kill me?" She glanced around the table but avoided Brex's eye. "I don't think so."

"Why haven't we just killed him yet?" Shaw demanded. Lathan's voice was grave when he replied.

"Despite everything he has done, we do still need him. The army follows him, as Lord Commander. I am only a vice commander. They won't follow me if he is still in power."

"And if they see us remove him from power, they very well could turn on us," Ravi added.

"So, what, we have to play nice for the next four days?" Shaw demanded, sitting back with his arms crossed.

"That is exactly what I'm saying," Lathan said. "It is also absolutely imperative that no one mentions that we know it was Amadeas who drove Brex out. It could cause him to do something worse, something we might have no knowledge of until it is too late." He looked around the table. "Something that could very well cost us our lives."

"This is going to be much harder than I thought," Brex grumbled.

"So good to have you back with us, Brexler," Amadeas said as Gaia and Brex joined the rest of the commanders at the large table in the Tallpian hall later that morning. Brex glanced at

Gaia and then Auggie. Every single person in the room knew that Amadeas was the one who had forced Brex into leaving. While he agreed with the logic of Lathan's plan, it grated on him to pretend otherwise. Brex just shook his head and gave Amadeas a grin, deciding to play the old man's game.

"I just couldn't stay away." Amadeas fixed him with a hooded look that only Gaia saw before he turned back to the group.

"As more and more of our reinforcements arrive, our Miwarman hosts…."

Parting ways at the Brotherhood's barracks that afternoon, Brex headed off to brief the newest batch of Brotherhood members who had arrived to take part in the attack, and Gaia off to train.

It was late afternoon by the time that Brex was free from his duties as Commander of the Brotherhood. He headed for the training green where most of the troops were drilling. He spotted the black-clad form of his lover in a far corner, sword in hand as she sparred with Alix. She had been good with the weapon before he left, but watching her now, he was astonished to see her progress. Every single movement was utterly effortless, and, within a minute of Brex watching, she had clipped the sword from Alix's hand and stood triumphantly over his prone form.

"She's lethal." Auggie stepped up next to Brex, also watching Gaia.

"She's terrifying," Brex agreed. "What did Ravi have to say?" They had decided it would be better if their Tallpian insider continued to meet with Auggie instead of Brex. Gaia had pointed out during their early morning meeting that not even Amadeas was stupid enough not to notice if one of his captains was meeting privately with Brex. It hadn't taken much, once Amadeas made his plans, to convince Lathan, Ravi and a handful of other ranked Tallpians to side with the Brotherhood. The men were committed to Gaia and her cause, and did not want to see Amadeas on the throne any more than Brex and Gaia did.

"Our favorite snake is spending quite a bit of time connected to his men still on planet. Ravi's only heard bits and pieces."

"Prepping for the invasion, I suppose?"

"Something like that," Auggie said, letting his eyes wander across the crowded training field. "How are you holding up?" he asked. Brex chuckled, and knew he wore the same sleepless look Auggie did.

"I'm fine, but you look like hell, dude."

"Speak for yourself," Auggie snorted, laughing. Brex chuckled again.

"At least I've got a good reason to be up at night. What's your excuse?" Auggie shrugged nonchalantly, but Brex knew his friend. "You sure you're good?"

"The waves make it hard for me to sleep," he finally admitted. Brex glanced at him suspiciously.

"Are you saying you miss the shit-hole of a planet that we were born on?"

Auggie laughed. "Sort of. Not a huge fan of this humidity either. I miss the dry heat," he said. "And Noria." Brex raised an eyebrow. He knew Auggie had been close to the girl but had no idea it was so serious.

"Don't worry, dude," he said, clapping his friend on the shoulder before staring back at Gaia. "This will all be over soon—one way or another."

# Chapter Twenty-Three

That evening Brex sat with Lathan on the training green as the sun dropped below the horizon. Gaia had gone to shower after her training session. It had taken all of Brex's self-control not to follow her, but she still needed some space, and he was willing to do what it took to get back on her good graces. Instead, he took the chance to connect with the Tallpian.

"I never did thank you," Brex admitted, "for keeping an eye out for Gaia while I was gone." Lathan's expression was contemplative, but he nodded in acknowledgment of Brex's words. "For standing up for her, even if it means going against someone you've followed your whole life."

"I'll admit that it is much harder than it looks," Lathan admitted. Brex raised an eyebrow in question, and Lathan sighed. "I guess I've turned a blind eye to Amadeas and his schemes over the years. I chose to only see what I wanted to."

"What do you mean?"

Lathan shrugged uncomfortably. "When Amadeas first confided in me that he wanted to rescue Gaia, I only saw the good intentions. I knew in the back of my mind that Amadeas had helped over-throw Yehuda, but convinced myself that he had only gone along with Nuweydon to save as many Tallpian lives as he could. I never dreamed it had been his idea or the lengths he would go to to maintain his control over the throne."

"He made me nervous the minute I set eyes on him," Brex confessed.

"You're wiser than me," Lathan acknowledged. "I've turned away from his flaw for years because he favored me but recent events have made them impossible to ignore."

"And Ravi and the others? How do they feel?"

"You know it was Ravi who first heard Amadeas plotting to kill Gaia?" Lathan asked, and Brex nodded. Lathan shook his blonde head in disgust. "I am eternally grateful he chose to do the right thing. Not all of Amadeas's men would have done so."

"Then we're lucky to have you both," Brex said with a significant look. Lathan nodded in reply, but didn't respond.

They lapsed into an amiable silence, watching the sun drop over Miwarma's tropical ocean landscape when Leona appeared at the far end of the field, marching towards them. Brex heard Lathan take a deep breath and exhale slowly as they watched his wife approach. She was beautiful as a redhead, but today, with rich mahogany curls cascading down around her shoulders and flashing grey eyes, Brex wasn't sure he'd seen her look better.

"I love her more than any being in this galaxy," Lathan breathed to Brex, "but, gods, sometimes she terrifies me." It was all Brex could do not to choke on his laughter. Lathan smothered a grin before turning an adoring smile to his wife. She beamed at Lathan with a look that Brex could only define as pure and unrestrained love. It was odd, Brex realized, because he'd never felt any kind of jealousy for that sort of thing until now. It wasn't their love he envied, but rather their surety. Brex and Gaia's future was so uncertain, they could only take it a day at a time. A moment later, Leona turned her iron-colored gaze on Brex, her eyes narrowing. He groaned. What had he done this time?

"You need to talk to Gaia," she without preamble, reaching them. Lathan stood and wrapped an affectionate arm around her waist, although Brex wondered if he was trying to prevent Leona from diving at him.

"About what?" he asked, raising an eyebrow. "She listens to you more than she listens to me," he pointed out, not rising. Leona tossed back her mane of dark hair, her eyes flashing.

"I'm worried about her." Brex felt his eyebrows knit together in confusion.

"Why?"

"She's pushing herself too hard," Leona said, and the concern in her voice was genuine. "She's strong, but I'm worried if she keeps up this training pace, she might do herself—or the baby—serious harm." Brex scrambled to his feet to look her in the eye.

"Do you think so?"

"I watched her spar with Njoroge today. She kicked his ass, but I worry that she is trying too hard to prove that she is fit."

"Her biggest fear is that we'll leave her out of the war," Brex said. They had not rehashed their old fight, at least not since he had returned. "And that people will die for her."

"That is going to happen either way," Lathan pointed out.

Brex shook his head. "I keep trying to tell her that, but she still hates the idea of it."

"That is the way of war."

"I know that, and you know that, but she still struggles with it."

"That can't be the only reason," Lathan said skeptically. "She can't win this entire war single-handedly."

"You saw how she was in one of those last meetings," Brex reminded him. "She thinks that we are going to force her to stay here and that she won't get to be a part of the fight. Her throne, her war."

"That is what needs to happen," Leona said fiercely. "We can't risk her getting hurt between now and when Nuweydon is dead. She is all we have left."

"I've already had this fight with her," Brex pointed out. "I am just barely getting back onto her good side. I'm not picking an old fight with her just for the sake of arguing."

"At least try to convince her to take it easy in training. If she strains herself too hard in the early days, she could do some real damage."

"Have you tried telling her that?" Brex asked.

Leona frowned. "She told me not to worry."

Brex laughed. "Welcome to my world."

"At least try, Brex. Please?" He was caught off guard by her pleading tone. Leona had made it obvious she didn't think much of him, but Brex wondered if maybe she was warming up to him after all. He shrugged.

"I'll try. But I can't promise any results. When she gets an idea in her head, nothing can change her mind."

Gaia was reveling in the rainfall of cool water in the shower when there was a knock. A moment later, Brex stuck his head around the door.

"So much for letting me have some peace," she called to him as he entered her cottage. Brex offered her a lascivious grin that made an explosion of desire erupt in her stomach. Even with all of the emotional turmoil, their physical attraction and passion had not diminished. Brex waited patiently until she finished rinsing before grabbing a towel and helping her from the shower. He dried every inch of her skin, taking extra care around her belly. She smiled down at him. Gaia had seen angry Brex, terrified Brex, cocky Brex, and despondent

Brex, but tender Brex was something new altogether. He helped her into her filmy sleeping robe before sitting on the bed behind her and began plaiting her wet hair.

"Where did you learn to braid?" Gaia asked as she luxuriated under the feeling of his fingers in her hair.

Brex chuckled softly. "My sisters. Someone had to keep them looking put-together when we were kids." He shrugged. "Most of the time it fell to me." She glanced over her shoulder at him.

"You don't talk about them." Another shrug, his eyes a shade darker.

"Mia is the only one I'm still in contact with. The others have gone in different directions. The last update I got was that Genevieve and Lynne had both died, Clara married and settled on the Core, and no one has heard from Gayle in years. I don't know any of my biological brothers." Gaia felt her eyes prick with tears. Brex didn't talk about his past much, but at least he had some semblance of family. Both of her parents were gone. All she had left in terms of blood relatives were Amadeas and Bronwyn—and of course, Nuweydon. Tying off the end of her plait, Brex pressed a kiss to her bare shoulder.

"I love this look on you," he said, running his hands across the plain of her shoulders before slipping them down her front to cup her breasts. She squealed and tried to swat him off but only succeeded in pressing herself back against his chest. He hugged her tight, re-wrapping his arms around her waist, just above her growing belly. "You've already gotten so much stronger," Brex said, admiring his view. Gaia gave him a sideways glance.

"You've been talking to Leona, haven't you?" she asked.

Brex didn't deny it. "She cares about you."

"And I her, Brex."

"And I care about you."

"Get to the point."

"We just want you to take it a little easier. I watched you kick Njoroge's ass earlier. You realize not even I can do that?" She spun so she could look him in the face and grabbed his hands.

"Brex, you have to give me this. I can't contribute anything other than my skills as a warrior. You can't expect me to sit by and let this fight happen, only to stroll in once everything is over. That doesn't make me a queen; that makes me a dabbler." Brex hadn't thought of it that way.

"At least agree to take it easy. We only have two days left here. You need your rest."

"No," she said, adamant. "I can guarantee you no one on Meidonna is telling Nuweydon to take it easy. He is going to come out at his best." She fixed her silver eyes on Brex. "I have to beat him."

"Gaia—"

"Brex! My life depends on this!"

"Alright," he said, holding up a placating hand as she colored in frustration. "I get it. You just have to understand that we worry about you."

"And I love you for it," she said pressing a gentle kiss to his lips. "But I'm not scaling back."

"Gaia," Brex started, but she shot him a steely glare that reminded him of Mia.

"Don't pick a fight you can't win, Brexler," she said, raising a dark eyebrow in warning. "You may not live to regret it."

"We are just worried about you."

"I know that, and I'm grateful, but if I'm going to be queen, I can't take it easy. Not now."

"Alright, I understand." Brex tried to swallow the lump in his throat. "I've got to talk to Auggie, but I'll be back before you go to bed, ok?"

Gaia kissed him again. "Good, I hate sleeping without you."

Brex strode into the Brotherhood's barracks several minutes later. He had left Gaia with a sinking feeling in his chest. She would be taking on the mantle of queenship within a few short days. He wasn't sure where that left him.

"Brex." Auggie sat at the table in the center of the room, the remains of his meal pushed aside. One look at the darkness in Brex's face and Auggie knew something was up. "You look like you could use a drink," Auggie offered as Brex sat next to him, but his friend and commander shook his head.

"I had enough to drink at Mia's to last me a lifetime."

"What's up, man? You look like someone just crashed your ship or something."

"Nothing." Auggie snorted.

"Nice try. Come on, let's walk." Auggie hauled Brex up by the scruff of his neck and pushed him out the door without waiting for an answer. They walked in silence along the narrow rope bridges that connected the entire town until they reached the large stone outcropping that anchored the village. Auggie jerked his head, motioning for Brex to follow him. They pushed through the lush foliage as they followed a thin track that lead up the steep hill. After another ten minutes of hiking, they emerged above the tree line to find a small, rocky outcropping with a wide, flat shelf. Auggie threw himself down comfortably, and Brex joined him, hanging his feet over the edge. Looking down, they could see the entire town spread out in front of them like a tapestry, the wooden buildings shining like gold against the flawless blue of the sea as the sun disappeared beyond the horizon, dusting the village in the shadows of twilight.

"It's almost pretty enough to make you not want to leave," Auggie said, shooting a sideways glance at his friend.

Brex started across the stunning landscape, his eyes unseeing. "I can't stay with Gaia."

Auggie turned and looked at him in shock. "What? What the hell does that mean? You just got back!" Brex turned his heartbroken eyes to his friend.

"She's going to be queen. Where does that leave me?"

"What do you mean where does that leave you? You're the father of her child."

"Yeah, and what kind of father am I going to be?" Brex's voice was bleak. "I never knew my dad. What if I screw up?"

"The only way you are going to screw this up is if you leave Gaia!"

"But what am I to her? Not her husband—just a lover."

"Just a lover? What the hell is going on, Brex?"

"Don't you see it, Auggie? If she's going to be a good queen, I can't stand in her way. Her people would never accept someone like me."

"As king?"

"As anything. Besides, I don't want to be king—I won't walk away from the Brotherhood again."

"Everyone has a day-job," Auggie reminded him.

"Yeah, I can imagine that going well," Brex said with biting sarcasm. "The new king of Meidonna who just happens to be a part-time criminal. I have almost as much blood on my hands as Nuweydon does." He snorted in laughter, the sound harsher than necessary.

"Not even close, Brex." Auggie's voice was cold. "You aren't a murdering psychopath."

"Doesn't matter. I won't give them any reason to doubt Gaia or her abilities."

"You're going to let her go aren't you?" Brex opened his mouth, but Auggie shook his head. "Don't lie to me, Brex, I know you better than almost anyone else."

"Don't say anything to her. Not until after."

"You can't do that to her. Her or the kid."

"Auggie, I have to. I won't risk her safety or th of her reign just for selfish reasons."

"What about the kid?"

"We'll figure it out."

"But you're not going to stay?"

"Maybe. But this is what she was born for. What was I born for? A skinny, good-for-nothing kid Kain scooped out of the gutter?"

"And the newest leader of the largest independent, inter-galactic force for good."

"I'll only ever be her watchdog."

"Where is that coming from?"

"I'm not Tallpian."

"Who cares, dude?"

"I won't hurt her chances of having a stable reign."

"You won't; you will only make her stronger."

"We'll see."

"Don't do anything stupid until after this invasion is over and we've won the war," Auggie growled, eyeing his friend.

Brex shook his head. "Why do people always say that to me?" he demanded, offended.

Auggie shook his head sadly. "Because, Brex, you always do something stupid."

They descended the hill in silence, but as they neared the village and Brex could see Gaia's white hair flashing in the setting sun as she leaned on the railing of her balcony, he collared Auggie.

"One more thing," he said as his friend raised his eye-brows. "You don't say a damn word to her. I won't distract her right now."

"She'll kill you either way," Auggie reminded him, yank-ing himself from Brex's grip.

Brex's dark blue eyes were far away as he stared at the woman he loved. "We'll deal with it afterward. Gods help me; I'm going to have to break her heart—again."

⁓

Miwarma was barely different from night to day. The gentle roll of the waves came and went, the tides rising and falling in a slow-motion dance. Instead of the brilliant tropical sun, the nights were dominated by a single colossal moon that seemed to take up almost the entire sky. The same tropical breeze wafted through open doors and windows, making wind chimes tinkle and sway.

That night, after his conversation with Auggie, Brex had a hard time dislodging the lump in his throat that rose every time he looked at Gaia. He could not get enough of the rosy glow that training and pregnancy had given her, and he did his best to push his feelings aside as she twined her arms around his neck and sealed her lips across his.

After making love, he lay next to Gaia, watching her sleep. Her long lashes created crescent moon shadows on her cheeks, and her full lips were parted, giving her a slight smile. Brex was so consumed by listening to her steady breathing that he barely registered the sound of the cottage door as it swung open. Gaia didn't stir as Brex glanced over his shoulder at the faint squeak. Sia, Gaia's diminutive Miwarman assistant, stood in the open door, her slight frame shadowed against the bright moon behind her. Brex stared at her, perplexed. It was the middle of the night— what was she doing there? The girl held a finger to her lips in a shushing gesture before starting to gather clothes from the floor. Brex felt his suspicion growing. There was no need for her to be taking care of laundry right now. He was just sitting up to ask her what she was doing when she drew a blade from behind her back; a wakizashi, a short blade sword, just like the one Gaia sometimes practiced with during the day.

"What the—" But before he could finish his sentence, the young girl let loose a war whoop and swung, bringing the blade down just inches from his face. With a shout, Brex shoved himself back across the bed, smashing into Gaia as the blade whipped past him. She awoke with a yell as Brex snatched his own long knife off the bedside table. "Gaia, get out of here!" Brex roared as he blocked the next strike. The young Miwarman let loose a shriek and dove at Brex, who narrowly dodged the blade, knocking it away with his own weapon. Gaia rolled off the bed, and Sia turned her attention to her mistress and moved to pin her in the corner. "No!" Brex dove towards the girl, but she spun and the very tip of the sword sliced into the bare flesh of his hip. Bellowing in pain, Brex charged the girl again, his knife raised. He dodged and parried another two strikes, but it was clear the girl was skilled with the weapon, which grated against everything Brex knew about the Miwarmans, who despised violence of any kind.

"Brex!" Gaia's scream was shrill and made Brex's blood run cold. While Sia was concentrating on Brex, Gaia edged towards the door and was able to yank her own weapon from its sheath. The young Miwarman saw the movement and rounded on Gaia with another feral shriek. The two blades met in midair with a deafening clang. While Sia was young, it was a frighteningly evenly-matched fight, and she held both of them at bay with considerable skill. Brex watched, helpless, just waiting for a chance to strike. Seizing an opportunity as Sia ducked back from one of Gaia's blows a moment later, Brex dodged behind her and slammed his knife into the base of the girl's neck, the blade shearing through her spine. She swayed for a moment, staggering several steps backward before the blade clattered to the stone floor and its owner collapsed, brilliant red blood pulsing from the wound in her neck.

"Brex!" Gaia flew across the room and slammed into him, her arms wrapped around his neck as she started to sob incoherently, weapon still in hand.

"Gaia. Gaia!" Brex had to shout to get her attention, and she pulled her face away from his shoulder, completely distraught.

"What just happened? How was she—"At that moment the cottage door crashed open, bouncing off the wall. Brex and Gaia spun, bringing up their blades defensively. Shaw, Lathan and Kyan came pouring over the threshold, weapons held aloft.

"What the fuck just happened?" Shaw yelled, sweeping the room with his pistol in hand. "We heard Gaia scream." Brex pointed to the body on the floor but found couldn't speak around the frozen lump in his throat.

"What happened?" Lathan's voice was deadly calm.

Finding his voice, Brex spoke slowly, holding on to Gaia, who was still shaking. "She attacked us. Came in and started gathering laundry, and before I knew it, she drew her weapon and charged. If I hadn't been awake, she would have killed us both."

"Jorah and Azir are both dead." Shaw's words were like an iron-clad punch to the gut. Brex hadn't even given thought to the two Brothers standing guard, and now they were dead. His men, dead. He bit down hard on the inside of his cheek to keep tears from his eyes.

"She must have killed them first before coming after you."

"What the hell was a Miwarman doing with a weapon?" Kyan demanded, his gun still trained on the corpse. Lathan knelt and inspected the spreading blood pool.

"She's no Miwarman," he said. "Step back." Everyone took a giant step back as Leona, Auggie, and Njoroge rushed into the room.

"What—"

"Just wait," Lathan snapped. As they watched, the small, skinny body started to expand, the limbs lengthening, skin losing its dark tint until it was a Tallpian soldier that lay on the floor, Brex's knife still buried in the base of his neck.

"That's Ezra." Leona's words shattered the icy silence that had descended over the small cottage. Gaia glanced at Leona, whose face was deathly white as she spoke. "He was one of the palace guards on Meidonna."

"What the hell is he doing here?"

"Isn't it obvious?" Gaia asked, a savage expression on her face. She looked around the small room. "He was sent here to kill me."

They did not go back to sleep. The Miwarman leaders were rousted from their beds, along with Amadeas and the rest of the Tallpians. The real Sia was confirmed to have been sleeping soundly in her own bed during the attack.

"There are only two possible explanations," Gaia said, her hands wrapped around a steaming mug of tea. They had moved from Gaia's cottage to the Brotherhood barracks while the body (its head completely severed, just to be safe) was removed and the Miwarmans began cleaning. A dozen sets of eyes stared at her. "Either Nuweydon figured out where we are or someone here told him where to find us. Personally," she added bitterly, "I am inclined to believe the second option."

"How could someone off-planet have known to impersonate your maid?" Brex demanded. "Someone who could move through town without suspicion? There is no coincidence in that."

"We have to think rationally about this," Lathan started, but Leona sputtered indignantly.

"Rationally, Lathan? We all know there is only one person on this planet who wants Gaia and Brex dead. Why haven't we done something about it?" she snapped. Lathan opened his mouth but was cut off again, this time by Cayson.

"Amadeas is still needed, as perverse as that sounds. We need him believing we are still working together. If we openly turn against him, he could derail our entire invasion," Cayson pointed out, dark mauve circles under his pale eyes. "Lathan, you said it yourself." The Tallpian nodded in agreement, but it was Brex who spoke.

"If he hasn't already done serious damage that we don't know about. Alix says he still doesn't have the shield codes yet." He exhaled hard. "I'll say something to him."

"I'll talk to him," Lathan offered. "Just the sight of you still makes him angry beyond reason," he said to Brex, who flashed an evil glare as he plunked back in his chair next to Gaia.

"Good. He deserves it."

"Brex," Gaia warned.

He shook his head. "Fine, sorry. Lathan, that'd be great. Let him know we want to meet first thing in the morning."

The Tallpian nodded. "I'll go now." He gave Leona's hand a squeeze before rising from the table and disappearing into the night. Auggie, who had sat in silence the entire time, looked at Brex, who at once noticed how red his friend's eyes were.

"Auggie?" the mechanic just shook his head, unable to speak. Brex felt the same agony.

"I know, buddy." Jorah and Azir were both young recruits and recent arrivals to Miwarma. They had selflessly and cheerfully volunteered to stand guard and take part in the fight afterward. "It's the middle of the night on Simma. I put a call into Jorah's parents, but they didn't answer. Azir didn't—" Brex choked and couldn't finish the sentence. Azir didn't have a family, so there was no one to notify. Gaia reached over and took Brex's hand.

"Azir might not have any living blood relatives, but he has a family," she said fiercely. "You are his family. You too, Auggie. And Kyan, and Njoroge, and Shaw. All of you." She paused, tears welling in her green eyes. "Just like you are mine. We are here to take care of each other. Azir and Jorah will both be given hero's memorials, and those responsible for their deaths will pay."

# Chapter Twenty-Four

They convened a final strategy meeting as the sun rose to deal with the unprecedented assault on Gaia and Brex. Gaia knew without a shred of doubt that it was Amadeas who had ordered the attack yet they had no proof and were forced to continue acting as though he was innocent of any wrongdoing. But the meeting quickly fell apart.

"We should consider relocating, Your Grace, to another secure planet within the system," Amadeas said. "For your safety, of course."

"No—" Gaia started, but Brex cut her off.

"What's the point of that?" he demanded. Amadeas contained his anger with effort.

"If they know where she is, they may send another assassin. If we remove her, she has a better chance of surviving."

"What is the point of moving an entire army literally two days before we leave? The memorials are tomorrow. We are not leaving before that."

"The Outer Rim Brotherhood would remain here, obviously," Amadeas said with a sniff.

Brex bristled. "Gaia goes nowhere without us."

"If you think that the inconvenience of moving is worth her life—"

"Did you hear me say that?"

"Well, no—"

"Nuweydon will expect us to try and move her," Auggie pointed out, trying to diffuse the argument. "Staying here will be the last thing they expect us to do. Gaia is sleeping in Brex's quarters now. To reach them, an assassin would have to murder over a hundred Brothers first." He sat back, an angry glint in his normally placid blue eyes. "We will not let that happen again."

"It should still be considered."

"If you want to tuck your tail between your legs and run, by all means," Brex taunted him, "go for it. As for the rest of us, we all are staying here and leaving in two days."

Fury consumed Amadeas's pointed features as he jumped to his feet. "Insolent fool," he bellowed, pointing a finger at Brex, who stood to look the general in the eye.

"Be careful who you insult, old man," he warned. "You won't win this battle without us."

"I refuse to work like this," the Tallpian shouted, throwing his arms in the air. They all watched in utter disbelief as the older man stormed away from the meeting table. The door slammed behind him a moment later.

"Well, that went well," Auggie said mildly.

That afternoon found Brex and Gaia taking a rare break, and they sat trailing their feet in the water off Gaia's cottage with Auggie and Leona.

Lathan was still with Amadeas, trying to persuade him to set aside his differences for Gaia and the sake of their people as well as ascertain if Amadeas had any alternate plans.

"I don't know why Lathan thinks he'll be successful," Leona muttered, training her pale feet in the crystal-clear water. "Amadeas swore he'd never work with you again." She nodded to Brex, who shrugged as if he couldn't have cared less.

"It's all pretense on Lathan's part," Auggie offered from his spot in the shade, leaning back against the bungalow wall. "Amadeas still doesn't know we're on to his plan to have Gaia die in battle—at least as far as Ravi can tell." He yawned. "As long as we make it look like we're still trying to work with him, he probably won't suspect anything, and we can make sure he isn't able to put his plan in motion."

"Once you're queen, do yourself a favor," Leona said to Gaia, "and just kill him. It will make everyone's lives much easier." Gaia tried to look stern, but she couldn't stem an evil snicker.

"Real mature," Brex snapped.

"I'm not even twenty-one," she retorted.

"And you're about to become not only queen but a mother as well," he rejoined. Instantly, Gaia dropped her hands to her stomach where the swell was getting more noticeable each day.

"I never officially congratulated you," Auggie said, leaning over and tugging Gaia into a tight hug.

"Thank you, Auggie."

"Hey, easy now," Brex said, pushing them apart. "Gentle on the future king."

"Is it a boy?" Auggie asked in surprise.

Gaia looked up, startled then shrugged. "I have no idea."

"Yes, he is," Brex said confidently, leaning back against the wall of the bungalow. "Because if I have a daughter, we are all screwed."

"Why?" Gaia demanded, staring at him with slitted blue eyes.

"If I—and when I say I," Brex said, giving Auggie a significant look, "I mean the entire damn Brotherhood—have to spend the rest of our lives chasing around a girl who is as beautiful as her mother and even half as stubborn, we'll all be driven to an early grave," Brex said laughing. Gaia smiled.

"Well that's ok then," she said, grinning at Brex, who wrinkled his nose at her.

"Have you thought of a name?" Auggie asked as he sat one leg crossed over a knee. Gaia glanced at Brex and saw he wore the same stunned look.

"No," she said honestly. "I haven't given it much thought yet."

"Caratacus or Kain. Something war-like," Brex suggested.

"Oberon or Breccan. Something majestic," Leona offered.

"Calix or Ahmet. Something unique," Auggie added.

"Stop, stop!" Gaia cried, laughing. "We'll choose something when the time comes. I'm content to wait until then."

She tilted her head in question at Brex, who shrugged. "All I care about is ten fingers and ten toes," he said, his eyes sliding over Gaia, stealing her breath away. "We can worry about a name later."

"I think we can manage that," she said, returning his smile.

"I wonder what a half-Tallpian will be like," Leona said. The other three turned to stare at her, surprised. "What?" she asked. "They are extremely rare. I don't think I've ever actually met one."

"I guess we'll just have to wait and find out, and meet the little guy when he arrives," Brex said with a fond brush of Gaia's belly.

Later that afternoon, Gaia was resting the shade after a sparring match with Alix. For someone who spent almost all of his time behind a computer screen, he was incredibly talented with the long-bladed sword. She could disarm him within minutes, but it was still always a good fight.

"You're far too good with that thing," he muttered petulantly as he flopped down in the shade next to her.

She laughed. "Its name is Sigur," she offered lightly, and Alix smiled in approval. He had suggested that her blade deserved a name. Many of the great swords carried one, named either for their purpose or their deeds. After many hours of thought, she decided upon Sigur which meant 'victory.' "But I've got a good teacher," she offered, trying to mollify him. He shrugged. "How did you get so good anyway?" she asked, eyeing his thin, lanky build. Another shrug, but more thoughtful this time.

"I went to a military academy on the Core. It was one of the weapons they trained us on. I just happened to be good at it. But put a gun in my hands, and I'm useless," he said with a self-deprecating chuckle. Gaia gave him a tilted smile and his black eyes crinkled as he smiled back. "Thanks, by the way," he said. "I needed a break. I can only stare at my screens for so long before my brain starts to turn to mush."

"Any time," she said. "Besides, we need you at your best."

He nodded in agreement. "I finally cracked their fleet codes," he said, his voice sleepy and satisfied. "A couple more lines and I should have their whole weapons system shut down right as we arrive."

"Wait," Gaia said her eyes wide. "Are you saying you've got the entire fleet codes figured out? What about the planet shield?" Alix made a face.

"I've asked Amadeas for the planet codes daily, but he says he's still making sure the ones he'll give me haven't been changed since we left. If he doesn't give them to me today, I'll just try and hack in myself. But they should still be relatively simple, compared to the fleet codes. It wasn't easy, but if I can't hack long distance, then what good am I?" His smile was triumphant. "Once we can get to the surface, we'll be able to do so without worrying about their gunships."

"Does Brex know?"

"Not yet," he said. "I had just finished when you showed up." Gaia jumped up.

"We've got to tell him and the others. Alix, this is huge!" She grabbed him into a hug as he stood, making him almost topple over. "Come on!"

They found Brex in the barracks, his revolvers on the table top with cleaning tools spread across the surface, chatting with Shaw and Kyan.

"Did she kick your ass again, Alix?" Brex asked, leaning back in his chair.

"You know I did," Gaia said with a wink. "But you'll never guess what Alix did!" Brex raised a lazy eyebrow.

"Cracked the fleet codes," Alix said with a modest shrug. "We may not have the planetary codes yet, but they should be a piece of cake compared to the whole fleet system."

"What?" Brex shot upright and managed to flip himself and his chair over backward with an almighty crash. Gaia and the rest of his Brothers burst into laughter as he struggled to right himself.

"Shut up, you guys!" He looked at his dark-haired Brother. "You did it?" Alix nodded, chewing on his bottom lip, trying not to look too pleased with himself. "Yes!" Brex's shout made their ears ring as he grabbed Alix in a bear hug. Shaw got up to slap Alix on the back as Kyan smiled broadly. None of them noticed the slight, dark-hair figured standing at the slightly open door at the other end of the hall.

"They said what?" Amadeas's voice was a deep growl. The girl's round face flushed with fear.

"They said he 'cracked the fleet codes,'" she said in a small voice.

"Damn them," he snarled. He glanced at the terrified girl. Again, he thought how fortunate it was that his wife had persuaded Kallideia's little Miwarman assistant to spy on her. It had gained them so much, even if it hadn't all gone according to plan. "Dismissed," he threw at her, and she scuttled from the room. If the girl was right and the Brotherhood hacker had succeeded in cracking the access codes to the Meidonna fleet systems, it could entirely change the tide of their fight. Since the assassination attempt had failed, he knew he was running out of choices. Weighing his options, he reached for his telelink.

The next morning, as the sun was rising, Brex gently shook Gaia's arm.

"Gaia, darlin', you've got to wake up." She peeled open one honey-gold eye and stared at him. He was already dressed, standing by the side of the bed.

"Why?" Her question was muffled by the feather pillow against her face.

"We have the memorials this morning." A sick, cold feeling surged through Gaia's stomach as she sat up. She had wept bitterly over her mother's death, but had also managed to cram a stopper into the well of her grief, doing her best to wait, and properly mourn once the war was over. But after having the bodies prepared, they were finally ready for the ceremonies. Kain, Azir, and Jorah were to be given hero's funerals, alongside Dyla, who would receive a memorial fit for a queen. "Bronwyn is here with your gown," Brex said, pressing a soft kiss to her forehead. "I'll go change and meet you back here, alright?" Gaia nodded and glanced at the door where her great-aunt stood, garment bag in hand. Gaia opened her mouth to speak but found there were no words.

Her great-aunt crossed the threshold and waited until Brex had left before offering Gaia a soft smile.

"I have your gown here. Leona is readying herself, and I offered to assist you instead," she said as she helped Gaia from the bed. Gaia managed a tight smile before the tears started to fall. Bronwyn made soothing sounds as she pulled the black dress from its bag and held it up for Gaia's inspection. Appropriately plain, it was simply cut and modest. Gaia sat and allowed her great-aunt to arrange her hair before she helped her into the dress. Covering the lowest skin of her throat, it left her arms bare, and a line of black satin buttons trailed down the back. When the last button was secured, Gaia turned and thanked her great-aunt with a small bow.

"Your mother was a wonderful woman," Bronwyn offered. "We were all sad to lose her. And I am sorry that she will not be with us to see you become queen." Although her modest behavior drove Gaia to distraction, her great-aunt was far gentler than her husband. Opening an unfamiliar black case, Bronwyn pulled a delicate circlet from the crushed velvet. She settled the diadem onto Gaia's head with a sad smile, before adding the black-netted veil. Gaia pulled the veil down under her chin before glancing in the mirror. After a thought, her hair shifted to the white blonde and eyes to the brilliant turquoise she knew Brex loved, and it contrasted nicely with the silver diadem and black dress.

"Are you ready?"

"I am." Lady Bronwyn opened the door and preceded Gaia to where Brex stood, waiting to escort her. As she stepped across the threshold, Gaia saw Brex freeze when he caught sight of her. After a beat, he recovered and offered her a low bow.

"You look beautiful," he said as he took her arm. She tried to thank him, but the words wouldn't come. He squeezed her hand knowingly. "I am right here," he whispered in her ear. "I won't leave your side." All she could manage was a nod as they traversed the paths that lead to the airstrip. Auggie, Shaw and the others stood arrayed, all dressed in black, with a black ribbon tied across the Brotherhood patch on the arm of their jackets. Brex helped Gaia into a waiting speeder, and their party headed off across the gentle, rolling ocean landscape of Miwarma.

Their destination was a small island far-removed from the town. They landed on solid ground, and Brex helped Gaia down. Feeling the tears surge, she bit down on her lip and grabbed Brex's hand as tightly as she could. He gripped back, his own face pale and hard. The crowd gathered on the small outcropping and stood, waiting. Gaia glanced around and noticed that Amadeas was not present. Bronwyn along with most of the Tallpian court were there, but she didn't see her great-uncle yet. Shaking it off, Gaia raised her eyes and let them settle on the reason they were there. Four bodies rested on the biers at the edge of the island, and though a layer of gauze was draped over each, Gaia could still see her mother's dark, rich hair and aquiline nose. The darkness threatened to overwhelm her, but she fought it back, knowing she had to be strong not only for Brex but the rest of her people. A Miwarman minister parted the crowd and climbed to a small dais. He spoke in a rolling voice about how those that they loved would never really leave them, but all Gaia could hear was the roar of the ocean in her ears. A black heat started to build in Gaia's chest as she stared at the four pyres. This was Nuweydon's doing, and he was going to pay for every single ounce of blood that had been spilt. She wanted him to die slowly and painfully, with the knowledge that she had been his undoing. A squeeze of her hand brought her back, and Gaia looked to see Brex staring at her.

"Are you ready?" he asked her. She gave a terse nod. He handed her a lit torch before taking one of his own. Auggie and Shaw stepped up behind them, bearing similar torches. Hand in hand, Brex and Gaia walked until they stood before Dyla's and Kain's bodies. Gaia had to swallow several times before the lump in her throat would disappear. Over the ringing in her ears, she heard Brex muttering a fierce promise to Kain, a whispered vow that he would be avenged. Auggie was silent on her other side, but Shaw mumbled a grim prayer under his breath. She tried to form the words, to thank her mother for her lifetime of suffering, just so that Gaia had a chance at life. But nothing would come. Finally, she just gave a single nod as her eyes burned, tears tracking silently down her cheeks. Brex glanced at her, and as one they touched their torches to the foot of each pyre. The flames took instantly, and almost immediately all four were completely consumed. Hearing a voice behind them, Gaia glanced to see one of the Miwarman shamans with his arms raised over his head, a loud prayer on his lips. But as she turned back to watch the fire, a soft wind began to build at their backs. As the breeze strengthened, Gaia saw a wisp of something shimmery rise from the fire where her mother's body had lain. Before long, there were four identical trails of what Gaia could only call dust that rose from each pyre, and they twisted and glittered and danced into the air, skipping and trailing over the surface of the gentle sea. They stood in silence, welded together at the hand, watching the smoke fade until the fire had died down. Eventually, Brex tugged on Gaia to guide her back to the speeder, but suddenly, she couldn't bring herself to turn her back on her mother.

"Wait—I need to be alone," she said, and he stopped pulling on her hand to look at her with hollow eyes.

"Gaia—"

"Brex, please." She couldn't bear to argue with him—not now. But she needed to be alone, to say her last goodbye to her mother.

"I'm not leaving you here alone," he said gruffly. "But I'll be over with the others." He squeezed her hand one more time as Auggie and Shaw ambled back towards the crowd.

"Wait, give me your dagger." Brex gave her a worried look but handed over the small knife without question. She took it and clutched it to her chest as she approached the smoldering pyre. She watched the flames for several long breaths before sliding the sharp blade across her palm. She felt no pain as the skin broke and blood welled in her hand. No physical pain could compete with the ache in her heart. She cradled her hand to her chest for a moment before holding it over the fire and let her blood drip into the coals.

"My blood for his," she vowed. "I swear I will take back our throne and that I will make you proud." A gust of wind blustered around her, and the low, still-burning flames guttered and danced in the breeze. She nodded with a grim smile. "I love you too." And only then did she turn her back on the fire and walk back towards Brex and the rest of their party with her head held high.

The entire ride back to the city was silent. Brex had raised his eyebrows at the sight of Gaia's bloody palm, but she shook her head at him, and he knew to stay quiet. Instead, he gripped the injured hand tightly on the ride back, and by the time they disembarked, the cut had healed itself.

"The joys of being Tallpian," she murmured.

Brex chuckled then froze, glancing at her with a surprised look on his face. "What did you say?" he asked curiously.

"The joys of being Tallpian," she repeated. "There is something about our advanced DNA that allows us to heal ourselves very quickly." She glanced at Brex's confused expression. "We talked about this, remember?"

Brex's handsome face was still unsure. "I know we did, but I didn't think of it at the time." He looked at Gaia, comprehension dawning across his handsome face. "So an injury that could possibly be fatal to a human?"

"Would take a Tallpian days, if not hours to heal, instead of weeks or months."

"So a massive belly wound—"

"Would take maybe a few days to a week, depending on how bad," she said, shrugging. "What is your point Brex? Elizar is dead, we know that."

"Auggie."

"What about him?"

"It didn't surprise you when he came bouncing up here less than a week after having his gut sliced open?"

Gaia digested that for a moment before looking at Brex in surprise. "Do you think?" she asked, sounding intrigued.

"That his father might have been Tallpian? I'm beginning to think so."

"I'm surprised it took us this long."

"His mother is terran, so he inherited half of his genes from her—maybe why it took him a few days to get better than just a day or two?" They both examined the back of their friend's copper-colored head as he ambled along ahead of them. "He's always bounced back from things fast, but I never really thought about it."

"Do you think he has any idea?"

"None," Brex confirmed. "He's wondered about it over the years, but his mother was a whore and his father took off long before Auggie was even born. I don't think he cares to know much about the man that left him."

"Should we say something?"

"I'll talk to him. Not right now, though. We still have a lot to do before tomorrow, and this'll keep." Gaia nodded and pressed a kiss to Brex's lips. Instantly his arms came around her waist and tugged her close. She had to drag herself away, a reluctant chuckle low in her throat. He grinned at her. "Go change."

They parted ways in the main quadrangle, promising to change and return for the final war meeting. Gaia entered her quarters and immediately shed her gown. As she paused, contemplating what to wear, she caught sight of her naked form in the mirror. The bump between her hips was becoming more prominent by the day, she thought as she caressed the swell. She had not thought much about her own child during the memorial, but now as she thought about it, she had a feeling her mother would have been thrilled at the prospect of a grandchild. She changed into a floor-length white dress, one that hid her growing bump and went off in search of her lover.

She was halfway to the barracks when Ravi rushed up behind her.

"Oh, Gaia! I'm sorry," he said, skidding to a stop, trying not to knock her over.

She glanced at his worried face in concern as he grabbed her shoulders to keep them both upright. "What is the matter, Ravi?" His young face was a mess of anxiety.

"Amadeas is gone."

She felt her eyes go wide in shock at his words. She shook her head. It couldn't possibly be true. "What did you say?"

"He's gone. His ship left for Meidonna three hours ago."

A shriek ripped from Gaia's chest, and she clenched her hands into fists at her sides. "Are you sure?"

"Yes. The flight tower confirmed it."

"Do you think he's betraying us?" she demanded harshly, looking at the young Tallpian.

"The only thing I can think of that makes sense," he said, still panting. "At this point, are we surprised?" he asked.

"We have got to tell the others," she said, spinning around and heading for the Brotherhood's rooms with Ravi on her tail.

They burst through the door, and a group of about sixty people all shouted, "SURPRISE!" at the same time. Gaia staggered back in shock, tripping over Ravi. Brex stepped forward, a wide smile on his face that faded the instant he saw her dark expression. The chatter behind him died down quickly as they all stared at Gaia's stricken countenance.

"What is the matter?" he demanded. "I'm sorry; I thought you might like a surprise birthday—"

"Amadeas is gone."

"What?" Brex's voice thundered through the silent room.

Gaia nodded in agreement as Ravi spoke. "I went to see him after we returned from the memorials. His office is cleaned out, and his ship is gone."

"Do we know where he's gone to?" Lathan demanded as he joined them, drawn by the tension.

"I think I have an idea," Brex muttered.

Ravi nodded helplessly. "He's gone back."

"To Nuweydon? How is that possible?" Leona snapped as she stepped up next to her husband.

"He'll say that we kidnapped him," Brex growled. "He'll say that we forced him, held him prisoner or something. He can probably worm his way back in, punishment free.

"And even if Nuweydon wants to punish him, he'll be able to tell him everything about us to make up for it," Shaw said. Everyone was crowded around them, all murmuring under their breath. Gaia saw Bronwyn's troubled face in the crowd, undoubtedly upset at the idea of her husband betraying them. "How much of the army is left?" Shaw asked, looking around at the pale Tallpian faces that remained.

"Almost every single Tallpian soldier is still here, as far as I can tell," Ravi said, gesturing to his fellows. "I passed the other barracks. Almost all of our infantry is still here. It's only about two hundred individuals, but it's better than nothing."

"How can we be sure he's betrayed us?" Njoroge asked.

"He thinks our cause is lost," Brex said with a derisive snort. "Is that not enough? Rats always abandon a sinking ship."

"Hey!" Gaia snapped. "We are not—"

"I didn't say I think we're a sinking ship," Brex interrupted her. "It is what Amadeas is clearly thinking."

"If he returns to Meidonna, he'll be able to give them our entire battle plan," Lathan said in concern, but Brex just smiled his cocky smile.

"Not all of it."

# Chapter Twenty-Five

In the hours following Amadeas's defection, the Brotherhood and the remaining Tallpians chose to forgo a night of celebration and sleep and instead spent the remaining hours readying themselves to leave as soon as the time struck a new day. Brex pulled Gaia aside in the midst of the drama.

"I'm sorry," he offered, brushing a strand of blonde hair out of her eyes. She tilted her head at him in confusion. "Your birthday? We won't really have much time tomorrow so I figured we could celebrate tonight," he said.

"Oh!" Gaia said in shock. She hadn't given it any thought past the initial surprise. Tomorrow was her twenty-first birthday. "I honestly hadn't even thought about it," she said with a small shrug. "But thank you for thinking of it." Standing on her toes, she pressed a soft kiss to his lips. He looked pleased, but the worry was clear in his face.

"You're sure?" She waved away his worry with a delicate hand.

"I'm positive, Brex. It isn't a big deal, and this invasion is far more important. We'll celebrate after this is over." Her lover nodded before kissing her back and taking her hand.

"If you say so. Come on, we have a war to win."

"You're still sure that splitting up is a good idea?" They were assembled on the floating airstrip, getting ready to board their ships, when Lathan asked Brex the question that was on everyone's mind.

"I'm positive," Brex said, fixing a long knife to his thigh. "Amadeas stormed out of that meeting before I proposed splitting the group. As long as you haven't said anything to him about it, we should be good." Lathan held up his hands in surrender while shaking his head. Brex nodded. "Good. As far as he knows, we'll still be fighting en masse as a single army. Not to mention we still have Alix, Amadeas has no idea how deep that kid has gotten. With enough time, he can disable their shields and ground their entire fleet— which they do not know about. That gives us the advantage."

"But it will disable our ship's weapons," Alix reminded him as he sat on the ground, hidden behind his ever-present screen. "It's a network-wide blanket so any ship in the vicinity will be affected." Brex shrugged.

"We never really planned on using them in the first place, so it's not like we're taking that hit like they are."

"Still doesn't feel right," Lathan said, shaking his head.

"Of course it doesn't," Shaw chimed in. He checked the bandoleers of ammunition he wore strung across his chest as he spoke. "We're charging into a fight where we know we're outnumbered, we know we're out-gunned, and one of our generals just pulled a fucking Benedict Arnold."

"A what?" Lathan asked politely, but Shaw waved him off.

"Never mind. The point is, it's a shit situation no matter how you slice it, but let's face it, just about every single member of the Brotherhood has come up against worse odds at some point or another, and we're all still here."

"Well most of us, anyway," Auggie offered as he loaded the clip in his pistol.

"You see my point, though."

"I do," Lathan said, "but it doesn't make me any less nervous."

"You and me both," Shaw said. "But we can't back out now." A couple of them glanced at Gaia, and Brex put a hand on her shoulder to keep her from stepping forward.

"We're committed to this," he said, speaking before she could open her mouth. "All of us. Now tell your men to load up," he ordered, looking at his time-piece before meeting the eyes of Cayson and Tyrell. "It's time." Both Brotherhood commanders nodded and moved away into the crowd, issuing orders for their men to begin boarding their ships. Ravi had been given control of the Tallpian army, and he had already organized his men into their units. The entire fleet would leave together, but at the last moment, Brex's ship would split off, and their elite crew would infiltrate the palace. Gaia offered Lathan command of the Tallpian army, but he had declined. No one else knew their way around the palace as well as him, he had pointed out.

"I never did ask you why you chose to support my claim in the beginning," Gaia asked Lathan bluntly earlier in the night. He had offered a graceful shrug, not offended. She knew that Amadeas's goals of ruling through her had made Lathan uncomfortable, but even before then, he had agreed to stand with Gaia and Amadeas against Nuweydon.

"Nuweydon has always been very suspicious of me, with my connection to the throne—" Lathan started.

Gaia gasped. "Your what?" she demanded, and Lathan had bowed to her.

"I apologize that I never told you before. Your mother and mine were cousins. So while it's tenuous, I do still have a claim."

"We've been here three weeks—your wife is my best friend—and you neglected to tell me that we're related?" She had to control her voice to keep from shrieking.

Lathan snorted. "I want it less than you do," he said, trying to reassure her. "There was a time when Amadeas sought to have me rule, but I refused. I have no desire to change my station in life.' Another shrug. "Not to mention Leona would probably have killed me if I considered it." A smile played at his lips, and Gaia smiled too, knowing and not doubting her friend.

"But you are my kin," she said, taking in his narrow face.

Lathan snorted again and waved an arm at the expanse of Tallpian soldiers readying themselves for battle. "As is everyone else. Just because we share a direct relation does not mean you should show me any special favor. I wish to be recognized because of my abilities, not because of our family tree." Gaia sighed in relief.

"How is it that you understand this and Amadeas does not?"

"Amadeas has been blinded by his ambition. He lost his ability to manipulate Nuweydon long ago and has since been searching for a replacement that would heed him. Since you have proven unsatisfactory—"

"Watch yourself, cousin" she growled in a dark voice, making both Lathan and nearby Brex laugh.

"You are capable of many things," Lathan said with another bow. "But being manipulated is not one of them, Gaia."

"Thank you," she said a little stiffly. Brex had wrapped an arm around her waist and pulled her away.

"Relax," he said, kissing her temple. "He's not like Amadeas."

"I know," she relented. "It just always surprises me when I find another relative I had no knowledge of."

"Wait until you're queen. This is only the beginning."

"Gaia, are you ready?" Brex stood on the ramp of the ship, his hand extended. She glanced at her lover before looking back at the sleeping planet of Miwarma. She was grateful for her time there and hoped that as soon as the war was over, she would be able to thank its gentle people for their support. Finally, she turned to Brex and took his hand as they boarded the ship.

"I'm ready." She took her seat next to Brex as the rest of their team arrayed themselves around the cabin. Brex readied the ship for take-off and waited until Cayson's face popped up on the telescreen.

"We're good to go. Tyrell is also set." Brex nodded.

"Good. We'll meet you outside the atmosphere." The screen went blank, and Brex slowly eased the throttle open until the rumble of the engine filled the ship, and it pulled itself free from the planet's surface. Gaia sat in silence as the ship rose through the clouds. The Brothers were chattering and joking: Their calm demeanors still surprised Gaia. She was sitting on the edge of the control console when she felt a sharp pain stab her in the stomach.

"Ugh!" she grunted in pain and doubled over, closing her eyes and grinding her teeth to ward it off.

"Gaia!" Brex's voice echoed in her ears as she tried to right herself. He dove out of his chair, abandoning the controls to throw himself to his knees in front of her. "Gaia, what is wrong?" He took her face in his hands and tilted it so she would look at him. She grimaced and took a deep breath.

"Nothing," she said, trying to wave him off. "Just a twinge. It caught me off guard, that's all." She could see that Brex didn't believe her. She placed a placating hand on his cheek. "I'm alright, Brex," she said, trying not to chuckle at the concerned look on his face.

"Brex, relax man. I get that this is your first time parenting but—" Brex rounded on Auggie with a snarl.

"Do you realize we are sending the future queen of Meidonna into battle while carrying the heir to her throne?"

he demanded. Auggie stood and clapped a hand on Brex's shoulder with an easy smile.

"Relax, dude. If anyone can handle themselves, I have a feeling it's this one here," he said, pointing to Gaia with his chin. She dimpled at him, trying to ignore the pinch in her stomach.

"Thank you, Auggie." Brex glowered between them before finally shrugging.

"Fine, if you two insist on ignoring me, then do whatever you want," he growled before booting Shaw from the command chair. Gaia did her best to hide her smile at his grumpy behavior. He was behaving like an overprotective parent, and it made her heart sing. He was going to make an amazing father.

"She's going to be queen," Shaw said as Brex nudged him aside. "She can do whatever she wants," he said with a teasing purr.

"Hey! That is the future queen you're talking to," Brex snapped, but Shaw didn't look at all ashamed as he rubbed the back of his head where Brex had swatted him.

"And what about you? Are you the future king?" someone asked, and the room went silent. Brex glanced at Gaia, whose face was a combination of surprise and what might have been horror.

"No. The throne is Gaia's—that is the most important thing," Brex said quickly. "I don't want to be king."

"We are changing all of the rules," Lathan said, stretching lazily. "No outsider has ever sat on the throne of Meidonna, but that means nothing now." The lanky Tallpian smiled at his cousin. "You'll create new traditions and new rules. You can do as you please." Gaia looked terrified, but Brex chuckled under his breath. He didn't have a doubt about his girl's ability to rule, even though she doubted herself.

"Oh," Brex said, snapping his fingers, pretending like he had just remembered something. "I forgot, I have something for you," he said to Gaia, and she smiled in relief at the distraction. "Come with me," offering his hand. They left the cockpit and the chattering members of their group.

"Thank you," Gaia said in the hallway. "I wasn't sure what to say to that." Brex shrugged.

"The throne is yours, Gaia. You know it holds no interest for me. We'll figure it out after we've won."

"What do you want? After, I mean," Gaia asked and Brex turned his blue eyes to her, looking sad. But only for a moment. He caught her look of concern and forced a smile to his face.

"What did I just say? Don't worry about it until after. Until then, we only have two things to worry about, and those are keeping you alive and killing that son-of-a-bitch." She looked like she wanted to argue, but Brex gave her a look, and she closed her mouth. They passed into his compartment, and he pulled a bundle wrapped in a large piece of coarse cloth from under his bunk. "This is for you," he said, offering it to her. Gaia took the gift, her face puzzled. She pulled the wrapping free and revealed a breastplate, forged from scales of a delicate, almost iridescent metal. It caught the light as she turned it over in her hands, glinting off the gentle, swirling designs delicately carved along the edges.

"What...." she trailed off as she looked up at him, at a complete loss of words. Brex smiled. While most women desired diamonds or other precious stones, he knew that wouldn't be it. So he had taken a different route.

"I had Auggie forge it during his first week on Miwarma. The guy has a touch for metal like no one else I know."

"Brex, it's beautiful!"

"I'm more concerned about the functionality," he muttered but smiled at her as she held it to her chest. "Here," he said, sliding the back piece into place and snapping the connectors closed. It fit her like a second skin. She turned and bent, the flexible scales moving with her.

"It's perfect." She beamed at him, and he knew instantly it had been the right choice.

"I had already planned to give it to you, but now I'm even more glad I did," Brex said as he slid his hand between the armor and her body, cupping her stomach. "It's iridium alloy, one of the strongest elements. Nothing can penetrate it." Gaia drew in a deep breath and held it before slowly exhaling.

"Thank you, Brex. I know this is hard for you, but I have to do this." She sighed as Brex furrowed his eyebrows at her.

"I still wish that I had made you stay, but there isn't anything we can do now. You just have to promise me you won't do anything stupid."

She quirked her eyebrows at him, laughter in her eyes. "That's rich," she said with a throaty chuckle.

"Hey!"

"You know it's true, Brex. Who had a bullet dug out of them last time we were here on Meidonna? Certainly not me."

"I had to do something!"

Gaia patted his cheek gently. "Of course you did, I'm just saying you have a tendency to be a little…impulsive."

"I'll show you impulsive," he growled, grabbing her around the waist and yanking her against him. He sealed his lips over hers and felt his bones dissolve.

# Chapter Twenty-Six

The trip to Meidonna was much shorter than Gaia remembered. All too soon, they had rejoined the rest of the fleet, just outside the planet's atmosphere. Transmissions were hurled between ships as the commanders readied themselves and their men for the fight. Alix sat in the cockpit of Brex's ship, hunched over a computer, his hands whizzing across the keyboard as he muttered to himself and watched the screen. None of it made any sense to Gaia, as she watched the lines upon lines of letters and numbers fill the screen, but after several tense minutes, Alix looked up at Brex with a triumphant smile on his face.

"We're a go," he said, flashing thumbs up. "The shields will dissolve in,—" he glanced at his timepiece,—"about thirty seconds. Their ships should all be disabled." Brex unwillingly released Gaia's hand as he returned to the captain's chair. She stood at his shoulder as their commanders reported in, confirming that everything was set.

"We'll follow you in," Brex confirmed as Cayson and Tyrell's faces shared a split screen. "But break off at the last moment. Nuweydon has to know we're coming."

"You better believe he knows we're coming. But he won't feel the hammer until it's already dropped."

"Cayson," Brex said, suddenly serious. "Thank you." The lavender-hued giant shook his head.

"This isn't about you, Brex. This is about her," nodding his chin at Gaia, "and the Brotherhood removing a bully from power. It is just another day on the job."

"I know. But thank you, nonetheless, for following me and believing in this."

"Kain trusted you. That speaks more for you than anything else, Brexler." Brex nodded, unable to speak. "We'll see you for the victory lap." Cutting the transmission, Brex glanced up at Gaia, her expression unreadable.

"Are you ready?" She turned her turquoise eyes to him, a serene look stealing over her fair face.

"More than I have ever been." After he had given her the armor, she had changed into a black, long-sleeved top that hugged her curves and fit under the breastplate and black pants, tucked into her boots. Her sword lay waiting, and she had both a pistol and a knife in holsters, strapped to her thighs. As a finishing touch, she had settled her glinting silver diadem into her blonde hair.

"She already looks like a queen," Auggie had whispered to Brex, watching Gaia as she stood in ernest conversation with Lathan across the cockpit as they were getting ready to exit warp and rejoin the rest of the Brotherhood. Brex nodded in agreement, letting his eyes linger on her stomach. Few things in life scared him, but suddenly he was terrified that he was going to lose the woman he loved—and the child they had created together. As long as she survived the fight, that was all Brex cared about, even if he lost her to her throne in the end. Auggie had fixed him with a sharp, knowing stare but said nothing.

An icy, rigid energy stole through the cabin as they waited the final seconds for the shields to drop.

"Five, four three, two—" Alix was counting down, his eyes glued to his screen, when the first hit rocked the ship. The massive comet-class ship bucked hard, slamming everyone to the floor. Brex swore and managed to cling to the controls by the tips of his fingers.

"Alix!" he shouted, trying to right the leaning ship and stem the screaming alarms. "What the fuck just happened?" he demanded, trying to pull the ship up away from Meidonna's atmosphere. Cayson's face appeared on the telelink as Brex barked at Auggie to get Gaia locked in, and more hits shook the ship.

"What the hell was that?" The Necosian demanded. The screen split, and Tyrell's face appeared, a large cut over his eyebrow pouring peacock-blue blood. Ravi's strained face appeared a second later.

"We're in trouble, Carrow," he howled. "What is going on?"

"I'm working on it!" Alix shouted back, furiously banging away at the keyboard.

"Brex, we can't take another hit like that!" Auggie yelled, his eyes on the gauges, most of them with needles leaning into the red.

"They knew we were coming!" Gaia screamed, watching through the massive windshield as more energy pulses shot up through the clouds towards them. Brex swore and narrowly avoided them but managed to dump most of the crew back to the ground. Gaia swore in her own language, clinging to Brex's chair.

"Alix!" Brex roared again.

"I'm trying, I'm trying!" he shouted back, fingers racing across the keys. "They knew we were coming. They had the codes open but changed them as I entered them. I didn't notice until just now. I just have to change them back to our frequencies. Two minutes."

"We don't have two minutes!"

"Just hang on!"

"Ground their weapons!"

"I am!" They watched as one of the Tallpian troop ships took a direct hit, and there was a massive eruption as the vessel was shredded by a fireball.

"Alix!" Gaia's voice was an octave too high as it cut through the air, shrill with panic.

"I'm almost there!" They waited with baited breath as more shots whipped past them.

"Their laser targeting must be down," Lathan said as another shot suddenly went wide.

"First thing I disabled," Alix muttered over the din. Gaia kept her eyes fixed on the planet, but after another long moment, the shots thinned out before they stopped altogether. Alix threw his hands up triumphantly, and Brex slumped back into his chair. Gaia cupped a hand to her belly, wincing. Thankfully, Brex didn't see her grimace.

"Fucking Amadeas," he snarled under his breath, glaring at the planet that was barely visible through the clouds. "He had them just waiting for you, didn't he?" Alix nodded, his pale face drenched in sweat and hands shaking.

"In the planet codes yeah, but what about the fleet? Everything should have been locked down. They shouldn't have known about that block."

"How did he find out about the fleet block, then?" Brex asked, eyes wandering darkly across their assembled crew.

"I have no idea. I only told you guys."

"He must have had spies—but who?"

"He found out I was pregnant the same day I did," Gaia reminded him. "And there was no one in my rooms other than Leona and…and Sia." Her thoughts immediately went to the young Miwarman girl who had been assigned to assist her. "May the gods damn him!" she growled, glancing at Brex. "It had to have been Sia. Leona certainly wouldn't have done it."

"Well, now we're fucked," Cayson said from the screen. Tyrell, who had Kyan hovering over him, trying to stitch the massive gash on his forehead shut, nodded, swatting the young medic out of the way.

"Not necessarily," Alix said, his fingers back on the keyboard. "I'm flooding their frequencies with static and junk codes. They shouldn't be able to get through everything and back into their programs anytime soon. This is our chance." Brex glanced at the screen where his commanders stared back at him.

"Are you ready?" he asked, and his commanders nodded. "Ravi? You alright, brother?" Ravi's face was the color of sour milk, tears glittering in his green eyes. He ground his teeth as he fought to hold himself together.

"My brother was on that ship." His voice broke, and he looked away for a moment before turning back to stare at them all. "I am going to rip Amadeas to shreds."

"Get in line," snarled Alix. "We're clear," he snapped at Brex. "I should be able to destroy their hold on both sets of codes by the time we hit the surface."

"We're clear?"

"You're clear," he said, looking up from his screen, his black eyes hard. "Go, now." Brex nodded and jammed the controls forward as the ship dove through the atmosphere.

The rest of the team spent the last, silent moments affixing their weapons. Gaia had Sigur slung across her back, her opalescent armor shimmering in the low light.

"Alright." Brex spun in his chair to face the rest of the crew after putting the ship into autopilot. "We'll be landing in just a minute or two." He looked at Murad. "I'll need you to get us as close to the palace as possible." The young Brotherhood member nodded.

"We'll enter the palace through a skylight in the roof," Lathan said. "As long as we can get into the palace undetected, we should be fine."

"And if we don't?" Shaw asked. Lathan shrugged.

"Fight like hell and hope at least some of us make it inside."

"And once we're inside?"

"There are really only two possible locations that Nuweydon will take shelter in. The council chamber behind the throne room is one, and the dungeons are the other. Since the dungeons are full of prisoners, my bet is we'll find him in council. As for Amadeas," he held up his hands in a helpless gesture. "I have no idea if he'll be with Nuweydon or not."

"What kind of resistance are we looking at?" Shaw asked as he double-checked both of his pistols.

"He'll probably retain most elite of the palace guards, but the major force will be concentrated around the doors into the throne room. If we use the roof, we should bypass them entirely. They will surrender once Nuweydon is dead."

"You're sure?" Lathan shrugged again.

"They follow the leader of Meidonna. Most of them are terrified of Nuweydon, as is most of the population. He has a small, loyal force that helped him with his original coup twenty years ago. Those are the ones who will be guarding him in the chambers."

"And you're ok with killing your own people?" Alix demanded. After his parent's murder, he was sensitive about people turning on their own. Lathan's face darkened.

"No, I'm not. But my father was also killed during Nuweydon's coup, and my mother lived as an outcast for most of my life. I joined the palace guards as a chance to someday avenge my father. Thankfully, Gaia's return has allowed for a full-scale takeover, instead of a single, lone soldier with a grudge." His smile was self-deprecating, but his voice was hard. "I vowed that I would seek revenge on Nuweydon if it cost me my last breath."

"Well, it might," Auggie offered, and the cockpit broke into nervous laughter.

"Shut up, guys," Brex ordered, his eyes on the dashboard where the gauges were showing the rapidly approaching surface. "This is it."

Every eye was glued to the massive windshield as they watched the rest of their armada flood to the surface, each door popping open to spill dozens of soldiers in dark clothing onto the planet. A distance away, they could see Nuweydon's forces, arrayed in grey formations, waiting.

"Don't worry about them," Brex ordered Gaia, watching the concern fill her face. "Cayson, Tyrell, and Ravi have this under control." He glanced around at the team. "Buckle up; this is going to get rough." As the final ships landed, Brex jerked hard on the controls, and their ship dove off to the side, roaring across the landscape, almost scraping the tops of buildings as they neared the palace. Guards poured out of the front doors and began firing at the ship.

"Get us out of range," Brex ordered as bullets pinged off the hull and he slid from the captain's chair. Murad took his place at the controls and immediately pulled the ship higher into the air and aimed for the roof of the palace, trying to hide the ship among the spires and towers. Brex grabbed his holster from the console and tightened the buckle around his waist as Murad maneuvered them towards their entrance point. Brex grabbed Gaia's hand as the ship rocked and pulled her into a tight embrace.

"I love you," he whispered fiercely into her ear, and her bright eyes jerked up to meet his. "Forever."

"I love you too," she breathed back before unlocking her arms from around his neck.

Brex looked at Lathan on one side and Auggie on the other, both of them nodded at him. "Let's do this."

The team streamed into the main bay, and Brex kicked open a small hatch in the floor. As soon as it swung open, the room was filled with the roar of gunfire and the howl of the wind. They dropped a rope through the hatch, and Auggie was the first to slide his lean height through. He offered Brex a salute, winked at Gaia, and was gone before Brex had time to bristle. Lathan followed, and too soon Brex was offering Gaia his hand so she could wriggle her way through the opening.

"I'll be right behind you," Brex shouted, his voice was almost lost in the wind. Gaia gripped the thin, black cable and slowly loosened her grip until gravity pulled her towards the roof. She could hear gunfire, and the shouts of thousands as the Brotherhood surged against the Tallpian army. Her feet slammed into the tiled roof as the wind buffeted against her. She staggered into Auggie as Brex came sliding down above her. The mechanic grabbed her and held her upright as they struggled to maintain their footing on the slippery tiles. As soon as Shaw hit the roof and completed their team, Murad jammed the ship into the air before dipping low to skim the ground, trying to draw away the attention of the guards. Unable to talk over the howling wind, Lathan gestured for them to keep low and follow him as they hurried across the roof. Gaia checked her weapons as she ducked after him, trying to stay low in the shadows. Meidonna's single, massive sun was just starting to sink below the horizon as they found their way to the skylight that Lathan had chosen. As her cousin knelt to pick the lock that held the grate shut, Gaia gazed east to where the infantry battle was raging. The smaller, darker force made up of her loyal Tallpian soldiers and Brotherhood members had surged forward, and while it was difficult to see individuals, the difference between the two forces was noticeable.

"They're holding their own!" Brex shouted, the elation clear in his voice. All Gaia could do was nod. She had an itchy feeling in her palms, and she recognized it as the need to feel a weapon in her hands. Only a few short minutes, she promised herself, as Lathan pried open the hatch and beckoned them to follow him, until Nuweydon would cease breathing and finally release his hold on her and her people.

The roar of the wind cut to a muted hiss as they slid into the attic of the palace. The long, low room they found themselves standing in as Auggie closed the hatch was dark and dusty.

"Don't sneeze," Lathan advised them in a whisper. "We're right above the throne room." They followed him through the dim landscape of broken furniture and discarded masquerade props until they reached a small door. "This leads to the rear staircase, just behind the throne room," Lathan whispered. "The door to the council chambers is at the bottom. Once we hit the stairs, we only have a few seconds until they will hear us coming. Be ready." Gaia pulled Sigur from its scabbard, and the others drew their weapons. Lathan listened before easing it open and gesturing for them to follow. He made it three steps down before a shout of alarm rang through the narrow hall.

"Now!" Lathan shouted, opening fire as he ran down the stairs, Gaia hot on his heels. A dozen guards poured from the door at the bottom of the stairs, some drawing guns, and others swords. Gaia plunged into the thick of them, letting her blade become an extension of herself, just as Alix had taught her. One guard brought his blade up the meet hers, and the impact stung as the blow rang through the metal. Growling under her breath, she slammed her blade back against his before pulling her pistol from her holster and shooting him point-blank in the chest. The staircase was too narrow for her to effectively wield Sigur without hurting any of her own people. Seeing another guard taking aim at someone above her, she fired again and again until her clip was empty. Pushing to the bottom of the stairs, she could hear their shouts and shots echoing through the massive throne room. One voice, in particular, made her blood run cold and she knew Lathan had been right: Nuweydon had taken cover within the council chambers. As more of their team pushed down the stairs, the fight spilled into the throne room, and the stone chamber was filled with the sounds of war and soon littered with bodies in grey Tallpian uniforms. Dispatching another guard, Gaia looked around to see most of their team engaged with other opponents, but Nuweydon was nowhere to be seen. Suddenly, as she was stalking around the base of the massive dais, a figure stepped from the shadows to confront her. But it wasn't Nuweydon—it was Arlo.

"Arlo!" It was Brex's voice that cut through the chaos like a knife, and the gorth's head whipped around to look at his long-time enemy. Brex's handsome face was filled with thunder as he head-butted the guard he was wrestling, knocking the soldier out cold before turning his rage to the gorth. Arlo raised his gun, but Brex was quicker, and he had drawn his revolver and fired before Arlo could even pull the trigger. Arlo staggered back in surprise, a red stain blooming on his chest. Brex fired again, his eyes like chips of flint. A second figure darted into the room, and Gaia saw the slim, rat-like features of Keon. Without even taking his eyes off Arlo, Brex raised his second pistol and fired again, the shot hitting home in Keon's neck. His narrow body collapsed without a sound as Brex strode forward to look Arlo in the eye.

"This is for Gaia, you son-of-a-bitch," Brex growled, raising his gun. Arlo tried to lift his weapon but coughed, dropping his weapon as blood dribbled from his lips. Brex sneered in disgust and pulled the trigger one more time, and Arlo's greasy head rocked back before his body crumpled to the floor, his malicious eyes open and unseeing.

Gaia looked around the room, the marble floor littered with the dead and injured but all of the Brotherhood remained on their feet, chests heaving in exertion, and except for a few minor wounds, mostly unharmed.

"Where is he?" Gaia screamed as she spun around, her voice echoing and doubling in the huge room. "Nuweydon, you coward! Where are you?"

"You have made a grave mistake, Niece." The icy voice cut through the room, and Gaia whipped around to see Nuweydon standing at the base of the dais, his red eyes glowing. He took in her weapon and diadem with a sneer. "So you stand before me, crowned queen already?" he drawled. Gaia narrowed her gaze, but as she glared at her uncle, she saw a flash of movement out of the corner of her eye. Lathan surged forward, dagger in hand. Nuweydon turned and delivered a swift kick to Lathan's midsection before her cousin could even raise his knife. Lathan was knocked back off the stone stairs and crumpled into a heap at the bottom.

The rest of the Brotherhood jumped forward, but Gaia whipped her hand up, freezing them in their tracks. "No!" she shouted, "He's mine."

Nuweydon offered her a mocking smile. "So noble, Niece, to give your life for this rabble."

"The only life to be forfeited tonight is yours," she spat back.

"And yet here I stand," he said, spreading his arms wide, laughing.

"Pick up a weapon," she ordered him.

"Gaia, no!" Brex's voice was like a white hot knife in her heart, but she shoved down the pain. She had to do this.

She waved a hand, cutting him off in a single gesture. "No, Brex. This is one fight you can't take for me." She threw Auggie a glance, and he grabbed Brex's arm to keep him from diving in before Gaia turned back to her uncle. "Pick up a weapon, Uncle."

Nuweydon smiled at her, the evil leaking from him like poisoned smoke. He eyed her for a moment, red gaze taking in Sigur, still tightly clutched in her hand. "The katana," he said, his voice like silk as he caressed the word. "So much like the father you never knew, Kallideia."

"Gaia," she spat automatically.

He offered a sarcastic bow as he drew the weapon strapped to his back. "As Her Highness wishes." Instead of answering, Gaia gave a kestrel shriek and dove forward, bringing up her blade. Nuweydon's face lost its mocking sneer as he raised his own weapon, and they met with a ringing clang. Gaia kept her grip light, wielding the blade with dexterity and grace just as Alix had taught her. Their blades met, again and again, the sound of metal on metal echoing through the marble room. The look on Nuweydon's face slid from confident to concentration as he realized she was far more capable than he anticipated. Gaia poured every ounce of strength she possessed into her blows as they clashed against one another. She was lifting her sword for an overhand strike when Nuweydon's blade suddenly flicked out and struck her, slicing into the exposed flesh just above her hip. Body singing with pain, she took a step back to glance down at her wound before looking up at Nuweydon. He wore a satisfied smirk on his face as blood, bright and glossy, spilled from the cut. Rage, metallic and white hot, flooded her body and burned her tongue. Gaia let loose a feral scream and dove back at her uncle, who took a startled step back before raising his weapon.

"You killed my father," she barked, punctuating the sentence with a hammer of a blow that caused Nuweydon to take another large step back. "You killed my mother," she yelled, slamming forward. "You tried to kill me, and you threatened the man I love." Another blow like a lightning strike. "But now, you have threatened the life of my child!" Her voice rose and rang through the room like a thunderstorm. "That

I will not stand for!" She began to rain down blows upon Nuweydon, and it was all he could do to keep his footing as he fled backward. Miscalculating a step, he stumbled backward against the steps of the dais and fell, landing on his back. She brought her blade down hard, clipping the sword from his hand, knocking it away. Suddenly prone and defenseless, Nuweydon held up his hands in surrender, but the gesture was far too slow and far too late as Gaia swung Sigur one last time. The blade, still honed to perfection, sliced into his neck and sent his head tumbling.

"Gaia!" The shouts broke over her like a wave as she staggered back from the dais where Nuweydon's blood was spreading in a glassy, crimson river down the white stairs. She turned to see Brex's handsome face, white with fear. He dove to his knees in front of her, slamming a hand against her hip. It wasn't terribly deep and was barely bleeding, but he still shouted for bandages. Auggie produced a small medic kit, and they slapped a bandage over the cut, even as the cut began to heal.

"Are you ok?" Brex finally asked, rising to his feet and taking her face in his hands, smearing her cheek with blood. They locked eyes, and the world dissolved around them. Gaia's heart expanded so much it hurt in her chest, staring into Brex's blue eyes. The man who had jumped out of the shadows in a bar to help a young woman in distress was now standing by her side as her lover and the father of her child. She would be queen, and their future was wide and open and free. Trembling but managing to stay on her feet, Gaia kept a smile on her face as she looked around the white throne room, awash in crimson blood.

"It's over," she said, her quiet voice triumphant.

"Not quite yet." As Gaia lifted her head and listened, she realized she could still hear the sounds of the battle raging outside, and there was banging and yelling coming from beyond the main doors to the throne room that were still barricaded.

"We need to end this," Gaia said, the panic surfacing in her voice.

"We will," Brex soothed her. "Once you're cleaned up."

"I'm fine," she said, brushing his concern aside. "We have to stop them before anyone else dies." The shouting at the door was even louder now. "Come on." Gaia stepped around the lake of blood that had pooled at the foot of the dais and had just bent to pull Nuweydon's head from the floor, his red eyes already clouded by the shroud of death, when the doors at the end of the hall burst open. Tallpian soldiers in their grey uniforms poured through the doors, guns trained on Gaia. Paused in the act of lifting Nuweydon's head from the ground, she froze, unable to reach for a shield of any kind. She twisted, turned her back, and ducked. The shout and the crack of gunfire were simultaneous—even later in life, Gaia would remember them as a single sound. The still-standing members of the Brotherhood immediately dropped down and returned fire, and it was Lathan's frantic gesturing and shouting that finally ended the barrage. The other Tallpian soldiers recognized him and laid down their arms once they saw Nuweydon's corpse on the dais. As silence descended, Gaia glanced down at herself: She was miraculously unhurt. But it was Auggie's shout a breath later that caused a jolt of pain to shoot through her; primal and animalistic, the sound hurt her straight down to the marrow in her bones. Jerking around, it took her several long seconds to process the fact that Brex had thrown himself in front of her to shield her from the gunshots and had taken several bullets to the chest.

"Brex!" Dropping Nuweydon's head, she dove the short distance to where he lay against the dais stairs, his shirt already soaked in blood.

"Get a medic!" A pale-faced member of the Brotherhood sprinted from the room as Gaia crashed to her knees next to Brex, her heart in her throat. She grabbed one of his hands, gripping it tightly.

"How could you?" she demanded as Brex looked up at her. "Damn it, Brex, how could you?" She howled as the tears began to fall, the sobs shaking her entire body.

Auggie was kneeling on his other side, trying to keep pressure on the worst of the wounds. "I thought I told you not to do anything stupid!" he growled at him. Brex chuckled weakly before coughing, coating his lips in blood.

"We need a medic!" Gaia shrieked at the men who were standing in a somber circle around them.

Brex lifted a weak hand to cup Gaia's cheek. "I love you, Gaia."

"Brex, no—"

"Take care of my boy," he said, dropping his hand to her stomach.

"Brex, please no. I can't lose you. I can't do this without you."

"You're going to be an amazing queen—" he broke off, coughing as more blood appeared.

"Where is that fucking medic?" Auggie snarled.

"You'll be an even better mother." Brex's words were soft, fading.

"You can't leave me, Brex," Gaia sobbed. "I can't do this alone."

"Yes you can, and you will."

He turned his hazy eyes to Auggie. "Auggie—"

"No, dude, shut up."

"Shut up and listen. Auggie, you're my best friend."

"I don't want it—don't do this."

"Take the Brotherhood. There's no one better. Kain should have given it to you the first time around."

"Brex—"

"Take care of Gaia and the kid."

Gaia and Auggie's eyes met for half of a second before they both looked back at Brex. "I will," Auggie vowed.

Brex nodded weakly and turned back to Gaia. "I love you so much. You changed my life. I am so sorry that I won't get to see you crowned queen. I love you."

"I love you too, Brex, I am so sorry." She cupped his hand to her cheek as his eyes stared at her hungrily, taking in her face one last time. After a moment, his hand went limp in her grasp, and his eyes became fixed, staring off into nothing.

"No!" Gaia's scream echoed through the silent room. She sat, rocking and sobbing, clutching Brex's hand for several long minutes before Lathan settled a gentle hand on her shoulder, but he recoiled when she snarled at him.

"Gaia, I am so sorry but the others—they're still fighting. And Amadeas is leading them."

"What?" She jerked around. "You're sure?" Her cousin nodded once and swallowed thickly. With a wild growl, she jumped to her feet and snatched up Sigur and Nuweydon's head from the floor in a single movement.

"Where are you going?" The look she threw over her shoulder as she marched towards the doors was that of a soul about to storm the gates of Hell.

"To end this."

# Chapter Twenty-Seven

As Gaia disappeared from the hall, Auggie looked up from his place at Brex's side to glare at his Brothers.

"You heard Brex. We have to take care of her. We can't let her go out there alone. Njoroge, stay here. Lathan, Shaw, we need to go after her." Auggie staggered to his feet, dragging a revolver from Brex's holster as he stood, and they rushed after Gaia's disappearing form as she strode through the castle towards the battle.

The sound of gunfire and men screaming met her ears as Gaia pushed through the two massive front doors of the palace. While Nuweydon's force was more significant, the Brotherhood had held their own, and the black mass kept their line firm. Striding down the steps towards the raging battle, she raised Nuweydon's head over her own, her fingers wrapped in his long, white hair. As she neared the battle, soldiers began to turn and look at her. Most of the Tallpians instantly hit their knees, and the Brotherhood stepped back, perplexed. She marched up the line that ran between the two forces, and the sound of gunfire began to fade out. Only a small core force of Tallpian soldiers continued to fight, and Gaia could see Amadeas's twisted, angry face as she strode towards them. As soon as his group caught sight of her, Amadeas's fighters dropped back, whether in fear or respect, she wasn't sure, but she didn't care. Soon Amadeas was the only being on the battlefield still fighting. When no further opponents stepped up, Amadeas whipped around glaring and finally caught sight of his great-niece. His eyes flicked from her face to that of Nuweydon. Drawing level with her former general, Gaia tossed the severed head towards him, and it bounced twice before coming to rest a foot from where Amadeas stood. He looked down at it before taking a step back.

"Amadeas!" Gaia shouted, her voice ringing across the battlefield. "You are hereby charged with desertion and treason. As the new queen of Meidonna, I sentence you to death!" Her voice rose and carried over the now almost silent battlefield.

"Crowned yourself already?" he snarled at her, contempt consuming his face. Gaia felt a smile spread across her lips.

"From the man who would have crowned me the moment he met me—provided I danced only to his tune!" Her shout carried over the heads of the men, and she could hear muttering behind her. She pointed at Amadeas. "This man is the one responsible for our fight. The Tallpian people and the Outer Rim Brotherhood have no quarrel! This is the man who plotted the death of my father, King Yehuda! He is the man responsible for the last twenty years you have suffered under Nuweydon." Gaia spun to face the Tallpian soldiers directly. "He sought to use me, to make me his puppet, so that he could rule Meidonna from the shadows behind the throne. But I refuse to be used!" She whipped around and addressed herself to the Brotherhood. "This man," she bellowed, "has caused the deaths of not only one but two leaders of the Outer Rim Brotherhood." The grumbling was getting louder as she spun back to face Amadeas. "Brexler Carrow is dead! Because of your plotting and scheming, he has been taken from us!" She dropped her voice and addressed Amadeas directly. "Not only have you robbed me of the love of my life, you have also robbed my child of the chance to know their father." Understanding flooded Amadeas's narrow face, and he twisted it into a grimace.

"Good!" he shouted at her, eyes crazed as he waved his arms above his head. "Good riddance of the mercenary scum! He was never fit to sit on the throne—" At his words, Gaia ripped Sigur from its scabbard and broke into the first steps that would have spelled Amadeas's death, but a single gunshot rang across the landscape, bringing Gaia up short. Glancing over her shoulder, she saw Auggie standing behind her, Brex's revolver in hand, its barrel smoking. His face was like thunder as he stepped forward.

"I warned you," he roared at Amadeas. "I warned you that if you that if anything happened to Brex, I would hold you personally responsible." Turning to look at Amadeas, Gaia saw a sparkling stain of bright red spreading across the shoulder of his jacket. "I told you there would be nowhere to hide because the Brotherhood is everywhere." The men in black behind them all chuckled in dark anticipation. "And here you stand surrounded by them, responsible for the death of our leader." Suddenly Auggie's normal, teasing tone was back, and he grinned a distinctly evil grin at Amadeas. "Your move." Amadeas whipped around, looking at his men, all of whom took large steps away from him as the black crush of the Brotherhood advanced.

"Defend me! Defend your kin!" he bellowed. But Amadeas's words fell on deaf ears. "You cowards!" he shouted as the first member of the Brotherhood grabbed the collar of his jacket and jerked him backward. His shouts turned into one long howl as he disappeared under a mass of black. Auggie and Lathan pulled Gaia back from the crush as both Tallpian soldiers and brotherhood members alike jumped onto the pile.

# Chapter Twenty-Eight

*Three Months Later*

"Are you ready?"

"I have been asked that question daily for the past four months," came the answering snarl. "If I weren't at this point, it wouldn't matter." The room broke into titters of sympathetic laughter as Gaia stood on a raised platform; the seamstresses were put the finishing touches on the royal-blue coronation gown that was wrapped around her. "I have unified my people, released Nuweydon's prisoners, traveled the planet, and created a new cabinet government. If that doesn't make me queen, a stupid piece of headwear won't change anything."

"Gaia!" Leona snapped at her, giving her an exasperated look. Gaia glanced at her chief lady-in-waiting and rolled her eyes.

"Yes, alright? I'm ready—oof!" Gaia suddenly doubled over at the waist with a grimace.

"What? What is it? Are you alright?"

But there was a smile on Gaia's face as she righted herself. "Yes, he's just stretching." She pulled aside the robe of state just in time to show the little foot that was pressed firmly against the wall of her distended stomach.

"Only another few weeks, Your Grace."

"And I thought running from Arlo was the longest few weeks of my life."

"Gaia!"

"Alright, alright. Yes, I'm ready." Leona flung open the doors and preceded Gaia into the hallway where Auggie and Lathan waited. Both men froze, surprise etched into their faces. Lathan was the first to recover, and he bowed over Gaia's hand.

"You look beautiful,"

"And fat," Auggie added with a snicker.

Gaia shot him a dark glare but couldn't help but join his laughter. "You have no idea," she moaned, rubbing the curve of her stomach. "He's so strong already."

"As if any kid of Brex's wouldn't be?" Auggie asked softly.

Gaia looked up from caressing her belly to stare into Auggie's eyes, her turquoise gaze full of tears. "Gods, I miss him," she whispered, her lower lip trembling.

Auggie and Lathan both nodded in agreement. "We all do. But you know he would be so proud of you too," Auggie offered.

She nodded in return. "Yes, I do. I think he knew I was going to be queen all along."

"He did," Auggie said in agreement. "And he was the one who figured out all this,—" he said, gesturing to himself. In the days following Brex's death, Gaia had finally gotten around to telling Auggie about their hunch regarding his heritage. He had been skeptical, but a blood test had proven he was indeed half-Tallpian, his father a long-dead mercenary. Gaia's new court had welcomed him with open arms, and in addition to leading the Brotherhood, he served as an ambassador of sorts between the Tallpian people and the rest of the galaxy. He now had a permanent place at court and had abandoned his shop on Cunat in favor of aiding Gaia and keeping an eye on the heir to the throne once he arrived. Noria, the beautiful half-Xion girl from Cunat that Auggie had long had feelings for, made the move across the galaxy to Meidonna and married Auggie shortly thereafter. She was already pregnant with their first child.

"Gaia, today is a happy day," Leona said, giving her arm a little shake as the queen's face filled with sadness. "The day that we have been waiting for all these years."

"You're right," she said, wiping the tears from her eyes. "You are absolutely right. I'm ready."

They took their places, Leona and Lathan in front, and Auggie at her side, her hand resting gently on top of his.

"This is it," he whispered as the doors were flung open and the light poured through. Gaia counted to ten as Lathan and Leona made their way in, and soon her steps were pulling her forward into the throne room. The once-dark pall was thrown off, and the room was buzzing; filled with light and color as the Tallpian court arrayed in all their finery to watch their new queen be crowned. Auggie guided her through the hall and up the few steps—much shorter than Nuweydon's towering dais with its dozens of stairs and lofty perch—and helped her arrange her robe and gown as she sat on the marble throne. At the foot of the stairs, the head priest of Meidonna stepped up, spread his arms wide and spoke in a rolling voice. The gods had, at last, answered their prayers, he said, and given them a beautiful, young ruler who was fair, just, and honest; who had freed them from fear, hate, and persecution. As Gaia listened to his words, she remembered something Brex had once said to her: "The best leaders are the ones who do not want their power." It was true, she mused, as she listened to the priest implore the gods for another long, peaceful reign under the bloodline of Yehuda. She hadn't wanted the crown, and even then, sitting in the flowing, gold-trimmed robes of state, the idea of ruling still made her a little queasy, although that might have had more to do with the little being doing backflips in her belly than becoming queen. A throat cleared, and Gaia realized she had missed her cue. Looking to her left, she saw Lathan bearing the crown, a heavy gold concoction covered in precious gems. She dimpled at her cousin who shot her a look, trying to remind her to be serious. She stifled a giggle and the urge to roll her eyes. She might be queen, but that didn't mean she was going to change who she was. The priest smiled as Lathan set the crown on her brow. It slipped perfectly into place.

"Do you, the Princess Gaia, promise to heed and uphold our laws, to honor and protect the people of Meidonna? To rule as your father did with a firm hand and a gentle heart? To live for your people and guide them? To train your heir in the spirit of the Tallpian people?"

"I do." Her voice rang clear and bright across the room. Only Auggie, who stood just to her right, heard the slight quiver. He knew he would have given anything to have his best friend standing next to him—he couldn't imagine how Gaia must have felt. But she had graciously inclined her head without wavering, and Lathan, as Lord Commander, settled the crown onto her blonde head. Auggie had noticed—but would never mention—how Gaia hadn't changed her appearance since Brex's death. She had gone into battle a platinum-white blonde with turquoise eyes, and nothing had changed since the day Brex had taken his last breath. Now she raised those same piercing, cerulean eyes to look across the room as it erupted into cheers, the light catching the stones in her crown and throwing rainbows across the walls.

"I give you Queen Gaia the First! May long be her reign!"

# Epilogue

*Thirty Years Later*

Behind the closed palace doors, the roar of the crowd and the glare of the white sun were both muted.

"We are late," the steward muttered, hovering at the doors, nervously checking his time-piece. The dark-haired prince glanced at him with an amused smile.

"A queen is never late," he offered. The steward gave him an obsequious look but said nothing.

"I'm not late, I'm here." A side door was flung open, and the queen ushered in by her chief lady-in-waiting. The Lady Leona wore an exasperated expression, as per usual.

"Mother."

"Darling," Gaia said, gliding forward in her black gown, her white-blonde hair interwoven with the elegant silver diadem that was settled onto her forehead. She pressed a kiss to her son's cheek. "Are you ready?" He smiled down at her, and as it always did, the look sent shock waves through her stomach. His smile was pure Brex.

"Are you?" he asked, that laughing smile never leaving his lips. "Giving up your throne already?" Gaia snorted in derisive laughter, and Lady Leona clapped a hand over her eyes. It didn't matter how many times she told Gaia that a queen did not snort, Gaia always ignored her.

"The throne I never wanted? Darling, please. You are ready. And it's not as if I'm going to flutter off and die. I will stay as long as you need me. But our people deserve a ruler who knows them and lives for them. I live for you, and there is a great difference in that." Another handsome smile. "You are making history, you know," she said, smoothing the sash that crossed the chest of his military uniform.

"First half-Tallpian on the throne, I know," he said, and in his voice, Gaia heard her wry sense of humor. How she had been blessed with such a perfect son,—the exact combination of herself and Brex—she might never know, but she thanked the gods for him every night.

"Your father would be appalled," she teased, but stopped short when the light left his eyes. "Haiden Brexler, you know I'm teasing you." Her son nodded, smiling again, but she could still see the pain in his face, longing for the father he knew everything about but had never met.

"I just wish he could be here." She took his hand and squeezed.

"So I do, darling, so do I." She squared her shoulders and smiled at him as he stood next to her and settled her hand on top of his own. Right before the doors swung open, she glanced up at him one more time. Her perfect, dark-haired, blue-eyed son, born of war and desperation and love, who was the spitting image of his father, with his mother's heart. Raised to be a good man by a horde of uncles, all of whom worshipped Brex and loved him as Gaia had. It was true: Brex would have been appalled to see his son about to take his rightful place as the king of Meidonna and not as a member of the Brotherhood. But he would have also been proud, proud of his son's heart and his drive, his passion and his strength.

Waiting in the crowd just outside the doors were Auggie, much more grey now than copper, Zaire, still bald and fat, his Aunt Mia, who shared her brother's dark eyes and sharp wit, and many others, all there to celebrate Meidonna's new king and to usher in the next generation of peace. Gaia looked to the steward with a nod, and he flung open the doors.

*The End*

# Character List

## Major Character List

In Order of Appearance
**Name:** Description || Race

**Prince Nuweydon:** Current ruler of Meidonna, murdered King Yehuda, uncle to Gaia || Tallpian

**Amadeas:** General in the Tallpian army, uncle of King Yehuda and Prince Nuweydon, great-uncle to Gaia || Tallpian

**King Yehuda:** Gaia's father, murdered by his younger brother, Prince Nuweydon || Tallpian

**Gaia aka Kallideia:** Princess and heir to the Tallpian throne on Meidonna. Raised in secrecy on Annui by her mother, Queen Dyla || Tallpian

**Arlo:** Gorth hired by Prince Nuweydon to find Gaia || Terrin turning cyborg

**Keon:** Arlo's assistant and crony || Stakorian

**Brexler Carrow:** Smuggler, mercenary, gun-for-hire, member of the Outer Rim Brotherhood. Born on Cunat || Terrin

**Zaire:** Wealthy collector and friend/sometime employer of Brexler Carrow. Lives on Xael || Terrin

**Auggie:** Mechanic on Cunat, life-long friend of Brexler Carrow and member of the Outer Rim Brotherhood || Half-Terrin, half-Tallpian

**Willa:** Owns and runs a brothel on Cunat, friend and former employer of Brexler Carrow || Terrin

**Maggie:** Prostitute, former favorite of Brexler Carrow || Terrin

**Drianna:** Slave, owned by Zaire || Orchidian

**Alix:** Central Core born member of the Outer Rim Brotherhood. Hacker || Terrin

**Shaw:** Chessmia born member of the Outer Rim Brotherhood. Gun-for-hire || Terrin

**Njoroge:** Soevaria born member of the Outer Rim Brotherhood. Gun-for-hire/bodyguard || Soevarian

**Thrain:** Dail born member of the Outer Rim Brotherhood. Miner/gun-for-hire || Dailian

**Ethen:** Landife born member of the Outer Rim Brotherhood. Courier/smuggler || Lafimen

**Kain:** Cunat born leader of the Outer Rim Brotherhood || Terrin

**Queen Dyla:** Gaia's mother, queen of Meidonna || Tallpian

**Lathan:** Captain in the Tallpian army, second cousin to Gaia, on their mother's side || Tallpian

**Kyan:** Kalki born member of the Outer Rim Brotherhood, medic || Terrin

**Cayson:** Necosia born Southern Quadrant leader of the Outer Rim Brotherhood || Necosian

**Bronwyn:** Wife to General Amadeas, great-aunt to Gaia || Tallpian

**Sia:** Miwarma born, Gaia's temporary assistant || Miwarman

**Tyrell:** Roomaja born Eastern Quadrant commander of the Outer Rim Brotherhood || Roomajan

**Bria:** Xoi born slave, escaped Xael with Brexler's help || Xoian

**Leona:** Lathan's wife, member of the Tallpian court. Friend and tutor to Gaia || Tallpian

**Mia:** Brexler Carrow's younger sister, married to Marcus Calixson, lives on Dail ||Terrin

**Ravi:** Sergeant in the Tallpian Army || Tallpian

# Glossary

*Terrin:* A human who can trace their ancestry back to the original Earth before the rest of the galaxy was terraformed.

*Central Core:* The location of the government that controls the universe - a dyson sphere created by the original members of the Core built around a massive star at the center of the galaxy.

*Orchidian:* A graceful, beautiful, flower-human hybrid from the greenhouse planet of Orchidia, located in the south-eastern quadrant.

*Gorth:* Bounty hunters, usually employed by the Central Core government, charged with hunting down and returning undesirables. Also hired by warlords and other shady outer rim powers.

*Tallpian:* Tall-pee-an - a humanoid race with the genetic ability to change their physical appearance at will.

*Meidonna:* May-a-donna - The homeworld of the Tallpians, located on the far-outer edges of the north-western quadrant

*Annui:* A-new-ii - An industrial central planet where Dyla and Gaia lived in hiding, located in the inner-rings of the Central System

*Xael:* A trading planet based half-way between the Central Core and the Western outer rim.

*The Outer Rim Brotherhood:* A Robin Hood-eqsue collective that spans the universe, fighting against the corrupt Central Core.

*Sovarian:* Soe-varian - A humanoid race from the planet Sovaia, located on the south-eastern edge. Characteristics include extreme height (7'+), dark skin and violet colored-blood.

*Landife:* A planet on the very south-Western edge of the outer rim - known for its three blazing suns that burn across the surface of each day which lasts 42 hours. Home to the Lafimen, or smoke people. They have evolved to survive the heat and often appear to move as smoke.

*Roomajan:* A reptile-human hybrid race, known for their color-shifting skills, similar to a chameleon.

*Necosian:* A giant hybrid people, known for their pastel colored skin that hail from Necosa, located in the northern quadrant.

*Miwarma:* A tropical ocean planet, part of the Leconus system - a galaxy wide neutral zone.

*Xion:* A humanoid race with skin made up entirely of precious stones

*Dail:* A mining planet in the South western quadrant

*Stakorian:* A rodent/human hybrid race created by the scientists within the Central Core designed as spies

*Imathine:* A vampire-like creature, known for its preferred diet of Terrin blood.

# About The Author

L.R. Oberschulte is a California-born author, specializing in science-fiction, fantasy and historical fiction novels. She lives in the country with her husband, dog, cats, horse and pigs.